When the Music Stopped

When the Music Stopped

Elisabeth Ogilvie

McGRAW-HILL PUBLISHING COMPANY

New York St. Louis San Francisco
Toronto Hamburg Mexico

1 2 3 4 5 6 7 8 9 DOC DOC 8 9 2 1 0 9

ISBN 0-07-047792-2

LIBRARY OF CONGRESS CATALOGING-IN-PUBLICATION DATA

Ogilvie, Elisabeth, 1917–

When the music stopped / by Elisabeth Ogilvie.

p. cm.

ISBN 0-07-047792-2

I. Title.

PS3529.G39W48 1989

813′.54—dc 19 88-28636

CIP

Book design by Sheree L. Goodman

Also by Elisabeth Ogilvie

The Summer of the Osprey
The World of Jennie G.
Jennie About to Be
The Road to Nowhere
The Silent Ones
The Devil in Tartan
A Dancer in Yellow
An Answer in the Tide
The Dreaming Swimmer
Where the Lost Aprils Are
Image of a Lover
Strawberries in the Sea
Weep and Know Why
A Theme for Reason
The Face of Innocence
Bellwood
Waters on a Starry Night
The Seasons Hereafter
There May Be Heaven
Call Home the Heart
The Witch Door
High Tide at Noon
Storm Tide
The Ebbing Tide
Rowan Head
My World Is an Island
The Dawning of the Day
No Evil Angel

Books for Young People

The Pigeon Pair
Masquerade at Sea House
Ceiling of Amber
Turn Around Twice
Becky's Island
The Young Islanders
How Wide the Heart
Blueberry Summer
Whistle for a Wind
The Fabulous Year
Come Aboard and Bring Your Dory!

When the Music Stopped

1

That August I was too busy finishing my book to pay any attention to what was happening on the planet, in the nation, or in the small world of Job's Harbor. I hadn't even read the *Tenby Journal* for weeks, and that's one of my most treasured sources of material. I didn't watch television, and I wasn't reading anything except those detailed and leisurely mysteries when I fell into bed at night, sometimes before sundown because I'd be up and working by four in the morning. I don't like to use up my summers like this, but once in a while I miscalculate, and the book, like a baby, will be born when it's ready, never mind the inconvenience.

For these last few weeks of hurrying toward the end of the final draft, I hadn't even been to Maddox, thirteen miles up the road; occasionally I went through the long ell chamber from the Hayloft (which is what my flat had once been) and down the back stairs for a meal with my grandparents and anyone else who happened to be there, but I'd never hear half of what was said. There were no long days on the water with Glen, no tennis at the Sorrells', just long walks with Chad, the black Labrador, early in the morning and sometimes a quick swim off the lobster car when the boats were all back on their moorings and the harbor quiet. But nothing was more seductive than the paper rolled into my typewriter. The family and Glen were used to this and respected it, what with the modest success of my first two books. There's nothing like being paid real money for something you've done to make your nearest and dearest take it seriously.

I finished late on a Saturday afternoon and sat there grinning like Chad. Then I shuffled everything together and dumped it into Job Winter's sea chest. I'd take it out after a few days, put it in order, and begin last-minute changes and corrections. But for now I was in the state of mindless bliss that follows writing those two magnificent words "The End."

I went out onto my deck and leaned on the railing like a passenger on a vessel entering her home port. The harbor opened before me in the loose embrace of Winter Head to the southwest and Fort Point to the northeast. Light seas broke infrequently around the base of the Head's steep prow. Across the harbor mouth a token surf, sent in by somebody's wake, frisked and sparkled about Job's Tears, the string of dark ledges that kept boats well off Fort Point when they rounded it from the river. A few natives and most of our summer people lived on the two long points among meadows and spruce woods; wharves of various sizes fringed the harbor.

Everything was remarkably quiet for high tide on a fine summer afternoon. Long afterwards I still recall that particular hush, when our world seemed to be holding its breath, waiting for something; it didn't know what. Flags hardly stirred on their poles. The children, for whom the harbor was one great playground as soon as they were trusted to row, were inexplicably absent; they were like the schools of tiny fish which were thick in the water under your skiff one moment and gone the next. All the lobster boats were at their moorings, occupied only by some contemplative gulls; by law there was no trap-hauling after four on summer Saturday afternoons, and none at all on Sundays. Three tall-masted yachts were anchored together in the lee of Winter Head, and a couple of cabin cruisers were using two spare moorings in the harbor. I didn't see anyone moving about on them. The boats were all regulars; the owners liked our small harbor, always quiet because it offered no special amenities besides a chance to buy soft drinks and candy and to use the telephone at the Job's Harbor Lobster Company (or, when it was closed, Grampa's house phone).

It was closed now, and the big wharf had a done-for-the-day look. A few gulls sat on ridgepole and hoisting mast. The lobstermen's parking lot, set off from the family driveway by a high and untidy rose hedge, was empty of pickups.

Outside the harbor the water was a velvety blue across the broad river mouth to the sunlit slopes of the St. David peninsula, and south to the horizon, flecked with sails. My cousin's herring seiner, *Juno,* dark red, broad and low in the water, with the seine boat like a kid sister trailing her, moved westward. She disappeared behind the Davids, that miniature archipelago lying straight to the south about ten miles out of Job's Harbor.

The sight of them jolted me back into a childhood when they had promised me ineffable delights. It took a certain blue in the sea, a specific slant of sun across them, to convince me that if only I could go there on the instant I would catch the enchantment in the act: white ruins of a hidden temple among dark woods; lithe maidens kneeling among unimaginable flowers by a reflecting pool; the sea-facing fields dappled with sheep and guarded by a flute-playing shepherd boy in an animal skin. (I'd been conditioned young by Gram's Maxfield Parrish collection.)

Since then I'd been on all the islands many times, from tiny Haypenny to Heriot, and my best and oldest friend lived now on Heriot. But whenever I beheld them in that certain radiance, the old magic was there, coexisting quite comfortably with everyone else's reality.

Juno appeared beyond the westernmost point of Heriot. How many times had Jon seined herring among the islands and neither guessed about the lithe maidens nor heard the flute? I laughed. He knew enough lithe maidens as it was. And maybe the islands were magic for him in their own way; he'd seined a small fortune in herring out there.

Someone was stirring out aboard the cabin cruisers. One gull called to another. The hiatus was over. The world still breathed for another day. And I was hungry, and it was baked-bean night next door. I turned to go in and saw the Temple boys careening across the parking lot on their skateboards. "Hi, Eden!" they yelled at me. It was too late to dodge. I'd been discouraging their visits, saying I had to *think,* and they were very respectful. Now I had the feeling that wherever they'd been this afternoon they knew by ESP the instant I typed "The End" and had shot home to see me.

They were eleven and thirteen, two slim boys in shorts and T-shirts saying "Job's Harbor" over an immense green lobster. Their blond hair was lighter than their tan, curling about their ears. They looked like idealized choirboys; all they needed now were those angelic frills around their necks. And they knew absolutely everything, whether it were true or not.

They left their skateboards, chased each other around the rose hedge, giggling and threatening, and came leaping up my steps.

"Book done yet?" Will's voice was just beginning to change.

"Yep," I said.

"Congratulations," Will said. He hoisted himself up onto the rail.

"You starting another one right off?" Ben asked. He still qualified as a small boy.

"Nope, I'm going to play for the rest of the summer," I said.

"Good," said Ben gravely, perching beside Will. "Hey, Eden, Richie was swearing something awful at Shasta today—we could hear him way over to our house—and throwing things around."

"*Richie?*" I said involuntarily. "Are you *sure?*" Richie Barry had a childish mouth and wore thick glasses behind which his blue eyes were innocent and vulnerable. He looked too young to be married and a father, but he was both.

"Sure I'm sure it was Richie," Ben said. "He's mad on account of her having another brat."

"That's what he called it, not us," Will said. "And Derek was crying like everything. I think Richie hit him. Mum was antsy about it, till she saw Toby take him down to the shore and let him throw stones."

I don't believe in encouraging kids to gossip, but the Temples never needed encouragement; for them it wasn't gossip, but reporting in its purest form. The Barrys were my tenants in the small house behind the spruces on the far side of the parking lot. The house had been left me by a spinster great-aunt who thought all women should own some property. I didn't want to live in it until I could afford to fix it up, and I didn't want it to stand empty, so when the young Barrys, from Amity, came to me, I let it at a small rent; enough to cover the taxes and the insurance.

Then Richie's older brother Toby had moved in with them, and, ever since, the neighbors and my relatives had been beseeching me to evict them before the brothers stole us blind. It seems they'd been practically run out of Amity.

Well, nothing had happened yet. If it did, I'd never live it down.

But—Richie cruel? Maybe a little dim upstairs, and easily led by that smiling extrovert Toby, but I couldn't believe him vicious. "I don't think Richie would ever hit anyone, especially a baby," I said firmly.

Two pairs of blue eyes pitied my innocence. "He hits Shasta," said Ben.

"How do you know?" I sounded no older than they were.

"I heard him slap her once. I was going right by the window."

"Maybe he slapped something else. Maybe he was killing a mosquito."

"She *yelped!*" he said indignantly. "You think he's a wimp, but he's some mean! Once she had a real black eye. You see that?"

I hadn't. Obviously I'd been too long in my book, and I wished I were still back there.

"She should have married Toby," Will said. "Then maybe he wouldn't get into any more trouble. When you have children, you have to set them a good example."

"She couldn't very well marry Toby," I said, "if she was in love with Richie. Besides, he's Derek's father."

Will disposed magnificently of that. "Toby's the uncle. Same blood and all."

"Maybe Toby wouldn't want to marry her," I suggested, seeing no delicate way of saying it's a rare man who wants to father another man's mistake.

"It would only be common sense," said Ben, sounding about eighty and teetering insouciantly over the lawn far below. "Toby may be a crook, but he's not mean. We know he likes Derek better than Richie does. I could never figure out why Shasta fell for Richie. He's a real creep."

"Oh, she probably thought he was cute and tame as a bunny rabbit," said Will cynically. "Till they got married, and he started baring his teeth." I could hear his father in this.

A police whistle shrilled from over beyond the parking lot, the spruces, and my little house, and the boys came off the railing, fortunately on the deck side. It was supper time, and Amy Temple's baked beans were almost as good as Gram's.

They went leaping down the steps, crying back, "So long, Eden!"

"Take the shore path," I called after them. "Don't use the shortcut by the house any more." They obeyed, while I was watching.

2

I went inside to shower and change. Those blasted kids had tarnished my euphoria. *Cheerfulness breaks in,* someone had written. So does ugliness. It's the Law of Surprise. Just how ugly the consecutive surprises were to be, I couldn't have imagined for a book on that lustrous afternoon.

I thought of Shasta and Richie as I'd first seen them; Shasta defeated and fat already in maternity jeans and faded secondhand tents, though it was early in her second pregnancy; Richie, the fumbling pathetic type born to live from hand to mouth. They'd had to get married, and Derek was still in diapers when they'd gone and done it again. Toby was clearly needed to help pay the rent. Both men dug clams out on the islands. (And cased the summer places for future visits, it was said.)

I hadn't known until after they were moved in that they had lost their lobster licenses after repeated offenses concerning possession of short lobsters and hauling other people's traps. Amity had hoped they would go to jail for awhile, but they were always given suspended sentences and a chance to earn the enormous fines. When there was a fresh epidemic of larceny in and around Amity, it looked as if the citizens would be indirectly paying the fines; so one night the Barrys were visited by a committee and invited to leave town.

Well, how could I have known what was going on way over there across Bugle Bay if nobody told me? The Job's Harbor men hadn't known either, until somebody from Amity warned Sprig Newsome that the people at the harbor should nail down all their possessions now that Snowy Winter's do-gooder granddaughter had rented a house to the Barrys.

"What should I be, a do-badder?" I'd snarled at Sprig and made his day. He said I was the sexiest when I was mad.

Doggedly I'd insisted that I wouldn't evict the Barrys as long as they paid their rent and behaved themselves. When they first moved in, I had taken Shasta some of Gram's turnovers one day and had a cup of tea with her, trying to discover some spark of spirit. She told me in flat weary tones that her parents and sister hadn't spoken to her since she'd taken up with a Barry; and that Richie's mother was a whore, and his father was the nearest to nothing that ever feet hung on and was called a man.

There'd been no pilfering yet among the boats and fish houses around Job's Harbor, and the jokes about my being a one-woman welfare department had died down. But this domestic ugliness was something else. If I gave them notice after she'd recovered from the next birth, then I wouldn't have to think about them any more.

Showered, splashed with my best cologne, wearing fresh thin slacks and a cool silk top, I felt so good again that I happily put the Barrys out of my mind. Two family cars were now in the driveway. I tried Glen's number to ask him to supper, and there was no answer. I was sharply disappointed, but not surprised. After all, he hadn't known I was going to finish the book this afternoon. Theoretically we had no strings on each other, and if I could isolate myself with my book, he was entitled to amuse himself however he pleased. I did see a difference between certain forms of amusement and writing to make a living, but I tried not to dwell on the possibilities and thus flaw a comfortable relationship. Darby and Joan, my brother and Glen's sister unkindly called us.

His boat, *Little Emily*, was in the harbor, so he wasn't taking someone out for a supper picnic on one of the Davids. But I knew at least three women who had their eyes on him, one summer and two native, and they'd had unlimited opportunities in the last few weeks. Who knew when Glen would suddenly get tired of our comfortable relationship and just not be in my life any more?

Richie Barry slapping his wife around and maybe his baby; Glen Heriot in the sack with some excitingly shameless bit of goods. I wished passionately that I were still in my book.

The trouble with you, Eden Winter, I told my reflection in my bedroom mirror, is that you don't have both oars in the water. The dark blue Winter eyes agreed. I glared back like the much earlier Eden Winter whose daguerreotype was in a family album. She'd hated the whole lengthy process, and especially the daguerreotypist. (Later she'd married him.) Remembering her, I was suddenly overcome with a tender amusement, and everything else glided away to its proper distance. The book was finished, I knew it was a *good* book, and I was starved.

I walked through the open chamber, which is the upstairs in the ell separating the barn from the house. It was full of assorted cultch being saved because some day something might come in useful; between them, Gram and Grampa knew just what was there and where it was. At the head of the back stairs I met a hot wave of heavenly scents from the open door at the foot. I sat down at the turn of the stairs to listen. From the time I could first manage those stairs, I'd heard many a fascinating, if bewildering, discussion from up here at the turn.

Gram was out of sight, but I could see my mother and Uncle Early's wife setting the table. Aunt Eleanor is big, not fat; a good-looking woman with Scandinavian coloring. She always seems to move in her own sunny atmosphere, giving off its warmth and light to anyone who comes into her orbit. Years ago when I was small, she and Uncle Early had lost their first son, my playmate, by drowning; they provided my first example of the possibility of surviving such a ferocious grief. She and my mother were laughing now like sixteen year olds, and I heard a burst of snickers from Gram's side of the kitchen. I must have just missed a good one.

By contrast with my aunt, my mother is a slight and tawny-skinned woman, who likes to think her dark eyes and strong aquiline nose came from the Penobscot Indian strain she is so proud of. "*Gypsy* is more likely," my father teases her; she would happily spend half the year traveling, and she expects to when they retire.

Unseen by me, the men would be over by the big window overlooking the harbor, with Chad lying among and over their feet, blissful in all this male company. The father and two sons looked alike with their wiriness and their dark blue eyes, the quick way they walked and the tilt of their heads. Their hair grew the same way. Grampa's was now a glistening white crest, and the sons' heads were well silvered over black. But each was indelibly different from the others in personality. They were born victims to nicknames; my father is Stormy, a misnomer for such a mild man. My generation has escaped, because there aren't too many more things you can do with "Winter." It is not true that a rather loose-living female Winter was known as "Open." It's one of my brother's yarns.

In the little hiatus that meant Gram was taking the bean pot out of the oven, with her daughters-in-law hovering as if attending a birth, my father said, "We met the Esmond girls up by the sawmill."

"*There!*" Gram exclaimed, and I knew she wasn't hailing the beans.

"It was like seeing a myth become incarnate," said my mother, who has an endearing capacity for awe.

"Incarnate is right," said my father. "A little too much so. Taking the curve at about sixty. I thought that Thunderbird was going to sail right out over Parsons' Cove and end belly-up in the river. I wouldn't have known who it was if Barney hadn't told me yesterday about selling them the car. He says you can't call them typical old ladies." He laughed. "Not Mrs. Rigby, anyway. Barney was impressed. And after seeing her take that curve like a professional race car driver, *I'm* impressed."

"She must have got used to driving like that in the south of France," my mother said wistfully.

"I haven't seen hide nor hair of those two yet." Gram sounded injured. "When I think how close Emmie and I used to be. . . ."

"Well, Mother, if you want to see her, you'd better make it soon," my father said. "The way her sister drives, she's not going to be around very long."

"What's going on uptown about Mary Ann?" Uncle Early asked. "Anybody organizing a picket line or putting out a contract on her?"

"There's a lot of scurrying in and out next door," my mother said. "Offering moral support to Beth Rigby, I suppose, and of course picking up any little bits of information lying around. Beth's very calm, a little tight around the mouth. The Harpies are doing all the talking. 'She's so *brave!*' they keep saying. You'd think Beth was the deserted wife, instead of the daughter-in-law who was just born when it happened. You can hear the clack-clack-clack wherever Clara Fitton is. '*That woman!* That Jezebel! How she dares! Brazen as ever. And for her to come to *that house!*' "

"Mary Ann must have known exactly what it would be like," Gram said. "She's been in touch with Clement Cruikshank all these years. Makes you wonder why she did come back."

"I suppose she thinks it's safe now," Grampa said dryly. "Talk doesn't hurt, and what's left of the old bunch aren't likely to tar and feather her or burn her for a witch. Not Clem Cruikshank or Sidney Carver, anyway."

"I saw Kenneth when I went into Rigby Marine the other day," said Uncle Early. "Wonder if he ever once raised his voice."

"I think he's been struggling all his life under the weight of his grandfather's sins," Gram said. "Beth must have told him the family shame before he started the first grade, and she's never let it die. Poor boy."

"They told him on his twenty-first birthday," I said, going down the steps. "They told him the secret of the monster in the attic, and it's really driven him insane, but nobody knows yet. Come on, what's the Rigby curse or sin or shame or whatever? And why is an old woman in a Thunderbird a Jezebel? Where is *that house?* Why have I never heard anything about it before in my whole life?"

"Well, most things that happened in a small town sixty years and several wars ago don't get discussed much around the average dinner table these days," said my father. "Has your chick hatched out?"

"Yep, it's out and cheeping."

There was an impromptu round of applause and congratulations. Chad threw himself at me in delight, but I was braced for the impact. "All right, I'm waiting," I said. "Who's Mary Ann?"

"Goodness!" Gram said in impatient surprise. "You've heard of Marianne Rigby and Emma Esmond! You never miss a thing in the paper, not even the Want Ads, and the *Journal*'s always kept up with her and Emmie."

"Well, I've missed a lot in the last three weeks." Then the penny dropped. "*That*'s Mary Ann? The *pianist?* Of course I know who she is! The hometown girl who became a big artist in Europe, and so forth. But there hasn't been anything in the paper about her for a long time."

"What about Emma Esmond?" Gram prodded. "You must have heard me mention her."

I plunged into memory and triumphantly retrieved a fact. "I remember reading once that Miss Emma Esmond was retiring after a long career in Boston. She played the violin, taught it, and toured with a string quartet," I told Gram smugly. "See? I *do* remember. So they must be the Esmond girls. Right?" (I hate people who keep saying "*Right?*" to me.) "Did either of them ever come home at any time?"

"Not Mary Ann," said Gram, "but Emma visited every summer as long as her parents lived, and we always had at least one day together, without fail. Then when Guy died, seven years ago, she went to France to stay with Mary Ann."

"All right," I said. "I've got that straight. But why the big flap because the quote Esmond girls unquote are back? Did I hear someone mention a deserted wife?" I looked at my mother, who smiled enigmatically. "Mary Ann married a Rigby. Which one? What's the connection with Kenneth Rigby? What happened sixty years ago? Come on, someone," I appealed to the others. But they all looked expectantly at Gram, willing to give her the floor. Only she and Grampa had been around sixty years ago.

"It was fifty-eight years ago," Gram corrected, "and Mary Ann's going on eighty-two. She may have come home to die. Has anyone thought of that?" Her grey-blue eyes accused us.

"I thought of it when we met her on the road just now," said my father. "She's going about it the hard way, isn't she?"

"Let's eat," said Gram flatly. "I'll tell you about it another time, Eden. Or maybe I won't. I'm scared you'll use it in a book."

"Wow!" I said fervently. "It must be terrific!"

She gave me a long and chilling look over her glasses. "It was terrible," she said.

That subdued me; it subdued everyone. Nobody brought up the Esmonds all through the meal. There was plenty else to talk about, and I took part, but I was determined to get the Esmond story. If Gram wouldn't tell me, I couldn't wheedle it out of Grampa—he was too loyal to her. But my parents knew it at secondhand. I could hardly wait.

I did know Kenneth Rigby, who owned Rigby Marine and lived with his mother in the old Jarrett house next door to my parents. He was an extremely quiet bachelor in his thirties, and his father had been Guy Rigby. But that Guy would have been too young to be married to Mary Ann. Obviously her Guy had been Kenneth's grandfather. I had to know about it. I was an addictive collector down into the marrow of my bones; even the simple phrase *that house* could lift the hairs on the back of my neck.

Was it simply the story of an elderly black sheep gamboling home or of a skeleton shambling up the stairs like the one in Robert Frost's poem? Whichever it was, I'd rather think about that than the people in my house across the parking lot. After all, it had happened more than half a century ago. The shock waves should have long since died away, no matter how powerful they had once been.

3

The conversation never did get around to ancient scandals, not even when we females took a walk at sunset. That was quite exciting because Chad treed a porcupine in the orchard. The porcupine was comfortable for the night, but Chad wasn't going to leave. He has made three trips to the vet with a mouthful of quills and still believes there is a way to get even. He is not a brilliant dog, though he makes up for this by being sweet and friendly, good to cats, children, and smaller dogs, even pugnacious ones. He is not a gun dog; Grampa got him for free from a disgusted owner because Chad hated guns and splashing overboard into cold water. It is my belief that Chad is some other kind of dog trapped in a Labrador's body. "A Chihuahua?" Uncle Early suggested.

What finally pried Chad loose was the sound of the seiner *Juno* outside Winter Head. He went by us like an ebony projectile and was down on the lobster car barking when *Juno* came around the Head, low in the sunset-colored water with a load of pogies for lobster bait.

When my parents went home, I tried Glen once more. Still no answer. I went to bed with a book, consoling myself with a plan for getting the Rigby-Esmond story from somebody tomorrow.

Glen came up my steps early the next morning and woke me up. The sun was an immense blood orange behind the spruce tips on Fort Point, and the boats were still black silhouettes on water the color of tangerine sherbet. After breakfast I packed a lunch, and we went out to set a batch of clean traps, which is legal on summer Sundays when hauling traps isn't. When they were all baited and set, we sailed out to Monhegan on a sea like blue porcelain, cleaning up *Little Emily* as we went. We gave Heriot Island a wide berth; his sister—(my best friend) Fee—and her lover lived there and were having a big crowd for the day. Neither of us wanted to get into that. Some of Julian's friends were as dim as he was, and most of them would be half-seas over in beer.

It was hot on the land, but perfect on the water, and we ate our lunch aboard the boat. I didn't ask Glen where he'd been Saturday night, and he didn't volunteer to tell me. I didn't care; being out with him now felt exactly right.

If Glenroy Heriot sounds like the name of a hero in a Victorian romance, it's only because Glenroy is an ancestral name on his mother's side. His twin sister was called Fiona because their mother thought she should have a Scots name, too. She died young, a girl herself, and the twins' growing up was anything but romantic, though they did have those lovely names.

Glen is tall and thin with light brown hair that never lies flat, because he has two crowns. His eyes are deep-set and grey, with sun creases at the outer corners, in an interestingly angular face. It has the long flat spaces between cheekbones and jaw that make women want to lay hands on them, when they aren't trying to smooth down his cowlicks. It happens a lot at parties after they've had a few drinks, and he always looks polite about it or, at most, mildly entertained. "Aye-uh," he drawls outrageously when someone half-smashed tells him he's gorgeous.

If the time comes when *he* thinks someone is gorgeous—well, that was the least of my worries on that perfect Sunday.

The next morning I took my manuscript out of the sea chest, spread it out on the floor, and separated chapters by paper clips as a first step. Then I laid it away again. Job Winter was quite a reader, they say; I liked to think he'd be happy to acknowledge a descendant who wrote books, but Gram thought it was just as well he couldn't know what went into books nowadays, even unsensational ones like mine.

Then I went across the parking lot among the pickups and through the spruces to my house. The weather was still muggy, and the windless heat made me sweat; Shasta looked almost sick with it. She was hanging out a wash, and Derek, in a diaper, was trudging around in the uncut grass, picking red clover.

"Hi, Eden." She gave me a weak smile, actually a sweet one; before she became so puffed up, she must have been rather pretty. Now she was lardy-white, thick around the neck, and swollen around the eyes. Her dark blonde hair was lank and flat with sweat.

"Getting close, isn't it?" I said."

"Yes, thank God. My back just about kills me." She leaned down awkwardly to pick a sheet out of the basket, but I got it first and gave one edge to her. We shook it out and hung it over the line together. "Thanks," she said, short of breath. I saw bruises on her left upper arm, as if someone had grabbed her there and dug his fingers in. What could I do or say? I couldn't humiliate her by mentioning the marks.

"I'm through with my book now," I said. "How about coming over for a cup of tea or a cold drink on the deck this afternoon? If the stairs are too much for you, we could sit on the front lawn."

Shasta said, "It's hard taking Derek anywhere. You have to watch him every minute."

"My grandmother keeps a box of toys," I began, but Toby spoke suddenly from behind the screen of the kitchen window. "We'll watch him, Shas. Hi, Eden." He grinned at me. "Sure she can go. We've already dug once today, and we won't be going again till supper time."

"That's right, you've got two low tides today," I said. "How are the clams holding out?"

"Finest kind out on the islands, long as we don't get the red tide. Great price, too."

"Good," I said. "Well, how about it, Shasta? Around two?"

"*No,*" Richie said gruffly, unseen behind Toby. "She ain't going nowhere. She's staying home with the kid. We got business uptown."

Shasta blushed the ugly color of a burn and gave me an embarrassed grimace. I wished that I hadn't come over and started this and that I could belt Richie right in the gut. Shasta bent panting over the clothes basket, groping blindly.

"What business, Richard, me boy?" Toby asked. "First I heard of it."

"We got business," Richie repeated.

"Bull!" said Toby. "I'll be here, Shas. I don't plan on going anywhere today, too goddam hot. Derek and me'll get along like a house afire. You go ahead."

Shasta's hands were trembling as she attempted to pin a small jersey to the line. Richie said in a low voice so packed with rage it gave me a chill, "You can pick up and get out of here any time. I won't cry about it."

"And then who'll pay your goddam rent?" Toby retorted, sounding on the verge of laughter. Something smashed; Shasta jumped, dropped the jersey and clothespins. She said breathlessly, "I'm sorry, I'd like awful well to come, but I can't."

"Oh, *hell.*" said Toby. He left the window. "You'd better sweep up this shittin' mess, every last goddam splinter of it," he said coldly to his brother, "before your kid comes in, unless you want him to slice an artery and bleed to death."

Shasta and I looked involuntarily at Derek's fat bare feet in the grass. I picked up the jersey and pinned it on the line.

"Listen, we'll do it another time," I said. I nodded encouragingly and escaped through the spruces, breaking into an unpleasant sweat. How had I missed all this misery next door? So much for my intuition, the kids were right; Richie *was* mean. I should never have gone over there; I should have taken my rod and gone down to fish with the kids off the lobster car.

The scent of the loose-petaled roses was heavy in the humid stillness. Gram and Chad were just coming from the mailbox up on the main road. Chad loped ahead with his perpetual air of holiday expectancy. He always seemed to be saying, "Isn't this *nice?* Isn't this *great?*" Gram walked quickly. She's on the portly side, very straight, and she wears fresh bright housedresses and aprons she makes for herself. The grey glitters like sun-struck frost in her short brown hair; the natural wave is one of her vanities. She came along through the mingled sun and shade, stopping to pick and eat a blackberry from the thorny tangle edging the road.

If ever there was an antidote to the scene behind the spruces, Gram and Chad were it. The dog discovered me and went racing in manic circles around me until he had to flop under the rose bushes, panting. Gram and I sorted out the mail on my steps.

"Come in for a blueberry turnover," she said. "They ought to be cool enough now."

I took my mail upstairs and dropped it on my desk, then walked through the house and down to the kitchen. The teakettle was heating, and Chad lay on the cool linoleum, beating his tail on it at sight of me. Gram had the *Tenby Journal* spread out on the table and was staring at it as if it announced that the world had ended yesterday afternoon.

"Well, I never," she said softly. "Never! Did *you* ever?"

"Did I ever what?" I asked. "There's plenty I haven't ever yet, but I have hopes."

"Come and look at *this.*"

This was a small item tucked away in the Social Notes, among the notices for the Shakespeare Club, the Friends of the Museum, and various bazaars and fairs. It announced that Mrs. Guy Rigby and Miss Emma Esmond would be happy to receive friends at Fox Point on Sunday afternoons from two to five o'clock.

"They're having 'Afternoons'!" I was happily incredulous. "It's straight out of Henry James and Marcel Proust! Oh, Gram, you've *got* to go, so I can go with you!"

She was looking at me as if I'd gone raving mad. Then she said with an infinitely sad little smile, unusual for her, "It can't be meant for people like me. We were only young girls when we were so close. Emma never came back home after her folks died, and that was more than twenty years ago. She's lived most of her life in a whole different world from mine."

I kissed her cheek and said, "I'm sorry, Gram. Let's just forget it, huh?"

Glen and I spent the evening together; most of the night, really. He left around three, and a sou'westerly storm was already blowing up. We knew by the sound of the rote outside Winter Head that there'd be no hauling traps today. I slept until around nine and ate my breakfast in a room surrounded by a soft roaring like the sound in my conch shell doorstop when I held it to my ear. The wind was unremitting, and rain poured against my seaward windows. Whenever I could see out, I saw the big greybacks rushing obliquely toward the harbor, with the crests blowing off them like smoke. In the harbor the boats were in perpetual motion, but almost all of them were sheltered by the long barrier of the Head. In the battle of wind and tide at the harbor mouth, Job's Tears were buried again and again under tons of white water, out of which geysers of surf shot high into the air at each fresh impact.

I put the *Amadeus* sound track in my player and settled down to work. Between manuscript and Mozart I was so far away that I jumped when Gram knocked at the ell chamber door. "Come on in!" I yelled, shutting off the music. Chad rushed at me, ready to damp me down with kisses which I fended off. Gram stood militantly in my kitchen and said, "I'm going to Fox Point on Sunday. It's pure greedy curiosity, that's all. I don't expect anybody to remember anything special from the past. I just decided I had as much right to take a look at 'em as anybody, and maybe more than some."

"Can I go?" I asked meekly, trying to keep a decently sober face.

"I want you to drive me." She was steel-eyed over her glasses. "I don't figure there'll be a crowd, but I'm not taking any chances on having to back and fill in a driveway full of cars. And I'll expect you to wear a dress. It'll be a Sunday afternoon and should be treated as such."

"Gram," I said solemnly, "I know what's due an Afternoon, Sunday or not. I've got just the dress for it, and if I had a hat to match, I'd wear it."

Mollified, she said, "You have pretty hair, Eden. Like black silk. Don't fuss with it."

"What if it rains?"

"It won't rain. Whoever said 'Into each life some rain must fall' didn't know Mary Ann Esmond was going to be born."

"Gram, I can't stand the suspense!" I said. "Everything you say makes it worse. Sit down and tell me about her right now, no matter how awful it was. I know the facts of life."

"I should say so," she said grumpily. "You know quite a few I've never heard of." She gave me one of those long looks. She's proud of my books when they come out and usually relieved, because she's apprehensive when I'm working, as if I'm typing up sexy exposés about the first families of Whittier, including ours. I haven't done it yet, but with my brother mischievously urging me to turn out some X-rated material and make our fortune, she's always nervous.

"Well, at least tell me why all the flap about Fox Point," I begged. The beautiful shingle-style "cottage" was the castle of my imagination for all my childhood, and the rich summer tenants were what I expected royalty to be when they laid aside their crowns and ermine for the hot weather.

"Guy Rigby built that house, and he must have left it to Mary Ann," she said, making for the door.

"You mean he's been the landlord for all these years?"

"Yes, and never set eyes on the place since 1927." She had her hand on the doorknob. "Clem Cruikshank Sr. handled it."

"Well, didn't this Guy have a right to leave the house to his wife? Why is everybody so worked up?"

"I haven't got the time right now, Eden," she said and shut the door smartly behind her. I half-expected her to push the bolt over to keep me from following her.

I went back to work, bemused by all the things hinted at but left unsaid. I could drive to Maddox and get one of my parents to tell me all about it, but I needed to do my work. Besides, I knew Gram; sooner or later she'd open up, now that she'd given me one small scrap. She was all of a simmer, I could tell.

4

I went out to haul with Glen the next day. There was a good bounce left over from the storm; the seas were a shining blue-green, marbled and crested with glittering white. Everyone was out to see how the gear had fared; we saw Fee and Julian's *Island Magic* far out by Davie's Rock, lunging joyously into the deep chop and taking white water over her bow. That would be Fee's doing; Julian had helped his brother build the boat, and he was as tender with her as he was with Fee and his cats.

Glen and I went into the lee of Heriot and tied up on Julian's mooring while we ate lunch. It was shimmeringly hot and still here, and we could look through liquid aquamarine at the little green and silver pollock and the sandy bottom. I'd have been tempted to strip and go overboard if it weren't for the probability of another lobster boat or some high-powered summer sports rig suddenly speeding into view.

I told Glen what I was going to do on Sunday, and he said indulgently, "Have fun."

"What are you going to do?" I asked, hoping he had firm plans to referee a ball game or take some men deep-sea fishing.

"Oh, I'll find something," he said amiably. There was no doubt of that; any one of those three predatory women would be full of suggestions.

Sunday afternoon I was standing by my big window, dressed in pale yellow voile for the Afternoon, and fastening Great-Aunt Noella's topaz locket, when Glen appeared on the wharf below. He looked up at the

Hayloft and waved; under his other arm he carried a carton of vegetables from his garden. So he was going out to Heriot. I waved with enthusiastic relief. Fee was so anxious for us to get married that she wouldn't have some nubile young beauty waiting in a bikini or one of those swimsuits with the legs cut out to the armpits.

He pushed his skiff off the float and rowed out to *Little Emily.* He's had three boats in the twelve years I've known him, the first one a skiff, the present one a thirty-eight footer, and they've all been named after a small beagle of beloved memory. A grown man who names one boat after another for a dog he had when he was a little boy should be very patient with other people's quirks, and he is.

Gram came in when she was ready. She was wearing pale blue silk with white polka dots and a narrow lace collar and cuffs.

"You look very distinguished, Gram," I said. "I'll be proud to be seen with you."

"Thank you," she said. If she was the least bit uncertain about going, she didn't show it. "You look very nice, too, Eden. You should wear dresses more often. Men like good-looking legs." Her own ankles were still slim. "And they never get over it. Your grandfather hasn't."

"I'll remember that," I said demurely. Maybe I should get one of those swimsuits.

We went in my dark blue Chevalier: I'd hired the Temple boys to wash and polish it. As we turned onto the main road by the mailbox, I began to nag. "Come on, Gram. Give me some background before we get there. What did the Esmond girls do to put everybody into a swivet? Run a call girl agency in Boston to finance their music studies?"

"Emma didn't do anything!" she snapped. "And she never went to Boston till Mary Ann was gone. Mary Ann never gave Emma a hint of it beforehand, and that just about broke Emma's heart. No, Mary Ann and Guy went straight to France. That was in 1927. They never came back, and Emma never went over there till Guy died. Then she up and went and has been there ever since."

"So the awful thing that Mary Ann did was to elope with somebody? I gather they got married."

"They went the same week in May as Lindbergh flew the Atlantic—I'll never forget that! Maddox nearly exploded with excitement, the two things happening in one week."

"But really horrible things have happened in the years between then and now," I said. "Local men have died in wars, and the world's trying to poison itself if it doesn't blow itself up first. They've arrested kids for drug-pushing in Maddox High. *Maddox High,* for God's sake! So what kind of bubbleheads are carrying on because of a scandal over half a century ago?"

Gram said in exasperation, "Well, for one thing, Guy Rigby left two little boys and a wife in that house on Fox Point. For another, sometime that weekend of the elopement he cleaned out the bank vault and took over a quarter of a million dollars with him." While I was still speechless, she added, "The bank fell long before the Crash."

I pulled the car off onto the side of the road. If Gram had wanted to shake me up, she'd done so. "Oh, my God," I said. "So *that's* it. And Beth Rigby, Kenneth's mother, must have married one of those kids. Right?"

"Yes, young Guy. His brother George married Naomi Wells, and they had a couple of boys and Edith. The boys both went out to California and settled there. They'd light back here once in a while, but not any oftener than they could help. Quite a batch of Rigbys out there by now, I guess, but I don't imagine that the clan'll come rushing across the country to avenge the family honor. They wouldn't care. They probably don't even know any family history."

"Daughter Edith married Jake Morley." I was filling in the blanks. "And they had darling Jane."

"Edith's not much of a producer," Gram said. "Good thing Jake already had a couple of boys by his first marriage, or Morleys would be pretty thin on the ground around here. Of course he got a real beauty in Jane, anyone could say."

"Anyone could," I agreed, "but not me, unless it's in a different context. How'd Guy ever get into the vault?"

Gram was enjoying herself now that she'd gotten into the swing of it. "He'd married Kitty Jarrett when he came back from the war—a real hero, genuine flying ace, and all. Until then the Rigbys were nothing much, an old family in Maddox gone to seed. But when Guy got Kitty, Earl Jarrett made him a partner in his bank for a wedding present. Well, Earl was the last of his line, and it was a blessing that he died before he could know what his precious son-in-law was about to do to his daughter, his bank, and his town."

"It must have been like an earthquake hitting the place," I said.

"It was. Guy ruined a good many people, so it's not only the relatives who have long memories. And Mary Ann's tarred with the same brush. Of course most folks or their young ones pulled themselves up by their own bootstraps in time, but it was a long nasty crawl through the Depression, I can tell you. One man hanged himself, and another blew his head off, but neither was much to begin with, according to Papa. *We* never banked with the Jarretts. Papa always kept his money, when he had any to save, in Tenby."

My mind was reeling. If I'd been avid before, now I was frantic to get a look at this phenomenon born Mary Ann and become Marianne. She'd have aged and would be impossible to imagine as a 1920s Helen of Troy, but if one could only tap her memories!

I started the car again, and Gram went on talking. "They couldn't get him back from France, and after a while Kitty divorced him. She got the cottage and the real estate, and then later he bought Fox Point from her. It was all done through Clem Cruikshank. If she'd had any gumption instead of being a born martyr," Gram said with some scorn, "she'd have hired somebody to burn the place down once she got paid for it. But she let him have it, and he must have got a good chunk of income from renting it all these years. Enough to pay the taxes and keep it up and hire Roy Thatcher full-time. Maybe he had dreams of coming home, who knows?"

"How did Kitty and the boys make out?"

"She moved back to the Jarrett homestead on Elm Street. She had some money from her mother, so she weathered the hard times pretty well. Never married again, though it wasn't for lack of attentions. Nope, she was a born martyr, as I said. I always thought she enjoyed being a tragic heroine and didn't want to swap it for being a plain wife." She had a funny little quirk to her mouth. "The way she raised Young Guy, he was the white hen's chicken, the crown prince, whatever. She picked out Beth for him, and then he died of a heart attack in a place he shouldn't have been." By another quick look at her mouth I knew I wasn't going to hear about *that.*

"What about the other boy?" I asked.

"George was neglected, and he was all the better for it. It was Young Guy's curse that he was the image of his father, but George was homely like his grandfather Jarrett. He had a happy marriage. He died of cancer, poor soul, but it was in his wife's arms."

I drove slowly in spite of my eagerness, so as not to get there too fast and shut Gram off. "Beth's raised Kenneth the same way his father was raised," she said. "It's a crime. And he's never kicked over the traces yet. He'd better, before he gets too long in the tooth. There's nothing sillier than an old bachelor kicking up his heels."

I grinned at the picture of Kenneth Rigby kicking up his heels. "Well, you can't really blame his mother much," I said. "One Guy robs a bank and deserts his wife and kids. Guy the Second raises hell in his own way and dies doing it so *his* wife and child are disgraced. That could warp a certain kind of personality. I'll bet she doesn't intend to let her son desert her."

"Or she'll hand-pick the woman, the way she was hand-picked. Somebody to take over from her and Kitty's ghost." She shuddered. "Gives me chills."

I didn't tell her what was said about Kenneth in certain quarters. It could or could not have been true: he managed his private life with the skill of a sorcerer. "He was so good to me when I was the pesty kid next door," I said. "I had such a mad crush on him. I took up tennis just so he'd coach me. Mrs. Rigby couldn't have been nicer until my breasts started to show. Kenneth kept on coaching me, but she turned so frozen-faced, the chill reached over the hedge, and Mother told me I'd imposed on Kenneth's good nature long enough." I laughed. "In my innocence I thought that when I achieved a body like a woman, Kenneth would see me as one, so I tried to feel lovelorn for all of a month afterward."

"Look at that!" said Gram. We came around a bend, and there was a new mailbox on our side of the road, with the names Esmond and Rigby on it in shining black letters. "No missing it, is there? She's right there in that house Guy built with Jarrett money. He stowed his wife away in it while he tootled back and forth to town in his merry Oldsmobile and took his train trips to Boston on so-called bank business while Mary Ann Esmond was studying up there. Of course nobody guessed a thing."

We turned in by the mailbox. "He sounds despicable," I said.

"He was a charmer," she said, which stopped my foot on the gas, the word was so strange coming from Gram. "When he came home from the war, there wasn't a girl in town who didn't have a newspaper picture of him stuck up on her bedroom wall beside the Prince of Wales—the old one, not Charles. Guy was marshal of all our parades, always so elegant in that uniform with all his ribbons, the whipcord britches, and the shiny boots. Oh, Lord!" Her gusty sigh broke up into laughter. "And it wasn't just the young ones! Going to the bank was an event, because if you happened to meet Guy he was always so courtly. That was the only word for it. I can see him now. . . ."

I was tired of the charmer. "Tell me about the Esmonds."

"Mr. Esmond worked on the railroad; he was the stationmaster for years. They were respectable people and strict even for that time. They had three girls, all talented. Susan, the oldest, had a beautiful voice. She married Thomas Hearne when she was sixteen. He was new in town then. He'd come to work as a ship carpenter in the Mackenzie yard."

"Then Morris Hearne is theirs. Do you mean to say that these two are Esmond Hearne's great-aunts? I loathed that jerk from the seventh grade on."

"And none of those Hearnes can sing worth a darn, either," said Gram. "Susan's gift died with her. But Susan never broke her parents' heart. I truly believe they'd have been happier if Mary Ann had died of TB or in a subway accident in Boston. Then they could have wept in public but still held their heads up. After the burglary and the elopement, Emma's eyes were nearly swelled shut from crying, but it wasn't so much shame as hurt because Mary Ann had told her nothing. She used to go off and meet someone whenever she was home, and Emma thought it was Sydney Carver, her violin teacher. Emma worshipped him, but she was just a youngster with her hair still in braids because her father wouldn't let her bob it.

She told me right afterward she was glad it wasn't Sydney, but that was the only redeeming thing about the whole mess."

"Guy Rigby was a rat," I said.

"Some people tried to find excuses for him. They said Mary Ann seduced him and got him to steal the money. Of course that made *him* out to be an absolute fool, which he was far from being."

"Well, I can see now why people wonder that she chose to advertise her presence like this, instead of coming quietly home. But if the stolen money and the wife and children didn't bother her then, why should it matter to her sixty years later? She must have been thick skinned from the start."

"Fifty-eight," Gram corrected me.

I turned around in the seat to face her. "Gram, did you *like* her when you were all girls together? Or was she like Jane Morley and Angela Fitton?"

"Well, Mary Ann was four years older than Emma and me, so she lived in a different world, you might say, and her music made it more so. She was always working at it. She'd outgrown Mr. Muir and took the train to Portland every Saturday morning for a lesson. When she was only fifteen she took over playing the organ at the Baptist Church for all one spring, Easter and everything, when Mr. Muir broke his leg." She was still awed by it. "*Fifteen!* Emma and I used to sneak into the back of the church to watch her practice. We worshipped her. . . . No, she was never stuck-up about her talent. It was just a fact of life with her, and she was busy going somewhere. None of us ever dreamed just where she was going, no more than she did in those days."

Gram was silent, and I could see the two little pig-tailed girls silent as statues in the back pew. I could hear the old hymns rolling out and the classical preludes and postludes I'd often heard in that church, and I tried to imagine a fifteen-year-old girl up there in the organ loft, but I couldn't.

"What did she look like?"

"She was skinny, fast moving, a music case always under her arm. Bright blue eyes, not dark blue like the Winter eyes. Black hair in one thick braid and a big tartan bow at the back of her neck. She always wore a middy blouse, and her tie was always tied crooked somehow, and her petticoat was always below her hem. Her stockings were always wrinkled, and her shoes scuffed." Gram laughed softly, as if to herself. "I remember different-colored lacings. One would break, and she'd grab the nearest piece of string or ribbon. Mama used to say she'd like to take hold of Mary Ann and shake and pull and tie everything into place. Emma swore Mary Ann left the house all in one piece in the morning, but when she came home, her mother would throw up her hands, and Mary Ann would look down at herself and say, 'What's the matter? Aren't I decent?'"

"Damn it, I *like* her!" I said. "I like that kid, anyway. She doesn't sound as if she'd grow up to be a *femme fatale.*"

"Oh, there were always a few boys she was driving away. Clem Sr., for one. There was something they saw, or guessed at, behind the way she looked at them as if she didn't really see them. Not stuck-up, as I said, but as if she was playing music in her head and listening for mistakes."

"How was she to Emma?"

"She always had time to accompany Emma when she practiced. She'd encourage her, and hug her. . . . I used to wish I had a big sister like that. She called us the Sunbonnet Babies."

I was liking Mary Ann more and more. But charming children can sometimes grow up to be monstrous or at least immoral adults. Now I was about to see the old woman who had been the dedicated prodigy, that marvelous big sister, that home-wrecker (as I'm sure they called her), that partner in grand larceny. And finally that concert pianist. The old woman was the veteran of one metamorphosis after another, and now that I was about to meet her, I had a violent fear of a crushing anticlimax. But I couldn't back out now.

One of those big motorcycles destroyed the silence on the black road behind us. I watched in the rearview mirror for it to go by the driveway, but it planed around the curve by the mailbox and then dared go past us, raising dust and echoing hideously from the woods.

The rider was made anonymous by his helmet. He flung out one arm in a backward salute to us as he charged up over the rise.

"I wonder what friend that is," I said. "One of those yearning lads caught in a time warp?"

"Let's find out," said Gram. "I told you I'm going out of pure greedy curiosity, and that's getting stronger by the minute."

5

Gram became abruptly quiet, and now that the motorcycle had stopped, the voices of the birds were clear. Monarch butterflies hovered over the goldenrod on the sides of the road. Then we left the trees and came to mown grass, with the granite bones of the earth rising out of it here and there like islets in a green sea. Ahead of us was the house. Its grey shingles, like the granite outcroppings, were subtly gilded by sunlight. It was as enchanting to me as it had been when I was small, with its odd angles and gables and its little unexpected balconies and porches.

I'd been there several times when Uncle Early took us in his pickup to deliver a special order of lobsters as a favor, not a duty. The truck had followed the drive past the recessed front door and around to the eastern end of the house to the kitchen, the garage, the woodshed, the clotheslines. Sometimes the cook was a local woman who knew us and gave us cookies; occasionally it was a woman who'd come with the family and treated Uncle Early as a delivery boy, which always put a new sparkle in his eye and gave him a farfetched twang that was never otherwise heard on land or sea. At Fox Point I saw children with a nanny; we'd stared wordlessly at each other, and probably they were as wildly curious about us as we were about them. Once there was a houseman in a white jacket, who joked in a strange accent with Uncle Early. Once there was a chauffeur who came to the harbor to fish for mackerel in his time off and was just like everybody else, except for that from-away (New York) speech.

Proust wrote that the essences of our most acute experiences are stored as if in jars, and whenever we take down a jar and remove the lid, we instantly become whatever we were when the essence was distilled. So I was that barefoot little kid again, tormented with curiosity about what lay behind the front door where the rich lived in their special atmosphere as gracefully as goldfish in their tank. And now I was going to find out.

I was also about to meet a Scott Fitzgerald heroine. I kept seeing her in peach chiffon with accordion pleats just to the knee, wearing a sequined headband and carrying a long cigarette holder and dancing herself around a room to *The Sheik of Araby* on the Victrola. At the same time she was one of Proust's titled old ladies who held Afternoons attended by only a few faithful friends and dutiful relatives, because long ago they had somehow disgraced themselves in society's eyes.

"You struck with Spanish mildew?" Gram asked tartly.

"I'm just deciding where to park," I said. I'd been so entranced I hadn't even seen the three cars and the motorcycle up ahead in a row where the drive passed the front door.

"Are you feeling all right? You look flushed."

"I'm feeling wonderful. Well, they've collected quite a few so far," I said. "Maybe they invited people personally, to be sure somebody came."

"Everyone was always fond of Emma," she reproved me, "and Mary Ann had her admirers, I told you."

"So did Lucrezia Borgia," I said. "But there can't be many left from that time."

"What do you mean, there can't be many?" She bridled. If you don't know how that's done, you should see Gram. "*I'm* here, and I can name you plenty more. We were a tough bunch."

I parked behind the motorcycle and turned the key, just as another car pulled up behind us. I recognized the station wagon, and so did Gram. "The Harpies!" she said in disgust. "Like a bunch of gulls after a cod head! If you hadn't lollygagged, we'd be inside by now."

"I'm sorry," I said, and I was. To call those three the Harpies might be a bit strong, but they couldn't be called the Three Graces by any stretch of the imagination.

"I told you Maddox is full of ghouls," Gram said. "Let them go in first. I don't want anybody to think I'm with them."

"Any of their families affected by the bank robbery?"

"All of them. But they got over it, didn't they? You can tell none of those three has missed a meal in the last fifty years."

They came around the car, borne on waves of merriment and assorted perfumes. Clara Fitton poked her silver-blond chrysanthemum head in on my side. "Hello, Eden dear! Don't you look nice! What's the matter, Vinca, don't you have the courage to go in? Come along with us, dear."

"Don't wait," said Gram with a grim smile.

"Are you still writing, Eden?" asked Dora Sayers from Gram's side; pink marshmallow with ruffles.

"I sure am," I said. "The new one's scheduled for spring. I hope you'll all buy it to give someone for Easter."

More girlish glee. You'd think I'd said something outrageously witty. If any of them had ever bought one of my books, she'd been careful not to let me know. Clara said sentimentally, "Angela's expecting her third at Easter. Isn't that a coincidence? Angela bringing a baby into the world, and you a book."

Impossible to miss the message. I smiled and said, "That's lovely! Angela always has such beautiful children!" I didn't know what they looked like, but the blatant flattery took the wind out of her sails. She spoke across me to Gram.

"Wouldn't you know that Mary Ann Esmond would be shameless enough to come back here in the face and eyes of everyone, take over this house, and then invite the public in?"

"Well, it's legally hers," Gram said unwisely.

"What about *morally?* If there were any justice she'd have been dead long ago, and he'd never have lived to enjoy the fruits of his crime."

Dora came in on time. "She's an offense to all decent people."

"You going in to tell her that?" asked Gram.

From behind Dora's ruffles Sarita Barron said plaintively, "Our family has always blamed her because Guy took that money and my poor great-uncle did away with himself. My mother said Mary Ann Esmond was always bold as brass. I suppose showing herself off in front of all kinds of people all these years has made her even more of an exhibitionist." She sounded as if Mary Ann had been a stripper.

"I tried to get Beth and Edith to come," said Clara. "To have his daughter-in-law and his granddaughter just walk right in and stare her down could give her a stroke or a heart attack on the spot."

"Oh, Clara, you're *awful,*" said Dora delightedly.

"It would work better if you dug up Kitty and lugged *her* in," Gram said. Sarita and Dora uttered little cries of horror, but Clara smiled steadily and said, "Don't I wish I could! No, Edith will never step foot in this house, and neither will Beth. But imagine—*she* had the nerve to call Jake Morley to go over the heating and plumbing. She must have known he's Edith's husband."

"It was nice of her to give him the work," I said. "Keep it in the family." She ignored that.

"He came himself to check things out, but he never saw hide nor hair of them, just the housekeeper. *Nurse* is more like it, they both must be pretty decrepit by now. Well, you can't live a life like that and not have it catch up with you."

"A life like what?" Gram said ominously; now Emma was being insulted.

"Oh, here comes Connie Wells!" Sarita happily changed the subject. "I have to see her about lending some of those wonderful quilts for the exhibit." She hurried back to the approaching car, Dora behind her.

"Well, Eden," Gram said to me, "we could have sat in the car in our own driveway if that's all we're going to do."

"Right!" I said with gusto. I opened my door, and Clara had to move back. "I'll wait for the girls," she said.

"There's strength in numbers when anybody's feeling a dite shy," Gram said.

"Who's shy?" Clara's laugh went strident. "*She* should be feeling shy! Nobody else!"

Gram had the grace not to grin. We walked rapidly up the driveway past the other cars. "Did I ever tell you how I hated Angela Fitton in school?" I asked. "She was Jane Morley's sidekick."

"Listen," said Gram, laying her hand on my arm. Then we heard the music floating out to us through the open windows. It was the first movement of Beethoven's "Spring" Sonata for violin and piano. I'm no musician, but I have favorites, and this is one. I tried not to make a sound as I walked, letting myself go with the familiar ravishing phrases, praying that those women would stay away gabbing until the movement was over. We let ourselves into the dim hall. I wanted to stay there in the shadow to listen, without the distracting spectacle of human performance, to the song of the violin and the exquisitely authoritative voice of the piano. But Gram was impatient to see Emma, and she went straight to the door of the long, light-filled room beyond and beckoned to me. I went reluctantly, trying to keep the music disembodied. I wasn't expecting fragility now, not from what I was hearing, but mountainous flesh packed hard into corsets or left comfortably unrestrained under elegant caftans. Mary Ann would, of course, be flamboyant; dyed hair, much makeup, including black false eyelashes, and long danglies swinging from her ears.

Gram sat down just inside the door, and I sensed without seeing a male figure leaning against the wall on the other side. I knew there were many other people in the bright room, but I saw only the two musicians. The woman in sea-blue playing the piano was thin to gauntness, her back so straight I stiffened my own, involuntarily. Her white hair was impeccably waved and shaped, and there were no danglies, but small diamonds twinkled like dewdrops in her ears. Her strongly aquiline face was without expression, only her eyes moved in it toward the violinist and then back to some point in space beyond this room.

The violin was the star here. The slight woman who played it with her cheek against the honey-toned wood and her eyes shut had no less authority than her accompanist.

The movement ended, and applause washed around the room like surf. The stranger beside me came away from the wall, clapping his hands and shouting, "Brava, brava!"

The other faces in the room now emerged for me as if from a dissolving fog. The Hearnes seemed to be applauding because everybody else was or with relief because the inexplicable music was over; Sydney Carver was standing up to clap. He was balding and a bit stooped, but in his happiness he looked nowhere near ninety. Jason Higham, band instructor at the high school, was also on his feet, his round face incandescent; his wife Tillie, a wispy, kiddish-looking girl, both mother and piano teacher, was wiping her eyes. The two Clement Cruikshanks were more moderate in their pleasure, but it was imprinted on their long, sharp features. The motorcycle rider turned out to be Robbie Mackenzie, who worked for Jake Morley and delivered oil and bottled gas to the harbor. They'd sorely missed his playing the piano at school affairs, now that he'd graduated. He stood alone against a far wall, a very skinny, sandy-haired boy, blinking and apparently trying to swallow his Adam's apple.

"God, but you're terrific, the two of you!" Jason Higham said fervently.

"You're just saying that," said the pianist in an unexpectedly deep voice, "because you're so astonished to find us functioning at all, let alone groping through Beethoven."

"*Groping!*" cried Tillie. She jumped up and kissed each sister on the cheek. "Excuse me, I just couldn't help that, I'm so *excited!*"

"Of course I haven't heard you two play together for over half a century," Sydney said, "but I wouldn't say you'd deteriorated."

"That's the Sydney we know and love," said Emma. She had a merry, youthful voice. "Never an overstatement. Thank you, my dear."

"Praise from Caesar is praise indeed," said Mrs. Rigby. "Whenever you told Emmie she'd had a good lesson, she took wing."

"And eventually she flew a long way past me. But I take pride in saying that I prepared her for flight. And as for you, Mary Ann—I mean Marianne—"

She rose from the bench and put her hands on his shoulders. "I've never stopped being Mary Ann, Sydney. Well, Tracy," she spoke to the overweight teenage Hearne, who sat between her parents on a sofa, chewing gum and looking as vacant as a cow but not so handsome. "Were you bored to stupefaction?"

The girl stopped chewing and stared through her fringe. She said without enthusiasm, "No, it was neat. I mean, like, you can really play."

"We do give a pretty good imitation of it, don't we?"

The Cruikshanks were like a pair of tall blue herons moving deliberately through the shallows. "Mary Ann and Emma, it's great to have you both home again," Clem Sr. said.

Esmond Hearne, who had helped make my school days memorable, cleared his throat and made a sortie into the conversation. "Is that violin a Stradivarius? I hear they're worth millions." A faint animation brightened him.

"No, dear, this is an Amati." Esmond subsided into indifference; evidently he thought there was no other valuable violin.

"But it sounds lovely," his mother anxiously exclaimed. She was a rather pretty, soft-eyed woman with an apprehensive smile that kept flickering on and off. Esmond, thick and dark, was sharply turned out, whereas Tracy, as if dedicated to making herself as unattractive as possible, was squeezed into skin-tight pink jeans and an outsize T-shirt. Her badly tinted hair looked as if it hadn't been washed or combed for the entire summer. Her mother glanced at her and quickly away. "The piano is beautiful, too," she said bravely.

Mrs. Rigby stroked the deeply curving side. "My treasure. The poor thing was woefully out of tune after the long journey home, and I thought I'd have to have someone come from Portland. Then Roy Thatcher suggested Gideon Wilkes. I must say I was impressed by the first sight of him on the doorstep." She laughed. "It doesn't seem right that he can be reached by mail. I should think a note in a hollow tree would be more his style."

Morrie Hearne heaved himself upright from the depths of the sofa. He's heavier and swarthier than Esmond. "You mean you let him *in?*" he demanded. "Was Roy here, too?"

"No." Mrs. Rigby sounded amused.

"But Gideon Wilkes!" he said angrily. "We won't have him in the house." His eyes seemed to swell behind his glasses, and he ground his cigarette hard in an ashtray. "This place isn't what it used to be, you know. There's a lot of weirdos around."

"I remember some from my day," she said. "And I lived through the German Occupation of France." It was quietly, pleasantly said. "Believe me, a Gideon Wilkes turning up at the door is a blessed sight if you've ever lived in terror of the Gestapo."

There was a short, shocked pause. Then Jason, the young band instructor, said cheerfully, "Oh, Gideon's harmless. Not many pianos to tune these days, but he's trusted in most of the houses that do have them."

"He and I always have a cup of cocoa together after he tunes ours," said Tillie. "With marshmallows. Gideon's got a sweet tooth."

"You're *alone* with him?" Annie Hearne leaned forward.

"Well, my cat's there," said Tillie. "And the baby in his playpen. He likes Gideon's playing better than mine."

"Just to see him on the street turns my stomach!" Mrs. Hearne said. "We have that man from Lewiston to tune our piano. And I tell Tracy to go way out around Wilkes if she meets him on that old bike of his and to speed up! I wouldn't trust him around young girls."

"Or young boys, either," Morrie said heavily. "Stuff you hear nowadays."

"He wasn't put away as a sex offender, Morrie," Clem Sr. said.

"But he was put away, wasn't he?" Morrie said belligerently. "And the rest of us all know what for, if my aunts don't."

"Your aunts know, dear," said Mrs. Rigby. The stranger laughed to himself, and I glanced at him. He wore white jeans and a red and white Rugby shirt. There was a small gold ring in his ear, and he had a black beard. As if he felt my look, he turned toward me, smiling; he had a good, strong nose, but the shape of his mouth was hidden by the short, elegantly shaped beard. His eyes were dark enough under peaked brows to seem actually as black as coal, or crows. Light glinted off them like reflections on a wet black road at night.

"Hello," he said pleasantly, and then we were discovered. Marianne Rigby was coming swiftly toward us.

"Welcome to Fox Point," she said. "I don't know any of you, but you're welcome." *Her* eyes were as blue as Gram had described them.

Gram stood up and said, "Don't you know me, Mary Ann?"

"Vinca! Good Lord!" She drew Gram to her, calling over her shoulder, "Emma!" Then she held Gram off, smiling and shaking her head. "It's heaven to see you! So you grew up and married Snowy."

"Yep, got him away from Allie Pease at the class picnic."

"Remember that naughty little poem based on 'Pease Porridge Hot'? She was precocious."

"She's 'born again' these days and thinks sex education in the schools is what gives young ones ideas. Makes you wonder where she got hers."

Marianne laughed and embraced her again. I was introduced and felt as if I should curtsy and call her ma'am. Emma came up, moving as lightly as a girl and laughing like one, and a new series of hugs began. "You have those lovely Winter eyes," Mrs. Rigby said to me. "Everybody used to say they were wasted on boys, but such boys! Those eyes could get them anything. And you're the girl who writes the books. But your picture in the *Journal* didn't do you justice." She raised her eyebrows at Blackbeard. "Are you the grandson of an old friend?"

"I'm afraid not." He had a deepish voice with a from-away accent. "I'm Nick Raintree, and I'm working at the Glenroy yard. I crashed the party, I'm not sorry to say. I couldn't resist a chance to see Marianne Esmond in person."

"You turn a pretty phrase, Nick Raintree."

"And you're marvelous," he said bluntly.

"Oh, people say that about anyone over eighty who can get out of bed by herself and put her shoes on the right feet. So you're a boat builder, of wooden boats, too. The Glenroys won't do anything else, I understand."

"That's why I'm here," he said.

"Mrs. Rigby!" Robbie Mackenzie's cheeks were bright red as if with fever, and his eyes were watery. I hoped he wasn't bringing some vicious summer virus into this house. "Please, could I talk to you for a minute?"

"Yes, of course. Excuse me," she said to us and took him by the elbow and walked him away to the side that overlooked the drive, well away from the others, who were now all talking freely among themselves, except for Tracy and Esmond Hearne. I was about to join Tillie Higham when Nick Raintree said to me, "So you're the writer. I hadn't been in town twenty-four hours before I heard about you. I wish I could say I'd read your books, but I haven't."

"Goodness, you mean you didn't rush at once to the library or the bookstore? Then please don't. You wouldn't like them."

"Why?" He sounded amused. "And why have you taken an instant dislike to me?"

"I haven't," I protested, blisteringly aware that I was making a complete fool of myself and for no discernible reason. "I mean you really wouldn't like my books. They're not very blood-and-gutsy. But they suit a lot of readers, who are very loyal to me."

"Then why do you need to defend them?" He was not quite smiling, but it was there. I hated that dandified beard of his and the one gold earring; he probably fancied himself the picture of an Elizabethan seadog. And what in hell ailed *me?*

6

"Eden!" Gram called to me from the sofa by the fieldstone fireplace. "Come and meet my old chum!"

"See you," I said to Nick Raintree as I turned away.

"I hope so," he answered quite seriously. So I hadn't offended him—he was too thick-skinned for that—but I had certainly offended myself. I headed for the fireplace, wishing it were the door. I had to go out around the grand piano and make my way among islets of conversation, and here I was held up for a moment when Jason Higham crossed my path to take some music off the rack and pass it to Sydney.

That's when I saw Guy Rigby watching me. If I hadn't been halted, the portrait would have done it. He had been in his middle years when it was painted, a man of robust good looks; there was a mere suggestion of white at the temples against tanned skin. His hair looked to be dark brown, and thick. Wearing slacks and sport jacket, his shirt open at the throat, he sat comfortably out of doors in a deep wicker chair, one knee slung over the other, hands loosely laced around it. Sun and shade speckled the scene, and his eyes picked up the green of the grass and his shirt. It's a cliché to say the eyes in a portrait follow one, but his gave that discomforting effect.

Discomforting because it was so agreeable, and he was supposed to be a scoundrel. Everything about him—the easy pose, dangling foot, relaxed hands, expression—invited you to sit down, take your time, and tell him about it. And if you just waited long enough, the incipient smile would come, and you *would* be telling him all about it, whatever *it* was.

The charisma came right off the canvas at me. Perhaps the artist had glamorized him, but from Gram's story the glamor had been there already. He was the sort of rascal who in an earlier century would have had ballads written about him. I wanted to stand and stare until I'd absorbed every detail.

Everyone else seemed to be consciously ignoring him, and I hoped they were all too involved in their talk to notice me. The uneven tides of assorted voices and subjects rose and fell about me. I looked away from the eyes to prove that I could, minutely observing the small table at his elbow under the tree, a pair of glasses laid on an open book, a pipe in an earthenware saucer, a glass half full of white wine.

I hope he died while he was still like that, I thought. Sipping his wine and listening to Marianne play. I hope he didn't fade away, but we'll never know, so I can go on hoping he went in full bloom.

"Eden, dear," Annie Hearne called to me, and I jumped, then became very attentive. "I've been telling Tracy she should invite you to talk to her English class this fall."

"Any time, Tracy," I said. It's still so flattering to be asked to speak anywhere, and schools are best; the kids ask such good questions.

Tracy's silent response looked like *Over my dead body* or, possibly, *Up your nose, sister.* "As soon as school starts and she talks with Miss Parnell, she'll be in touch," her mother said.

"You do that, Tracy," I said. Her brother Esmond, who'd been yawning through his father's lecture to Clem Sr. about the iniquities of the planning and zoning boards in Maddox, launched himself into my path.

"Let's take a walk, Eden." Chad does it with much more charm.

"Sorry, my grandmother wants me," I said, moving on.

"You're Snowy all over again," Miss Emma told me. "Prettier, of course." She looked fluffy and delicate, but her hand was strong. I wanted to hold it and examine it as if it were a jewel or a precious artifact. "We have your books, we sent for them. I can hardly wait for the next one, to see what happens to that upstart Ione!" Brown eyes sparkled with humor behind her glasses. "Goodness, what is *that?*"

"You don't want to know, Emmie," Gram said.

The Harpies, forgotten for a blessed interval, had finally come in. I thanked the gods of music that the meeting of the coven had lasted long enough to spare Beethoven. The room fell expectantly silent; there was no way to talk above Clara Fitton.

"Oh, I've been in this house often!" she was trumpeting in the hall. "Remember the years the R. J. Fennells rented it? And they were so generous to our Bicentennial Fund? Many's the cup of tea I drank here with Mrs. Fennell. Quite the grand dame she was, a *genuine* lady."

She arrived in the doorway and faced a roomful of people who were all looking at her. She stopped so abruptly that the three behind her were taken by surprise; for an instant the doorway was jammed with them. Nick Raintree moved farther along the wall.

"Well, here we are!" she cried.

"And so you are," said Mrs. Rigby, rising from the window seat where she'd been talking with Robbie. At sight of her Clara was clearly knocked off balance, and while she struggled for an even keel Connie Wells, a stooped sprite of a woman with a cane, slid around her elbow, smiling luminously. "I told you I'd be here, Mary Ann! Now where's that kid sister of yours?"

Marianne bent and kissed her. "Connie, I'm glad you came," she said. "Emma's over there." Miss Emma met her halfway with glad little cries and sat her down on the sofa between her and Gram.

Clara was steady again, as if buoyed up by rage because Marianne was not a tremulous little old woman who was easily cowed.

"I'm Mrs. Henry Fitton," she announced. "These are my friends, Mrs. Edmund Sayers and Miss Barron. You don't know us, but most of our parents went to school with you. So we're representing them, you might say."

"It's so nice of you to do that," said Mrs. Rigby. "Later we shall have to sort them out. Let's find chairs for you all. You must know everyone here, I'm sure." Dora and Sarita murmured and ducked their heads. Clara looked pointedly at Nick Raintree's earring and then turned her back on him.

"I suppose I must go and make hospitable noises," Miss Emma said.

"I managed to keep them outside prattling about quilts until you finished playing," Mrs. Wells said. "But I hated them for making me miss hearing you."

Emma gave her arm a little squeeze. "You'll hear me, Connie. We'll drown ourselves in music." She went across the room, and Lydia Carver joined Mrs. Wells and Gram. Annie Hearne talked to Tillie Higham about Tracy's piano lessons, and I went looking for a door to the front veranda. I discovered that the room was ell-shaped, and Clem Jr. had gone around a corner into a generous alcove, walled with filled bookshelves broken by the door onto the porch and a wide window on the western side. Clem sat on the window seat by an open casement, smoking his pipe, and Fiona Heriot sat cross-legged beside him, grinning at me.

"Lah-de-dah! Aren't we the elegant one!"

"An Afternoon with a capital A calls for a dress," I said.

"Well, I couldn't compromise myself that far," said Fee, "but I've got on my fanciest pants and my frilly shirt, and I washed my hair and my ankles. And I couldn't wait, so I was here before anybody else, and I met the ladies *first,* so there."

"Gloat, gloat, see if I care, so there," I said. "I think Glen went out to see you, unless he's plying some woman with lettuce and eggplant."

Fee laughed. "Well, he can keep Julian company. I didn't think either Julian or the ladies would appreciate his presence here today." She held a stoneware sleeping kitten on her palm and stroked it with a finger. "He'd be crazy about this. I'm going to get him one."

Clem watched her and smoked his pipe. If it hurt him to hear her going on about Julian, it didn't show. I hoped he'd given up a long time ago.

I sat down beside Fee. "Gosh, I'm glad to see you, but I didn't expect to."

"You don't think I'd miss a chance to meet a living legend, do you? My dad used to talk about her when he'd had just enough booze to make him poetic. He must have inherited that nostalgia from our grandfather—Dad was an infant when the you-know-what hit the fan. Does your father ever talk about it, Clem?"

He shrugged slightly. "She's one of our clients."

"I wasn't asking for *secrets,* for heaven's sake!" She slapped his knee. "But to hear Dad talk, she was a cross between Nefertiti and Lily Langtry, only with genius. He'd found a photograph of her in Grandfather's strongbox and had it framed under glass. She was a handsome girl, and she's a handsome woman now. I'll probably look like a witch at that age, if I live so long," she said blithely. "My God, listen to it out there!"

The arrival of the Harpies had raised the decibel volume in the main room. It was mostly Clara, who was talking about her difficulties with her septic system.

"From Beethoven to sewage," said Fee. "You know where I'd like to ram her head, don't you?" She slashed her fingers across her throat. "Let's go out there and take charge of the conversation."

"Listen," said Clem, and we realized the room was suddenly growing quieter, until only Clara was left. Then that stopped abruptly. Marianne's deep voice said, "The Aeolian Harp Etude." Fee slid off the windowsill and pulled at my arm. We walked out to where we could see, and Clem came and stood behind us. The music rippled exquisitely through the room, and I wished it would go on forever. It redeemed the afternoon; it wiped out Clara, without a smear left on its luster. Fee's grip kept tightening on my arm.

Across the room Nick Raintree sat astride a chair with his arms folded on the back and his chin resting on them. Robbie Mackenzie was still on the window seat. The last note had barely died away before he was blundering out past Raintree as if he were blind, knocking one shoulder against the door frame. In the midst of the applause the motorcycle started up and roared away, the sound mercifully cut off by the first curve.

"My God, that was some reaction," Fee said. She let go of my arm, saying sheepishly, "I've probably left marks on you, and I didn't even know it. You'd think I'd never heard good music before."

"But you've never heard it played by this person," Clem said.

"This person," said Fee, "seems to be setting Maddox on its ear for the second time in her life. Clara Cluck clapped like mad, did you notice? If she can't out-talk, she'll out-clap."

"I think it's time for a cup of tea," Miss Emma was saying. "Or if anyone would like wine, it's on the console table over there, just serve yourselves. Tracy, dear, would you like to help me?" Tracy sat in bovine obstinacy, then arose so quickly I suspected an unseen pinch from her mother. She rolled toward the hall door on her high heels.

"Come on, Eden," Fee said, "let's make ourselves indispensable." But Nick Raintree was already on his feet. "I'm good with heavy trays," he said. "I used to be a busboy."

"Who's he?" Fee asked.

"His name's Nick Raintree, and he works at Glenroy's. He's got a from-away accent."

"You sound pretty curt. What else is wrong with him?"

Clem Jr. had gone back into the alcove, where I could see him cleaning out his pipe into an ashtray. "Did you ever take a dislike to anyone on first sight?" I said. "Maybe it's that gold earring. Wait till you see it."

She widened her eyes at me. "My!" I'd just made a fool of myself again, and Fee wasn't likely to forget.

Mrs. Rigby and Tillie were clearing music and magazines off a low table. "Mrs. Rigby, you play beautifully," Clara Fitton informed her.

"Thank you," said Marianne gravely. "That's very kind of you." Clara sat back with a satisfied smile; *I'm not afraid to give credit where credit is due.*

Nick came in with a tray holding the tea service. Miss Emma and Tracy followed him with smaller trays, and Miss Emma established herself behind the teapot. Tracy was excused the task usually allotted to the youngest, the handing around of napkins and teacups; Miss Emma must have distrusted that dangerous wobble on spike heels. I felt an atavistic call to duty, but Nick Raintree had taken over again.

"I think he's an escaped butler from California," said Fee. "He probably took the silver when he left. They'd better watch out around here; he may be casing the joint."

"He's enjoying himself," I said. "He's got everybody wondering just who he is and how he happens to be so much at home here. It's a kind of exhibitionism." I didn't want him bringing me a cup of tea. "Let's go and get our own."

"Wine for me," said Fee. Clem was back, and she hooked her arm in his. "Let's go, old friend. I hate to drink alone."

A glass of chilled white wine would have suited me, too, but not when I was with Gram. I wandered toward the tea table, stalling till Nick was a good distance from it. Then I took my cup and went to sit down beside Tillie Higham. "Isn't this fantastic?" she whispered. "I'm just afraid it won't last."

"Why?" I whispered back.

"Because it's too perfect. Or else *some* people will barge in every blessed time and take over."

Clara was on her way for a refill, shrugging off Nick. "You needn't wait on me, young man," she said. "I always do for myself."

"I could tell," he said solemnly.

"Attractive, isn't he?" Tillie murmured. "Who is he?"

"All I know is he says he crashed the party because he wanted to meet them. Works at Glenroy's, or so he says."

"Well, he's making the most of this, isn't he?" Over by the console table Fee lifted her glass to me and then drank.

Miss Emma was urging Clara to have more of those delicious little things Mrs. Thatcher had made. Tracy, supplied with a tall glass of something, was working her way steadily through the delicious little things. Esmond chomped mechanically on them, not a pretty sight. Clara gave the plate a look that should have shriveled the contents.

"My maternal grandfather was Lionel Corbett," she said loudly to Mrs. Rigby. "You must remember him."

"Oh my, yes! They used to say that anyone who *was* anyone had to be seen off by Mr. Corbett, or they weren't well and truly buried."

"Mr. Corbett had a great flair," Miss Emma said. "With him a funeral was almost a performance. So elegantly stage-managed. And what a presence he had! I can see him now, the way he'd take off his hat and bow to the ladies on Main Street. So *gallant.*" She gave it the French pronunciation. "Of course," she rambled on, "none of the Esmonds could afford Mr. Corbett. We always went to Mr. Johns, in Tenby." She might have been comparing dentists.

"My grandfather lost his reason after the bank failed," Clara said starkly.

"Talk about rattling old bones," Fee muttered in my ear with a warm, sherry-scented breath.

"All his savings went at once," Clara continued. "He wouldn't eat—he thought he couldn't afford to. You could say he starved himself to death."

"How tragic." Mrs. Rigby sounded sincere.

"It was too bad," Miss Emma said innocently, "because you'd think that with people dying all the time he could have continued to make a good living, no matter what." Fee poked my shoulder. "Father always said that as long as human beings kept on being born and dying, the doctors and undertakers would never be out of work."

Lydia Carver burst out laughing. She was a lean, raw-boned woman, taller than Sydney, and she'd been one of the first women doctors in the county. "I don't know how undertakers were paid, but a country doctor in those days could always be sure of plenty of chickens, bacon, eggs, and potatoes. And *turnips!* Lord, I got so tired of turnips! And if a baby was born in the summer time, you could anticipate be sure of a good mess of green peas and all the corn you could eat."

Clara's cup rattled dangerously in its saucer. "Some of us were wondering, Mrs. Rigby," she said, "how you had the courage to come back."

My scalp tightened with shock. It was one of those moments when you are so appalled by someone's conduct that you can't meet anyone else's eyes, but the common embarrassment is like a stench in the room.

Marianne, gently stirring a cup of tea, said, "Oh, you know the Maine winters aren't nearly as brutal as their reputation. I've endured some absolutely horrible winters in Europe, even in the south of France. We're having a whole new heating system installed, and this house is just full of sunshine, so I know we'll be snug."

Clara said in a queer, half-throttled voice, "Of course you will be." She turned away, slopping tea. Her ears were red among the silver-gilt curls. Fee tweaked a hair on the back of my head, and when I looked around at her, she winked.

7

That wink of Fee's! She winked at me the first time I met her, and whenever it had happened since then I was eleven again and experiencing the incomparable joy of friendship discovered.

I couldn't wink like Fee then, and I thought it was because I lacked her nonchalance, her dare-anything spirit, and the satirical humor of someone who, at eleven years of age, could invite you with the flick of an eyelid to share a joke nobody else in the world knew.

The world on that day was the seventh grade of Maddox Junior High, of which my father had just become principal. Until then he'd been principal in a small inland school, and my mother had taught in the elementary school, as she would be teaching here. We were *from* Maddox originally, but I knew Job's Harbor best, because I had spent so many summers there with my grandparents.

The first day in a new school can be traumatic when you don't have an arm-in-arm chum. My brother Zack was welcome in senior high because he was such a great athlete. My father was settled into his new job. My mother would be teaching beside a couple of friends she'd grown up with and with whom she'd gone to Farmington. Back in their youth both parents had been woven into the fabric of the town. *I* was the miserable alien, wishing on that bright September morning that they could have been something else but what they were.

I could hardly eat my breakfast, my stomach was in such upheaval. I wished I could throw up at will—one of my cousins found it extremely helpful. Then I could have put off the awfulness for another day.

My mother and I were the last to leave the house. She was looking very pretty in an autumn-leaf print with a full skirt and wearing a maple-red sweater over her shoulders. Gram had made my dress, a crisp linen patterned with little ripe apples. My long straight hair was held back by two new barrettes. I shall remember both outfits till the day I die. I thought my mother was callously ignoring my misery, but she told me later that she knew one word of encouragement would have broken the dam.

We parted at the gate of the elementary school, where the happy little kids ran screaming around the playground in their new clothes. "See you after school, dear," my mother said briskly and kissed me. I watched her go away from me as if she were about to disappear into the Fifth Dimension, and then I walked on alone under the elms to the guillotine.

I wished it were pouring and blowing, but the late-summer day tortured me with its brilliance and fragrances and raised memories of summer freedom only two days back. My throat swelled shut as I imagined how blue the harbor looked this morning, and I felt as if I'd never see my grandparents again. The thought of Uncle Early whistling on the wharf started sentimental tears. The gulls, the cat, and the dog; I couldn't bear to think their names.

I knew nobody would ever want to hang out with me, because I was the principal's daughter. Even the Job's Harbor kids I'd played with for years would now see me as one of the Enemy. Sure, they called, "Hi, Eden," but that didn't mean a thing; I was sure of it. We were divided forever.

I found my home room and then my locker and stood gazing blindly into it, listening to the heartless confusion all around me. A violent thump on my back made me jump and gasp. There were snickers. From the next locker a chunky dark boy in snug corduroys and a bright new argyle pullover poked his face into mine and said, "You the new head honcho's kid?"

I'd have denied if I dared. As I opened my dry lips, the two girls at the next locker snickered again. One said, "That's all we need around here, a snitch."

"Like having a police spy," said the porky boy.

The other girl said, "Well, nobody *has* to *include* her in *anything.*" She was one of the prettiest girls I'd ever seen, and now I knew what "willowy" meant. I could take that in even while I was sick with fury and pain, fighting to keep the tears from showing. Once the three saw those, they'd move in for the kill. I wanted to slam shut my locker door and walk away, but I knew their laughter would follow me like an arrow in my back. If I could just keep my face marble-hard and out-stare them until the bell rang, then I'd leave this school forever. Nobody would get me inside it ever again.

The cheerful tides swirled out around us, uncaring. The three were watching me with greedy fascination, torturers waiting for the first whimper to burst into a scream.

"I'm glad *my* father isn't warden of this jail," said the pretty girl. "I wouldn't be able to hold my head up."

"You know he's going to shorten *lunch?*" The other girl wasn't as pretty, she wasn't tall and willowy, but she'd already had her ears pierced and was wearing lipstick—not very well, probably put on fast after she got out of the house this morning. "And he believes in *long* detention. And lots *more* demerits! And *going through lockers!*"

"If he searches mine, my father will take him to court," said Porky (a nickname that was an insult to an animal far more noble than Esmond Hearne would ever be).

I would have told them none of it was true, if I could have spoken. Off to my left, out of my line of vision, someone had stopped; I could feel the presence. They saw it, and as their gleeful eyes instinctively shifted, it was my chance to duck into the nearest classroom. But instead I looked around, too, at a skinny, tanned girl wearing jeans and a boy's shirt. Her straight light brown hair had been carelessly chopped off around her neck. She winked at me.

The wink said, "*Get them!*" At once it turned their nasty little voices into the vain crackling of thorns under a pot. It didn't make me at once brave, arrogant, and contemptuous, but the well of tears dried up in a fire of joy.

"My, don't you look nice today, Jane!" she said to the pretty girl. "Washed your hair, have you? I hear horse piss really makes it shine—that what you use?" She sniffed loudly. "I can smell it from here. But maybe it's old Porky. And that *is* Angie behind the clown makeup, isn't it? I hear you got into the seventh grade because now you can count to ten. Too bad you haven't got more fingers, but you can always use your toes. Do you have more than five on each foot? Gosh, Porky, what are you going to do over here without any second graders to feel up when you can grab 'em?"

The surprise attack was so outrageous, we left them inarticulate and snarling when she pulled me into the classroom. It was a wonder they weren't lying in wait for us that night with baseball bats.

Fee and I had different homerooms, but we ate lunch together outdoors. She told me that if I'd learn to twist a few wrists it could help with Jane and Angela. "And I've sent that tub of lard in the fancy sweater home bawling more than once. Just get hold of the hair on the back of his neck, and you can bring him to his knees. Or get his little finger, like this." She demonstrated enough so I got the idea. I didn't think I could make it work, but I had no doubt that she could, and had.

"It's not your fault your dad's principal, any more than it's my fault my dad's the town drunk. Or one of them." She grinned at my expression. "If you haven't heard it already, you will. Might even meet him. He's harmless, though." She crunched away on an apple. "There, we've got it over with; we know all our family scandals."

A lean brown boy in jeans and a Maddox Mariners sweatshirt joined us for a little while. Glenroy, her twin. They were so casually friendly I wished lunch could last forever. As it was, Fee and I did eat lunch together every day all through junior high.

I never gave Jane and Angela and Porky another fearful thought. I might never scald them with words as Fee did, let alone twist wrists and little fingers, but I knew it could be done. Henceforth they were nothing more to me than annoyances.

Jane and Angela weren't wildly popular, I found out, and they stuck together for mutual comfort. Esmond Hearne had hips and a fat behind, and the other boys called him Lard-Arse. He had to pass the torment on, but not to me; as Fiona Heriot's friend, I was safe. In time I could be sorry for him, but I never liked him.

Even when I'd made myself comfortable in school and realized that most kids didn't care if my father was principal as long as he was fair, I never stopped being grateful for that wink. I had a friend, and Fee acted as if she'd just been waiting for my arrival. She told me that she'd had no close friends other than her twin brother, because even the nicest parents weren't keen on their kids going to the Heriot house, where there was a drunken father and no mother; she had died when the twins were small.

"I could go to *their* houses all I wanted," she said, "but I felt like a charity case. You know, not equal. They were sorry for me, but *I* wasn't sorry for me. Glen and I can always manage alone. Some people are dying to get us away from Dad for quote our own good unquote, so we steer clear of them, and we behave ourselves so nobody ever has a chance to say we're neglected. If we need advice we go to the Cruikshanks. They're in charge of the estate... such as it is."

Her twin, that long, thin amiable boy, always ambled along as if half in a dream. He worked around the waterfront, doing any chore he could get: running errands, sweeping floors at Rigby Marine, painting skiffs, filling bait bags for a couple of lobstermen, and cleaning up their boats when they came in. Fee walked and groomed dogs, sat with them, gave them pills and drops when their owners couldn't get by the teeth and the growls.

She weeded gardens and mowed lawns she'd gotten away from boys. No one ever needed to feel sorry for the twins, as she said. If either of them ever experienced moments of self-pity, nobody else knew it.

She liked my parents because they acted as if she and Glen were fit to be in charge of themselves. The only restriction was that I couldn't ever spend a night in the Heriot house because of the fire danger. Their father used to wander around in the attic, carrying a candle because the top floor had never been wired. The Cruikshanks insisted that the twins sleep on the first floor and know exactly how to get out fast if they had to.

After I made other friends, Fee was always "The Friend," and I meant as much to her. When we were sixteen and she was spending the night with me once when my parents were away and my brother in college, she told me that she and Glen were Maddox Heriots by adoption. Their father had been the illegitimate child born to a relative somewhere in Maine or perhaps out of state.

"Glen and I used to make up all kinds of stories about his real parents," Fee said in the dark. "Not that we didn't love Grandma and Grandpa, but you know how kids are. We were so curious. Dad said he felt so safe and loved that he never gave his birth-parents a thought. But then why did he become alcoholic after our mother died?"

"Maybe because of that," I said. "Or maybe it's something chemical in his system. An allergy."

"It's a fifth of whiskey a day," she said cynically. "And what's he looking for, night after night, going through the old trunks and boxes again and again? I wish there was a way to find out, for him as well for us. But I suppose it's too late for him. This instant he could be dropping a candle, and—"

And Glen and their father could be about to burn to death. We had to get up in the middle of the night, dress, and walk over to the Heriot house. But it was all dark and quiet.

Their father, a gentle, boyish man, drove around the countryside when he was able, buying junk that he kept in the carriage house and sold as antiques. Some of it really was. These sales and the twins' jobs kept them going. His father had left the house to the twins, and there was a fund from which to squeeze out the taxes, but none for repairs. My parents suspected that the Cruikshanks put their hands in their own pockets literally to keep a roof over the Heriots' heads.

Then in the twins' last year of school, the winter after Fee told me about the adoption, Ronald Heriot died. On one of his scouting trips in the old van, he was caught in a snowstorm and skidded off a lonely hilltop road into some trees. Waiting for the snowplow, he'd kept himself warm with the heater on and a pint of whiskey. He died drunk of carbon monoxide poisoning.

Glen cried at the funeral, but Fee didn't. Some said she couldn't believe she was really free of the burden the two had taken on when they were still so young. Still, he had been a lovable man, and their father, and all they'd had besides each other. A tight trio had been destroyed when the van went into the snowdrift.

We brought them home afterwards for a good meal. I wanted to put my arms around Glen, I was so shaken by his grief, but Fee's stiff square shoulders defied anyone to hug her, even her best friend.

By then my father was principal of the high school. The twins turned down his pleas and those of the guidance counselor to apply for scholarships. Glen could go to work full time at Rigby Marine, and save toward a decent boat; Fee had a job with a vet and was still a gardener on the side. They had been so self-reliant and free to act for so long, Fee said, they couldn't have pinned themselves down to a tight academic schedule and the obligations of scholarships. My father didn't try to argue.

The Cruikshanks suggested selling the house before it was too far gone, so they could live somewhere less haunted by memories, and they agreed. The buyer, a local man, wanted to turn the house, including the carriage house, into four apartments and still keep its nineteenth-century character. What was left of the estate was Heriot Island, which a much earlier Heriot had taken for a bad debt back when islands weren't worth much. They were offered a phenomenal price for it, but refused. They used the house money to buy Glen an almost new twenty-eight-foot lobster boat and two hundred traps. They hired carpenters to repair the old island house. They had to live somewhere—why not the place they loved, which had no ghosts but brief, glowing memories of happiness? They'd never had much time to stay on it because of their jobs and not wanting to leave their father alone too much. To go there to stay was all the joy they could imagine.

The first summer when they were camping out there, with the work being done on the house, I went out often to stay and loved it. Glen was lobstering full-time, Fee was his partner, and they sold their lobsters to Grampa.

Glen always had girlfriends, or hopefuls—even then he had that mysterious laid-back charm—and Fee had boyfriends in quick succession. By the time I'd finished my first year at college and was feeling pretty learned, I decided that because of her devotion to a father, who had been more like her child, and her close companionship with her twin, she'd have a hard time finding a man who'd suit her.

There were plenty who wanted to try; my brother Zack was among them, and my cousin Jon, and of course Sprig Newsome. Later, Clem Jr. Then she fell in love with Julian Hardy from across the river, one of the men who had worked on the island house. Sprig Newsome said she'd at last found a man she could boss and who liked it, because if Julian had any more brains he'd be a half-wit. That was unkind, because Julian, though not very articulate, was an excellent carpenter, and that's what you need in a family, even more than a doctor.

Fee and Glen spent only that first winter together on Heriot, with Julian going back and forth between St. David's and the island in his twenty-footer in all kinds of weather to finish the inside work on the house. Finally he stayed, and Glen was relieved; he was too much of an extrovert to enjoy the island winters with no neighbors, but Fee loved it, and he wouldn't have left her there alone. He made his share of the island over to her and bought himself a woodlot on the road a little way up from the harbor, facing Bugle Bay over on the northwest side of our peninsula, and built a log cabin on it. He had a mooring in the harbor for his boat.

In a year he had his thirty-eight-foot boat built, for lobstering eight months of the year and shrimping in the winter. He sold his other boat to Fee and Julian, who used her until Julian and his brother built *Island Magic.* Glen and I had settled on each other without any fanfare. It was always a pretty relaxed atmosphere; he found no fault with my writing, and I had no complaints about his never mentioning marriage. Fee kept asking him if he wanted to be the last of the Heriots, but we both ignored that.

The shattered trio had been replaced by a quartet. I remember a long, unblemished, leisurely happiness. And it had all started with a wink.

8

It has often been suggested that Grampa hire someone to keep the store open on Sundays, adding ice cream and packaged snacks to the candy bars and cigarettes and putting in a bigger soft-drink cooler among the coils of rope, rubber boots, cans of paint and engine oil, and other gear and tackle of the fisherman's trade. Grampa always listens with the contempt (polite) that it deserves. Local summer people and natives know enough to gas up on Saturday if they want to use their boats on Sunday. And with everything closed up and no public landing, the harbor isn't a gathering point for the speed freaks who like to roar downriver in a squadron and then raft together at anchor with ghetto-blasters rending the air and beer cans flying overboard like autumn leaves in the line storm.

Grampa never wants to go anywhere on Sunday. "I'm happy to sit at home under my own vine and fig tree," he says. But he'd invite all the world in for a mug-up if it came to his door.

On the Sunday night following the Afternoon the world consisted of four of my grandparents' friends who'd driven down to the harbor knowing they'd catch someone in. They'd waited for Gram to come home and had been invited to supper. I begged off and took Chad for a row around the harbor in the lovely melting blue and gold hour when everybody else was eating and thought about the Afternoon. I wanted to come back to earth like a feather floating downward from a passing gull, not like a stone dropping into a well. When I got back to the Hayloft, I would set down impressions of the afternoon like a series of watercolor sketches. I was both exhilarated and starstruck.

It was very quiet this evening in the small white house across the empty parking lot. No radio or television blasted through open windows. They'd gone somewhere; they came and went by the right-of-way that went with the place, so they parked on the far side of the house. I hoped unrealistically that Shasta had gone into labor and was even now having the baby, so I could give them notice in a few weeks. Of course nothing is ever that simple.

I didn't owe them reasons, but to salve my conscience I could say I wanted to live there myself. Then I'd feel duty-bound to start the remodeling. Something small and inexpensive but necessary, so I wouldn't be a liar. Much had to be accomplished in the house before I'd want to move in, and for some reason, I always shied away from imagining myself actually living in Great-Aunt Noella's house. I ought to sit down with myself and talk it out, I thought glumly. After the elation of the Afternoon I became depressed, and when I feel like this, I'm convinced that whatever I'm working on is no good, and even my agent will hate it. I couldn't bear even to think about the manuscript in Job's sea chest.

I called Glen. He was home, and alone. "Come on over," he said. "I've been mackereling. We'll broil up a dozen."

We ate the little broiled mackerel with our fingers out on the deck above Bugle Bay, in the light of a flaming sunset. Conversation was unnecessary except to praise the food. The birds sang as they do on summer evenings; the gulls were flying seaward, the brown young ones close to their mothers. Late mackerel-fishermen dallied on water so dazzling we could hardly make them out in the fire of a dying day.

We cleaned up the dishes—Glen is far neater than I, and with no effort—and went up to his sleeping loft. At first it held a bronze light from the afterglow, and the blue dusk came on without our noticing it, until we opened our eyes to the dark. I felt wonderfully sure of myself, the world was back on its axis, the book was *good.*

So was life. It often occurred to me at moments like this that if we were married nobody would ever have to get up and go home, but usually the balance of my mind was restored once I was back at the typewriter. If anything works well, why fix it?

Glen lifted his face from my neck and said drowsily, "How was the capital A Afternoon?"

"Didn't Fee tell you?"

"Fee didn't have much to say. When we picked her up at Fox Point, she came down the dock ladder smelling like a wino and saying, 'Don't speak to me, I'm in another world.' She fell asleep before we reached the island. You know how Julian is about booze. He looked like the entire WCTU rolled into one. He's probably not speaking to her yet."

"Maybe the sherry helped," I said, "but she and I were both dazzled out of our skulls by the famous Esmond girls. Miss Emma's a darling and a super musician, but Marianne is magnificent just to look at, as well as listen to."

"What's so wonderful about some old bird who ran away with a bank robber when she was a flapper? Oh, hell, people being what they are, I suppose Bonnie and Clyde would have a fan club, too, if they'd survived to be eighty."

My euphoria was being rapidly blasted away. "They've got one anyway," I said. "Even dead. But this is hardly the same thing."

He turned over on his back and spoke quietly to night-hidden rafters. "She was accessory to a crime that ruined half the town, maybe more. She lived damn' well on the proceeds during the worst of the Depression, and I understand he was a genius at investing what he had left, or his broker was. Now she's back here owning a house and land worth a million or so at today's prices. What's so handsome about that?"

"OK," I said. "I know what you're getting at." Though we were touching, I felt that we were suddenly too far apart, and I was eager to cross the gap. "I've been going over it myself," I said. "Would I be so impressed by her if she were an old crone with a malicious expression? Or a sentimental one, which would be worse? And would it matter how striking and straight she is, if she couldn't play music in a way that melts my bones? *No.* But if she looked like Old Lady Witch crouched over the keyboard and played the way she does, I'd be terribly moved and impressed. The fact that she looks so handsome at the piano is a plus, but I honestly believe I admire her talent as a musician. Music doesn't call for moral judgments."

He said, "Mm." Encouraged, I went on. "If she'd been a mass murderer, I wouldn't want to be in the same room with her, no matter what. But for Fee and me she's a character from a great twenties novel, suddenly popped out of the book where she's been gracefully aging all these years." I was really charmed by the simile. Glen was so quiet I thought my dissertation had put him to sleep. Then all at once it hit me that the Heriots or his mother's people could have been badly injured by Guy's act.

I turned over to him and embraced him with my free arm and asked him straight out. "If it's so," I went on, "Fee's never mentioned it. She called Marianne a living legend, and she said your father used to go on about her as if she were this great romantic heroine, and that he caught it from your grandfather."

I felt rather than heard him chuckle. "Grandfather Heriot was quite a sport around town when he was young, and not so young, too. Liked horses and raced a couple of trotters at all the fairs. He was a buddy of Guy's, but who the hell wasn't in those days? I always figured he was in love with her, too, and wanted to think Guy seduced her and carried her off to Europe by force. Never would hear a word against her. Our grandmother knew better than ever to make a crack about Mary Ann Esmond."

"But what about the bank failure?" I persisted.

"Never touched us. The Heriots could ruin themselves without any outside help. Grandma saved the Heriot homestead when she married Grandfather, because her old man made so much money with his schooners. Before Grandfather died, he had the house made over to us kids so Dad couldn't lose it the way *he* almost did."

He was silent again, and I wondered if he was thinking of his mother, the girl who hadn't lived to see her twins into the fourth grade; of the life he and Fee had lived in the old house with a boyish father whose existence, for all the time they knew him, had been a long slide toward destruction. I tightened my arm protectively around him, and he roused himself.

"So Dad passed Mary Ann on to Fee. For God's sake—no, for mine and your own—don't *you* go catching the itch and acting like a teenager starting a cult about some gone-by movie star."

"I don't intend to," I said haughtily. "But Marianne Esmond's gift has nothing to do with her alleged crime."

"Alleged!" He snorted. "There you go, making excuses."

I sat up, and he hauled me down again and wrapped his arms around me, pinioning mine. "Where the hell are you going?"

"Home. And if I ever mention that woman to you again, I'll—"

"You'll what? Oh, shut up. I asked, you told, and then I made a speech. That's what comes of being chairman of the board of selectman and having to hold forth at Town Meeting. I was always shy before."

"Funny, I never noticed. You certainly hid it well."

He ignored that. "I guess I didn't want to hear you making a fool of yourself. It was bad enough seeing Fee with that silly grin, breathing out sherry fumes, when she and I both know what it was like with Dad. I took it out on you, and I apologize."

"That's very handsome of you," I said. "But Fee's got too much common sense about liquor. She didn't have a lot to drink. I was there to see, and we left about the same time. I think she just didn't want to break her mood. Being in that living room today was exactly like being in a novel. Spoiled only by Clara Fitton in full cry."

He had relaxed enough to laugh. "And what about the Hearnes? Breathing hard about the place, I suppose. Having to wipe away the drool. The way things are today, Fox Point could be worth more than a million as a condo site."

"That word turns my stomach, don't say it!" I protested.

"Who's this Nick Raintree?"

"I thought Fee didn't tell you anything."

"She yelled his name at me when I left the wharf out there. Told me he'd take the wind out of my sails. So he must be an eligible male."

"I don't know how eligible he is," I said. "He may be married. He could even be a polygamist. We talked for about five minutes. He's from out of state, but he didn't say where, and he's working at Glenroy's."

"That black beard and earring turn you on?"

I rose up again, but he held on, squeezing. "I'm not letting you go home tonight."

"Let's see, who'll be the audience when I let the car roll in at the crack of dawn? Uncle Early will probably drive in at the same time. Grampa will be just letting Chad out the back door. Sprig Newsome will be ready to go haul before sunup for the first time in his life. Then there'll be the usual early birds. You'll be hearing about it on your boat radio all day long."

He shut me up by kissing me and then rolled out of bed. "You've made your point." He didn't mention marriage as a solution to these problems. He pulled on his jeans and went down the ladder. "Have a cup of coffee and a piece of pie before you go?"

"Where did you get it?" I asked, with foreboding.

"It was on the table when I came back from the island. I don't question gifts from the ravens."

"Well, Elijah, that particular raven will probably come flapping around looking for thanks when she thinks she can catch you alone," I said. Casually, I hoped.

"Then I've got something to look forward to," said Glen. "Come on down and eat in your birthday suit."

"I will not," I said.

He drove my car up the winding dirt lane to the black road as if I would find it dangerously difficult after dark; a bit of male chauvinism I didn't challenge because it might mean he was trying to postpone our parting. We hugged and kissed by the mailbox. "Going out with me tomorrow?" he asked. "I guess it's today now."

"I have to work on my book," I said. "Once I get it sent off, you just try getting rid of me."

"OK," he said agreeably. "I'll try." He gave me a comradely squeeze.

I drove home carefully in case deer or raccoons were crossing. When I came down our own bit of dirt road, the barn rose big and black between the driveway and the security light out at the end of the dock; a sign of changing times, that light. If it hadn't been there, I'd have walked out on the wharf in the starlight and listened to the small mysterious sounds of the harbor at night and seen the brightest stars reflected just beyond my feet. We all hated that light and hated even more the need for it.

I didn't slam my car door, lest it rouse Chad, but left it unlatched and went up my steps and so to bed. It had been quite a day.

9

I awoke to the cries of the gulls and the sound of oarlocks as the men rowed out to their moorings in the topaz light. There was an orchestra of other noises; pickup doors slamming in the parking lot, engines starting—I knew whose, I knew them all. That quarterdeck shout echoing from mooring to mooring, that bray of laughter. The expert whistler. Someone's radio went on, and I got every word of the Coast Guard weather report. I knew each boat without seeing her as she went out the harbor mouth. I heard the voice of *Little Emily* and wished I were with Glen. Yachts followed the lobster boats, going out by engine power because there was no wind yet to fill the sails.

I made coffee, toasted an English muffin, and got to work at my table beside the big window. On the wharf below, Uncle Early hosed down the floor of the bait shed, Gramp went into the store to work on the books, Chad stood on the car and barked at any sea pigeon who had the temerity to paddle with its little red feet to within ten yards of him. The Barrys' outboard motor coughed and choked all the way across the harbor as they headed their dory toward a day's clamming on the Davids.

A red sunrise burned briefly behind Fort Point and dulled to a harmony of greys. Yesterday's perfection and this hush meant a weather-breeder; the land was looming, and the seabirds were washing themselves.

I did three hours of work with the dictionary and the thesaurus, a yellow legal pad and my favorite pen. Then the Temple boys came to mow the lawn, and I decided to drive to Maddox to have lunch with my parents.

There were at least two hours between now and lunch, and Gram gave me a shrewd look when I asked if she wanted any errands done in town.

"Nope. Visiting the scene of the crime, are you?"

"Ay-uh," I said. "Now that you mention it. This Rigby-Esmond business is a living novel, and even if I haven't read it yet, I want to get all the settings straight in my head. Whenever I read a book, I draw a map for myself. It helps the imagination."

"Save your imagination for making your living," she advised me.

The day was cloudy and still, predominantly green and silver, with the yellows leaping out like flares from a sun in hiding; on either side of the black road the golden rod was gaudy against the woods.

I slowed down when I came to the Fox Point mailbox. There was nobody else in sight, so I stopped, staring up the driveway. All right, so I was behaving like that teenager Glen had warned me about. But who was to know but me? How I longed for the nerve to drive up there right now. I imagined them having mid-morning coffee; they would ask me to have a cup, and I would thank them for yesterday and try to say what the music meant to me. They'd ask me to sign their copies of my books. It would all be so comfortable, and Marianne would repeat Miss Emma's invitation to come often. A wondrous new dimension was about to be added to my life.

But I didn't have the nerve to intrude like that. One didn't just "drop in" at some houses after one meeting. Besides, it wouldn't have been like my cozy fantasy; they might sleep till noon. Or they'd be practicing. I thought of leaving the car and walking up and listening from outside, but if Roy or Nell Thatcher caught me, I'd look like an imbecile. I sighed and drove on.

Around the next bend I met Gideon Wilkes free-wheeling down Sunday Hill on his elderly bike; a scarecrow in old army fatigues, hair like grey straw poking out from under the cocked-up brim of the Allagash hat he'd probably found in the town dump. He was laughing to himself like an exuberant ten year old and included me in his triumph, waving one arm so hard I thought he'd hurl himself into the ditch like a pile of dead branches lost off a truck and break every limb. But he kept his balance, and I watched him in the rearview mirror going out of sight around the turn. Perhaps he was on his way to tune Marianne's piano again. Why hadn't I ever considered piano tuning as a career?

The River Road ends when you cross the bridge at the Narrows below Maddox proper. Jake Morley's plumbing and heating business is on the left as you come off the bridge; General Mackenzie's lime kilns still stand at the back of the lot where Jake's trucks park. Robbie Mackenzie (not a direct descendant; many Mackenzies had come to Maddox) was just taking an oil truck out. He waited for me to pass and waved without smiling. What had so upset *him* yesterday?

I thought I knew, having been way up there myself, and I wasn't a musician. To listen to Marianne could be hell for a young pianist who was still struggling with the perplexities and insecurities of growing up. Never mind if she'd been playing for seventy years or so, compared with perhaps ten for him. He hadn't been, and there was no more reason for dreaming of Olympus. *Ah, but a man's reach should exceed his grasp, / Or what's a heaven for?* What had Browning meant? That Heaven would make it all up to you? Cold comfort when at eighteen you stand among the slain dreams and see a long bleak life ahead of you.

I'd faced something like it, and still do when I read certain writers. But I have my tough Winter heritage to anchor me, and I'm thankful to be able to make my living doing something I love. And if I don't make the *New York Times* best-seller lists, I'm spared their lethal reviews.

The business section of Main Street is short. I found an empty slot in front of the First National Bank of Maddox and sat there looking at it. There was no trouble seeing it as the Jarrett and Rigby Bank, because I'd seen that in old photographs. I wanted to know how Guy had looked committing the burglary and then letting himself out the back door into the May night, carrying all that money. The Oldsmobile must have been parked out there, and he'd driven straight out of town.

What was the weather like? Pouring rain, thick fog, so nobody was likely to be out after midnight? What did the Maddox police force amount to in those days? I doubted that a policeman had patroled the business section all night, trying doors and flashing a light through the windows.

If Guy had robbed the bank on a Friday night, it gave him a couple of days' head start. Whatever had he told Kitty when he left Fox Point that night? That he had to see someone in town for an hour or so? Was his conscience already dead when he kissed his small sons good night, knowing he was leaving them forever?

By Monday morning he must have already picked up Mary Ann in Boston and sailed for Europe. The burglary was timed for this sailing; they'd have had tickets and passports ready, so she'd known she was going. OK, wrong of her, but she still might not have known about the theft. I had to hang on to that, for some weak-minded reason.

But how could I gloss over the wounds to the sister, the parents, the wife, the children? If I were using Marianne's life for a novel, I'd have a hard time making that young woman a sympathetic character. By tradition she'd have to suffer greatly to expiate her sins. If Marianne had suffered, who knew? Maybe it had all been worth it. I thought of the portrait. *A face to lose youth for, to occupy age/ With the dream of, meet death with.* Browning again.

Across Main Street, between the Craft Corner and the gift and card shop, there was the Hearnes' in-town office. Morris Hearne and Son, Contractors, the show window said. The display was a model of the condominium development they'd wanted to build on a point just down the river from the bridge. It had been vetoed last year by the town and the DEP, but they still showed the model. Could they now be dreaming of Fox Point?

A bright new panel truck pulled up in front, and Esmond got out on the traffic side. He looked fixedly at my car and then up and down the street. When two gravel trucks came slowly through, hiding me from him, I left my car rapidly and walked toward Sawyer's Grocery.

I didn't know why Esmond even had hopes of a date, but he liked to catch me alone and ask me why I didn't like him. "I know I was a rotten kid," he once said mournfully, "but I've changed. Besides, everybody knows Glen Heriot only likes his sister. He'll never marry you." He never had a chance to say that again; not to me, anyway.

I passed the entrance to the Cruikshanks' office; their names were in gilt letters on a black board. Two girls came out of the drugstore licking ice cream cones and exchanged giddy comments with the boys taking up the bench out front. One of the girls was Tracy Hearne, wearing shorts that were even worse than the jeans. But she was laughing and looked astonishingly pretty; I'd never have believed it possible. The other girl had a blond Dutch cut and pink cheeks and the small, compact body of a gymnast. I'd seen her before but didn't know her name. Tracy looked fatter than ever beside her, but the two of them seemed to enjoy each other's company and the joking with the boys. They didn't see me as I went out around them.

At Sawyer's I bought some black grapes for my parents. When I came out, Esmond had disappeared into the office, and the Harpies and some auxiliaries were having a meeting outside the card shop as if they hadn't convened for a month. I backed out and turned off Main Street by the Baptist Church to go down the hill toward the river again. Here I passed the Carver house, where Lydia was working in her herbaceous border and a young girl with a violin case was going up the walk. Sydney still took a few pupils whom he considered worth his efforts.

I'd have loved to visit the Esmond house, but I didn't know where it was; perhaps it had been burned or torn down. I could find out and at least visit the site. There'd be other houses that had been standing when it had all happened. Halfway down to the river I turned left and drove through to Ship Street. The mast flagpole is at the head, up on Main, and Rigby Marine is at the foot, occupying the old Mackenzie sail loft; they haul boats out for the winter where once the General's vessels were built.

Off to the left, the white chimneys of Strathbuie House gleamed through the trees. At the foot of Ship Street I turned right onto Water Street, parked a little way beyond Rigby Marine, and walked back. Two fiberglass runabouts were on display on the wooden walkway that led from the sidewalk to the open doors.

I'd known Kenneth Rigby since I was eleven, when we moved into the house next door. He'd been a quiet young man who'd had nothing much to say and was now an older young man who still had nothing much to say. He sailed a Friendship sloop, skied in winter, played tennis in summer and poker once a week. He had no women friends, but if he was a homosexual it was the best-kept secret Maddox ever had. Even those who suggested it, for lack of better things to do, couldn't point to evidence.

When I was inside the shop, I tried to figure out what I was there for. The other people consulting with clerks, or looking around, seemed to have some idea in mind, but mine was pure nosiness. I joined the browsers among the varnished oars and dinghies, then inspected the ranks of outboard motors along one wall as if I couldn't decide what horsepower I needed but was tempted by seventy. Kenneth was in the office finishing a telephone conversation.

Now that I'd seen his grandfather, the phantom of a resemblance was inescapable: the way his hair grew, the hazel-green eyes. No stunning glamor, but that expression when he came toward me from the office doorway. *Sit down and tell me all about it.* I wondered what *my* expression was, to get that look from him. Maybe it was the result of my sudden guilt attack.

I turned to leave, but he called my name and caught up with me. "What can I do for you?"

"I don't know," I said honestly. I used to hope he had sworn a vow to himself to marry me when I grew up. Now I was was truly grown up, and if he nurtured any passion for me, it was another of those best kept secrets. He was waiting now, pleasantly unhurried; though I was no longer enamored, I felt no older than in the days when *with his own hands* he corrected my grip on my tennis racket. This time, however, my heart didn't jump about.

I lied. "I want to give Glen a birthday present for his boat, and I don't know what. It has to be something useful, not gadgety."

"What about those?" He pointed at the mats draped over a rack; they were made of closely woven narrow strips of rubber tire and lacquered a shiny black. "A local man makes them. The fishermen like them; it makes a difference having something like that under their feet all day. Come and try one." There was a sample on the floor, and it was thick and springy to stand on. In my relief at finding a legitimate object I had to try not to overdo my enthusiasm.

"That's great, just perfect! I'll take one."

"What size?"

"Oh, gosh." By now I could swear he'd seen through me and was secretly laughing at me. I seemed to be having a premature hot flash. "I can't ask. I want it to be a surprise."

"Take a three by five. You can still surprise him, and then you can change it for a larger one if you have to."

"That's a good idea. Thanks, Kenneth."

He rolled up the mat and tied it with twine while I wrote a check. "Too bad I can't gift-wrap it," he said. "Maybe I should stock some of that paper with Snoopy on it."

"Or teddy bears," I said. We both laughed. He carried the mat out and put it in the back seat.

"When's the next book due, Eden?" he asked.

"In the spring sometime. Maybe around April."

"Good," he said. "I'll be looking forward to it."

"*Really?*" My astonishment was genuine.

"Why not? You get your history straight but keep it lively. Besides, I never stop being surprised because the little girl next door grew up to be a writer and a good one."

"What did you think about me then? That I'd make a career out of being a nuisance to you?"

He laughed out loud. "You were never a nuisance, Eden. Sort of unnerving at times, I'll admit, with that silent stare."

"It must have been a relief to you when I started falling in love with boys my own age," I said.

"I remember the day it hit me, 'Kenneth, old boy, you're over the hill,' I said to myself. I thought of taking to drink, but I resisted." More laughter, and it came so easily to him, his eyes were so candid, that I could believe he was not at all perturbed by the return of Marianne Esmond. Maybe he was even relieved because his mother had something else to concentrate on beside him.

When I arrived at my old home on Elm Street there were three cars in the Rigby driveway, and Clara Fitton's station wagon was one of them.

"I think they're all making little wax dolls and sticking pins in them," my mother said. "I wouldn't put it past some of them. They're so *outraged.*"

"Does anybody ever hear Kenneth say anything?" I asked.

"Oh, he comes and goes as he's always done," my father said. "Never a change in him that you can see." There was a slight emphasis on the last word. "But who'd ever know what Kenneth is thinking?"

My parents are both active in the historical society, and my mother was on the committee to choose the pictures to make up another book in the "Old Maddox" series. She spread out a collection for me to see, and there was the first Guy Rigby on his Shetland pony outside the Jasper Rigby house. He was a pretty little boy with dark curls and a charming smile, in which I could see Kenneth.

"Two people who shall be nameless," said my mother, "and one of them a man, object strongly to using this. Well, it's no great loss, there are plenty of photographs of cute kids. But *these?*" *These* were photographs of the 1912 hockey, baseball, and track teams, and a group of young men at the depot in 1917.

"One objection to *that* one was, verbatim, 'My grandfather never came home from France—he's been just a name on the honor roll—but that one came home to rob widows and orphans! And now his whore's back in town!'"

I didn't wince. The word had no association with the woman who had played Beethoven and Chopin yesterday.

"You know," Dad said, "we have a murderer in the Grand Army collection, and I didn't hear any objections before the book was published, or after. But it wasn't because nobody knew about it. It was because nobody wanted to talk about it and embarrass the descendants."

"Tell, tell!" I demanded.

He got out the book and showed me. "There he stands in his uniform, looking like Abraham Lincoln's trusty right hand. He was court-martialed and hanged for robbing his dead comrades on the battlefield and using his bayonet on one who wasn't dead and objected to his actions."

"Oh, my God!" I said. "Who was it? Scout's honor, I'll never use it. I'll never talk about it. Just tell me."

"Josiah Blackburn," said my father. "He sent his parents in sorrow to the grave. One of his great-great-granddaughters is next door right now, digging up Guy Rigby's scoundrelly bones." He smiled wryly. "You'd think that by now Mary Ann Esmond would be more of a curiosity than an object of hatred. But it's as if they hate her for being alive and healthy."

My mother and I simultaneously knocked on wood. "It's pathetic, in a way," I said. "If that's all they have to do and think about."

"It's infuriating!" said my mother. "Thank God the rest of the committee is sane. We can't leave out all the other boys just because Guy Rigby is in the pictures, too. And he wasn't an embezzler and a wife-deserter when the photographs were taken."

"Didn't they ever try to extradite him?" I asked. "They might have got some of the money back."

"Pressure was put on somewhere and somebody to prevent it," said Dad. "He knew where too many bodies were buried. Too many people had confided too much in him. He could have blackmailed half the town, but he just took the money and ran."

"You should see the portrait at Fox Point," I said. "'O villain, villain, smiling, damned villain!'" I was rather smug about remembering it.

"*Hamlet,*" Dad capped me. "Act 1."

10

Home again. The Temple boys had mowed, and the place smelled of fresh-cut grass. I made a pot of tea and sat down to write out what I'd heard and seen today. I described my tour and the key characters, not leaving out Gideon Wilkes and Tracy Hearne; they were part of the Fox Point novel, because Gideon was the piano tuner, and Tracy was a grand-niece of the Esmonds. I reported the mild touse about the photographs and included the hanged soldier, though I didn't write his name.

I wished that I'd known when I was twelve that Jane Morley's great-grandfather had robbed his own bank. Fee couldn't have known, because she'd have used it without a qualm. I could just hear her. "What makes *you* think you're something on a stick? Go home and ask your mother what her grandfather did!"

While I was working, a northwest breeze sprang up, and when I emerged from a good hour of note-making, with digressions, everything was almost achingly brilliant in the light of that yellow dwarf star we call the sun. The boats were coming in, and Grampa and Uncle Early were on the lobster car. I went down to the wharf, feeling as if I'd been a time-traveler in the past for hours.

A coastal warden was on the car, too, checking hauls for short lobsters and V-notched egg-bearing females. The Temple boys were in *Woodstock*, their bright yellow skiff, hanging on to a corner of the car to watch the inspection. The men were cleaning up their boats and talking. Chad had to stay up on the wharf, where he lay by the gas pumps and yearned audibly over the edge.

The Barrys' dory came in loaded with full hods, outboard clattering as usual. Richie never looked around as he ran the dory's bow up on the scrap of gravelly beach below the house, but Toby yelled across to the car. "How's business over there, Ralph? You caught any of them Job's Harbor high-binders yet?"

"Mind your failings, Toby," the warden called back.

"Want to check my clams, officer?" Toby asked cheekily.

"I'll leave that to your buyer. Tom Pease knows what's good for him."

Toby laughed, swinging out two heavy hods at a time. Richie looked sullen and exhausted. Shasta appeared on the bank, holding Derek; he was fighting to get free, yelling, "Boat, boat!"

"You want to be careful, dear," Sprig Newsome called to her. "Don't let that kid bounce up and down on the other one's head. Likely to make it foolish." She gave him an apprehensive little smile and looked quickly back at Richie, but he was slogging up the beach carrying two hods of clams and didn't lift his head.

When Toby had slung his load up onto the bank, he took Derek from Shasta and set him in the boat while they moved the rest of the clams. Caroling his ecstasy, Derek climbed over the seats, gathered up loose clams, took hold of the outboard motor throttle, and made engine noises. Shasta folded her arms on her belly, hugging herself as if she were cold. Her mouth looked swollen and red in her pale face.

"Jesus, Shas," Richie said, "you could at least back the truck down here instead of standing around picking your nose."

She turned and walked heavily back up the lawn. "That boy," said Sprig Newsome loudly, "has got the prettiest way with words in the county, I shouldn't wonder." Richie didn't look around; he climbed the bank as if his rubber boots were loaded with old flatirons. Toby took the baby out of the boat and put him on his shoulders and ran up the beach with him, yelling, "Everybody dodge, here comes Daredevil Derek!" The baby's half-fearful laughter trailed behind him.

When they'd all disappeared, and the truck hadn't yet come to get the clams (I was wishing Shasta had simply gotten into it and driven away), Ben Temple said to the warden, "If you find any shorts or a notched female, do you arrest the guy right off and take him away in handcuffs?"

The warden laughed. "Nothing so spectacular."

"You kids watch too much TV," Steve Wilmot said.

"We never saw anybody get busted by a fish warden," Ben explained.

"That's because this is a law-abiding community," said Grampa.

Ben persisted. "Well, can you arrest anybody you see doing other kinds of wrong, like hurting someone? Because if you did, you could arrest Richie because he hits Shasta."

Will turned solemnly to me. "He did it again, Eden, and we saw him. Yesterday." My stomach lurched around a bit. I didn't want to hear this today, or ever. "We hear him cussing her all the time, but yesterday we *saw* him hit her right across the mouth." He touched his own mouth, tenderly. "She almost fell down, but the truck was in the way."

With what he clearly considered the best part, Ben burst in. "Then Toby came rushing out of the house, and he said, 'By God, Rich, you do that again and so help me I'll flatten you so anybody could slide you under a door to wipe their feet on!'"

For once even Sprig was at a loss. Grampa austerely handed Ira Neville his money. Putting it away in an old billfold, Ira looked steadily at the two youngsters as if he had something to say. He was a small man, like a jockey, his bony face prematurely lined; his youngest son was in a correctional center for breaking and entering. Whatever he was thinking, he didn't say it but backed his boat away from the wharf and circled out to the mooring.

"Probably wondering how come Sonny didn't get a suspended sentence," Uncle Early said. "But he's locked up, and that little bastard is out and slapping his wife around."

The warden shook his head. "It's not my fault he's out. Blame the judge."

"Mum wanted Dad to go over there the other day when we could hear Richie swearing and Derek howling, but Dad said he couldn't walk into somebody else's house unless somebody was screaming for help, and Shasta wasn't, and he said—" Will punched him in the ribs, and Ben said furiously, "*Hey!*" Then he gave me a round-eyed stare and said on a long breath, "Oh, boy, I goofed."

"And he said he wished Eden would throw them out, right?" I asked. They nodded silently.

"I want to be sure Shasta has a place to go with the babies," I explained. "It wouldn't be fair to put her out because Richie hits her, would it? That would be like my hitting her, too."

"I guess," said Grampa, "you'd better start house-hunting for them yourself, if you ever expect to move 'em."

"I wish I could move her away from that rotten Richie!" I said furiously. "But she's the only one who can do that."

"I like Toby even if he is a crook," said Ben.

"Everybody has some good points," said Grampa. "Just don't take pattern from the bad ones."

The pickup next door sounded as bad as the outboard motor. Richie backed it down over the lawn with enough impetus to send it straight overboard if the brakes failed. It stopped short of the bank and shuddered noisily while the Barrys got out and loaded the hods into the back without speaking to each other. Toby dourly ignored us this time. Ben and Will watched openly with the merciless curiosity of children. The rest of us didn't, but I think we were all conscious of every motion over there. The tension was as pervasive as the cloud of exhaust from the truck. When it had ground its way up the slope again, Grampa said, "Good thing you got ledge under that lawn, Eden, or there'd be nothing left but ruts by now."

"That's why I haven't objected," I said absently. That stupid Shasta. Too stupid to think of either herself or the children.

"Hi, Gorgeous!" Sprig Newsome saluted me. "Haven't even spoken to you yet, have I?"

"Gosh, Sprig, I thought you'd never get around to me, but I hate to beg."

He's as homely as a hedge fence but not at all handicapped by it. A free spirit. His motto is "No harm in trying," and it works; there's a certain honest outrageousness about him that some women go for. He always has at least one on the string, if not more. He claims he was broken in at fourteen by a grown woman. (Of fifteen, probably.)

"When you figgering to start writing up my biography?" he asked.

"My publisher doesn't specialize in that kind of material."

"Hell, going by what I've seen on cable, there shouldn't be any problem. Gawd, I keep finding stuff even I didn't know. Like the other night—"

"Spare our sensibilities, Sprig," said Grampa.

"I would never say a word or do a deed to corrupt the innocent," Sprig raised his right hand. "And I'm talking about you, Snowy, as much as these two pure-hearted young ones. I'm taking it for granted that they're pure. You can't tell about kids nowadays."

"Nor back in your time, to hear you tell it," said Uncle Early.

"Well, I couldn't help it if I was precocious," said Sprig. "You find anything in those crates of mine that hadn't ought to be there, Ralph?"

"Not yet, but I have hopes," said the warden. "It's been my lifelong ambition to see you trying to out-talk a judge."

"Let me know when you come to that coke I've got stashed away in one corner," said Sprig.

"Is that how you keep your soda cool?" Ben asked. Sprig laughed. "You're a corker, Ben," he said. Ben looked pleased but puzzled.

"You're clean, Sprig," the warden said. "Dammit."

"What a relief. Thank you, Doctor. And I promise to stay away from them bad women in the future."

The boys looked more mystified. Grampa made out Sprig's slip; Chad whined sadly up by the gas pumps. *Little Emily* came in around the Head. She is grey and white like a gull, and I think she is the prettiest boat in the Job's Harbor fleet.

"I don't know why that one always shows up just when I've got you alone," Sprig said to me.

"If you call this alone, what do you call *real* alone?"

"Meet me tonight, and I'll tell ye."

"*Auf Wiedersehen,* Sprig!" I went up the ramp to the wharf, and he called after me, "Going to get all dolled up for him, I see."

"Yep, wrapping myself in a see-through coffeepot." Chad greeted me as if either he or I had just brought the serum to Nome and pranced around me all the way up the wharf.

By the time Glen's lobsters had been checked and sold, his gas tank and bait barrel filled, his boat cleaned up and put back on her mooring, his rubber boots changed for moccasins, and he'd rowed back to the wharf and come running up my steps, the coffee was made and a pizza was in the oven. He was whistling a jig, which meant he'd made a very good haul. But no veteran lobsterman will ever admit that in words. He knows he'd be inviting a sudden dearth of lobsters, if not the irrevocable disappearance of the species from the planet.

We kissed inside the door. I love the scent left by the day's work aboard the boat, and I put my nose against his shirt sleeve and breathed deeply. "Heavenly," I said. "I wish I'd been with you today."

He didn't say he'd missed me. None of that flowery stuff from *him*. "Get your work done?" He took off his shirt and began to wash up at the kitchen sink.

"I made a good start. When I turned stale I went to town and had lunch with the folks. Hey!" I had just remembered. "I bought *Little Emily* a present."

We went down and took the mat from the car. He was pleased. "Steve's got one of these; he's been talking about it. Thanks, love." He gave me a quick kiss. "That's from her. I'll reward you later. Where'd you get it?"

"Rigby Marine."

"Kenneth look any different?" he asked, straight-faced.

"I didn't go there to find out," I lied with dignity. "But now that I've seen Guy's portrait and some photographs, I couldn't miss the resemblance. So because of that, he does look different. But he acts just the same.... That pizza will burn!" I bolted for the steps.

Until now there had never been any subjects either of us had been forced to pussyfoot around, but it seemed that the Esmond-Rigby story was about to become the first one. The censorship would be hard for me, because I'd always been used to talking to Glen almost as freely as I talked with Fee. At supper I couldn't think of any other subject that was worth the breath and the effort, and apparently Glen didn't even notice. Maybe I've been talking too much all these years, I thought in exasperation. If I take a vow of silence, I wonder how long it'll be before he catches on. Maybe he'll be relieved. That irritated me, too. Oblivious, he got up and brought the coffeepot to the table and filled both our cups.

"I met Fee and Julian just outside the Head," he said.

"What were they doing this far in? They hadn't been in here."

"They'd taken some lobsters up to Fox Point," He sat down again. "Had tea up there, all cozy as a batch of coons in a den. Talk about starry eyes," he said cynically. "Fee was lit up like the whole Milky Way."

My anger was a knee-jerk reflex. It shocked me. It lasted only for a moment, but resentment remained. I'd wanted so much to stop at Fox Point this morning, but I'd been afraid of intruding. The picture of Fee laughing and talking with them, at home in that house as if she'd known them all her life, made me wish I hadn't eaten the pizza; damn, she'd been there first on Sunday afternoon, too. Got to meet them before I did. I'd laughed then, but—

"What the matter?" Glen said. I looked up from my plate, and he was leaning forward studying me. Actually concerned. That touched me.

"Too much pizza," I said ruefully. "But it was so good.... I wonder what they did with Julian. I can't imagine him in the living room holding a bone china cup. How would he ever manage those thin little handles?"

"I guess they had it at the kitchen table like common folks, and his tea was in a mug. He never says anything, so they probably think he's deep as well as handsome."

My jealousy was burning off like morning fog under a hot sun. I was too fond of Fee to resent her because she'd gone ahead and done something I was too timid to do. She was simply Fee, dashing and daring as always, and I had been boring old Eden, always hanging back. It was a wonder I'd ever had the courage to send off my first book. When it was accepted by the second publisher to see it, I was flabbergasted by the success of my own temerity.

Changes were due. I could ruthlessly edit my own manuscripts, why not myself? Beginning now, I wouldn't pass up the next chance to leap without looking.

"I picked up some fascinating stuff in town today," I said chattily.

"For instance?... You make these brownies?"

"Yup. Back in 1927 the scoop was that Guy wasn't extradited from France because he knew too many family skeletons by their first names. People who went to him with their money troubles sometimes confided too much. So he must have known he was safe across the ocean."

"Son of a bitch, wasn't he?" said Glen, taking another brownie.

"And did you ever hear of Josiah Blackburn?"

There were steps outside, and we both looked toward the screen door. Nick Raintree stood there, a dark apparition against the sun-washed blues and greens beyond him. The gold earring in his right ear caught the western sun and glittered between black hair and beard.

"Hello in there," he said. "Anybody home?" Glen raised his eyebrows at me. I shrugged and shook my head.

"Yes, come in!" I called, getting up. He was already halfway in, and he had my books under his arm.

"Hi!" he said. "I brought you some books to sign for my sister—" He stopped when he saw Glen rising from the table. "Sorry! Am I busting up something? Shall I back out?"

"Come on in," Glen said cordially. "Have a cup of coffee."

I introduced them, and they shook hands.

"Does Glen stand for Glenroy?" Nick asked. I had a feeling that he knew that about Glen already. "Any relation?"

"Distant," said Glen, filling a clean cup. "Have a brownie."

"Thanks." Nick was bigger all over than Glen, who looked as skinny as an adolescent beside him. "I'm surprised you're not in the firm. They seem to want to keep it in the family."

"They'd have a job taking us all in," said Glen. "I'm not a boat builder at heart, but I let them build mine."

"I think I picked her out a minute ago, by the bow. *Little Emily?* She's a beauty."

Glen looked quietly pleased. They talked boats and boat-building for a few minutes, and then Glen rose to go. "Nice meeting you, Nick," he said. He sounded sincere, and he is not devious. "Right now I have a meeting of town officers, but we'll be talking."

"I'd like that," Nick stood up, and they shook hands again. "I have a room over the Bains' garage, and Charlie Bain swears you're the best chairman they've had since somebody named Snowy Winter."

Glen grinned and pointed a thumb at me. "Her grampaw. And I'm flattered, but Charlie Bain always did draw the long bow. See you, Nick." He went out, and I followed him. We kissed on the top step. When he ran down the flight he began whistling "The Rakes of Mallow" again, and I watched him walking away from me between Nick's Charger and the rose hedge, in time to the music. I kept expecting him to look back and say, "I'll see you later." But he didn't. I watched him into the parking lot, and he still didn't call back.

This was one of the times I thought he was a little too happy-go-lucky about us. One of the assessors was a good-looking woman, recently divorced. I liked her—I'd voted for her—but she and Glen were the only unmarried members on both boards, and I hoped she was passionately in love with another man. I didn't watch Glen out of sight, true to a seafaring tradition we all think it's safer to observe.

11

I returned to the kitchen and said efficiently, "I'll sign those books for you now. What's your sister's name?" I cleared a space on the table.

"Nice chap, Glen," he said. "He didn't bristle up when I came barging in. I liked that."

"He didn't have any reason to." I fished around in the stoneware marmalade jar for my favorite autographing pen.

"How did he know I wasn't going to fall on you like Byron on that chambermaid?"

"Not being a rapist himself, he doesn't automatically expect every strange man to be a rapist. Not around here, anyway. *Are* you one?"

He gave me a buccaneerish grin. "Never had the slightest inclination. I'm not a violent man, even if I look it. The books were just an excuse, by the way." It was said so simply, it was disarming. I sat down and he pushed the two books toward me. "Sally Raintree."

He watched me with those black-diamond eyes as I inscribed the flyleaves. His attitude was benignly alert, that of an observant but peaceful cat. I finished signing and put the books aside. "Is she older or younger than you?"

"She's the kid sister. Twenty."

"Where do you come from?" I asked abruptly.

"'Baby dear? Out of the Everywhere into the Here; Where did you get your eyes so blue? Out of the sky as—'"

"I know that one," I said, "so you don't have to run through the angel kisses, and so forth."

"If you know it, too, it shows we're soul mates. Of course you're the one with the blue eyes, but I couldn't think offhand of a rhyme for black."

"Somehow I don't remember wishing for a soul mate," I said. "Not recently, anyway."

"Some people never know what they want until someone else tells them."

"Thank you for buying the books," I said formally, "but if they were just an excuse, what's your real reason?"

"I wanted to see you again. Curiosity. You're a novelist, and I've never known one before, male or female."

I leaned back in the captain's chair and folded my arms. Fee would have thought of something audacious to say back, but though I can write good dialogue, I'm no better at sparkling spontaneous quips than I am at crossword puzzles. Silence and a contemplative gaze work as well, though. It makes me look deep, like Julian.

"For me," he said, "meeting my first novelist in a perfect setting for a novel seemed more like a preordained event than a provocative coincidence."

I was incredulous, then overjoyed. Someone was actually using that line on me! I started to laugh. "It was meant—it was destined—it was Fate! Oh, Lord! You disappoint me, but it's hilarious. Did you really think it would get to me?"

"But I made you laugh, didn't I? And wasn't it fantastic for coming right off the top of my head?"

"You mean you didn't compose it beforehand? Lovingly shape it and burnish it to a fine luster I could see my face in?"

"I solemnly swear I did not. It just came to me like *that.*" He snapped his fingers. "But seriously, as a writer, don't you think that sentence would make a great opening statement for one of Henry James's novels?"

"It's still a dite too simple," I said judiciously. "How about adding a few conditional clauses and some parenthetical phrases? Otherwise it's fine. Do you actually *read* Henry James?"

"Doesn't everyone?" he asked and then grinned. "Is it safe to admit it here, or do the walls have ears?"

"It's safe. You know, I never talk about Henry to anyone except at home, because most people I know have never heard of him, or else they can't make sense of him unless he's done on Masterpiece Theatre. But my father taught English and American literature before he became a headmaster, and he used to assign 'The Turn of the Screw' to his seniors every year, along with Poe and Bierce. At home, he had a good collection of books from his college days, and that's how I got hooked."

Why was I telling him this? Why had I bristled at him like a porcupine yesterday? I wished he would go away so I could try to make some sense out of it.

"You see how much we have in common," he said. "We can discuss our favorite James novels on a long rainy afternoon before your fire." He nodded at the Franklin stove. "For now, how about a ride up into the country to watch the moon rise?"

"I can watch it right here from my deck," I said, "and often do."

"Have you ever been to the Birch Mansion?"

"Nope." I started carrying dishes to the sink, and he got up and helped me, which added to my discomfort; he was too much *there.*

"A place like that, with a wonderful romantic story, only about thirty miles from here, and you've never been there?" His astonishment put me on the defensive again.

"You'd be surprised how many people have never been to Birch Mansion," I said. "Almost as many who've never been to Job's Harbor."

"But you're a writer! You must know the story of the place—don't you have any desire to see it for yourself? How parochial can you get?" He seemed more earnest than scornful.

I widened my eyes and spoke with exaggerated patience and clarity. "All I said was that I'd never been to the Birch Mansion. I didn't include the rest of the state, or the nation, for that matter. My brother lives in Maryland, and—" I caught myself before I started naming off all the places I'd been. What the hell business was it of his? "Also, someone's always living in the mansion," I continued. "Whatever you do at home, whereever that may be—Alpha Centauri, for all I know—around here we don't go tramping across private property to stare at a house where people are living, no matter how famous it may be."

"Then let's get cracking! There's just a caretaker couple now, and I know them."

"I'm not surprised," I said. He wasn't offended; I didn't know what it would take to offend him. "And where will you go when you've left no stone unturned around here?" I asked.

"It's hard telling. There are too many places I want to see before one supposedly extinct volcano after another comes to life in a chain reaction and blows the world up. That's what'll do it, not the bomb. Whatever is out there in space will say, 'That place had its chances, and used them all up,' and put a cosmic match to us. Or maybe the end was programmed into the beginning. Let's go!" He rubbed his hands vigorously. "We're wasting the shank of the evening! Do you realize this may be the last full moon we'll ever see?"

Of course I went. Twenty-four hours ago I'd have made excuses; now I wasn't missing any opportunity to launch the new Eden. The Esmond sisters were responsible for more than they knew.

All my life I'd known the inland roads behind Maddox and Tenby, and the road to Parmenter best of all, because of the Grange Hall dances, the big annual fair, and the ski slopes. I'd been on the road in all seasons; every dip and turn, stone wall, pond, meadow, house, and barn was known to me, as well as the names on mailboxes, the farm dogs, individual horses, and a prize Holstein bull. But tonight it was as if I'd never been on it before. Neither the old nor the new Eden had ever traveled it with a stranger. He didn't talk or turn on music, so it was a swift and quiet ride through one of those George Innes landscapes all awash with sunset.

Almost into Parmenter we turned off to the right onto a dirt road whose entrance was nearly hidden by trees. There was no gate or mailbox, and I'd always thought it led to a deserted farm or somebody's woodlot.

We left the amber light for dense blue shadow; maples crowded us in and closed over our heads. Nick drove slowly, stopping for a squirrel and then for a cock pheasant who unhurriedly exercised his right-of-way. I knew we were not far from the village, but I was experiencing the nearly physical sensation of dropping deeper and deeper into the Unknown. I looked sidewise at Nick; he seemed oblivious to me, the talkative wanderer replaced by another personality. The discomfort in my gut sharpened to a cramp, and I was gripping the door handle. Could I throw myself out and get away through those woods? One of my heroines had escaped like that, but I'd been in charge, so I could save her. Now I was willing to jettison the new Eden for good, if the old one could just get safely home.

Good God, how could I have made this fatal error? What was I *doing* here? I couldn't believe I'd become one of those idiots who goes for a ride with a stranger and becomes a statistic, whether they find the body or not.

Suddenly enough to make me blink, we came out of the shadow into light from a still radiant sky; and there was the Birch Mansion facing us across a field of wildflowers that must have once been a lawn. It was a Greek Revival gem, tenderly tinted warm ivory by the transparent medium in which it was submerged.

Along both sides of the driveway, shrubbery had gone wild into explosions of roses of all colors, brushing against the car and dropping petals and pollen on us. The fragrance was almost overpowering. We parked by the broad, shallow steps running the width of the house below the pillars. With the engine silenced, we were in a jungle for birds, and we could hear and see the bees getting all they could in this last hour of heat and light.

"*Rosebower,*" Nick said. "That's what he named it."

"Nobody home?" My voice scratched a dry throat.

"Feels like it. But that's all right, the Meachams won't mind."

I heard low growling like the first warnings of thunder. Two German shepherds stood on the steps, their heads lowered, their hackles visibly rising. I sat back a little harder in my seat and didn't unbuckle. Nick got out. "Peter, Philip," he said. "It's me."

The fur flattened, tails began to wave, the growls were replaced by toothy tongue-lolling grins. The dogs bounced toward him like a pair of pups. He played with them and told them to sit. They did, still laughing, ears laid back.

"Get out, Eden," he said to me. When I did, they shut their mouths and stared at me, and their ears came up. Nick put his hand on my shoulder. "This is Eden. *Eden.* Come and say hello to *Eden.*"

They came to me and sniffed at my extended hand, courteously waved their tails. Would you save me from him? I silently begged. But Nick was the good old uncle who always brought something for the kids, and they knew it. He took out a candy bar, one of the nutty sort, and gave them each a half. Some murderers adored dogs. Leaving them crunching ecstatically, he took me by the hand and walked me around past more wildly flowering shrubs to the opposite side of the house.

We crossed a swath of mown grass to a fieldstone parapet. Sickish, coldly perspiring, I looked out on a landscape utterly foreign to me. A wooded slope fell steeply away from the parapet to a pond far below, the exact blue-white of the zenith and reflecting small pink flecks of cloud. The perfect reflection was shattered into kaleidoscopic fragments of color by a bird paddling across it; the bird was invisible to us, but not its coruscating wake. Opposite us, forested land rose beyond the pond to a ridge on a level with us. The tops of its tallest pines were still faintly illuminated by the light from the west, but it slowly died as we looked. A loon called on the pond below. A series of pure tones exquisitely echoed.

The dogs had come after us and were sniffing interestedly at Chad's scent on me. I put my hand on a warm head before I remembered to be nervous about the owner's teeth. Sometime in the last minute or so, the panic had washed away as quickly as it had come. Nick was no killer. I'd *know,* wouldn't I? Or would I?

"It's another country. Another world," I said lamely.

"Yes, it is, and I'm glad you've never been here before, so I could be the first to show it to you."

"Thank you, I'm glad I came. That's weak, but—"

"Why should we need words? Come and sit down and watch for the moon."

A porch on this side of the house held a collection of unmatched furniture; the caretakers must have spent a lot of time out here. Nick and I sat on the steps, and the dogs lay on the floor behind us. One of them was noisily washing up.

"The moon's about to show right over there," Nick said, pointing to the ridge. "We're facing just the way your deck faces."

"I can't place the ocean there," I said. "I'm disoriented. Does that ridge have a name? What's on the other side of it? What road could I see it from?"

"Quiet," he cautioned me in a whisper. "Don't wake whatever's lived in the valley all these centuries. There's nothing beyond that ridge but space and stars, and we're dipping, dropping, turning toward the moon—there she is!"

We sat silent while the enormous orange moon cleared the ridge. The loon called again and was answered. The antiphony continued like a hymn to the ascending goddess. I turned to him as one does to share, and he took me into his arms so easily, into such a gentle embrace, that I was responding to the kiss before my mind snapped to attention. I was still half-mesmerized, but when I felt his embrace shifting to a firmer one, and my own arms going around him, I was as shocked as if someone had just flung a pail of water over us. I wrestled to get free and backed off, bumping into a dog.

"What's the matter?" Nick was both surprised and amused. "Never kissed a man with a beard before?"

"I don't know anything about you!" I protested. "Just your name, and that could be made up. Come to think of it, it *sounds* made up. You could be anything. You could be a Mafia prince from New Jersey."

"Good God, woman, what is it with you? I don't want to be the father of your children, I just want to celebrate the rising of the moon!"

I was tired of feeling like a fool, and it was my own fault, nobody else's. Why shouldn't I welcome my own healthy response to a friendly gesture? I was damned sure Glen never had any such inhibitions. I smiled at Nick and said, "Why not?"

This time we moved into each other's arms as if we'd had a long experience of it. The kisses were firm, but not intrusive. I thought it was a grand way to watch the moon rise, though we weren't watching it that attentively. Once he held me off and muttered, "New Jersey! Whatever became of Alpha Centauri?"

"I notice you don't deny the Mafia part."

"It's not worth the dignity of a denial. Come back here." We settled in closer and tighter. The kisses went from friendly to enthusiastic, and a building tension sent disquieting impulses through my body. When we finally broke apart, it was with a conscious effort of will, and I was winded.

"*Well,*" I said stupidly. Nick repeated it, and we both laughed. The dogs got up and came to touch our ears and cheeks with their cold noses; their eyes shone in the moonlight, their gently waving tails made a breeze. The moon had changed, as it climbed, from Proust's big juicy thirst-provoking orange to luminous mother-of-pearl. The rose fragrance was even stronger than before.

"*Rosebower,*" Nick said.

"It had to be a bower of roses because her name was Rose," I said. "Wouldn't it have been something if she'd turned out to be allergic? She'd have been going around with a perpetual cold in her head." I was babbling; I felt shaky and confused, as if I'd just had a last-minute deliverance from disaster and was less relieved than I should have been.

Nick filled and lighted his pipe to discourage mosquitoes, and we talked about the romantic history of the robber baron who'd fallen in love with a maid at a Bar Harbor resort, married her, and built her a mansion in her hometown so she could be near her family. It had been a happy story, not a tragic one, and their heirs still owned Rosebower.

12

We sat there long enough for Nick to smoke one pipe. We didn't talk. The loons called back and forth, and a fox barked across the valley and was answered from our side. The dogs listened with pricked ears but otherwise were not disturbed. "They don't need to guard the house against four-legged folk," Nick said.

The dogs went with us to the car, and I called each by name and stroked his head. They saw us in, got out of the way while we turned around, and were lying in the moonlit driveway when we left. In the long black tunnel our headlights picked up luminescent eyes at the edge of the road, one pair high enough to be a deer's. A constellation low to the ground became a raccoon and her kits. A rabbit crossed before us.

We drove home through a country of Browning's "silent silver lights and darks undreamed of "; roofs glittered as with hoar frost, tree shadows were flung like black lace across a road like a frozen stream. Wherever a light showed in a window, it was a hot orange shout in the moonstruck hush. We met only one other car.

When we passed the Esmond mailbox, Nick spoke for the first time. "Do you suppose they're making music up there?"

"It's midnight," I said.

"Mrs. Rigby told someone yesterday they stay up half the night. She joked about being afraid to go to bed, for fear of not waking up again."

"Some joke," I said. "I hope neither of them has a weak heart or high blood pressure."

"They're superb, aren't they?" he said. "Mrs. Rigby is pure steel with elegance, and Miss Emma is no faded bunch of violets. And if I hadn't gate-crashed yesterday, you and I wouldn't have watched the moon from Rosebower tonight. I wonder what else they're responsible for, just by being here. What other good or evil will result from these Sunday Afternoons."

"You're sure you aren't a writer, too?" I asked. "Or a closet poet?"

He answered seriously. "You don't have to be a writer to have a sense of drama."

I didn't want to go on with it. I wanted to keep the evening sufficient unto itself, and the Esmond sisters to themselves. "Will you let me off at the mailbox? I'll walk in. I don't want to rouse Chad if they've gone to bed."

"All right," he said equably. He got out when I did, but he made no move toward me, and I realized I'd been expecting some gesture to follow up the interlude on the porch. Now the expectation embarrassed me.

"Good night," I said formally, "and thank you again. It was a lovely drive both ways, and moonrise from up there was unforgettable." Talk about drama! I was speaking the lines like a pro. Bright and brittle, if not quite Bette Davis. "I loved the dogs. I've never been that friendly with German shepherds before."

"They were thrilled, too. They've never been that friendly with an author before."

What he thought of the evening was now too evident, the buccaneer's grin gave him away. He'd been trying me out, and I'd been as obligingly ardent as a teenager. I was ashamed of myself and infuriated with us both. How was I supposed to pass the test? By some act of sophisticated aggression like unbuckling his belt?

"So long!" I said abruptly and turned away. He caught me by a shoulder and turned me back to him.

"*Eden.*" It was just audible. "Why are you so angry?" He took my face in his hands and kissed me. "Don't be. It was perfect." He kissed me again and then let me go.

"Nick," I began, but I didn't know where to go from there. "Yes, it was. Good night again." I walked away.

When I was well into the driveway, I stopped and listened to the car turning and going away. The quiet flowed back and surrounded me. I walked on the wet grass at the side so as to make no sound. Fireflies winked on and off around me. There were no lights in our house or the one across the parking lot, which looked like a skating pond in the moonlight. This was bright enough to dull the security light on the wharf, and I could almost read the names on the boats.

A familiar old bicycle leaned against the railing at the foot of my steps. Gideon Wilkes was likely to turn up anywhere in town on moonlit nights; he'd be down on the lobster car now, trying for mackerel.

Glen wasn't in the Hayloft, and if he'd come earlier, he had left no note. I was relieved; I can tell white lies with ease, but I've always been inept with a really guilty conscience. Though I didn't know why I should have one now, when Glen had quite possibly gone home for coffee with the lady assessor. Probably he wouldn't even care what I'd been doing, he was that sure of me, and I was suffering from guilt simply because I'd enjoyed myself.

A fresh unpleasantness began to crawl nastily around and around in my stomach, where earlier the cramp of panic had come. What if this little adventure tonight was not so little? Supposing it was the beginning of the end between Glen and me, a warning that we had become only each other's habit, that time would inevitably drive us apart.

As a kid I collected sentimental bits of verse, and these snippets have a way of coming back to be sickeningly appropriate.

Alas, how easily things go wrong!
A sigh too much, or a kiss too long,
And there follows a mist and a weeping rain,
And life is never the same again.

I went to bed depressed and woke up late to thick fog against the windows and muffled, sporadic activity in the harbor. Between the fog and the hangover from last night, I was more tired than when I'd gone to bed. I wondered glumly if Nick would call, and decided he wouldn't. I was doubtless just one of a long list of girls he'd taken to Rosebower or some other beauty spots to watch the moon or the stars, and it was pretty depressing to realize I'd probably behaved like the rest of them. Oh, put a sock in it! I thought nastily. You didn't get drunk with him, you didn't give your all, so forget him. Or else use him and the experience in a book sometime.

I got the manuscript out and began going through *Roget's Thesaurus* for synonyms. Ten minutes into the search I felt my life slipping back into place; there's a kind of magic in the thin pages of my old secondhand thesaurus. I worked away happily and even began revising paragraphs. When somebody knocked at the door I jumped and swore loudly.

It was Toby Barry. I was so surprised at seeing him through the fog-beaded screen I must have looked stupid.

"Hey, did I get you up?" he asked. He was carrying a clam roller.

"Nope, I was just far, far away. Come on in. Everything all right over there?"

"Oh, sure." He rapped on the door casing as he came in. "Just in case. I brought you some clams. Got a bucket?"

I held a pail, and he turned clams into it. He smelled of soap and water and his clean shirt; his fair hair was neatly trimmed, and the back of his neck looked young. I almost thought *innocent.*

The clams were large, white shelled, glistening with wet, and clean. "They're beauties," I said. "Where did you get them? You didn't go outside in *this.*"

"We went out around Job's Tears and up along the shore to Fox Point. You can kind of feel your way along with one foot on shore." He laughed, "We crawled some old slow and did a lot of paddling around the ledges. Took us a while, but it was worth it. So I thought we could spare some for the landlady."

"Well, the landlady appreciates them," I said. There was a good pailful. "Look, this would be money in your pocket—"

He held up his hand. "They're a present," he said solemnly. "You've been so good to Shas."

"I haven't done anything."

"It's not for want of trying," he said. "That's what counts. Richie's a cantankerous cuss, always was." He took cigarettes out of his shirt pocket, lit one, and leaned himself comfortably against the wall; his light blue eyes weren't missing a thing. "You writing another book?" he asked. I nodded, and he said admiringly, "And some folks say clamming's a hard way to make a living."

"Well, writing's easier on the back," I said. "But you can always be sure of selling your clams. It's different with a book. I'm never sure of anything till I sign my name on the contract."

"Yes, but if we get red tide for a summer it can sink us."

"Sit down and have a cup of coffee," I said. Obviously he wanted to talk, and after accepting the clams, I couldn't freeze him out.

"Thanks!" He sat down at the clear end of the table, and I gave him an ashtray. While I was getting a mug out and a turnover from the crock, I reflected that the Barrys had another trade if clamming went bad, but it wasn't one that you'd mention to Toby. If anybody else around here knew they'd been clamming at Fox Point, the inference would be that they were scouting out the best approach to the house from the water. I'd already inferred it.

"You must have dug those clams in the sand," I said. "They're so white."

"Ayuh, but not on that real sandy beach by the dock. We were to the south'ard of it. Quite a long stretch of sand and gravel mixed, in between some big ledges. . . . Thanks!" I put the mug and plate before him and pushed the sugar bowl and creamer nearer, and poured fresh coffee for myself.

He took quite a while getting his coffee right, frowning at it as he stirred, and I hoped he wasn't about to ask for a lease on the house. He was clean, personable, and well-mannered sitting opposite me, and he was a thief.

As if that word had struck him like a dart, his head came up and his eyes locked into mine. "There were three other guys digging there," he said. "We've seen 'em on the other side here, in that cove near your uncle's house, and on the outside of the Head and the Point, too. We know they aren't from Amity, or from across the river, or upriver, as far as we can tell. They've got a blue boat with a big Merc."

"Are they cutting into your territory?"

"We've never seen them out around the islands. And never that close to Fox Point before those rich old ladies moved in."

"They aren't rich-rich," I said. "They've probably got enough to take them through the rest of their lives, but I'm sure they don't have a lot of things in the house anybody would want for a quick sale," I said with quiet emphasis, just in case Toby was dreaming of sugarplums. "Like televisions and VCRs and machine tools. And I know they're too smart to keep large amounts of money in the house."

"Who does, nowadays?" The voice of experience. "What about this guy that robbed the bank way back when? Got a couple of million, didn't he?"

"There wasn't that much money in Maddox," I protested. "About two hundred and fifty thousand was what I heard. Of course, that was an awful lot of money then."

"What do you mean, *then?*" His eyes had a child's shining greed. "It's a hell of a lot of money now."

"I hope nobody's dumb enough to think any of that actual cash is still in Mrs. Rigby's hands, all these years later."

"He probably played the stock market with it," said Toby, "and made a fortune, and all the principal's in a Swiss bank account. God, I'd like to be rich enough to live on interest! If I ever win the lottery—" He gave me that innocent, luminous smile which inspired Sprig Newsome's parody: *when Barry eyes are smiling, sure they're stealing your hide away.* "Beggars on horseback, huh? But people like that, they'd have silver and jewelry, wouldn't they? Fur coats? Little antique doodads? Plenty of crooked dealers around to buy anything really old."

"I wouldn't know," I said. "All I saw that looked valuable was a grand piano, and it'd be hard to lug that off." I didn't mention violins in case Toby was knowledgeable about them.

He agreed about the piano. "But I don't like the look of these foreigners. It's damn funny, them starting to hang around Fox Point now that somebody's living there they think is loaded. They could terrorize two old ladies. Probably scare 'em to death. Have they got any dogs? Or some man sleeping in the house nights?"

I couldn't believe he was being that brazen.

"They're talking about dogs," I lied. "Trying to decide between Dobermans and Rottweilers. And their nephew wants them to have somebody in the house besides."

"Gorry, I *hope* so!" he said fervently. He stood up. "Well, thanks for the coffee and the turnover. It was as good as my mother's."

"Thanks again for the clams, Toby," I said. "Look, if you really have bad vibes about those people, why don't you speak to Ralph?"

His pitying gaze said he knew now that he'd overestimated my intelligence. "You can bet old Ralph's checked them out and their boat registration long ago. Oh, they're all legal, and even Ralph can't read their minds. No, you just tell those old ladies to be careful."

"I certainly will," I promised sincerely.

13

Nick had been steadily retreating all morning, and Toby's visit put him practically out of sight. I took the clams down to the other kitchen, and my grandparents and I ate them steamed at noon. They were delicious; none of us looked this gift horse in the mouth. But there was a discussion as to whether or not the sisters should be warned that breaking and entering was as common these days as it had been uncommon in their youth.

"If they've been reading the *Journal* all these years they ought to know it," Gram said. "And last Sunday Morrie Hearne was having conniptions about their letting Gideon in without Roy Thatcher standing by armed to the teeth." She and I giggled. Roy looks as much like a cuddly rabbit as any human being could.

"That's quite a picture," Grampa conceded. "But there's too much going on these days that isn't funny. If Mary Ann's anything like what she used to be, she thinks all those things happen to other people. If she thinks of them at all, that is. You'd better have a few words with Emmie."

"Are we going again on Sunday, Eden?" Gram asked me.

"But you don't have to wait until Sunday," I said. "She's your old friend; you can call her any time."

"Sure, get her down here!" Grampa urged. "I'd like to see her again, but I don't plan to go to Fox Point and drink tea.... She was a pretty little thing," he said. "Used to wear pink a lot and looked about as delicate as an apple blossom until she tucked her fiddle under her chin and gave Mary Ann the nod. She was no fragile little blossom then!"

"It was a funny thing about Mary Ann," Gram said. "When she played alone, she owned the stage when she set foot on it. But when she played for Susan to sing, or for Emmie, she—" Gram's hands groped for the word. "Erased herself? Effaced herself? I don't know how she did it, but she did. I'll tell you *one* thing," she said emphatically, "I was in awe of her then, and I still am. In the same room with her I'm one of the Sunbonnet Babies again, just like *that.*" She snapped her fingers.

"So when are you going to have Miss Emma to yourself?" I urged.

"When they get settled in a bit more. They must have a lot of things to tend to. Besides, I like the idea of Sunday Afternoons. Must have caught it from you," she said. "I like seeing who's turned out and how they act. I'll get tired of it eventually. But if a Rigby ever shows up, I don't want to miss it."

"Sometimes I think she's still eleven years old," Grampa said to me.

The fog had retired offshore to wait until dark, but the day was still grey and muggy. Some of the men who didn't like fog were going out now. Fog had never kept Glen in, even before he had radar; he was one of those who, like seals or gulls, have a built-in sense of direction. But *Little Emily* lay deserted at her mooring.

My bad humor returned. I didn't try to analyze it, but I took a notebook and headed for Maddox, where I could turn negative energy into positive results by doing some research at the library toward a book I wanted to do when (and if) this new one was accepted. Besides, grazing in the meadows of the past was always a great escape. After that, if I still felt cranky—"pudgicky" was Gram's word for it—I'd buy myself a pizza with everything on it and go home and eat the whole thing, whereupon galloping indigestion would relieve me of all other annoyances.

When I saw the Fox Point mailbox up ahead I thought bitterly that if I were a nonstop Sunshine Girl like Fee I'd go dashing up that driveway right now, merry as Mr. Toad, even if I couldn't bring lobsters. I turned off the road before I could talk myself out of it. If they'd gone somewhere, at least I wouldn't be kicking myself for not stopping and wondering what I'd missed.

There was no car in the driveway, and I expected Nell Thatcher to tell me they were gone for the afternoon, but before I could lift the knocker, the door swung open and Miss Emma cried radiantly, "Eden dear, how providential!"

What a welcome! I could have bounced without a trampoline. "What can I do?" I asked.

"The car won't start, and there's something we'd like very much to do today." She took my hand and drew me in.

"I don't know anything about fixing cars," I said, "but I'd be glad to drive you."

"That's what we'd like," she said. "Roy knows what's wrong, and he says it needs more than his tinkering. Mr. Sparrow's coming from Maddox to tow the car to his garage. Mary Ann!" she called down the hall toward the kitchen. "Eden Winter is here, and she'll drive us."

"Heaven be praised," said Marianne's deep voice. She appeared in the kitchen doorway, looking extremely tall and narrow in dark blue slacks and blazer, a bright-figured scarf tied in a loose bow at her throat. I hoped I'd look that good in my eighties. As I'd done the first time I saw her, I stiffened and pulled up my spine, lengthened my neck, and lifted my chin. She came toward us with that swift, long stride.

"Mrs. Thatcher and I are agreed that to use Roy's car could be traumatic for us *and* the car. There's some peculiar rapport between it and him. So you're a happy surprise, Eden."

"Well, my parents say I was one almost twenty-five years ago, but I haven't heard anyone say it since, not in so many words. Where are we going? San Diego? China?"

"I'm glad you're prepared for a long journey," she said. "It'll be all the way to Maddox, and then out to Muir's Corner."

"To the old Esmond house, dear," Miss Emma said, "or rather to the Esmond family burying ground behind it." She picked up a rose cardigan from a chair; her dress was rose-and-pink plaid gingham. *Used to wear pink a lot,* I could hear Grampa saying. *Looked about as delicate as an apple blossom until she tucked her fiddle under her chin.*

"Trust Emmie to wear pink when she's going to dig in the dirt," Marianne said. "My sister hasn't changed in seventy years except that she's a better fiddler."

"I wore my new best dress once to whitewash the henhouse," Miss Emma said proudly, "and never got a spot on it."

"She did it to impress the neighborhood, because she couldn't wait until Sunday to show it off, and Mother and Susan were downstreet to the dentist, and I was practicing and didn't know what she was up to. Oh, yes, the dress was spotless afterwards, but I can't say the same for the new Mary Janes."

"I shouldn't have worn them," Miss Emma admitted. "They're what gave me away. Mary Ann, did Susan ever do *anything* wrong? Or were we the only ones?"

"When Susan sang we forgave her everything." Marianne turned to the hall mirror and began retying the silk paisley scarf. I realized that she must never have seen her family graves and this could be an ordeal for her; conceivably the whole weight of her past could come down on her all at once. I did not want to see that elegant composure threatened. But I was in it now; it was too late to run.

She was watching me in the mirror, and I didn't know what she'd seen on my face. "I hope you don't have any hang-ups about cemeteries, Eden. But you needn't come in, if you'll just take us there."

"I have no such hang-ups," I answered truthfully. "I've spent plenty of time locating old family plots and trying to read the stones. But you might prefer not to have an outsider along, so I'll stay outside anyway."

"Oh, but there are some really interesting and very old stones," Miss Emma said eagerly. "From the first people to clear and settle the land. You must see those."

Flowers were waiting outdoors in the shade of the porch: a broad flat basket of variegated phlox, dianthus, some little blue flowers I didn't recognize, and violet plants. I put them and a bundle of old newspapers into the trunk. Too bad, Fee, I thought smugly. Maybe you can supply lobsters, but not a ride.

Miss Emma waved Marianne into the front seat and nimbly settled herself in the back. I handed in the small basket of trowels, clippers, and cotton gloves. "This is so nice of you, Eden dear," she said. I tried not to beam too obviously. Marianne was efficiently strapping herself into the front seat.

"Fiona Heriot is a charming girl," she said when we were driving out. "I'd say you two are lucky in your friendship."

"She's so witty and lively," Miss Emma said affectionately. "We so enjoy her dropping in." How often can she drop in from ten miles away? I thought. "You must feel free to come too, Eden," Miss Emma went on. "When you can leave your work. Come often."

That made me as blissful as Chad looks when he's having his back scratched. How often was good manners? I was willing to bet that question didn't confuse Fee, whose motto always was "Go for it!"

"It's pleasant to know the grandchildren of old friends," Marianne said. Well, Guy hadn't robbed either the Heriots or the Winters, so no cruel wind from the past blew here.

The quickest way to Muir's Corner was to drive up Ship Street to the flagpole, across Main, and out on Oakwood Street. Muir's Corner had long since ceased to be a country crossroads, even if farmland lapped at the northwestern boundaries. But many of the old houses remained; they made the ranches and modern boxes and mobile homes look like urchins. The Esmond place was one of those huge square hip-roofed houses now turned into apartments. The bride and groom elms had been taken down a long time ago, probably because of the Dutch elm disease that had destroyed so many Maddox trees. But here nothing else had been planted. The paint looked like badly peeling sunburn, the lawn mere patches of grass tough enough to survive in hard-trodden dirt littered with children's battered plastic toys. If there'd once been flowering shrubs or fruiting trees, there were none now. But in spite of everything the house maintained a massive, patient dignity.

The neighborhood children and dogs gathered to watch me turn the car into the elder-bowered lane between the Esmond house and its left-hand neighbor, a cellar hole and two stark chimneys. The dirt lane was an old right-of-way to the private cemetery. The thick growth of alders showed it had been a long time since a hearse had gone through, probably when the third Esmond sister had died many years ago.

When we were clear of the alders, there was open ground behind the houses and their neat or ramshackle outbuildings. A goat pasture was roughly fenced off; the rest was unmown grass as thick with late summer flowers as a calico print. The far border was a stand of spruces and hardwoods.

The way was deeply rutted, and the ruts were studded with embedded rocks. I found myself clenching my jaw as hard as I was gripping the wheel. "Don't try to go any farther than Wolcotts'," Marianne said. "You should be able to turn around."

Ahead of us on the left was a small old farmhouse with a sagging ridgepole. The clapboards were weathered almost black, and against them the red and white pickup in the yard looked flamboyant. A little way behind the house the skeleton of a barn being taken down gauntly dominated everything else.

"The Wolcott land all lies to the northwest," Miss Emma said. "What hasn't been sold off. We own the land on this side of the right-of-way. When Clem Sr. sold the house for us, we held onto the field."

"It was our paradise when we were small," Marianne said. "It could be anywhere we wanted it to be. I couldn't bear to think of its ever being dug up and built upon."

Morrie and Esmond must be salivating about it, I thought. They must see it carpeted with dollars. "I hope the neighborhood youngsters appreciate it," Marianne said.

"I wonder if any of them know about the wild strawberries," Miss Emma said wistfully.

Two brown and white hounds were barking hysterically, and we could see them running back and forth between the pickup and the woodshed.

I could tell they were chained, but they sounded so bloodthirsty and raced around in such a frenzy the chains might snap at any minute.

"Listen," I began. "I don't think it's safe—"

"I don't believe the dogs are dangerous," Marianne said calmly. "The Cruikshanks would have warned me—they knew we were coming here today. Lucas Wolcott takes care of the cemetery."

"He's the last of the Wolcott men, and one of those valuable people who will do odd jobs," Miss Emma said. "A heavy drinker, I'm sorry to say, but Clem says he's a good worker and gives value for his pay. We knew his grandparents," she said nostalgically. "They were so good-hearted. Whenever there was a burial, Mrs. Wolcott always hurried out with her homemade wine to restore the mourners on the way back."

"It had quite a bang," Marianne said. "Some of the mourners would be feeling very restored by the time they reached the funeral meats."

"The dogs are barking at the house, not us," Miss Emma said. "I wonder why."

I stopped the car, but the dogs didn't give us a look. Lunging on their chains, they strained toward the ell kitchen, half-strangling themselves into convulsive coughs and then beginning again. Through the din we heard shouts and crashes from inside and a stabbing yelp of pain, at which the dogs seemed to go insane. I expected gunshots and a madman to rush out firing at anyone in sight. I'd never felt so defenseless in my life, and my throat was trying to seal itself tightly shut against voice and breath.

"Duck down," I said hoarsely. "*Hide.*"

Neither spoke. Perhaps they're too terrified, I thought, panicked by the awful weight of responsibility for saving them before we all became bloody corpses. A girl appeared behind the screen door, fighting with the latch; she got the door open and ran down the steps and past the dogs toward the road, her torn shirt flying open. A man tumbled out after her, swinging a belt like a lasso and yelling, "Whore! Whore!"

The dogs leaped at him, and he slashed at them with the belt, swearing. The girl looked back, tripped, and fell headlong into the road in front of the car. I have no memory of getting out; it begins with the three of us surrounding the girl, with that obscene apparition coming at us, and the girl curled up into a moaning ball, her eyes squeezed shut and tears running from under the lids.

"Oh, my dear," Miss Emma said softly. She took my arm to steady herself and knelt down in the dirt in her pink dress. The man lurched toward us; he was not big, but he was well built and muscular in the tight T-shirt and snug jeans of a vain man. He was as blond as the huddled girl on the ground trying to protect her belly. His face was so darkly flushed and so contorted it was impossible to see what it was really like.

"What are *you* gawking at?" he demanded thickly. "This is no goddam business of yours! Go on, get out!" He flourished the belt at us. He was just barely keeping his balance, which is why I was not afraid of him, and Marianne watched him approach as if he were some harmless, though unattractive, curiosity.

The dogs had quieted to rapid panting, probably because the beating had stopped. It *had* been a beating; as the girl twisted onto her back, her shirt fell open and the belt marks were clear and bloody across her small breasts. The dogs strained to reach her.

"I told you to get the hell off my property!" He ignored me and threatened Marianne with the belt, sneering and swaying. "Who the hell do you think you are?" She regarded him with a cold objectivity. "You think you're some shit on a stick, don't you? You old bag with your head way up there somewhere!"

She was taller than he was, which must have rankled. "I'm Mrs. Guy Rigby," she said without raising her voice. "I am not on your property—I'm on the right-of-way. I hired you through Mr. Cruikshank to take care of the Esmond cemetery, so your pay is my business."

"So you're the slut who ran away with the bank robber!" he said. "Got him to do it before he could get you in the sack. Christ, you must've been the most high-price lay since—since—" He wobbled back and forth, grinning foolishly. "H-hope it was worth it," he said, his voice running slower and slower. "Wrecking a town for one go-o—good f—"

"*Shut up!*" I heard myself in a glorious explosion of passion beyond mere rage; nothing was impossible for me in that instant. I felt as if I had the strength to strangle him into silence. I made a grab for the belt, just as Miss Emma said quietly, "She's bleeding."

I looked down and saw the blood-soaked crotch of the faded blue jeans and then back at that vacant red-eyed smile.

"Get in there on the telephone and call an ambulance," I snapped at him. "No, you can't talk straight, I'll do it."

"I'll s-s-set the dogs on ye—"

"Then I'll go somewhere else, and I'll be back with the police," I said. He took a step toward me, trying to swing the belt, his mouth working without audible words. I gave him a push, and he staggered backward. Then trying to come at me again, he stubbed his toe and fell on his face. He didn't move. The dogs ignored me as I walked by them. They were whining and still trying to reach the girl.

14

"Find a blanket," Miss Emma called after me. "She's as cold as ice."

I went into the kitchen. It was scantily furnished and hadn't been painted for years, but it was clean. There were red and white checked curtains at the windows and a white ironstone jug of goldenrod and asters on the table. I took a folded army blanket off the couch and handed it out to Miss Emma. The wall telephone was also in the kitchen, and I called for the town ambulance and said the police would be needed, too.

When I went outside, Lucas still lay flat on his face, and I hoped that he'd broken either his nose or his jaw against a rock when he fell. The dogs sat at the ends of their chains staring at the huddle under the blanket, which was making little whimpers. Miss Emma kept patting and murmuring, "There, dear, someone's coming to help you and make it better. . . . Tell me your name."

"Janine." It came out on a gasp.

Marianne sat down on a wheelbarrow. A hound put his chin on her knee and looked mournfully at her. "You tried to stop it, didn't you?" she said to him.

"I'm losing my baby," the girl gasped against Miss Emma's skirt. "It'll kill Sonny! We want it so bad. I thought Daddy would sign for me. Sonny's folks would for him." Sobbing with grief and pain, she curled into a tight ball again. We could hear the ambulance coming, and the cruiser whooping along with it.

"Tell us where Sonny is," Miss Emma said, "and we'll find him and bring him to the hospital."

Janine only cried harder. I knew who Sonny was; Ira Neville's boy. "He's been in the Youth Correctional Center for a couple of months," I said in a low voice to Marianne. Daddy lay snoring face down in the dirt.

Lonnie Sayers, the police chief, who'd been in high school with my brother, had the ambulance crew check Lucas to be sure he had simply passed out and not collapsed with a stroke or a heart attack. "Drunk as a skunk" was the succinct report. Janine was taken away, wrapped in reassurances as well as blankets. A large patrolman tranported Lucas by fireman's lift to the cruiser.

Lonnie took our telephone numbers and departed, carrying the bloody belt. We were left with the dogs and a pair of neighbors. One was an elderly man in overalls who said he would look after the dogs, and they went along with him quite happily. The woman was enormously fat, but she moved with surprising ease. She locked up the house and shed, told us her name, and pointed out her house. She owned the goats, who were now crying across the field at the sound of her voice.

She stood in the dooryard with her arms folded under her overflowing bust. "The hell of it is, Lucas ain't half-bad when he's sober. But cross him when he's got enough in him and then he's some ugly. He's been really pouring it down lately. It's gonna kill him some day."

"If somebody else doesn't do it first," I said.

"Does he beat the girl often?" Marianne asked.

"When she was little he'd never even slap her, any more than he'd hit the dogs. The first real time was last year when she struck out to a ninth-grade dance with Sonny Neville. Lucas used to go to Legion meetings regular then, and he'd stay and play cards. So she thought she'd be back before he was." She smiled reminiscently. "She stopped to show me her dress. One of her friends had made it for her. My, she was some cunning, all in blue, with that yellow hair of hers. Like a doll. Well, Lucas didn't stay to play cards that night, he went drinking instead, but he was there when she got home. She *knew,* poor young one. They were walking home from the high school when the pickup went crawling past 'em. He must have recognized her, but he never let on. She wouldn't let Sonny drive her in, made him leave her out on the street. Well, that bas—excuse me—was lying in wait. It was real quiet that night, and we could hear him cursing her, and her crying, and the dogs going crazy. My man and Ted—

Ted took away the dogs just now—and a couple of others came out here and told him some ideas they had." Her long mouth quirked over the gaps in her teeth. "Quieted him down something remarkable for a long time. Dunno what set him off this time. It wasn't a date with Sonny, that boy's been put away for a while. And Lucas has kept her real close. But it seems as if he can't stand to see her growing up."

Miss Emma, who had been given the wheelbarrow to rest on after the long time on her knees beside Janine, said with asperity, "If he's trying to hold on to her, he's going about it the wrong way."

"Ayuh, he's a little crazy," the woman agreed. "Been that way ever since his wife died when Janine was three or so." She left us to go and talk to her goats.

"It gets sadder and sadder, doesn't it?" Marianne remarked. "Have you unstiffened sufficiently, Emma, to go on?"

"I can hardly wait to get away from this place," Miss Emma said. "If I had to hobble on bare feet like a religious pilgrim, I'd do it gladly."

We took the flowers and tools from the car and walked on toward the trees. The sun was trying to break through and cast a frail gleam, like a distant memory of itself, into the little clearing. Lucas Wolcott had kept the stone wall in repair; the gate hinges were oiled; and the grass was clipped short around the stones. We could have been miles out into the country, it was so quiet except for the birds and the steady hum of the bees in the banks of goldenrod outside the stone wall. I offered to take a trowel and dig, but the sisters refused. They knelt on the newspapers, put on the cotton gloves, and got to work.

"Don't you have to save your hands?" I asked.

"For heaven's sake, Eden, we're not brain surgeons," said Marianne. She sat back and looked up at me. "I don't mean to sound ungrateful. You were sensational back there, you know."

"Yes, you *were,*" said Miss Emma. Basking in all this, I went off and sat on the wall facing out, to give them privacy. I was kept company by a chipmunk who dodged in and out of the wall as close to me as he dared. He and the sociable chickadees were a good antidote for what had just happened, but something like this is never tidied up without a trace, like a television drama.

The plants were all set out, and the sisters helped one another up, joking about their stiffness. "I'm a dite winded," Miss Emma said. "And drier than a cork leg, as Papa would say."

"Listen to her," said Marianne. "She's left Boston far behind. She's reverted to pure Maddox, and old Maddox at that. I'm a little parched myself. Thirsty work, confronting drunkards and so forth. Still—" She stopped by the gate and looked around. "He's kept it beautifully. Some handsome, as Emma would now say. Are we holding you up, Eden, or could you drive us straight home?"

"Come down to my parents' house and have a cup of tea first," I urged, anxious to draw out the time with them. "If my mother isn't home, I'll make it."

"Let's take her up on it, Em," said Marianne. "I think we need it."

Several cars were in the Rigby driveway, but if a curtain so much as twitched when we went up the front steps, I didn't see it. Neither sister glanced toward the house, though they had to know who lived there.

My father was holding a faculty meeting at the high school, but my mother was at home. Afterward she told me that for a moment she'd felt like a cottager being visited unexpectedly by the local Great Lady. But it had been for just that one moment. "I'm still Mary Ann Esmond," Marianne said. "I had only to stand outside the old house today, even the way it looks now, and I was that leggy child again, all long black stockings and starched ruffles, doing 'Für Elise' for Mama's callers or playing for Big Sister Susan to sing 'In the Time of Roses' or for little Emmie and 'Humoresque.' The place was suddenly crammed with ghosts, even the big elms were back! And those people living there didn't even know it."

We had tea and cinnamon toast comfortably at the kitchen table. The sisters showed no signs of falling apart from delayed reaction, but why should they? Neither had been sheltered from the world; they'd been out there living in it. Except for the overshadow of the ugly scene, we were having a good time. Now and then I was aware of the house next door, where Guy Rigby's deserted wife had lived out her years as Marianne's heroic victim. It wasn't likely to bother Marianne's conscience now, if it hadn't all those years ago.

"I wonder what they've done with that man," Miss Emma said.

"Tied him hand and foot and dropped him off the bridge, I hope," said her sister. "By now the tide should be taking him downriver and out to sea."

"Alcoholism is a *disease,* Mary Ann," Miss Emma reproved her. "It can cause dreadful personality changes. Perhaps that's what's happened in this case."

"Lucas was a high school athletic hero twenty-odd years ago," my mother said. "We were living inland then, but we knew all about him through the *Journal.* If you'd ever seen him in the yearbook, you'd never dream he could look as he does today. He went into the Marines straight from school, and he was a first sergeant when he finally decided not to reenlist but to stay home and marry, and they had Janine. He should have stayed in the service. His parents were dead, and without a firm hand over him, he was a ship without a rudder, and he couldn't stick to anything. He was drunk the night Janine was born and telling everybody who'd listen that he wouldn't let his wife go through *that* again."

"Did she survive?" Miss Emma asked.

"Oh, yes, but when she got pregnant again he was infuriated, blamed her, wouldn't let her go to a doctor, and threatened anyone who came near."

"Why didn't I know all this?" I demanded.

"You were about twelve," she said. "And we were fairly selective about our dinner-table conversation. Anyway, his wife begged people to stay away. She said she would handle him. She did it by drinking with him, and she died drunk giving birth to a premature, and dead, boy."

"What a tragedy," Miss Emma whispered.

"A son," I said. "He must have hated himself."

My mother shrugged. "I don't think he was ever sober enough to think about it, for a long time. The little girl was taken away and put in a foster home for a few years. After he pulled himself together, he got her back. He was holding a job, going to AA meetings, and everyone thought he was on the right course at last."

"Until the girl began to grow up," said Marianne. "May I call the hospital from here?"

She identified herself on the telephone as one of the women who had interrupted the beating and was told that Janine was resting comfortably and was in no danger.

"Does the child have any other relatives?" she asked my mother.

"No, Lucas's people are gone, and her mother came from out of state to work at the Mackenzie Inn one summer. I doubt that Janine knows anything at all about her mother's people."

"Well, she cannot go back to that house," Marianne said. "I'm going to call the Cruikshanks."

I drove them up to Main Street. Clem Jr. was waiting on the sidewalk for them and said he would drive them home; I took myself back to Job's Harbor.

When I drove in past the rose hedge, Chad gave tongue from up on my deck and then rushed down the steps. Glen sat on the railing watching me impassively, as far as I could tell. After my afternoon, I didn't really care what that foretold. I was feeling the backlash now, an overbearing tiredness, and my stomach was queasy. Yes, I'd stood up to Lucas, yelled at him, pushed him, but I wasn't proud; it was a sordid business, and I was depressed. Leaning over to quiet Chad, I was annoyed to have tears come into my eyes.

"Hi," said Glen to the top of my head. "You look all shot. You didn't run over a cat, did you?"

That made me laugh, though feebly. When I first learned to drive, hitting an animal or a bird used to be the worst thing I could think of, and it still rates pretty high. "Come in and I'll tell you," I said.

He listened without any comment, and when I had finished, he said, "Let's go to Tenby, get something to eat, and go to the movies."

"But you don't like what's on now."

"Don't argue. You said once you wanted to see it."

No consoling, no philosophizing, no advising me to forget it because it wasn't my problem. Instead he was offering to take me to a movie he didn't want to see. I appreciated the sacrifice, and it wasn't in vain; he liked the movie after all and handsomely admitted it. We drove home in a mellow and affectionate mood and finished off the evening in the loft of his cabin.

15

I slept well and woke early in spite of the dark drizzly morning. *Little Emily* was just leaving the harbor, in company with two others. Everybody was going to work, including myself; I could hardly wait to get to it. Yesterday was still as brutally vivid and tender as a new scar, but I didn't intend to keep fingering it. Janine was safe, if unhappy, and some good things had happened yesterday; the hours I'd spent with Marianne and Miss Emma, *Amadeus* with Glen, and the postlude.

Over a late-morning mug-up with Gram I told her about the beating and put her into a fine lather of indignation. "Why, Lucas Wolcott's mother and father were the nicest people you'd ever want to meet! They used to come down here to Grange, you know, and *she* could play the piano to beat the band. They must be turning over in their graves!"

When I left her she was putting on her raincoat to go down to the wharf and tell Grampa and Uncle Early.

By noon I was complacent about having done nearly five hours of work, and Janine was my legitimate excuse for driving to Fox Point. I gave them time for a late lunch, and when I reached their road, the mail driver was at the box. "You going up there, Eden? I got this package that's too big for the box, and I hate to take it back to the post office and make 'em come for it."

"Sure, hand it over," I said. "Give me the rest of their mail, too." He gave me the parcel and a sizable bundle held together by a thick rubber band.

"Those ladies get a pile of mail," he said admiringly, "and it's not all catalogs, either."

"Like mine," I said.

I wasn't really expecting to find Fee in the living room being witty and lively—she should have been out hauling with Julian—but I wouldn't have been surprised either. When I drove clear of the dripping woods, there was a dark green Cutlass at the front door, and I thought *Damn.* Whoever it was, I'd have preferred Fee.

Miss Emma answered the door. "Eden, how nice on a dark, dank day! And you've brought our records!"

"I'm not staying," I said, for manners' sake. "You have guests. But I'd like to know about Janine, if you have news of her."

"We do, and of course you're staying. Come straight in to the fire. It's the first one of the season, so it's rather special. Applewood, too." She went confidently ahead, and I followed her into the living room, carrying the package and quietly rejoicing. One in the eye for you, Fee! Then I was ashamed of myself, but only slightly, and in the next instant astonished, as Kenneth Rigby arose beside Marianne from the sofa before the fire.

"Hello, Eden," he said. Drama, Nick Raintree said, and this was drama: Kenneth standing under his sinful grandpa's portrait and looking, in his own reticent way, much like him.

"Welcome, Eden!" Marianne said warmly. "You're just in time for a cup of tea and some wonderful surprise of Mrs. Thatcher's."

I hoped I didn't look as witless as I felt. Kenneth seemed entirely at home. Kindly ignoring my bemused state, he took the package from me. *If a Rigby ever shows up, I don't want to miss it.* Well, everyone was missing it but me. A complacent satisfaction took over; Young Friend of the Household roosted informally on hassock by the hearth.

Kenneth slit the tapes of the package with his jackknife, and turned back the cardboard flaps. "Cassettes and compact discs are fine, I know," Miss Emma said happily, "but I love *records!* Just to handle them takes me back to the time when to own a Heifetz record was pure ecstasy."

"We're trying to replace lost treasures," Marianne explained. "Some of these will be collectors' items one day, if they aren't already. . . . Kenneth, will you have a cup of tea with us? Or would you like a drink?"

"I'd like to stay," he said, "but someone's coming to look at a trimaran two other brokers haven't been able to move."

"You'll sell it, Kenneth," Marianne said authoritatively. He smiled at that, said goodbye to Miss Emma and me, and Marianne arose and walked out to the hall with him. I watched Miss Emma reverently remove albums from between sheets of plastic bubbles. The others spoke quietly out in the hall. Kenneth as a used-boat salesman challenged the imagination, unless his low-key approach was such a novelty that it charmed the credit cards out of the billfolds. After all, there was a time when *I* would have walked on my hands up Ship Street for him, and shinnied to the top of the flagpole to perch on the crosstrees.

Mrs. Thatcher came in with the tea tray, and we swapped such family news as there was. She must be six feet tall, and is solidly fleshed. Roy looks minute beside her, but has never seemed depressed by this. They've been described as Peter Rabbit and Mrs. Macgregor.

The Cutlass drove away and Marianne returned; Mrs. Thatcher rather grandly accepted praise for her blackberry tarts, and left us. While Miss Emma was pouring the tea, her sister replenished the fire. Gazing into the flames she said, "He looks so much like his grandfather. It comes out more and more. He's very quiet, almost too quiet, but the smile just now, as he looked back at me from the steps—that was Guy's." She wasn't sad or vaguely sentimental, just matter-of-fact. "Well, Eden, it's good to have someone young to tea on a rainy day."

"Without young people in and out of the house, we might as well be dead," Miss Emma said. "I can't imagine any worse purgatories than one of those retirement villages. Can you? Fiona Heriot was here this morning for a few minutes with that handsome man of hers. She brought us two pounds of fresh crabmeat she'd picked out herself."

I was spared any twinges of jealousy. I'd had yesterday, and today I'd seen Kenneth Rigby at Fox Point, a little gem I would keep hidden in my bosom as my own until somebody else found out.

"Now what about Janine?" I asked.

"She's recovering nicely from the miscarriage," Marianne said, "but of course she's very unhappy about it. The loss seems to be worse for her than the beating. Lord, when I think of those two infants and their fantasy of playing house with a live doll!" She shook her head.

Miss Emma touched her nose with a handkerchief. "No matter if it is a fantasy, it's been terribly real to that child."

Marianne looked indulgently at her and went on, "Clem Sr. got very busy on the telephone while we were with him yesterday. Talk about your Old Boy Network! Clem Jr. is now Janine's guardian pro tem, and she is coming here from the hospital."

"She'll think she's in heaven!" I said from the heart.

"Unless she thinks she's been stashed away in the Old Ladies' Home," said Marianne. "We'll find out who her friends are and have them come out to see her."

"Mrs. Rigby, have you thought any more about what I asked you? Everybody will tell you I'm *good. I* know I'm good!" His voice cracked. "Jesus, Mrs. Rigby, I've got five pupils of my own! I play for the community chorus and sub for two church organists! But I've gone as far as I can with anybody around here, and I can't afford to go away to study without a scholarship. If you'd give me lessons I'd—it would make my life over. You don't know what it would do for me!"

I knew I ought to go outside, but I couldn't make myself. Miss Emma wordlessly handed me a signed first edition of *Tender Is the Night.* I'd have been dazzled if I hadn't been so enthralled by Robbie's passion.

"I'd have a better chance at a scholarship if I was your pupil," he bumbled breathlessly on.

The stoneware money-cat, serene on her windowsill, invited fingers to stroke her curved back. Her eyes looked drowsily half-open, as if she knew I was there. I concentrated on Julian, the gentle giant hovering like God over his basket of kittens and agonizing about their names.

"Robbie," Marianne said austerely. "I have talked with Jason and Tillie Higham, and they tell me you're as good as you say and will probably be better. But I am not going to give lessons to anyone."

It was as if he hadn't heard her. "I'll play for you right now! You can judge!"

"You're in no condition to play well now—you're far too agitated. I'm being completely honest with you, my dear. There will be no lessons for anyone. I have enough to do to keep in practice so I can play for my own pleasure, as long as possible in the time I have left."

"All I'm asking for is two hours—one hour—a week," he pleaded. "So little for you, such a hell of a lot for me. It would mean the world. I'd pay anything you asked."

"Money is no consideration. I am not a teacher. I never was. There are advanced teachers in the major cities of Maine and in the college towns. You can work toward your scholarship with one of them if you can take off a morning or an afternoon once a week for a lesson."

"But none of them is Marianne Rigby! *You're* the great one! You could inspire me. You *do* inspire me—" He started to choke. In a moment he would be bawling like a child. Miss Emma and I looked unhappily at each other, and I opened the door onto the porch.

"Wait," she murmured. "It's been dreadful but it's over."

"At my age," Marianne said, "I don't want to be an inspiration to anyone. I thank you, but it's only a burden. Now you are to go back to the kitchen, and Mrs. Thatcher will give you a cup of coffee, or a soft drink if you'd like that, and a large slice of her special chocolate cake. It's absolutely delicious. I don't want to hear anything more about lessons," she said quickly, as if he'd opened his mouth to begin again. "Otherwise you are welcome here on any Sunday, and we would all like to hear you play then."

We heard him walking away, and then a door closed down the hall. Marianne sighed. "Come back, you two," she called. She looked tired. "I don't think he's given up yet." She lifted the padded cozy off the pot and poured tea for herself. "You two, help yourselves. I'm drained. That boy is a *taker.* If he put that much fire into his music, it could be a great help to him. But I'm afraid the fiery ambition right now is to be taught by Marianne Rigby." She spoke with objective simplicity.

The truck went out rather faster than it had come in, and she shrugged. "If he has it, he doesn't need me as a midwife. Emmie's too soft; she can't refuse to listen." She gave her sister a mocking grin which took years off her.

"Emmie's not soft enough to refuse to send them away with a flea in their ear!" Miss Emma retorted. "The mother's ear, anyway. Mummie *adores* the violin; she plays records and tapes by all the great ones and tells little Lottie she will sound like that one day if she will just practice. Little Lottie, who can carry a tune but that's about it, is buried under the avalanche of Mummie's expectations. And little Lottie knows that not even a fairy godmother is going to make her play the fiddle like Yehudi Menuhin."

"Or Emma Esmond," said Marianne.

"Thank you for putting Yehudi and me in the same box, Mary Ann," said Emma dryly. "I'm sure he'd be flattered. What can this child see ahead of her?" She lifted eloquent hands. "Years of penal servitude with disaster at the end, and she's only eleven now. Her teacher's robbing them, and Mummie should be drawn and quartered." This spoken in Miss Emma's soft fluttery voice had quite an effect.

"The child was miserable and played miserably. Mummie said they planned to get her a really good violin, with my advice. I took the violin and played a Bach partita and proved there was nothing wrong with the instrument. I left Mummie with Mary Ann, while I took Lottie for a walk to the shore and asked her what she would really rather be doing instead of practicing. She said, 'Playing outside with all the other kids.' We talked about what games she liked to play. She really brightened up, and we had a good talk. Then I had the satisfaction of telling Mummie that Lottie's lessons were a waste of time and money and Lottie's childhood." She smiled reminiscently. "You should have seen her trying to be polite while she seethed."

"My sister is a closet sadist," Marianne said.

"But what if Mummie keeps pushing Lottie?" I asked.

"She won't. I called her father at his office. Being more sensitive than his wife, he'd been having misgivings for some time. All he needed was confirmation from an expert to make him put his foot down."

"So Little Lottie has a fairy godmother after all," I said.

"And at my age I'm receiving flowers from a young man," said Miss Emma. She pointed to the elegant arrangement on the top of the stereo cabinet, glowing like a Monet painting against an ivory wall. "Lottie's name was on the card with her father's."

"Of course the mother will tell everyone that you're so jealous of your position that you won't even encourage a small child," said Marianne.

Miss Emma shrugged airily. "*You* may not have taught, but that's how I earned my living. Touring paid for the desserts, but teaching provided the bread and butter and paid the rent. So I've run into ambitious parents before, though usually with older pupils. They'd be adequate; quite good, in fact; able to give much pleasure to themselves and others. But not star stuff, if you want to call it that, any more than I was. Sometimes the youngsters believed in it themselves. It was their right, then, to drive themselves and take the chances. But some were relieved to have the pressure lifted."

She sprang up. "Oh, never mind them; it's too depressing. Let's give Eden that little tune."

"Yes, please," I said, trying not to sound like Oliver Twist holding up his empty bowl.

It was more than one little tune. They were all old, all exquisitely played, simple, and inexpressibly moving. If Beethoven and Mozart could put me under a spell, these could put tears in my eyes. No one noticed; I had the sensation of invisibly overhearing something very private. I was not excluded by rudeness. I had simply been left behind while they went back to the Esmond house and the long black stockings and the elms still standing; the little boy fiddled on the street corner, and angels showered St. Cecilia with roses. The secret communication of two younger sisters was made up of glances, nods, single words, an exchanged smile, or a smothered laugh. And always the music flowed on from one melody to another, with no discernible signals given. They were thinking as one.

They finished up with a fast and joyous version of "The Ash Grove" and were back at Fox Point, smiling and bowing to my passionate applause. "I did the neatest curtsy in those days," Miss Emma said dreamily and demonstrated.

"She played the infant prodigy to the hilt, the little show-off," said Marianne. "I was *much* more modest."

My inbred sense of propriety got me on my feet. It was time to go, and they didn't press me to stay. I thanked them—inadequately, I thought—and they thanked me for bringing in the mail and told me to come again. I wanted to get home and up into the Hayloft without encountering anything to knock this particular jar of essence out of my hands.

When we walked out into the hall, Gideon Wilkes stood just inside the front door like one of Tolkien's Ents, with his Allagash hat crushed under his arm.

Between his frowsty beard and his overhanging thatch, his eyes had the wet luminosity of a dog's or of human eyes full of tears about to run over.

"Listening for a false note, Gideon?" Marianne asked.

"I hope you don't mind my letting myself in," he said in the cultivated baritone voice which was always such a surprise coming from a scarecrow in old army fatigues. "I didn't want to break into the music, but I didn't want to miss it, either."

"You're always welcome. You know that, Gideon," said Miss Emma. "Well, how did she sound to you today?"

"She's holding her course, Miss Emma. True as a clipper ship flying home."

They all laughed as if they had an established joke among them. "How are you, Eden?" he asked courteously.

"Very well, Gideon. Did you get any mackerel that moonlit night?"

"Three. Two for me and one for the cat."

"You must charm them in. I've never caught a fish in the moonlight yet. Goodbye," I said to the sisters. "So long, Gideon." I went out and left them. The jar was still in balance, undisturbed by Gideon.

16

On Sunday the wind was northwest and giving us a breezy, scintillating, Septemberish day. Gram and I were late starting and when we drove up the Fox Point driveway, there were five cars; the Highams', the Sorrells' station wagon, Sim Trescott's cherished 1967 Coronet; Clem Jr.'s unpretentious late model, and a long, extremely handsome affair in gunmetal blue that made everything else look meek and lowly.

"I can't park behind that. It'll give my poor critter a permanent inferiority complex," I said. "It's done that to me already." I drove to the head of the line and pulled in ahead of the Highams' Volkswagen with the children's safety seats in the back.

"Who do you suppose owns it?" asked Gram.

"Maybe we're about to meet some millionaire from Camden. I hear the place is crawling with them."

There was no music when we reached the house. Conversation and occasional laughter flowed out the open windows. The instant we were inside the door I felt as if I were walking into a new chapter of the novel or onto a stage set for Act 2. Over to you, Nick Raintree, I thought, wondering if he was here. I stayed back in the hall, and let Gram go alone into the living room, where she was affectionately hailed by Miss Emma. I tried discreetly to review today's cast.

Edith and Jake Morley sat on the sofa Kenneth and Marianne had occupied a few days before. Edith is handsome in a New England Gothic mode; her dark blonde hair has no grey in it yet, and that day it was brushed harshly back from her high forehead and done up in a smooth elaborate knot at the back. To use one of Gram's earthier similes, she was sitting up as straight as a cat in a pan of ashes. She was facing the portrait and trying not to look at it, though her grandfather persisted in watching *her*. Perhaps she had never seen him before; the family would hardly keep his pictures on display. It must have been a shock for her to be inescapably faced with the Devil and realize how much Jane looked like him.

There *was* something weird in the way the portrait had brought Guy Rigby alive in both Kenneth and Jane, yet they looked nothing alike.

Miss Emma now took Gram to Edith—here was a genuine Rigby for Gram. Jake was jovially telling Ed Sorrell what challenges this house had presented and how he'd met each one. He has high color and crew-cut grey hair and wears heavy-rimmed glasses which he often takes off and aims at his listener to make a point. He is husky without being fat, and his face and gestures are expressive, emphasizing Edith's bleak impassivity that Sunday.

Marianne and the Trescotts, from Winter Head, were discussing the portrait. There could be no tacit covenant to ignore it with Sim in the room. He was excited about it; he knew who the artist was, an expatriate mid-westerner.

"Either the Boston or Portland museum would be over the moon to have this," he said. He couldn't take his eyes off it. "I can feel the texture of the tweed from here. And those hands are going to *move.* I could swear it."

"It will eventually go to the artist's town in Michigan," Marianne said. "They're making quite a nice collection of his work."

Edith was listening to them, not to Gram and Miss Emma. God, how I wished I knew what she was thinking as she lifted her eyes once again to that face, those eyes. I was sorry for her, which she would have considered an insult.

Deb Sorrell and Tillie Higham were on a window seat across the room. Clem Sr. was sunk in a big chair, his fingers laced under his chin. He was watching and listening, or dozing; you couldn't tell what went on behind those glasses.

Walking through the room unnoticed, or taken for granted, I looked through a seaward window and saw Clem Jr. and Jason Higham out on the porch, smoking and talking. Fee sat on the railing apart from them, wearing white slacks and a faded blue middy. I could tell her hair was newly washed, because that was when the brush of foxy red in it shone coppery amid the brown. The wind lightly stirred it. Her face was turned away from the men, so I saw it in profile. Seen like this, she was the very young Fee whom I had sometimes (not often) taken by surprise. Before she realized my presence, I found an extraordinary sadness about that dreaming gaze. Early on, without having the words for it, I sensed the unattainable wish for a strong and protecting father and a tighter hold on the tenuous memories of her mother. "I can't even remember her voice!" she had cried out once when we were young. But she'd taken care never to show that anguish again.

I speculated on the significance of today's wistful melancholy. While I watched her, wondering if I could will her to look at me, Clem Jr. spoke to her. She turned her head, smiling at him, and I saw how he responded. For that moment he was unwary, vulnerable, and I had no business here. I turned back to the main room, carrying the memory with me. He was a widower with teenage children; he'd always had a great affection for Fee, and after she reached twenty-one, he'd proposed to her once a year until she took up with Julian.

"Mary Ann!" Jake called in a quarter-deck voice, holding Ed Sorrell by the arm. "You mind if I take Doc down cellar and show him the new system?"

"Heavens, no! It's so handsome we had half a mind to entertain down there today."

"What about you, Clem?" Jake asked Clem Sr., who waved him off with one hand. On their way, the men met the Carvers, and Jake invited Sydney to come along. Sydney declined, amiably. Out in the hall Jake boomed another invitation. "*Hello,* Morrie! You and the boy come on down and see the new heater! It's just the thing you should put in your new houses."

Annie Hearne and Tracy came in, Tracy in red jeans and a gaudy top. An elaborate makeup weighed down her eyelids. Her mother was smiling apprehensively and gave Edith a nervous nod. She went to Marianne as if to safe harbor. Morrie had gone with the other men, but Esmond entered with a woman holding his arm. Her hair was a tightly curled golden fleece, and she was very dressed up, even carrying white gloves. She was a well-known realtor, and Fee poked me in the back. I hadn't known she'd come in. "Love or money?" she asked. Esmond was possessively introducing her to his great-aunts.

"This is a privilege," she said, sounding more sincere than effusive. "Esmond is so lucky to have you ladies for his aunts." Esmond actually smiled, which didn't improve him.

Seeing the Hearnes, Edith Morley had suddenly become very animated with Gram and Nancy Trescott. By now Fee was trying to suppress giggles, and when Clem Jr. raised a warning eyebrow at her, she nearly blew up. "They'll try to outstay each other," she said. "Jake's already got the inside track—I'll bet he's had mug-ups with them all week while the work's been going on. No wonder *he's* so happy. I wonder how he persuaded Edith to come into *this* house and meet *that* woman."

"Watch it, Fee," Clem murmured.

"OK, Clem." She patted his arm. "I'll be good. Come on, Eden, let's talk to Deb Sorrell and Tillie." I didn't want to mix, afraid of missing something, but I compromised by letting the others do most of the talking while I observed.

Edith's rigidity was softened by Nancy Trescott's flattering interest in Jane's career. Jane was Edith's favorite subject, as if she could never get over her astonishment that she and Jake had produced this beauty. While Nancy admired the sheaf of photographs Edith took from her handbag, Edith said with a rush of forced laughter, "Your husband should be painting *her* instead of weird characters like Gideon Wilkes!" She leaned forward and tapped Nancy's knee. "Now you tell me what's so beautiful about *him!*" she said roguishly. "You must know his *background.*"

"Yes, we do," said Nancy, "but background has nothing to do with it. You'll have to take it up with Sim sometime, he'd love to discuss it with you." And how I'd love to hear that conversation, I thought.

"Well, I certainly shall!" Edith was practically jolly now. "When I think that people are willing to pay thousands for portraits of our local bums and lunatics!" Unfailingly ladylike, Nancy would never explain that people paid their thousands for her husband's signature.

Esmond took his girl outdoors to walk. The men came up from the cellar; the doctor and Jake were in a good humor and Morrie in a glum one. Fee and Deb Sorrell joined the group around Marianne. Miss Emma was with the Carvers.

"I wish to God they'd play again." Jason Higham drifted up to me. "But it would take a hell of a lot of nerve to ask. Being in the same room with those two is like starving in the midst of plenty. When I think of all those years behind them, with everybody else hearing their music, and we don't get to know them until—oh, forget it!" he said abruptly and walked over to his wife. I finished it silently for him. *And we don't get to hear them until it's almost over.*

The atmosphere in the room turned chill and grey, as if my brain had put on glasses designed to wash color out of everything. Brightness falls from the air, a man had written in time of plague, and this was what he meant. Gooseflesh rose on my arms. I even wished that Nick Raintree would walk in with his buccaneerish grin; *he* would understand what I was feeling. Instead, we heard the motorcycle coming up the drive, and everyone turned toward the sound. Robbie Mackenzie parked across the drive from the cars, slung his helmet over the handlebars, and came toward the house, scowling prodigiously and kicking at pebbles in the driveway, unaware of his audience.

Miss Emma moved swiftly and met him out in the hall. "Robbie, you're just the lad I wanted to see! I need those strong arms to carry a heavy tray for me," she said. "Tracy dear, will you join us?" she called.

Tracy arose, urged by her mother's hand, and sidled around the side of the room. She probably wished she were invisible. I wished *I* were, so I could freely circulate, listen to everything, and do a little mind reading, too.

Miss Emma returned, with Robbie behind her carrying the big tea tray, and Tracy behind him with two plates of confections. I thought that she looked a little happier than when she'd left, but I couldn't say the same for Robbie. When he lowered the tray to the coffee table, Marianne smiled at him and thanked him, calling him by name. He was quite pale, and I hoped he wasn't going to keel over onto the tea service. He backed carefully away as if looking for a space in which to faint, but he made it on his own two feet to a chair near the door.

Tracy *was* more cheerful. She was actually passing out napkins while her mother watched with a touching pleasure. Tracy's mouth kept turning up at the corners as if she was trying to smile, or trying not to. I remembered seeing her in town that one day and how attractive she could be when she laughed.

Esmond was back again, pouring wine for himself and his realtor friend, and they kept cozily to themselves down by the book alcove. "Figuring out the money," Fee said to me from the corner of the mouth, as she continued on her second trip to the bar table. On the way back she said, "What do you bet she's been appraising the grounds?"

"Shsh," I said.

"You and Clem must come from the same planet, you speak the same language. Lots of sibilants in it and no vowels."

"I'll add a few," I said. "Like *shut up!* Come on." I took my cup to one of the window seats.

"Why are you drinking tea when you could be drinking Dry Sack?" she asked.

"Because I'm driving Gram, and liquor on my breath makes her nervous."

"Right," she said. "Look at Robbie. Why is he smoldering, do you think? You can practically see the smoke puffing from his nostrils, like a volcano getting ready."

"Who knows?" I said. Robbie was mutely refusing everything offered to him. Miss Emma left her friends to go to him with a plate of chocolaty things, and his response was a violent shake of his head. She patted his shoulder and left him. Tracy apparently asked him quite civilly if he wanted the kind of soft drink she had in her glass. Whatever he said—it was brief—sent her away with her chin in the air, which improved her posture.

In a little while, without any previous discussion, Tillie and Sydney went to the piano, and he took the Amati from the case. "It's a put-up job," Fee said. "God, I wish I'd stuck with the flute. They'd be asking me to play." She sounded genuinely disgruntled. When I looked around at her in surprise, she dragged her hand down over her face in a clownish gesture and winked at me. "I take it for granted that I'd have been playing like James Galway by now."

"When did you play the flute?" I asked skeptically.

"Before your time, sweetie. It was Dad's flute, and he tried to teach me. He was good or used to be before he ruined his wind and got shaky hands. *I* was lousy. I never could get all the way through my one piece, 'The Dancing Doll,' and finally he sold the flute. He must have been disappointed. I wish now—" The music began, so I never knew whether her regret was for disappointing her father or for not persevering with the flute.

The music was not familiar, but it was nostalgic and charming. Edith Rigby could listen with pleasure because Marianne wasn't playing, and her gaunt face lifted toward the sound, nearly smiling, her eyes half-shut. Then Tillie played the Black Key Etude; when she finished, flushed and happy with the applause, she said, "I feel as if someone should put a gold star on my forehead."

"We shall have to get some in," Marianne said.

Robbie's chair was empty. He must have pushed the motorcycle down the drive, because he had gone away in silence.

17

The hall clock struck four, and Clem Sr. levered himself from his chair and moved stiffly to a position before the fireplace, under the portrait. He took out his pocket watch and looked at it. The gesture reminded me of the moment when the tide turns and all the seaweed floating above the ledges suddenly begins to stream the other way. Departures, mostly reluctant, commenced.

Esmond Hearne was convoyed by his friend to take a courteous leave of his great-aunts; she made up for his lack of finesse with her own tasteful raptures about the lovely Afternoon. Jake Morley was expansively proprietorial, as if becoming so familiar with the house's insides had given him certain rights. His wife could not bring herself to shake hands with either Esmond; she nodded stonily at each and was getting into the big car before Jake was through the door. He still wanted to show Sydney the new heater, but Sydney refused again, this time explaining that he had a bad knee for stairs.

"But nothing bad about those hands of yours, Syd," Jake told him. "The old maestro's still got it!" He hugged Tillie with one arm and gave her a smacking kiss on the cheek. "That ought to make up for the gold star, darlin'!"

Gram was in no hurry to leave, so Fee and I went out and sat on the porch steps facing the ocean. She was very bright-eyed and quietly merry. "Dry Sack on an empty stomach gives you a great buzz in an insidious way. I'd go back for more, but I don't want to be conspicuous."

"You already have been," I said.

She snickered. "Julian preached me a sermon last week on the Demon

Rum. I don't know why he and Glen think a few sherries are going to turn me into Dad the Second." She jabbed a finger at me. "And don't you say what *you're* thinking. I can read it. *Petit à petit,* etcetera."

"Actually it was *C'est le premier pas,* etcetera."

"I might as well. Everybody thinks Julian and I booze ourselves out of our skulls anyway. They can't imagine he's really a teetotaler. And I don't *care!*" she said blissfully. "Right now I feel all loose and happy. And I brought myself in today, so I won't meet the WCTU when I step aboard the boat."

"It's a good thing you aren't driving a car home. You've got the whole bay out there to ramble around in."

"And it's time I started rambling. I must mind my manners and bid the ladies adieu. Come along and watch my style."

There was still an impromptu court at the front door. Fee waited until everyone else had gone but Gram and then became *une jeune fille bien élevée.* I half-expected her to curtsy, slacks and all.

"Fiona Heriot," said Miss Emma, retaining her hand. "You have such a romantic name, like a Sir Walter Scott heroine."

"I meant to ask you the other day," said Marianne. "Do ospreys still nest on Heriot Island?"

"Yes, there is," said Fee. "They come back every spring. I'd kill anyone who bothered the nest, if Julian didn't do it first."

"Your grandfather Heriot had the prettiest little yawl, *Sea Swallow,*" Marianne said. "On summer Sundays we'd often sail down the river to the island for a picnic. We'd have quite a fleet sometimes, but *Sea Swallow* was the queen. She skimmed the water like the bird she was named for. She outsailed them all on a cupful of wind."

Fee watched her with an unguarded adoration. She said shyly, "I have a model of her on our mantelpiece. It was one of the few things I wanted from the old house."

"What finally happened to her?" Marianne asked, then shook her head quickly. "No, don't tell me. Let me remember her running before the wind, with 'Youth on the prow, and Pleasure at the helm.'"

I'd look that up when I got home, if I remembered. "Speaking of boats," Fee said. "I missed the Elizabethan seadog today. Young Frobisher with the ring in his ear." She looked at me sidewise.

"Oh, I don't suppose we'll see him again, now that he's visited the Old Curiosity Shop and seen the Old Curiosities," said Marianne. "He was an interesting young man, though. An anachronism in these days of the IRS dossiers and Social Security numbers." She nodded at us and walked away to where Gram was looking at a particular plant in the herbaceous border, and told her its name.

"Did you know that the one small earring is an old charm against drowning?" Miss Emma asked. "Oh yes, Father used to tell us that in his youth it was quite common for seafarers to wear them. Right in Maddox. Eden dear, I've asked Vinca to stay on for a bit so we can have a quiet cup of tea together. Would you girls have some with us?"

"Not me, thank you," said Fee, "but I'd love to wash up for you afterward. Eden and I," she corrected herself.

"You already did so much, Fiona," said Miss Emma. "You arranged the trays so nicely."

"I think I'll walk her to the shore," I said.

"Preferably with a bottle of Dry Sack," Fee said under her breath, as we walked away across the lawn. Under the capricious northwest breeze the cat's-paws flashed like diamonds. Wherever they didn't touch, the water was that incredible blue which can still stun the vision and turn the islands Greek again.

"It's like her eyes," Fee said. "They aren't faded; they aren't old. Guy must have drowned in them and never came up again."

"That doesn't excuse his cleaning out the vault," I said.

"Oh, you're just sour because Young Frobisher didn't show," she said gleefully. "Now tell me the truth, don't you think he'd be a fantastic change from old cold-molasses Heriot? He might even shake my twinnie up a dite."

"Well, we aren't going to have a chance to find out, are we? Young Frobisher is probably off to plow uncharted seas."

"Do you mean that in the Freudian sense?" Fee asked.

"Probably," I said. I had him nicely disposed of, no fuss, no muss, and didn't intend to dig him up again. The metaphor was macabre, but he deserved it.

Island Magic lay off the end of the wharf. "There's my sweetheart," Fee said dotingly. She jumped in and fell against the bait box.

"Try not to plow head-on into your wharf out there," I said. So she'd set the trays. On the way to making herself indispensable. Eden, you're a sarcastic rat. It's *not* a competition. And you know about Kenneth and Janine.

"None of your sarcasm now." She gazed up at me with her hand shading her eyes because I stood against the sun. "It's the whole—what's the *in* word now? It's the *ambience* up there that gets me. The music, them, and what they know, what they've lived through. Marianne's the great romantic heroine and the famous musician, but I'll bet Miss Emma has her own stories locked behind those twinkly eyes. She wasn't Miss Mouse up there in Boston. She's had her own grand tragedy—I could swear to it."

"'The oldest hath borne most,'" I said. "'We that are young, shall never see so much, nor live so long.'"

"You're giving me gooseflesh!" She started the engine, and above its beat and the swash of water astern, she said, "Want to know what happened to that pretty little yawl?"

"Tell." I sat on the edge of the wharf and dangled my legs above the boat.

"Great-grandfather built her and took care of her as if she were his daughter. Grandfather inherited her and had a fine time—all those picnics were just part of it. Then one windy night he took her out for a moonlight sail and kept going and going and ran her hard ashore on Davie's Rock. Shattered her. He sat on the peak all night drinking from his jug—he'd saved that—and was picked up at dawn by a lobsterman. After a three-day crying jag, he stopped drinking for good. He whittled out the model, made the tackle, sewed the sails, everything."

"I'll look at her differently next time I go out there," I said. "She's a whole book in her perfect little self."

"It happened in the summer after Guy and Marianne went away. I always thought they broke his heart. I think he was in love with Marianne, and Guy was his best friend. He married on the rebound, poor old Grandfather. Carried a torch for Marianne the rest of his life and passed it on to Dad. Cast off, will you?"

"Ayuh," I said, doing so.

"Listen, come soon," she said, squinting up at me. "Julian's going to beach the boat out at his brother's to paint her and overhaul the engine. So we can have a day to fool around, the way we used to. I miss you."

"Just let me know," I said. "I miss you, too." It was true.

I had to be with Fee for only an hour to know the bond was as tough as it had been in the first hour of its forging.

"What do you make of Edith Morley?" Gram asked me as soon as we were out on the black road. She didn't give me a chance to answer. "Morrie was some black. Likely never thought a Rigby would ever go within twenty miles of the place." I thought of Kenneth on that drizzly afternoon. "Bunch of ghouls," Gram said bitterly. "Waiting for them to die." Her voice trembled. "Then they'll fight for the best pickings off the bones."

I myself didn't want to be reminded of the sisters' mortality, or hers. To change the subject I asked if she remembered *Sea Swallow.*

"Yes, I do, and I know what happened to her, too."

"Fee just told me about her," I said.

"Fee made four trips back for wine," said Gram. "She should be careful, knowing her family failing."

We didn't speak again until we turned down our driveway. Chad barred the way, barking his fool head off. Gram put her head out and shouted, "Move, you idiot."

He spun himself around like a top, dashed into the yard, grabbed up a mouthful of what looked like dirty laundry, and brought it out to us, tripping over the trailing ends. It *was* dirty laundry.

"Here he comes with champagne and orchids," I said.

"If a dog can have only one trick," Gram said plaintively, "why does it have to be opening the bathroom hamper and hauling out the contents?" She got out, and he undulated from stem to stern. "Maybe we can say your accomplishments are liking cats and not chasing deer," she said.

"And he's got a bark that would make anyone think twice." When I spoke, Chad's reaction was a canine interpretation of "My Heart at Thy Sweet Voice."

"He might scare anyone who doesn't know him," she said cynically. "But the whole town knows that Chad Winter would invite anyone in, anyone at all." She tilted her head toward the house behind the spruces.

"Well, at least he can let you know if anyone's pussyfooting around." I examined the laundry. "It's mine," I said.

"How do you suppose he got at that?"

"I can guess."

Glen was sitting at my table reading *The Writer's Handbook.* "Be quiet," he said when I came in. "I'm learning how to be a writer. I'm going to reveal the truth about lobstermen. We're a bunch of horny bastards, and it ought to make good X-rated stuff."

"Yup," I said. "When the media discovers the author, one of those sexy magazines will want you for a centerfold."

"I can't do that. I'm saving it all for you."

I returned my clothes to the hamper. "You must have been entranced, if you let that dog out without noticing what he took with him, let alone not hearing him rummaging around in the bathroom first." His grin told me he *had* noticed. "He wouldn't give any of it up." He leaned in the bedroom doorway while I took off my dress and hung it up. "How was Fee?"

"That's a funny question. Didn't you see her before she left? She was enjoying herself like the most of us."

"But I left the island before she got back." He came across the room before I could reach my slacks and took me into his arms. "I'm glad to see you," I mumbled into his neck, inhaling the scent of him and enjoying the feel of his hands moving over my skin. "You think I could be here awhile tonight," he said, "and then leave without the sentry turning out the guard?"

"We can manage," I said. We kissed, and he let me go. Dressing, I asked, "What did you and Julian do all afternoon?"

"Well, we didn't chase women or each other. We built a fireplace on the beach at High Ledge Cove. A surprise for Fee. He was as tickled with it as a kid, and I left before she came back, so he could have the big moment for himself. I hope she wasn't foolish from too much wine."

"Fee can get high on happiness," I said.

"Julian's racking his brain for names for his kittens. He didn't like any of my ideas. He says the right name is important, and maybe you can help because you're some smart and educated."

"I'll make a list," I said, rather touched. Julian was something like Chad; huge, handsome, and lovable, if not bright.

"Your friend Raintree show up?"

"He's not my friend." Did I say that too fast? "No, he wasn't there, and he's not likely to be there again. Are you staying for supper or coming back later?"

He pulled me to him and gave me a long, hard kiss. "If I can't rassle you down right now, I'll be back later. I'll go home and take a cold shower, or split a cord of wood, or both."

I hung on to him, not wanting to let him go. Not for the first time I envied Fee and her island. "I'd go back with you, but you're just as likely to have people dropping by. All those female ravens leaving pies and so forth."

"How about that?" His grin was shameless. "When are you going to move next door? If you plan to get them out as soon as she's had it, you'd better move quick before Richie jumps her again. He's quicker than a damn jackrabbit."

18

Lucas Wolcott made the *Journal* in a brief notice at the start of the District Court news. It simply gave his name and said the case was transferred to Superior Court. The case was not described. Meanwhile, he was out on his own recognizance. If he became publicly intoxicated or attempted to see his child, he would go back to jail.

Sonny Neville was one of my father's Not-Quite-Lost-Causes. Even after Sonny violated his probation by driving a car for a couple of older boys who'd broken into a filling station and were now in prison at Thomaston, Dad still hoped Sonny would begin using his considerable intelligence to realize this was no way to live. He came of decent people who were bewildered by his wildness. They had known Janine was pregnant and were prepared to welcome her, innocently hoping that marriage would straighten Sonny out. (He was sixteen, Janine fifteen.)

Now the Nevilles came to my father, nearly inarticulate with embarrassment, and asked him to go to the Youth Center at South Portland to tell Sonny what had happened. They had never known how to talk to their youngest boy, even under ordinary circumstances.

Of course Dad went. Sonny was stunned at first. Then, child that he was, he wept for his child and its mother. Dad had him write her a note which he would himself deliver to her. He tried to assure Sonny that it wasn't the end of the world; he and Janine had their whole lives before them to build into something strong and good, and they would have other children.

"I don't know how much help I was," he said. "Sonny's desperate to be with her. He'll be allowed a call from her. If only she doesn't cry...I expected him to explode about Lucas—he must have hated the man's guts for a long time. But all he talked about, when he could talk, was Janine and the plans they'd had, and the baby."

"Do you think he'll run away?" I asked.

"Lord knows it's easy enough. It happens all the time up there. But I advised him not to try it, and I hope I convinced him that she's safe with people who care for her. If she tells him that on the phone and then keeps writing it to him, it ought to work."

Lucas's beating was the accepted reason for her being in the hospital, so the aborted pregnancy might not have been general knowledge, but it was no secret that the Esmond sisters had been involved in the business from the start (I might not have been there at all), and that Janine was taken from the hospital to Fox Point.

"I wonder," said Gram, "how long it'll be before the Harpies start stewing about how Marianne managed to get into the middle of it, just more showing off, and is she *fit company* for a young girl?"

When I thought Janine was settled in at Fox Point, I had another happy excuse for going there. I went through my things and chose a pink sweater with a lacy yoke and some costume jewelry never worn, three little goldfish pins with flirtatious eyes and tails. When I was driving out, I met the Thunderbird coming in, with Miss Emma driving. She was going to spend the afternoon with Gram. It was hot, with a haze over the distances and the smell of thunder in the air.

At Fox Point Janine opened the door to me. At once I recognized the girl I'd seen with Tracy Hearne that day in Maddox, eating ice cream and laughing. She was thinner now. Most of the welts were hidden under her blue-and-white checked blouse and blue shorts, and the blond Dutch cut was as lustrous as buttercup petals. But her eyes were slightly sunken and shadowed with the palest mauve. They had become much older than fifteen.

She exclaimed at the sweater and the pins and gracefully thanked me; she'd brought herself up well. Then she directed me to the porch. "Mrs. Rigby's out there. I'm learning from Mrs. Thatcher how to make this real fancy casserole." Still she hesitated; then it came out. "I want to thank you for helping me. And Mr. Winter's been so good to us, too, both Sonny and me." Her eyes filled with tears. I patted her shoulder.

"We're all plugging for you, Janine, and with a cheering section that big, there's no way you can go but up."

She made a sound that was half-laugh, half-sob and pulled a wad of tissue from her blouse pocket and wiped her eyes. "Daddy wouldn't let anybody in to get my things, so Miss Emma gave Tracy money to buy me anything I needed." So that's why Tracy had cheered up on Sunday. "I never in my whole life dreamed of living in such a beautiful place! You should see my room, and then to hear the kind of music they play! When they practice it must be what angels sound like." She blew her nose. "Everybody's been so good to me." The tissues were too soaked by now to be effective.

"You'd better go back to Mrs. Thatcher before you dissolve completely." I gave her a little shove and got a faint, reassuring chuckle.

I walked through the living room, giving Guy a good hard stare on the way, now that no one could catch me at it. To hell with charisma, the latest overworked word. I was warmed more by the presence of the piano and Miss Emma's violin case open upon it, the pencil-notated music on the rack and scattered on the nearby sofa.

Out on the lawn, the flag hung limply on the pole. Heat waves shimmered up from the turf, blurring the islands. On the porch Marianne lay in an old-fashioned white-painted deck chair, a book open on her knees, her dark-rimmed reading glasses down a little on her nose. When I saw her alone, I knew I'd been half-expecting to find Fee figuratively at her feet. It wasn't exactly relief I felt, but it was certainly pleasure.

"Hello, Eden. Sit down." She waved her glasses at the wicker chairs with squashy blue cushions. "Do you ever read P. D. James?" She held up her book.

"Is that a new one?" I asked greedily. She laughed. "There's my answer. You can have it next. It's superb for a long hot afternoon."

"Gosh, I'm sorry to interrupt," I said insincerely. "I came around to see how Janine was. She says she's doing fine."

"She's very courageous. She really feels the loss of her baby; she'd never once considered an abortion. She hadn't seen a doctor yet, wanting to be married first so she could act openly, with pride. Of course she had to ask for her father's consent to marry. She waited until he was sober, thinking he'd be reasonable even if he was angry with her. Instead he went into an insane rage about jailbirds, convicts, his name as a good Marine besmirched—though that wasn't the word he used, I'm sure—by a daughter who was a whore."

Gazing out at the pallid, hazy sea, she was quiet for so long I thought that was the end of it, but then she went on, still looking out. "Finally he shut up and drove off, and she went up to her room. You can imagine her state of mind. She wanted to run away, but she was afraid she'd be sent back to him. Then the bleeding and the pains started. She crept downstairs to call Tracy—"

My expression made her smile. "Yes, I know. It seems my grandniece has depths of which I never dreamed. Well, Tracy has her license, and Janine thought she could drive her to the hospital. Lucas came in, drunk, while she was dialing, and he knocked her away from the telephone. She was doubling up with pain and begging him to help her, and he took his belt to her. Then *we* came."

"No wonder she thinks it's heaven here," I said.

"Yes, it's heaven, except that she lost the baby. But at the hospital they were able to convince her it was probably going to happen anyway, that she'd do better when she was older. So at least she doesn't think her father murdered her child." She turned the pages of her book without looking at it, as if to occupy her hands, and spoke in a detached manner. "Now she's Emma's ewe lamb, and for my part I could honestly tell her I know about the sense of loss. I lost two babies in the third month, just as she lost hers, and after that it was decided I shouldn't chance it again. But I wasn't a child myself, and my husband was with me. She can't mention this boy Sonny without filling up."

"I don't think she could be in a better place right now," I said. "She says you and Miss Emma play like angels."

"It's a good thing she can't hear me swearing under my breath sometimes," she said. "Emma goes so far as to say 'Oh, drat!' but I say much worse." She held up her hands and looked skeptically at them. "Some mornings they're not quite as nimble as they used to be, and I have this horrid lead weight in my stomach, thinking Aunt Maisie's old Arthur Ritis is sneaking up on me. Then a few stretches and wiggles—"she demonstrated—"and it wears off, and I'm comfortably safe for another day."

The screen door swung open, and Mrs. Thatcher came along the porch carrying a tray. Janine followed, carrying a plate of something in thin slices.

"I thought you'd be ready for this by now," the housekeeper said. "Good Lord, it's hotter out here than it is in the kitchen. I've been convincing this child that a cup of hot tea is better for the stomach on a day like this than gulping down all that ice-cold stuff full of chemicals. I thawed out one of my pound cakes for you. Nothing fake in that, either. Hello, Eden."

"Hi, Nell," I said. "Your poundcake, huh? I'm glad I came."

She nodded without false modesty. "I'm going home now with Roy, Mrs. Rigby. Dinner's all ready, just needs to be heated up, and dressing dumped onto the salad."

"I'll tend to all that," Janine said importantly. "And I'll clean up everything afterwards. I love handling those pretty dishes."

Janine loved everything; she was pleased just to be placing a little table beside my chair and bringing me a cup of tea and a napkin. Already she had a favorite cup, patterned with Scottish bluebells. "Like in the song, see?" she explained to me. "Miss Emma has been teaching me that and some other old ones."

"Janine has a very true voice," Marianne said. Janine exuded contentment. It was plain that she felt safe here, cosseted, the child of the house. She sat on the steps sipping her tea from the bluebell cup; ladylike, but coming back often to the cake. At least she wasn't heading for anorexia.

We heard distantly the Thatcher car belching its way down the drive. "I think they must make it home by their combined faith and will power," Marianne remarked. "Eden, when you write a book do you begin with an outline, or do you simply start off and follow your nose, so to speak?"

"I used to think that was the way to do it when I was a kid, but it isn't if you're doing it for a living," I said. "I decide on the beginning and the end, and then I plot out the best way to get from one to the other."

"You make it sound so simple."

"So do you make a Chopin etude sound simple."

Like Mrs. Thatcher, she was above spurious diffidence. "I was a long time getting there. A few days without practicing, and I know the difference."

"I've got acres of room for improvement," I said. "I hope *I* get better."

Janine sat looking out across the lawn. The back of her fair head, her shoulders in the thin blouse, the elbows propped on the tanned bare knees as she held her cup in both hands, looked so young. But she had conceived and lost a child, which made her older than I in experience. She had lost the child while her father was beating her, which meant that she had to accept a double trauma. I wondered what she was thinking; maybe she wasn't thinking, but simply basking.

Lucas Wolcott came around the western corner of the house without our seeing him until he was standing by the steps. Janine's indrawn breath had the high whoop of strangulation. She was on her feet, slopping tea, coming toward us in a blind rush, then veered toward the door, still carrying her cup; incongruously I noticed the flowery saucer and thin silver spoon left on the top step.

"Janine, notify the sheriff's department," Marianne called after her, without perceptible alarm.

Lucas wore clean jeans and shirt and had a blond stubble of new beard. He was drunk; when he shouted at Marianne, the stench was raw in the hot moist air.

"There you are, you old bat! Get my kid out here, or I'll go in for her myself if I have to kick down the door and drag her out by her hair."

I knew the same hatred I'd known before, as if murder would be easy. I rose up and seized the teapot in both hands, ignoring its heat, took a pace toward the steps and raised the pot to throw it in his face. I had the satisfaction of seeing his mouth sag open and his eyes widen before Marianne said quickly, "Eden, *no.* Mr. Wolcott, if you are not off these premises in five minutes, you will be taken away and locked up."

"You send my brat with me," he said with a repulsive grin, "and I'll clear out." He wasn't drunk enough this time to sway and stammer. "But keep her here for your unnatural purposes"—that phrase took some doing, but he managed by going slow—"and I won't answer for the consequences." He liked that and said it twice, still grinning at his cleverness. "Answer for the consequences, you bitch."

"Are you completely without intelligence?" Marianne asked. "Or do you really want to go to jail before you have to? That day's coming soon enough, but if you want to go now, just stand there spewing out your dirt until the officers come."

"I'll spew, all right!" He hawked revoltingly and spat at her. The gob fell short of the deck chair; she hadn't flinched but just kept on gazing at him as if he were an ugly curiosity. He became a bright hot pink up into his blond hair, and he kept narrowing his eyes, widening them and then squinting again as if trying to clarify his view of her.

"My kid would never set the cops on me," he yelled at her. He put one foot on the first step. "Maybe she's a little slut, but she's still my kid. And I'll tell you what you are—"

I saw Nick Raintree appear around the corner, and Lucas's vision was too blurry to catch Marianne's involuntary eye movement, if she made one. Nick went wide so he could come up behind Lucas, walking without sound on the grass. He took Lucas by the back of the neck with one hand and with the other twisted Lucas's right arm behind him.

Taken by surprise in the midst of an obscenity, Lucas sagged back with his eyes rolling up, and I thought for a moment he'd either fainted or died. Nick gave him a light shake and said unhurriedly, "You want to go straight off the wharf or into your truck and away from this place forever?"

He looked neither sadistic nor personally angry, but deadly. In another context Lucas could have been on his way to being flung against a wall in front of a firing squad. He had turned greyish and sick; Nick apparently knew just where to press with one set of fingers and twist with another.

"To his truck, Nick, please," Marianne said. "Mr. Lucas, goodbye."

"She's my child!" he protested. "Nobody can take her away from me." He started to snuffle.

"You drove her away with your belt," she said implacably.

"It's all a lie," he mumbled. He tried to move his head but couldn't. He grimaced and grunted with pain. "I'll sue you for everything you've got, you old whore, and I'll sue this son of a bitch, too."

"Sure you will," said Nick. "March." He turned Lucas around and headed him toward the corner of the house. "Don't give me any trouble, and I won't give you any. Agreed?" Lucas yipped sharply, and Nick walked him away out of sight.

I was shaky, but I couldn't see that Marianne was. "I'm glad Emma wasn't here," she said composedly. "She'd be expecting him to come back at night and burn the house down over our heads."

"I'd be nervous myself," I said. "Are you going to have him arrested? I don't think Janine called, or there'd be someone here by now."

"I didn't expect her to call. I think she ran straight to her room and locked herself in. I'll ask Clem Jr. to have a word with Lucas's lawyer, and if he can keep Lucas in line and away from here until the case comes up, I'll be satisfied."

"But he can't be watched twenty-four hours a day," I objected. "And when all that rage is mixed up with liquor, it can explode."

"My dear Eden, I refuse to think I'm not safe here. A drunk making vicious and obscene noises is nothing new to me. We had one next door to us on Oakwood who was always threatening his wife with a carving knife, but my mother could walk up and take it out of his hand. His wife survived him," she added. "He didn't kill anyone but himself, with his drinking."

"Well," I said, gloomily unconvinced. I felt as if Lucas's violence had left an all but visible entity behind.

"You see, Eden, I know what fear really is," she said. "For a number of years I lived in terror that either Guy or I would be taken away. We never went to bed without thinking it could happen that night, and each new morning meant it could happen that day."

For a wild moment I thought she was going to mention the bank theft, the police, fear of extradition. So when I heard the word *Gestapo* it was as much of a nauseating surprise as Nick's grip had been to Lucas.

"If you haven't lived under those conditions," she went on, "you can't possibly know what it's like, no matter how vivid your imagination is. Some people still believe we sat out the war comfortably in Switzerland, snuggled up to our fabulous bank account. It wasn't so, any more than the bank account was fabulous. Unless you want to use the original meaning of the word as pertaining to a fable."

I couldn't think of a thing to say after that without sounding foolishly naive. She rose from the deck chair almost as easily as I could have. "I'll take this pot to the kitchen and make us some fresh tea. Will you go up and speak to Janine?"

We went into the house, and she told me where the room was. When we separated in the front hall, she said, "You know, we haven't even mentioned Nick Raintree's sudden appearance. We seem to be taking miracles for granted these days." She laughed and went on.

Janine hadn't locked the door. She was curled up sobbing convulsively in the middle of a delicate brass bed, in a room of faded flowery chintzes. I sat beside her and smoothed her head and gently rubbed her back. "It's Eden," I said. "You don't have to talk. But he's gone."

"I couldn't—call—the police." The words jerked out in chest-hurting hiccups. "He's my *father.* I hate him, but I couldn't call the police."

"It's all right, Janine. Mrs. Rigby didn't expect you to. She only said it to make him go away."

"I can't stay here and let him do this to them," she wept. "I'm so ashamed. I can't ever look them in the face again!" She wailed forlornly into a pillow for a few moments before words became distinct again. "You don't know! *Your* father's Mr. Winter! You'd never have to feel like this, wishing your own *father* were dead."

Oh, I'd learned a lot about my own innocence today. "Tell me about Sonny," I said. "Is this his picture?" A small framed photograph stood under the lamp; nothing done in a studio, but a candid shot someone had liked well enough to frame. I knew Sonny by sight—I'd seen him with his father—but I wanted to get her talking about him.

She lifted her wet and blotched face from the pillow. "Tracy got it from his mother for me. Daddy's probably smashed mine and burned my album." She smiled tenderly at the picture through a fresh rain of tears.

"He looks nice," I said. "Is he tall, or short, or medium?" Sonny was far from handsome, but he had an engaging smile along with his big ears and mouse-colored hair which looked as if he'd combed it with his fingers.

"He's real tall, with big feet. I tease him about that. And he *is* nice. I don't condone what he's done, and he's got to quit that, but he'd never hurt anybody with a knife or a g-gun or even try to scare them. And he's always been good and kind to me."

Another Toby, though with less artful charm. Why couldn't they be all good or all bad and make things simpler for everybody? "Have you talked with Sonny?" I asked.

"Yes, but it wasn't very good. I kept crying. I was ashamed, but I couldn't help it. The baby and all... I've written him every day since." She sat up and blew her nose. "His folks still want us to be married; they say I'll be his anchor to wind'ard." A wan, watery smile. "Only Mr. Cruikshank—he's my guardian now—he says my whole situation depends on what the judge does about Daddy. Maybe I'll be a state ward till I'm eighteen. But I can probably stay here," she said, brightening. "They said I could stay. He told me not to count on getting married so young, where there's no baby involved." The last three words nearly did her in. "I can't believe it. It was so *real.* Sometimes a boy, sometimes a girl. We had a list of names, and I started collecting little things. I suppose *he's* burned them all up now."

I waited in silence while she struggled to quiet herself. "Oh, I'm so tired of crying!" she burst out. "If I can keep mad enough, it helps."

"Be mad, then. Shout and swear. Up here, of course, and into a pillow."

"Daddy does enough shouting and swearing for both of us," she said mournfully. "The names he called me—I can still hear them. But I'm *not* those things! I never went with anybody but Sonny, and we only did it—you know—*once.* Then he went and drove the car for those creeps because they said they'd pay him plenty, and he got caught."

"You and Sonny can get married as soon as you're eighteen," I told her. "But you can be his anchor to wind'ard now, if he loves you enough to want to behave himself for your sake."

"He does want to!"

"All right. Now go wash your face and come downstairs for another good cup of tea."

She bounced off the bed. "They said I could stay and go to school from here," she called back on her way out to the bathroom.

I sat there in the pretty room with its old-fashioned white furniture and its faded roses and violets and bluebirds. It had been quite an afternoon. Another one on you, Fee, I thought shamelessly.

When we went downstairs and out onto the porch, Nick balanced on the railing with his back against a post, his legs straight out on the railing and crossed at the ankles. He was holding a tall glass. He looked Mediterranean-dark against the bluish mist of heat.

"Hello, Eden. Hello, Janine," he said without moving. "If I turn my head I'll fall off. Otherwise I'd offer to make a drink for anyone over twenty-one."

My, you're at home here, I thought. Making drinks and all. "Gosh, I hate to turn down such gallantry," I said, "but I'd prefer tea. I was brought up to believe that a good hot cup of tea was a specific for everything."

"For almost everything, anyway," said Marianne. "Janine, did you bring your cup back? Come and let me fill it. And there's plenty of cake left."

"What brings you around here on a working day?" I asked Nick. In fact, I continued in silence, what brings you around here at all? But of course you didn't expect to meet *me* here. His glance slid sidewise at me in a manner that suggested he'd just read my thoughts.

"We had a launching today, and the bosses decided there was no sense in everybody going back to work juiced up with champagne. The boat's owner was uncommonly generous."

"Are you juiced up?" I asked.

"Champagne isn't my drink. No, I was on my way down to take a look at the harbor, but I saw a familiar pickup parked by the mailbox here, so I thought I'd take a look at Fox Point instead."

Janine quickly sat down on the step again and turned her back on us.

"It's always nice to see you, Nick," Marianne said. So, like Fee, he didn't need the Afternoons; he came at other times. It was unreasonable to resent his presence, because his appearance had ended something very nasty. But then why didn't he go, instead of hanging around to show me how much at ease he was here? It was petty and childish of me. But this was also the first time I'd seen him face to face since the night at the Birch Mansion, which accounted for some of my dislocation. Dammit, he could make me feel so juvenile.

I drank my tea quickly and arose. "Well, I'd better be going," I said.

"Must you, Eden?" Marianne sounded honestly regretful.

"Yes, I have something I should do," I said quite sternly. Nick swung his legs off the railing and stood up. "I'll walk you to the car."

You're in a hurry to get rid of me, I thought. Not taking any chances on my hanging around; I might take the wind out of your sails.

I said goodbye to Marianne and Janine and went down off the porch. He caught up with me at the corner.

"How've you been?" he asked chattily.

"Fine. Busy." I tried to be sufficiently discouraging to drive him away, but he was apparently insensitive to vibrations, auras, emanations, or plain unsubtle hostility. When we had almost reached the car he inquired pleasantly if the cat had got my tongue.

"Oh, *really!*" I said—hardly a rapier thrust.

"I was on my way to see you," he said seriously. "Then I recognized Wolcott's truck. Not hard; it's got his name on it." He opened my car door for me.

"Janine didn't call the police," I said. "Not this time. I don't like to think about a next time."

"If we're lucky, they'll grab him today when he goes wobbling across Main Street. He set off at a slow crawl, and if he keeps that up, everybody ought to be safe on the road between here and there. Look, I'll call you, OK? If I don't see you next Sunday?"

I heard myself saying "OK." He shut the car door and stood back. When I made the turn around the loop, he was no longer in sight in front of the house. He had gone back to the porch and Marianne.

19

Miss Emma was just about to turn the Thunderbird into the driveway as I left it. She waved sedately, keeping her eye on the road. When I got home most of the pickups were gone, and a large refrigerator truck had been backed down onto the wharf to collect lobsters for a long night haul. Chad was tied out of harm's way, up by the store, and unhappy. There was quite an audience of youngsters in skiffs hovering a little distance off the lobster car, where Uncle Early and Julian were dragging out the heavy crates, one by one, from the long string of them tailing off the car. Grampa stood by smoking his pipe; Julian had taken over his job. Each crate was hoisted up, swinging and dripping, to a height where the truck driver and Toby Barry could reach it and guide it through the doorway into the truck body.

Toby wasn't a surprise; he was often around the wharf, gregarious as Chad and genuinely useful at times. The firm wouldn't strike away a willing hand, though Uncle Early said he always wished he could frisk Toby when he left the premises, especially if he stopped off in the store when Grampa wasn't in it. But evidently Toby had his code of honor; he didn't steal from the next-door neighbors. If he took cigarettes, gloves, gum, or soda, the money was always scrupulously put into the clean ashtray left on the counter for the purpose.

But Julian and *Island Magic* weren't usual sights in Job's Harbor. He and Fee sold their lobsters across the river in St. David where his family lived, and Fee kept her car in his brother's yard. Today *Island Magic* was tied on the far side of the wharf, below the bait shed, and Fee was up in the Hayloft drinking a glass of milk and eating a brownie, with my *Maine Times* spread out on the table before her. Glen lay on the couch reading *The Smithsonian,* which Aunt Eleanor passes on to me.

"Well, look who's here," I said. "The Gold Dust Twins."

Fee gave me that burnished, expectant look which sometimes makes her beautiful. "Hello, love! What put the roses in your cheeks? Or rather *who?*"

Glen lifted his gaze from the page long enough to recognize my presence. "Where the hell have you been?" It wasn't quite a snarl, but from Glen it was near enough.

"Oh, what a loving welcome," said Fee.

"I was going to say 'courtly,'" I said. "Let's see, what can I think of to stand your hair on end?"

"You're daylighting in a bordello," said Fee. "It's hidden away in one of those new log cabins at the end of a private road. You'd never guess it about those people; they look so respectable. Retired librarians *indeed!*"

"But they're the best, because they're so refined," I said. "They say I lend a touch of class," I preened. "For the more literate clients."

"Oh? What do they like to talk about, after? A spot of Chekhov?"

Glen threw down the magazine, swung his feet off the couch, and slammed them on the floor. It wasn't like him, any more than his surly greeting had been, and I knew Fee must have been plaguing him. I have this instinctive impulse to soothe, especially Glen; it knocks my world slightly askew whenever he behaves out of character.

"I went up to Fox Point to see Janine," I said. "She'll be fine as long as Lucas leaves her alone. He showed up there this afternoon, full of liquor and threats. . . ."

Fee sprang up in a fury. "It's true, then, what Julian's sister told me! I couldn't believe Clem would shove that kid onto them. Is he *crazy?* Doesn't he realize the danger? He's got no right to put them at risk like that! Lucas could come after them in the night with an axe, or burn the house down over their heads!"

"It was their choice to have her," I said. "Calm down, Fee. Do you guys want to hear the rest or not?" I addressed this to the top of Glen's head; he was studying the floor between his moccasins. He uttered an ambiguous sound.

"I just wanted to tell you how marvelous Marianne—Mrs. Rigby—was. I would have thrown the full hot teapot at him," I said modestly, "but she wouldn't let me. Of course I'd already knocked him down once. . . ."

"This afternoon?" Fee rose up again.

"Drink your milk," I said. "It was the day he beat Janine. Well, I didn't actually knock him down, I gave him a shove and he fell down, being very drunk."

"You were *there,* and with *them?*" Fee cried in the torment of betrayal. "Why were you there? What was going on? How could you keep such a secret from your best friend?"

"I told Glen right afterward, and I was going to tell you when I had a chance out on the island and could give you all the details. And I still intend to. So will you please *shut up* and let me tell what else happened today?"

She sank back into her chair. "All right, tell me how she was marvelous," she said enviously. "Dear God, I wish I'd been there!"

"She never jumped, or twitched, or showed anything at all but the most perfect dignity, even when he spat at her."

"I'll bet, I'll bet," Fee whispered. *Radiant* is almost too weak a word to describe her. Glen turned his head and gave her a long, cold look.

"Did anyone think to call the police?" he asked in a caustic tone. "Or did she simply turn him to stone?"

I ignored that. "We told Janine to call when she ran into the house, but then Nick Raintree materialized like Captain Kirk just beamed down from the *Enterprise.*"

"Was he marvelous too?" Glen asked disagreeably. "Or merely terrific?"

"Put a cork in it, Glen," said Fee. "Did he lay Lucas out, I hope?" She could be an extremely satisfactory audience.

"Nope, he took him by the scruff of the neck, twisted one arm behind him, and ushered him off the grounds. He watched Lucas drive away, and then came back and had a drink."

"Been fired from the yard, has he?" Glen got up and walked to the door and stood staring through the screen. "Or quit, because now he knows everything there is to know about building wooden boats?"

"They had the afternoon off after a launching," I said. "Lucky for us. I was never so glad to see anybody in my life," I added pointedly. Fee winked at me.

"But just the same, they shouldn't keep that kid there," she said soberly. "Why doesn't Clem keep her at his own house, where the police are handy?"

"They asked for her, and *she* thinks it's heaven."

"I'll bet," said Fee derisively. "They'll probably want to adopt her next. They're so good, it's easy to take advantage, and she probably knows that if she's at all bright."

"Don't be so uncharitable," I said. "All she wants is to be old enough to marry Sonny Neville and keep him straight. Lucas tried to break them up, that was why he beat her."

An authoritative whistle pierced the gentle medley of harbor sounds. Julian stood outside the store on the wharf, his hands on his hips, looking up at the Hayloft. He was bare to the waist, shining with sweat.

"What a lovely hunk!" Fee said. "He looks like burnished bronze, and he's all mine. If beauty is its own excuse for being, Julian shouldn't have to do anything but exist. Be right there, lover," she called down to him.

He smiled and waved, then hunkered down and began playing with Chad.

"Look, Eden," Fee said. "The reason we came over is to tell you the boat's definitely going ashore Monday morning, and they'll be working on her all week, putting in so much electronic stuff she won't be safe in a thunderstorm, I keep telling them. So I'll be looking for the Old Man of the Mountain here to drop you off bright and early some morning. And I want to hear *everything* about that day, not one comma missing. Promise?"

"Scout's honor," I said. "I'll be out as soon as the book's mailed off."

"Fiona!" Julian called. His bass voice goes with his size, but he hardly ever raises it.

"I'm on my way!" she yelled back. "It's supper time for his babies," she said to us. "They're beginning solid food now. If he's that protective of Polly's kids, what'll it be like when he has one of his own?"

She slanted a gleaming, enigmatic glance at us and went out. "'Lullaby, and goodnight,'" she sang on her way down the steps. "'With roses bedight, Creep into thy bed—'" We didn't hear the end of it; she was running down over the lawn to Julian.

"She pregnant?" Glen growled at me.

"She hasn't told *me.*"

"They'd better get married. I'll tell Julian—he'll never think of it himself. Where did you go with Raintree the night I had a meeting?"

"Apropos of what? We didn't get married, if that's what you think."

"Very funny," he said grimly. "I came back here around ten, sat all by myself in the moonlight for a while, went home, called around eleven, gave up at midnight."

"I didn't expect you to get away very early from the social hour after the meeting."

"What's that supposed to mean?"

"The way you walked out of here that night, without a backward look, I thought—" I stopped short of naming the lady assessor. It would have been silly and snide, and I made an attempt to return us to reasonableness.

"We drove up to the Birch Mansion," I said. "He knows the caretakers."

"Is there anybody in the county he doesn't know?"

"I doubt it," I said. "He sure gets around."

Island Magic was leaving the harbor. Fee and Julian were side by side at the wheel, his arm around her. He never questioned her; he just worshipped. I opened the refrigerator and began studying the shelves. "I really should clean this out," I remarked.

"I don't like the son of a bitch," said Glen.

I counted slowly to ten, shut the refrigerator door, and spoke with what they call a studied calm. "Probably I wouldn't like some of the women you're with when I'm busy. So what's the difference?"

"He's got something in mind, I can tell. I'm a male, too, remember."

"I've never forgotten it for an instant. . . . Let's see, you've met him just once, haven't you? And you were pretty civil to somebody you hated on first sight."

"I don't usually call a man a son of a bitch to his face the first time I meet him, even if I'm thinking it."

I shut the windows and the door, as I don't like making my point in whispers. Besides, it's impossible. "You weren't thinking it then—you can't fool me. You liked him because he admired *Little Emily.* You never thought it until you didn't find me sitting here with my paws tucked in, like a good little tabby."

"All right, I had an open mind about the bastard until you disappeared with him for half the night. He's what my father used to call a womanizer. He's like a loose cannon aboard a man o' war. I don't want you getting run down by him."

"You're not only impugning my morals, but my intelligence!" I snatched dishes and cartons out of the refrigerator, and slammed them on the table regardless of slops. "You're saying that if anybody looks lecherously at me I'll go all mushy like an overripe banana. I *like* Nick," I said, "what little I know of him,—which isn't a hell of a lot. But I've no burning desire to throw myself into his arms and moan, 'Take me!'" I demonstrated, and Glen should have laughed, but he didn't. He walked out.

I was left wounded, ashamed of myself, and righteously indignant because he'd started it and yet wanting to laugh at the whole ludicrous scene. I stared at the assortment of leftovers on the table, some of them unidentifiable. I felt as if I'd been running in a dream and was now completely winded. Glen and I had had scraps before this; we'd been having them since our teens. *Scrap* sounds better than *fight; squabble* is even better—it reduces a battle to a skirmish where nobody got killed. None of them had ever left me with this awe, this weird hollowness, as if I'd opened a door expecting a room and found myself teetering on the brink of space.

Had Glen and I broken off? It was ridiculous not to know. Ridiculous to stand here at my age, dithering. I wouldn't allow one of my heroines to behave like this.

Even his truck sounded angry, whipping around in the parking lot and tearing out to the black road. When sixteen year olds used our road like that in their first pickups, Grampa and Uncle Early muckled onto them and forbade it.

20

I slept that night in fits and starts and woke up before dawn, certain that Glen wouldn't go out to haul this morning without coming to me first. We could both admit to being idiots and agree to go on from there, with no apologies or explanations necessary. I'd go out with him, and a day on the water together would shake him and me back into Us.

Lying in bed I recognized the pickups as they came along the road, Uncle Early's first. Doors slammed; rubber boots went thumping hollowly down the wharf. There were voices, and the rhythmic click or creak of oars and engines turning over. Then I heard Glen's truck and lay waiting for his footfall on the steps. I wasn't apprehensive; I'd never been apprehensive about Glen in my life until last night, and that was only a temporary aberration, like his anger.

But his step never came, and in the next little zone of silence between engines, I heard the distinctive sound of sculling. Glen always sculled his skiff out to his boat, standing up, using only one oar, out over the stern both to propel and steer the skiff. I've never been able to do it.

I knew exactly how he looked, a spare silhouette in the filmy light as the sun rose huge and magnificently scarlet in the morning mist, and the water took the color like a sheet of smooth foil. I flounced over in bed and gave in to self-pity for about five minutes. After that I got up and kept my back ostentatiously turned to the harbor while I prepared and ate my breakfast, hoping that his engine wouldn't start. But *Little Emily* was always faithful.

A sort of escape was possible for the next few days. My grandparents were leaving this morning for their annual August visit to some old friends over in Hiram and wouldn't be back until some time Wednesday. After the men had all come in this afternoon, Uncle Early wouldn't be back until the working day began early Monday morning, unless Jon came in with a load of pogies.

Up in Maddox my parents had plans of their own, and everybody assumed I had mine, so I was left in blessed solitude, except for Chad, who behaved as if life were full of exciting possibilities for us both. I took him for a long walk while the territory was still quiet and cool. Then I settled down to work. The Temple boys were playing elsewhere. Toby and Richie had gone out with their load of empty hods. Derek wasn't crying over beyond the spruces, but making peaceful noises in his playpen in the shade. I could hear faintly Shasta's radio, and sometimes she sang along with it.

I did so well on the book that another day or two would see it ready to go to my agent. In the late afternoon I found myself growing tense about Glen's return; would he come in, or should I go out to meet him and those cold grey eyes? I took Chad for another walk, out through the field by my uncle's house and through their spruce woods. When we came back to the harbor, Glen had come in and driven away.

On Sunday morning the Barrys had all disappeared, and the Temples must also have gone away for the day. There was plenty of activity around Winter Head and Fort Point, and the yacht people rowed their dinghies for exercise or lay reading on their decks. I was perfectly happy to be the only human resident at home on our side of the harbor. It was too hot and still that morning to take Chad for a walk, and he wanted only to lie on the cool grass in the shade. I put in another good morning's work. *Work*, that was the thing; I wouldn't be the first writer to dedicate my life to my profession.

In the afternoon I dressed in a sleeveless cotton dress with a cool print of blueberry clusters and left Chad to take care of the house while I went to Fox Point. The Morleys weren't there today, and neither was Esmond; perhaps he and his realtor girlfriend were out scouting other potential properties or visiting the infestations of condominiums to the west and south of us. But Esmond's parents were there. Morrie Hearne was either wretchedly bored or stupefied by his Sunday dinner. Still he managed to keep his eyes sternly open, as if he'd come only to guard the silver spoons. Annie was touchingly happy to have Tracy welcomed into the house. Tracy and Janine sat on the front stairs; a third girl was with them, who looked shyly at me from behind huge glasses. The three were charmingly partified in dresses. Tracy being a friend was as different from the other Tracy as rose from thorn. She even smiled at me when Janine did.

The Sorrells had brought some eagerly respectful guests, and there were a few more elderly friends from the Esmonds' pasts; they were holding a high school reunion with the sisters when I came in. Fee was with Clem Jr. and the Highams at the far end of the room. When she saw me, she jumped up and came to meet me. She was as lithe and thin as a poplar sapling, and her pale green dress developed the simile. It was not only a genuine dress, but a very feminine one, sheer and full skirted over an eyelet petticoat. She had pulled her hair back into a ponytail that emphasized her long neck and the sharp distinctive structure of her face.

"Look at you," I said softly. "They've done what nobody else could do since graduation—get you into a dress." With her cupped hands tucked under her chin, she pivoted provocatively from one side to the other, like a model. "Like it?"

"Your waist makes me sick."

"That's what the girl in the store said.... Well, look, I can't disgrace them, can I?" She turned those luminous and expectant grey eyes on the sisters across the room.

"Whatever the reason, you look smashing," I said.

She was carrying the little stoneware cat tenderly in her curved fingers, as if it were a very tiny but living kitten.

"If I were a kleptomaniac I could steal this for Julian without a qualm," she said.

"You can buy one for him. I've seen them advertised."

"Not like this. Miss Emma had her made in France for Marianne. It's really a sculpture of a cat they had there, named Phronsie Pepper after a money-cat they had when they were little. So this one is special. Where's my twinnie this afternoon?"

"You know he doesn't care anything about this sort of thing." Miss Emma had spotted me and was waving past an elderly gentleman's ear. I waved back.

"Isn't she darling?" Fee murmured. "Wouldn't you love her for your own great aunt?"

Someone had come into the hall behind us, and the girls' voices sang out, half-mocking, half-flirtatious. "Hi, Robbie! Gosh, you look sharp, Robbie! Who is she, Robbie?"

"Glen had a woman out with him yesterday," Fee said portentously. "She was stunning and looked Swedish, and she was wearing one of those swimsuits that my Puritan Julian thinks are immoral, for public view, anyway. It was white, and her skin and hair were all gold."

"King Midas's daughter," I said. "I know who she is. She's been visiting the Eubanks on Fort Point for a week. She's a mathematician."

"That won't make any difference to Glen, you nut," she said. "You know how those Scandinavian blondes are. They start young over there. We got big waves from both of them, and they seemed pretty damn jolly, if you ask me. I wouldn't go so far as to say they'd been having it off in the cabin, but—"

"Any woman who understands binary numbers deserves my unquestioning admiration," I said. "If she can tell me why it needs an equation about three inches long to say '58,' I'll even call her a genius."

"I'm going to twist your wrist, stupid!" she hissed. "Where do you suppose they were last night? His place or hers?"

"His place, because she couldn't take him to bed at the Eubanks'. They're conservative." I wasn't as blithe as I sounded, but with a little practice I'd be doing it well. I smiled at Fee and patted her shoulder. "Thanks. But Glen and I understand each other."

"Pure apathy!" she retorted, just as Robbie appeared in the hall doorway, looking as usual very hot and harassed, as if besieged by a swarm of black flies.

"Hello, Robbie," I said to him. "Gosh, you look sharp. They weren't kidding."

"Brats," he said. "Not Janine, poor kid, but the other two." His gaze went roving around the room, and I knew without turning when it found Marianne.

"Blue's your color, Robbie," Fee said solemnly.

"Thanks." He was making an effort to calm down. "What have you got there?" he asked with a twitchy nod at her hands.

She showed him the kitten. "Isn't she a love?"

"How do you know it's a she?" he asked, frowning at the kitten. I left her explaining about three-colored cats and went alone to be welcomed by the sisters.

The shy girl on the stairs was the special guest of the afternoon. She was a clarinetist, and with Tillie Higham at the piano, she played the adagio from a Mozart concerto. She was very good, and even Morrie Hearne applauded heartily, showing that he could be touched by music after all, or perhaps it was her youth that did it. She blushed becomingly at the applause and the praise, fetched an awkward little bow, and was possessively taken away by Janine and Tracy.

Jason Higham was talking to Robbie, who was gazing across the room at Marianne, while all Clem Jr. wanted to do was gaze at Fee, who was putting herself out to be winsome. It was shamefully unfair of her because he'd had no chance beside Julian. Even if Fee had ever seriously considered him, in spite of fifteen years' differences, she wasn't foolish enough to think she could manage him. It bothered her because I couldn't, or wouldn't try to, manage Glen. When she found out we'd broken off (I was numbly accepting that as a fact now), she'd suffer, not silently, and demand that I should be in agony also. Well, if agony was inevitable, I was going to be the Spartan boy holding the fox in his bosom, never making a sound while it chewed away on him.

When I saw Miss Emma going toward the hall, I drifted obliquely away from a group and followed her out there. "Can't I help?" I asked. "I'd love to."

"Thank you, dear, but I have the girls all lined up." She waved a hand at them, and they headed for the kitchen; giggles trailed them like bubbles in a boat's wake. "Isn't it nice to have them here?" Miss Emma asked. "And it's lovely to hear Janine *giggle.*" She laid a hand on my arm. "I'm so glad you were here when her father came the other day."

"I didn't do anything," I protested. "I don't know how we'd have gotten rid of Lucas if Nick hadn't come along. But Mrs. Rigby didn't show even a tremor. She told me afterward about the Gestapo."

"And did she tell you about playing Beethoven sonatas for German officers and Guy serving them wine, while there were French Jews and American and British flyers hiding in the cellar?" She nodded at me. "Oh, yes. During the years I spent in France with her, people came often to see her and thank her. She said it had been happening frequently ever since the war. Even one of those German officers had come. Ex-officer, of course. He'd been real army, dear, not Gestapo or SS. Quite a gentleman; he told her he'd known all along what was in the cellar besides wine."

"It sounds like a novel," I said inanely.

"My sister's entire life sounds like a novel," she said. "Well, I must go and make the tea. I don't trust that to Janine yet." She flitted after the girls. When I went back into the living room, Robbie was standing against the wall, and Marianne was talking to him.

"Come here, Eden," she said. "Help me to convince Robbie that he should be our special guest next Sunday."

"I'd love to hear him play," I said. He threw up his head like a panicky steer and gave me a wild-eyed look. "I mean it, Robbie," I said. "You were good when you were back in high school. I *know.* I went to most of the concerts and operettas, and I'd love to hear you again, on that wonderful piano."

"I'm through!" he blurted. "I'm never going to touch a piano again, mine or anyone's." His voice rose recklessly, and she shook her head at him.

"Out in the hall," she said, tapping him on the chest. He backed out and almost managed to trip himself up on the sill, which didn't help what was left of his self-control. He looked about to make a dash for the front door, but Marianne's authority held him in one spot.

"So you're giving up, just like that, simply because I won't take you on as a pupil. Perhaps you're wise to stop now if you're so easily discouraged."

"*You* discouraged me!" Someone began to play something loud, and familiar with plenty of arpeggios and thundering bass chords. I guessed it was Tillie, being tactful. "It's *your* fault!" Robbie accused Marianne.

"You wanted me to hear you play, and I'm willing," she said imperturbably.

"But not like this!" He jerked his head toward the living room. "Why can't I come alone?"

"I am not going to give you a private audition, Robbie. I am not taking pupils, or *one* pupil, no matter how gifted he is. But I would like you to take part in our gatherings here. So we'll expect you next Sunday, prepared to play anything you'd like. Have at least two things ready, because we'll call upon you twice."

He flung himself savagely away from her and slammed out of the house.

"I am so sorry for that boy," she said. "He refuses absolutely to accept a *no,* which is fine in some respects but not in all. The instant he's alone with me he resumes the siege."

"Does it happen often?"

"Oh dear, yes," she said ruefully. "He's been around several times, and now and then he calls me. I understand he left home because he and his parents can't agree on anything. They must be glad for the rest." The motorcycle starting up almost drowned out the piano. The procession of girls came from the kitchen, carrying trays, Miss Emma following.

The young clarinet player was called upon after tea and played Schubert's Serenade. Then Marianne accompanied Miss Emma in the poignant, too-short violin solo from the winter section of "The Four Seasons," and Marianne played Debussy's "The Girl with the Flaxen Hair."

"That was for Janine," she said at the end. "She's our girl with the flaxen hair."

I walked to the wharf to see Fee off; we were each humming parts of what we'd heard, and they didn't match, but we didn't care. "I wish the Sundays could go on forever," Fee said.

"*Carpe diem,*" I said.

"Who he?"

"'Seize the day.' Where's your Latin? You used to be queen of the Latin Club once."

"That was before my brain came to a stop. What was with Robbie out in the hall? Everybody was trying politely not to hear, and then Tillie began playing like mad, and the next thing he's roaring down the driveway like a Hell's Angel late for a rape."

"Mind if I use that some time? Robbie wants to be a pupil, and he can't take a straight no."

"People should leave her alone," Fee exploded. "They all think someone like her is fair game. What are they trying to do, kill her?"

"Robbie could work himself into a nervous breakdown, and he still won't break Marianne Rigby down. She's a survivor." I thought of the Gestapo, Beethoven, and the fugitives in the cellar. When I went to the island, I would tell Fee; a story like this about her heroine would put her over the moon.

"I suppose she knows how to protect herself," Fee said grudgingly.

I went aboard the boat and sat on the washboard while she took off the pale green voile and matching sandals and put on shorts and a blouse. She remained barefoot. She folded the clothes with a care unique for her and laid them away in a box from Tenby's most expensive specialty shop. "They cost the earth," she said. "And I went to Tenby on a Saturday, too, which ought to prove something. Do you know what it's like up there on a summer Saturday? You wade neck-deep in tourists and out-of-state cars. I had to park four blocks off Main Street."

"I think the ladies should know what you've gone through for them," I said. "And you stayed away from the sherry, too. More or less."

"If I come home breathing alcoholic fumes, Julian gets upset. When'll you be out? We'll have some fun with the old Ouija board!" That had been one of the secret thrills of our early adolescence. We'd each had a spirit lover and had talked with Lord Byron, Bonnie Prince Charlie, and other heroes.

"I'm surprised Julian hasn't split it up for kindling by now," I said.

"He would if he could find it. How about tomorrow? You can get somebody else to drop you off if you and Glen are going through a silent spell. Sprig, for instance."

"Oh, my God," I said. "He'd think I was propositioning him. Look, in two days I'll have the book ready to go. Maybe I can mail it off by Tuesday afternoon and come out Wednesday. I'll hitch a ride with somebody, if I can't catch Glen."

"That blonde mathematician may have squashed him down to a common denominator by then," she said. "Maybe I overdid it, needling him about Nick."

"Forget it," I said. "If we can't stand kidding, there wasn't much in the first place." I sounded more nonchalant than I felt.

I watched *Island Magic* head out across blinding silver under a freshening breeze and then went back to the driveway and my car. All the other cars were gone but the Carvers', and I could hear the piano and violin through the open casements. The sisters were playing now for their old friends, and Janine would be sitting on the stairs thinking of angels.

I listened to the end, drifting with the music, and then drove away. The instant I left the drive for the black road I began wondering if Glen would be at home, if I would be excited and overjoyed at sight of him or ready to pick up the fight where we'd left off.

But only Chad was there. At sight of me he ran in lunatic circles yipping like a puppy, picking up and throwing anything he could get a grip on. Grampa's rubber boots were getting a mauling. I rescued them and sat down on the steps and took Chad's big head in my hands. His eyes went moist with pleasure.

"I love you," I told him. "I can see why Fee finds Julian so satisfactory. He just limpidly adores her." Chad tried to give my nose a lick. "Chad, my boy," I told him, "I'm one of those ineffectual souls who are forgotten the minute they're out of sight." I was too sad even for the relief of tears.

Chad wrenched himself free, pounced on a slimy pot buoy he'd brought up from the shore, and tried to shove it into my hand. It was a much better offer than advice. "Thank you, darling," I said. "How about supper?"

21

On Monday Chad and I went for a walk just before sunup. All the fishermen, including Glen, had come down and gone out. We went for two miles up an empty road, as far as the Beaver Dam, which doesn't exist any more except in the memories of the times when the dip in the road flooded sometimes hubcap deep in a rainy spell. Game wardens had finally live-trapped the beavers who'd blocked the culvert where it ran under the road; I was sorry when they were taken away and relocated. The alder swamp still floods in wet times, but the runoff now flows through the culvert and into a noisy brown brook on the other side, which rushes through woods west to Bugle Bay. I'd still rather have the beavers, flooded road or not.

This morning the swamp was merely damp and busy as always with chickadees working on alder cones. The cold shade where the road ran through the woods and the ringing cries of bluejays combined to produce that end-of-summer atmosphere, though Labor Day was still some distance off. I didn't stop at Glen's mailbox that morning, and Chad was disappointed. I did consider going down to the cabin and leaving a note, if I could think of a few words either cryptic or provocative, but I was deterred by the prospect of its being read by one of the yearning ravens who brought him pies.

We went back to the Hayloft and to work; Chad's job was to monitor all arrivals and departures. Once, when I went out on the deck to stretch, I saw him helping the Barrys unload their clams. I thought briefly of Shasta, then went back to work and forgot her. She was not my responsibility.

In the afternoon when Chad was busy on the wharf with the men coming in, I kept my back to the window so I wouldn't be watching for Glen. They say that if you're a smoker, it takes so many days for the nicotine to leave your system, and after that it's a matter of habit. Sounds simple, doesn't it?

Having to rewrite a difficult chapter is a great way to take your mind off withdrawal symptoms. When at last I found myself staring vacantly at the same sentence for about five minutes, with my neck aching and my eyes burning, the parking lot was empty, and the westering light lay richly on land and sea.

Groaning, cautiously stretching, I shoved my material over to one end of the table. I was trying to decide whether to take a long hot shower before or after I ate, and what I would eat, when the telephone rang.

"Want to watch stars with me tomorrow night?" Nick asked.

"Where this time?"

"That's what I like, a direct response," he said. "No argument, no whys, no dithering."

"My resistance is low," I said. "I've done about ten hours' work today, and my brain is a jellyfish stranded on a beach for the gulls to pick at."

"You sound irresistible. What about Marr's Grant? I've got a special aerie picked out among the rocks, just about three feet above high water. When it's calm, that is. Otherwise it's *under* high water."

"OK," I said. It was relaxing to be acquiescent.

"I'll pick you up around six-thirty then, so we'll be sure of the spot. It's too perfect not to be popular." His energy flowed along the lines to me like a transfusion. "I think I know where it is," I said. "I'll fix us some supper."

"Humor me," he answered. "Let's be people in a book, you know the kind—vagabonding through Upper Mildew, tramping through Lower Mold, or something. They buy hard bread and cheese and wine and fruit and picnic in a meadow among the cowflaps."

"Have you found a cow willing to leave a few around?"

"They're all Maine cows, independent as hell. Look, I'll bring some French bread and a hunk of that good Cheddar they slice off a wheel at Whittier's, some peaches and grapes, and a bottle of wine. What do you like?"

"They have a good Rhine wine at Sawyer's in Maddox." I was light headed, and I didn't feel like myself, but like another novelist's character, and I rather enjoyed it; it was so simple just to say the dialogue. *Let's be people in a book.*

"Maybe we'll meet Marr's ghost," I said.

"I hope so. I always wanted to meet a ghost," he answered seriously. "So long until tomorrow, then."

He left me bemused, but enjoying it. I didn't anticipate a repeat of what had happened at the Birch Mansion or the chance that he'd want to take it further; not in an aerie among the ledges, with other stargazers in the vicinity and mosquitoes. That reminded me to set out a can of repellent where I wouldn't forget it tomorrow night.

Then I put a frozen lasagna dinner in the oven and went to take my shower.

Marr's Grant is about twenty miles southwest of Job's Harbor, named for a Richard Marr who built a fortified dwelling on it around 1635 and bought furs from the Indians. The current owners had just given the state the point where the house had been, and by next summer there'd be state archaeologists camping and digging there, but for now it was as free as it had ever been. I put myself to sleep trying to decide how to use the site in a story: I even played with the idea of a ghost.

I slept well and woke up with the assurance that my next twenty-four hours were accounted for. Finish my work and mail the book sometime today; go out with Nick tonight and to Heriot Island tomorrow to spend the day with Fee. What the heck, I thought recklessly, it might even be fun to have a go at the Ouija board, this time with nobody cheating. I needed to regress to the Age of Innocence, just to rest up from being an adult.

Tuesday afternoon I took the book to the post office and had a social few minutes with our postmaster, who's the fifth generation in his family to have the job. From there I went down the hill to the store. For some time now I'd been too busy to stand around after I bought my groceries, and standing around in the store is a legitimate local occupation. So today I ate two ice cream bars while studying the summer renters and day-trippers, and passing the time of day with the people I know. I bought a box of eclairs for Fee and me to eat tomorrow, a couple of pounds of grapes, and two sweatshirts printed with pictures of the store back in the 1920s, with a Ford touring car parked beside it. I chose green for Fee and blue for me. As an afterthought I picked out an extra-large maroon one for Julian, which would please him immensely.

Then I went home and dug out an outfit I hadn't worn yet this summer, blue sailcloth slacks and blazer, worn over a red-and-white-striped jersey. I fed Chad and took him for another walk. At six-thirty I was ready for Nick, the mosquito repellent waiting on the top step so I wouldn't forget it.

He didn't come. At seven I gave up allowing for unexpected delays and waited for a telephone call. When none came, I called the Bains, his landlords. All they knew about him was that his car was gone. They'd both been out when he must have come home from work.

It was still broad daylight, so if he'd had an accident between here and there, it would be known. By eight o'clock the first and brightest stars were showing while the afterglow still lighted up the west; there was a gentle southwesterly breeze that would keep the water splashing softly against the rocks below the special aerie. I wondered who was occupying it. I was not angry, just weighed down with an enervating lack of surprise, as if I'd never really believed he'd come but had hoped I was wrong. My first opinion of him had turned out to be correct. Was he smiling now, wherever he was?

I lay on the couch listening to the gurgles and splashes around the wharf below as the tide crept up. Chad breathed deeply in his sleep on the floor beside me. I thought about the humans beings who slept so much, drugging themselves out of life simply by the power of their longing to escape it. My limbs and eyelids grew heavier. I was sinking down and down through layer after layer of cloud, feathers, petals—what?—numbly wondering when I'd strike bottom or if I ever would. Suddenly my body gave one of those convulsive starts, violent enough to wake Chad and completely arouse myself. I came up all standing, as Grampa would put it.

I'm *not* dropping out, I thought fiercely. Not *ever.* They'll have to knock me down first and *drag* me out.

I washed my face in cold water and brushed my hair; my clothes weren't too wrinkled. I shook them out. I told Chad to be good and drove up the road to Maddox. It was a little before ten.

The car seemed to slow of her own accord when I came to the Fox Point road, but I wasn't going to use the sisters as my escape tonight; that would make me a taker, like Robbie.

After I crossed the bridge into Maddox proper I turned right. The Old-fashioned Ice Cream Parlor is down on the the river shore, where the old brickworks used to be in General Mackenzie's time. Everybody loves the ice cream parlor. You sit in authentic bentwood chairs at little round tables, unless you want to sit up at the counter where they compound ambrosial ice cream sodas and frappés. The Barrons make their own ice cream, and when you buy a banana split, you are buying one of the most elegant creations in the country. I understand that in Gram's youth their banana splits were a lot cheaper, but she never says they aren't as good as they used to be.

I left the car in the limited parking area—local people all walk there—

and stood looking out at the starlit river. The boats anchored in the pool rocked in the breeze. On this side of the pool the narrowing river came sparkling toward me, ran on past the next wharf toward the bridge and under it, to disappear on the other side in the shadows of the steep, narrow gorge below Jake Morley's buildings.

I went into the ice cream parlor and ordered a banana split before I could change my mind. In the mirror behind the soda fountain I saw the room. It was full, and I knew many of the people by name or by sight, but there was no one close enough to make a claim on me. Two high school couples left, and I took my dish to their table. I ate every bit of the banana split, which was quite an undertaking, and I scraped the dish with my spoon. When I went out to the car, I sat behind the wheel for a few minutes willing everything to settle. My view of the sequinned river was somewhat fogged, leading to meditation on what a sudden assault by all that sugar and cholesterol could do to a bloodstream used to a simple life.

A few hiccups later, I was going back across the bridge and up the hill onto the Whittier road. I drove conservatively, not only because of animals but because going around curves too fast caused disturbing reactions inside me. I looked forward to being blessedly unbent in the middle.

The garage flat where Nick lived was dark, and so was the house, and there were no vehicles in the driveway. "And to hell with you, too, brother!" I said jauntily.

It wasn't original, but it did me good, and the effects of my orgy were wearing off, too, so I began to enjoy the night. I was almost back to normal when I passed the Pringle house, which was dwarfed by the tractor-trailer rig beside it. When we were in high school Wayne Pringle wanted to own his own rig and go trucking, and I wanted to write a book, and we'd done it. I was even feeling mellow as I began the long gentle coast down Sunday Hill to where the red cat's-eye shone at me from the Fox Point mailbox. Where was that woman who'd promised herself to leap before looking? I hadn't done much of that lately. I turned off the road and drove in. Now I wasn't looking for refuge or a poultice, I was my own whole self again. Just before the driveway started to climb, I stopped the car. I would walk up to the house, and if it were lighted, I might knock. Or I might not; I'd decide when I got there.

The breeze was stirring through the spruces, and the shivering poplar leaves sounded like light rain. I was in sight of the house before I heard the music of violin and piano floating out into the night. It was something lovely and unfamiliar. I walked on toward the subdued glow of of the windows like a woman in an enchantment. About me there were crickets and the fragrance of white nicotiana blossoms inviting the night-flying moths. Ahead of me, drawing me on, there was the music. In spite of everything else that was happening in my life, for that instant I was almost unbearably happy. I would stand outside and listen and then go away, trying to hold onto it all.

22

I walked on the wet grass so I wouldn't make the slightest sound on the driveway, though the breeze in the branches would have drowned my footsteps. I would grant myself one look, from far enough away so they wouldn't catch a startling glimpse of this face staring in at them, and then I would sneak around in the shadows to sit on the front doorstep and listen. If Janine wasn't asleep, she was probably lying in her bed with the door open, thinking of angels.

I walked in dew-drenched sneakers across the grassy oval in the loop of the driveway until I came abreast of the one open window. The light fell across the driveway but couldn't reach me; it came from the big table lamp, its shade patterned with red rosebuds, that stood at one end of the sofa facing the fireplace. It shone on the piano where no one sat on the bench playing or stood beside it with a violin; I had been fooled by recorded music.

It ended while I stood there. No other sound succeeded it, and I knew that the room was empty even though I could see only this end of it, because no shadows moved against the other windows.

Disappointed, I waited in hopes they'd come back shortly and still might play. It was then that I saw the irregular splatches of red paint flung on the ivory wall to the right of the fireplace; it was on a direct line with me and stood out like a scream. How had I ever missed it? I ran across the driveway to the windowsill; the scent of crushed nicotiana rose up in a cloud around me. I pressed my nose against the screen. The vandals had splattered red paint everywhere. The spots on the lamp shade weren't rosebuds; now I remembered clearly that it was a plain white silk.

"They can't come home to this," I kept saying as if to a companion. "They mustn't." I wasn't afraid for myself. I was so appalled I was beyond fear, and I kept seeing other things. The mantel swept clear of the gold ormolu clock and everything else. The portrait; my eyes blurred as I tried to see it. And I couldn't tell if they'd damaged the piano; I couldn't see the keyboard from here.

Vandalism is far more of an outrage than straight burglary for gain; even the softest of us aches to destroy the destroyers. I didn't want to go back to the Pringles' to call the police, for fear the sisters would come home to this all unsuspecting while I was gone.

Unless they were already home, had called the police, and were in the kitchen competently making strong tea for shock treatment. I started for the kitchen wing, but I tried the front door anyway, expecting it to be locked; it wasn't. I let myself into the dim hall, calling, "Anyone home? It's Eden!"

There is an emptiness that is more than the mere absence of other warm-blooded creatures. It is as manifest when you step into it as rain or fog, and you are almost afraid to disturb it for fear of rousing the Something. It's a legacy from our beginnings; the Neanderthals must have experienced it. A dog's hackles rise for no reason you can guess. Cats stare into corners where you can see nothing, and then they watch some invisible progress across the room, and *your* hackles rise.

I had to work up saliva to wet my mouth. I took a few steps toward the kitchen and said timidly, "Mrs. Rigby?" No sound from there. "Miss Emma?" I went back to the front of the stairs and called, "Janine?"

The sound waves cast wide by my voice washed back against my ears; that, and the beating of my own heart, was all that I heard. I went across to the living room.

They had tossed their red paint around by the canful. It was thrown across the piano keys. It spattered the sofa. It had been dripped on the books and music on the coffee table and sank into the carpet. On the piano the neckpiece of a violin stuck up at an angle, like the mast of a wrecked vessel. I forced myself to look up at the portrait; it had been knifed through in a giant X.

Keeping my eyes on Guy's ruined face, I sensed something below which I must have seen without allowing myself to accept it. I shut my eyes and immediately the emptiness was closing in on me; I gasped and opened my eyes. I saw a hand lying palm up at the end of a pink sleeve. A hand palm up, from between the sofa and the hearth. I knew it was Miss Emma's. One is blessedly insulated from reality for those first moments. And one always hopes for life even while knowing that this is death. I went to the hand and found Miss Emma flung down on the hearth rug which was soaking up not paint, but blood. Her face was a mask of it, and one brown eye looked at me through the red mask. It could have been a doll's eye. Her shattered glasses lay nearby.

Backing away, searching with a peculiarly clear vision, I saw Marianne's head, white hair dyed red, in the shadows beyond the piano bench and behind the sofa. I had to walk all the way around the piano to reach her.

Holding onto the nearest chair I looked down and saw no face, only more blood. I thought quite calmly, she must have been struck first when she was at the piano. That's why the keys are spattered with blood.

Lucas, I thought. *With an axe.*

People have their devices to save them. You're a Winter, I said. Winters don't faint. Winters don't scream. Winters don't fall apart. Winters are *winners.*

It got me out into the hall to the telephone. I had to turn on the lamp beside it on the table, averting my eyes from the mirror above as if I were afraid of seeing something else in it besides myself. The emergency numbers were tidily posted on the phone.

I called the State Police number and spoke with extreme care, like an acrobat walking a wire across Niagara Falls. I gave my name and told him where I was, even remembering to mention the tractor-trailer rig as a mark.

"I'm alone, and I've just walked in on something. Two people are dead." I heard myself with disbelief. I was having a nightmare, and if I worked hard enough I could wake up.

"Someone will be there very soon, ma'am," the man said. "Are you sure no one's hiding in the house?"

"I'm sure," I said. I hadn't thought of it until he mentioned it. "But I'll wait outside in my car."

"Are you sure they're dead?"

They couldn't be Marianne and Miss Emma. "Ma'am?" he said.

"Yes, I'm sure. There's no way they could be alive." I hung up.

I didn't know how I could make myself go up the stairs, but it was the picture of Janine huddled in terror, or badly hurt but still alive, that got me moving. I held myself stiffly together, arms at my sides as if they were bound there. I didn't touch anything on the way.

Janine wasn't in her room. It didn't look disturbed in any way, and she hadn't locked herself in the bathroom or a closet. I didn't know the way to the attic, and I wasn't going to look for it. I ran down the stairs so fast my momentum almost threw me headlong. Outdoors I went across to the trees and threw up the banana split and kept on retching when there was nothing left to come up. After that I was soaked with sweat and freezing. I walked down to the car and rolled up all the windows, locked the doors, and sat there with my knees hugged up to my chest. The wind had increased; the night kept lightening and darkening under blowing clouds, and the woods were full of movement. I kept seeing motions at the edge of my vision, but I stared rigidly ahead.

I saw the blue lights flashing through the trees, slowing down, and then the cruiser turned into the driveway and drove up abreast of me. I rode up to the house with the trooper and told him everything I knew, but I wouldn't go in with him. Through the window I watched him walk into the living room and then leave it without touching anything. He came back out again and used his radio.

My teeth were chattering, and he kindly put up the heat for me. "Janine may be safe in the attic," I said. "I don't know the way to it, and I was afraid to go looking."

"We'll check," he said.

After the other cruiser came, and I had talked to a man in plain clothes, I was told I could go home. A sheriff's deputy had arrived, and offered to drive me. "I'll be around all night if you're worried about leaving your car," he said.

"No, thanks, I'm all right," I said. "I need the activity."

"I'll turn her around for you." I guess I was glad of that, because my hands felt as if all the nerves and sinews had become loose strings. But once I was in the car, the habitual set of motions took over.

The way home was familiar the way a nightmare landscape is familiar. I drove into the yard and sat there a few moments collecting myself for the effort of climbing the stairs to the Hayloft. The kitchen in the house across the parking lot showed a lighted window; faintly and unevenly through the gusting breeze I could hear Derek crying. I tried to fix my mind on Shasta shuffling around in run-over slippers, wearing a housecoat that didn't meet over her belly, bleary-eyed, tangle-haired, maybe tearful, warming a bottle for Derek who was probably cutting whatever teeth appeared at his age.

It was sane and earthy, but it didn't work. What fortitude I'd had was trickling away like sand in an hourglass, with the difference that I couldn't be stood on my head to reverse the process. Finally I got myself out of the car. I went up the steps hanging onto the railing, which dripped with dew.

The artificial moonlight of the security lamp on the wharf gave me my shadow for company. The moon was hidden by now, but Chad was waiting for me inside the door. Weak as I felt, I didn't dare let him out alone because of porcupines, and I fastened his leash with my cold and trembling hands while he tossed his head around like a restive horse, impatient with my fumbling. He towed me down the steps and tried to drag me to the orchard, where the porcupines as well as deer came for apples these nights. The contest was probably good for me; I was less shaky when I got him back into the Hayloft.

But I was so *cold!* The room was warm with stored heat, but I was still cold. I drew the curtains as if to draw the Hayloft snugly about me and brought out my Hudson's Bay blanket from the bedroom and wrapped myself in it. I gave Chad his handful of dog biscuits, blessing the glossy, greedy, crunching life of him.

Then I went to the telephone and called Glen.

"I don't give a damn if you have two girls in bed with you," I said as I dialed. He answered on the first ring and got the last word.

"Who *is* this?" he asked irritably.

"Glen, can you come over here right now?" My voice sounded peculiar even to me. "Quietly?"

"I'm on my way." He hung up.

I turned on the gas under the teakettle, holding my blanket around me with one hand; I set out mugs. Because of the way the rising wind sounded up here, I didn't hear the pickup coming down the black road. I didn't know he was there until he was at the door. I met him there, and he took me into his arms and heard it all before he'd gotten in over the threshold.

The teakettle was shooting out clouds of steam. "*Cocoa,*" he said. "Sugar's good for shock." He dumped heaping spoonfuls of hot chocolate mix into one of the mugs. "I can't stand the stuff, but you need it." He poured the boiling water, found a package of miniature marshmallows in the cupboard, and sprinkled them all over the surface.

"My feet are so cold they're numb," I said foolishly. He sat me down on the couch and, kneeling before me, took off my wet sneakers and rubbed my feet. He brought out more blankets from the bedroom and bundled me up, leaving only my hands free to receive the hot mug. Then he sat beside me with his arms around me. Chad got up on my other side and leaned heavily against me. He was loving all this.

The first sip of cocoa burned the inside of my lower lip, but I didn't mind the pain, and the mug was warming my hands. Now I could see how pale he was. "You're upset yourself," I said. "Here, take some." I held out the mug.

"It'll make me sick. My guts are doing the high fantods at the thought of you walking in on it. If you'd been a little earlier—*Christ!* Things like that aren't supposed to happen around here!"

"I can't believe it did happen. I keep thinking it was all hallucinations. I'd rather think I was off my head than that it was real."

"Lucas," he said thoughtfully.

"Who else could it be?...Oh, *Glen.*" He took the mug away before I could drop it and held me tightly while I clung to him with my eyes shut. "I'll never stop thinking about it. For the rest of my life I'll always see it. Nothing can ever wipe it out until I die myself."

He didn't tell me I'd get over it or forbid me to think of it or order me to be brave. He simply held me. After a while he said, "I can't get warm myself. Let's go to bed."

We got in between blankets and wrapped our arms and legs around each other. Chad wanted to join us, but there was no room, so he lay beside the bed. As the shared body heat commenced to enfold us, lassitude crept over me like a narcotic, and I felt myself beginning to float, but I was afraid to shut my eyes. I knew what was lying in ambush. Thinking of what they endured before they died at last. What they must have been thinking, after the first hideous surprise, knowing there was no help.

I wrenched myself out of his arms and sat up. "Glen, I can't *bear* it for them, and I don't know what I'm going to do! And I don't know what's happened to Janine!"

"When they find Lucas, they'll find her."

"Supposing he's killed her, too!"

"She's his child. He won't." But I didn't believe that.

We slept after a while; exhaustion swept me under like one of those tidal bores that catch victims unawares.

23

I was awakened in a few hours by the crows' dawn patrol down in the orchard. For an instant it was a securely familiar clamor; they'd perhaps discovered an owl who was tardy about going home from his night-hunting. In the next instant all security and familiarity were gone. I remembered.

Glen had released me in his sleep, and it was as if I'd dropped from his arms into an abyss. Down there with no hope of clawing my way up again, I saw *It* all over again. The fight-or-flight reflex is a kind of killer in itself when you can neither fight nor fly. I suppose this is how we will feel when we face the ending of the world and know there is absolutely nothing we can do.

I had been too shocked last night to believe that I would have a tomorrow, when all their tomorrows had been scythed away. Then Chad pressed his chin heavily on my side of the bed, his brown eyes looking imploringly into mine. He breathed hard. I rolled out, shivering, and gave him a hug just to touch Life; Chad was certainly full of it. The air was cool but not enough to make me shake like this. When I was dressed in pajamas and my wool bathrobe and had pulled thick winter socks onto my feet, I let Chad out; the porcupines should have gone by now, and Uncle Early's truck was coming down the road.

Shaking in my wrappings, I was trying to make coffee quietly when Glen got up and went to the bathroom. When he came out, he said, "You go on in and wash up. I'll fix breakfast."

I retired mutely and stood in a warm shower, letting it hypnotize me until he pounded on the door and yelled, "What are you doing in there?"

"Not drowning myself!" I yelled back, which surprised me. I hadn't thought I had the strength.

He had made oatmeal with raisins and sprinkled mine with brown sugar. "No coffee till you get that into you," he said tyranically. I expected the first mouthful would make me vomit, but I must have needed the warm sweet bulk of it. We ate in silence. He didn't ask any questions or turn on the radio, which fishermen usually do when they get up, to hear if the weather has any surprises for them.

"Come on out to haul with me," he said. "Just leave the whole thing behind you for the day. It'll be pretty out there, with a little bounce the way you like it." The wind was still southwest and could whip the seas up into something more than a nice little bounce by noon. *They're gone. They will never see another pretty day.* Glen's easy voice went on through the words in my head. "Or I can leave you with Fee for a while."

"I was going out there today," I said, "but not now. I don't want to be the one to tell her, and if she's heard anything on the news, we'd be no help to each other. You talk to her."

Glen stood looking down at me with such concern that I was forced to prove I wasn't falling apart; if I'd given in, I'd have become a soggy mess, and the day hadn't even properly begun yet.

"Besides," I said, "I have to be here. I gave the police my number. I'll make you a good lunch, though."

"But will you be all right?" he persisted.

"Yes, I will. I have to be. What kind of sandwiches do you want?"

Chad scratched at the door and came in all of a wriggle at the sight of Glen upright and conscious. He smelled of wet dog and salt herring, meaning he'd been in the bait shed. I savored it; the scent of the nicotiana had been coming back to me in suffocating waves.

I put up a big lunch for Glen and would have gone down to see him off, but the other men were collecting. Instead of rowing out to their boats, they were standing around on the wharf with their hands in their pockets, talking, shaking their heads. Now and then someone glanced up at my windows.

Glen and I kissed inside the door, then I went out on the deck with him. Chad accompanied him down to the wharf. I knew there'd be no twitting Glen about spending the night in the Hayloft; this wasn't an ordinary morning for Whittier. Even Sprig was subdued.

Richie and Toby were poling out to deep water, and someone on the car shouted at them, "Hey, where were you last night?"

"What the hell business is it of yours?" Richie shouted back.

"You better be able to prove you were tucked in snug under the kelp," Sprig said. "And I'm not kidding. You had your radio on this morning?"

"Nope!" Toby answered with a grin. "We didn't need a feller in a suit and a tie to tell us it was a good day; we just looked outside." But something about the men's faces alerted him, and the grin went. "Why? What happened?" He poled toward the lobster car.

I went back inside and sat at my table with my chin on my hand, watching the boats go out between Winter Head and Job's Tears. This is the way I sit when I am working and stop to think out a sentence or a scene. Sometimes I try to describe a duel of wills between two gulls over a dead fish, with their brown youngsters bobbing and whistling at them, or the way a wet roof dazzles blindingly among spruces at sunrise. Now a sentence slowly arranged itself, spoken in Marianne Rigby's deep voice. *I sleep through sunrises, I am ashamed to say. But I can proudly claim that I've missed very few midnights in the last sixty years.*

I hadn't noticed my uncle crossing the lawn back to the house, and when he knocked at my door, I jumped. He said apologetically, "I should have hailed you from below instead of sneaking up on you. But I thought you saw me."

"I was miles away, that's all." Chad rushed in ahead of him as if he'd been gone a year, and I gave him half a dozen dog biscuits for his breakfast.

"You shouldn't be here alone," Uncle Early said.

"I'm not alone. Chad's here. I called Glen as soon as I got home last night, and he came right over."

"Good." He was not his brisk, buoyant self; there are times when he looks more like Jon's older brother than his father, but today he had been badly jolted.

"Sit down and have a cup of fresh coffee with me, Uncle Early," I invited, for his sake as well as mine.

"I could stand it. My first cup this morning didn't taste like anything on earth, when I was hearing the news along with it."

I put the teakettle on to boil. "We'll have it by the pot, maybe it'll taste better."

"Yep." He sounded preoccupied. "Did you notice—no, you wouldn't, not with what you've got on your mind. Well, Ira Neville didn't come down this morning."

"So?" I put some of Gram's doughnuts into the oven to warm.

"He and Blanche must be half-crazy, poor souls. Sonny walked away from the Youth Center late yesterday. That was on the early news, too. They didn't name him, because he's a minor, but they called him a local youth, known to be a friend of the young girl who lived with the—" He stopped and snapped his finger at Chad.

Keeping his head down and scratching the dog's ears, he went on. "Living at Fox Point. She's disappeared, and nobody's seen him since a truck driver left him off at a wood road somewhere to the west'ard of Maddox, in the afternoon. They've got an APB out on them, descriptions and all. . . . Makes it sound as if they think Sonny did it.

"He couldn't have!" I cried. "He knew they were her shelter, her refuge! He'd never have wanted to harm them! No, it was Lucas. Lucas is the one who hated them." I was back in the bloody living room again. I ran to the bathroom; so much for the oatmeal. When I came back, Uncle Early had made tea and dry toast for me and had taken the doughnuts out of the oven. The smell of them made me feel sick again.

"I wish I hadn't been the one!" I burst out. "I wish I'd heard it like everybody else, on the early news!"

"I know, I know," his voice soothed me. "What you see is printed on your eyeballs forever, you think, and you see everything else through it." His little drowned son. "You think it won't ever go away, and you'll never see anything clear and pretty again."

"And it *won't* ever go," I said angrily.

"No," he agreed, "but you'll be able to put it away sometimes. You won't think about it every minute. If you can't stop thinking about it, you can go mental. But Winters don't go under."

"Winters are winners," I said ironically. "That's what got me to the telephone last night."

"Drink your tea while it's hot. It's better for you than coffee. I have something else to tell you, Punkin, and you won't like it."

"What is it?" I sat down and took up my cup. "I don't care. What can it be after last night? 'No worst, there is none.' That's from a poem," I explained.

"Lucas was picked up yesterday afternoon for being drunk and disorderly," he said. "He was in jail last night."

"Damn it!" I exploded. "It *can't* be Sonny! He and Janine ran away before it ever happened!"

"You could be right. You probably are." He carried his mug to the sink. "All they have to do is show up. What are you going to do with yourself today?"

"I'm staying right here. The police may want to talk to me again, and I want to be here when Gram and Grampa get home."

"Oh, God, I forgot about them! This is going to knock Mother four ways for Sunday. She's been so damn' happy, finding her chum again. They've been like a couple of school kids." He said in dismay, "This is likely to make an old woman of her."

"We won't let it," I said brashly.

"If they haven't heard it before they get here, I'll tell them," he said. "Spare you."

"That's a handsome offer, Uncle Early. I admit I'm a coward." He patted my shoulder and left, Chad with him. The telephone rang, and it was my mother calling; she sounded out of breath. "Were you alone last night? Are you all right? If we'd known about this earlier, we'd have been down there by now to get you. But we didn't get up until now. We were at the Caldwells' all evening."

"Mother, don't sound so guilty," I said. "I'm not fine, but I'm all in one piece, and I wasn't alone last night. I called Glen, and he came and stayed with me."

"God bless Glen," she said emphatically, "and we're blessing him, too."

"He's gone to haul, and then Uncle Early came up and had another breakfast with me." This was poetic license, but it reassured my mother.

"Your father and I," she said, "will never believe Sonny Neville is a psychopathic killer."

"Who says he is?"

"No one—officially. And certainly no one who knows him. But you can't escape the connection through Janine, and with Lucas out of it. Your father's gone now to see Ira and Blanche. Are you coming up to stay with us?"

"I'd rather not," I said. "Gram's going to need me, and I'd feel better here, if there is any better in this."

"You know what's best for you, dear. Tell your grandmother that we'll be down tonight, and we'll bring supper."

I was grateful because they weren't going to treat me as an invalid or emotionally fragile. I might have felt it, but I wasn't going to act like it. There was no way in which even the most loving souls could share the burden of my experience; I had to get over it all by myself, and the only way I could manage to live with it now was to concentrate this frenzy of horror and grief and hatred on the killer. When I'd confronted Lucas, I had been uplifted on a surge of power in which all things were possible, and it seemed that what I felt now was a force so magnificently potent that it could seek out and destroy. It *had* to. There was nowhere else for it to go but straight to him.

And like a medieval headsman, the black-clad, masked, symbolic murderer roved through the pastels of the living room and the tunnels of my mind with his great ax over his shoulder. *I'll get you,* I promised him. *I'll get you yet.*

24

I didn't know what to do with myself; there was this awful, frantic aimlessness, like a sickness in itself. I gathered a load of washing and took it into the main house to put it through Gram's machine. While that was working, I began hurling stuff out of my bureau drawers; I hadn't tidied them for a long time. I knew everything would be hurled back into the drawers again. I hadn't the patience to do it properly. The harbor was quiet, and I was about to take Chad and go rowing when the telephone rang.

I was going to ignore it. Then I thought it was the police, so I answered. Nick's voice fairly leaped out at me. "Are you all right? Christ, I blame myself for you walking into that—that—"

Nick at a loss for words was a phenomenom I couldn't appreciate just then. "Why?" I asked. I'd honestly forgotten until this moment that we'd had a date planned for last night. "Oh, *that,*" I said unflatteringly. "Forget it, Nick. I might have gone there after we came back from Marr's Grant, who knows?" It was exhausting to deal with him, with anyone. "It's hard to talk, I'm sure you must understand. . . ."

He broke in before I could hang up. "Something idiotic happened to hold me up last night. I swear I'll never help another goddam drunk. Are you all right? Who's with you? Where the hell *is* everybody?" His energy bombarded the room. I felt as if I were spinning at the center of it. "They're not leaving you alone, are they? Look, I'm on my way over right now."

"No, you are *not!*" I had to shout to get through. "I'm alone for a little while, but it's the way I want it. You stay on your job. You're at work, aren't you?"

"Yes, it's coffee break. But I'd quit in a second if you needed me, Eden." He sounded badly shaken up. "What *can* I do?" he persisted. "I've got to do *something*. Just thinking of you alone with your thoughts is. . . ."

"Listen, Nick, if you have a few more minutes, you can tell me about the idiotic drunk," I said. "It'll give me something else to see in my head, maybe." I was tired just standing there, aching. I dropped onto the couch, put my feet up, and let my head sag back.

"It's a long story, but I'll try to keep it simple." He was quicker now. "When I left work yesterday afternoon, I drove to Tenby to get some French bread for our supper, at the Brookside Bakery. You know where it is, on South Main Street, in the same block as the Harborview Hotel."

"Mm," I said. I put my head back on the cushions. Gulls were coasting over the harbor, the effect was hypnotic, and I kept my eyes on them. "Harborview Hotel," I said. "Cheap rooms by the day, no questions asked. But good food downstairs."

"Yup. And a very busy bar. When I came out of the bakery with my bread, one of the bar customers was arguing with a cop on the sidewalk. I thought the officer was being pretty patient with him, because he sure as hell wasn't safe enough to drive or walk across the street under his own power. But he could *see*, and he gave me a shout as if I were a sail and he was a castaway. In fact," Nick said, "he did yell 'Sail ho!'"

I'm a storyteller and a listener to stories; in spite of everything, the instinct reacted to that opener.

The man, whom Nick called Gilly, had been fired from the Glenroy yard about a week ago for being drunk on the job, when he'd run out of second chances. As Nick walked out of the bakery with a long loaf of French bread under his arm, he should have pretended he hadn't heard his name and quickly left. But he stopped and was lost. Gilly kept telling the officer that his old friend and best pal would take him home; the officer said that if Nick would do this, he wouldn't lock Gilly up.

He pleaded with Nick to save him from jail; it would kill his wife, she'd divorce him for sure, and so forth. He wept. Nick agreed because there wasn't any other way out of it, but he insisted on using his own car so he could go straight home after dropping off this unappetizing parcel. The policeman would make sure that Gilly's car was locked, and Gilly could pick up his keys at the station the next day.

All this time Nick had believed that Gilly lived in Tenby, or just on the outskirts. It turned out that he lived a long way out of town. What with missing landmarks which Gilly could not clearly describe, having to back out of old logging roads, and coming to unpopulated dead ends of ancient town roads, Nick expected they'd soon be in Vermont or even Quebec. He'd never realized there were so many acres with so few people on them in the hills back of Tenby.

Finally Gilly shut up and fell asleep. They were then up on a rocky dirt road on the side of a distant hill, and Nick decided to navigate back to Tenby by the first stars and leave Gilly in a hotel room. But where the dirt road joined a black road he met a station wagon full of youngsters on their way up to the hilltop. He asked them where he was, and if they'd ever heard of Dunbarton Road. They gave Nick concise directions, and in a half-hour or so he was there. He identified Gilly's place by the name on the mailbox. The nearest house was about five hundreds yards away and dark.

The wife wasn't at home; Nick had to search Gilly for the key and then get him out of the car and drag him into the house. He was big, and now he was a dead weight. It was like handling a two-hundred-pound sack of sand.

"I huffed and I puffed, and I dragged and heaved and shoved, and I swore," Nick said. "I came out with a lot of picturesque speech I wish I could remember. We must have been quite a sight, but we'd need a sound track to make it really good. I could almost laugh about it, except that now I know what was going on at Fox Point."

At last he got Gilly into the living room, where he put a pillow under his head, took off his shoes, and covered him with an afghan from the couch. Then he looked for a telephone. From the appearance of the house, he guessed that the wife had been away for some time. There were no telephones; she must have unplugged them and taken them with her.

"So I headed home, and I tried to call you from the telephone at the corner of Ship and Main in Maddox," he said.

"It's such a wild and wonderful story," I said, "that if you made it up you're in the wrong business. You should be a writer."

"The only creative part of it was my language."

For a little while I'd escaped, but now that chase was over and *he* was back, the black-masked prowler with the ax. I could hear his footsteps disguised as my heartbeat.

"I headed straight for Job's Harbor," Nick was saying. "I called you first, still no answer. So I had something to eat and set out to be on your doorstep when you did get home. But when I was going down Sunday Hill I met the ambulance coming up, and then I saw the cruiser from the sheriff's patrol parked by the mailbox. The deputy flagged me down, but I was stopping anyway; I had this god-awful sensation in my gut. He asked for my identification and wanted to know where I was going and where I'd come from. Whatever I said must have convinced him," he said wearily. "I can't even remember. I asked him what happened and he said—" There was not quite silence; I could hear him breathing as if he'd been running. "He said the two women who lived there had been found dead, and I could tell by the way he said it that they just hadn't—died. You know what I mean. He wouldn't tell me anything, except to get moving, and then he flagged down another car, I don't know whose. I kept on going all the way down to the harbor, stopped by your mailbox, and walked in. I felt so damned peculiar, I was *there* and not there. Trying to reject facts, I guess. . . . There was one pickup in the parking lot, and Glen was going up your steps. So I went back to the car." There was another long pause. "This morning on the five o'clock news I found out you found them."

"Please don't ask me any questions, Nick," I said.

"I won't. Jesus, I can't take it in! I didn't sleep the rest of the night, and I've been working in a trance all morning. Part of me knows what to do; so far I haven't maimed myself or anybody else. Nobody can talk about anything but that, and everybody's got a candidate. One kid, or the two of them. The piano tuner. Some junkie caught ransacking the place—that's the one almost everybody believes in, but they've got candidates for that, too. So many it makes this whole community sound like a whited sepulcher."

"I've got to hang up, Nick," I said. "I appreciate your calling. I believe your story, I really do. But I can't talk about it. I don't mean your story, Nick. The family's gathering here for supper tonight. Why don't you come and be with the crowd?" It was another of my involuntary reactions; he sounded in need of company, and we could supply it, like food or drink. One more wouldn't matter in in the Winters' kitchen.

"Thanks, Eden, but no," he said hurriedly. "I'd better keep to myself tonight. Goodbye for now." He hung up before I could answer. My skin twitched as if invisible fingers trailed over it. The sense of the murderer's nearness. . . . It seemed that if I closed my eyes and put out my hand, I would touch him. What if Nick's whole story were a lunatic fantasy?

I went downstairs and took my washing out to the clotheslines at the far end of the house. The birds sang, Uncle Early was gassing up a cabin cruiser, everything was beautifully ordinary. The murderer vanished. Chad began barking out at the Hayloft end of the house, raising impressive echoes. I walked through the yard, whistling to him. He came running down from the deck, but not to me; with his hackles visibly raised he kept barking at the man leaning back against the hood of his car beside the rose hedge. When the man saw me, he straightened up, dropping his cigarette and stepping on it.

"Chad, stop that!" I said, and he rushed at me with joyous relief.

"Is that a real Labrador or a bull mastiff in a Labrador suit?" the man asked. He was the plainclothesman from the night before.

"The family has a lot of opinions," I said. "It's either a Chihuahua or a rabbit in there, or even a dear little pussycat. Call him Chad, and he'll be your friend for life."

It worked. Chad escorted him up the steps and through the door, then lay down with his chin flatteringly on the detective's foot. The man seemed to take it as natural. I didn't remember much about him from last night, when everything had been a surrealist dream.

His name was Jensen. In daylight he was a rumpled, stocky, slightly overweight man, dark but with a vaguely Scandinavian cast. He was starting to turn grey. I was pleased to be able to be so observant. It was reassuring, and it used up the nerve-straining interval while he read his notes.

The interview was much easier than I'd expected. His mild offhand manner helped, and he knew what questions to ask to start me searching for details I might have taken in without knowing. I don't know how he did it, but I was able to go through the story without coming apart. I *wanted* to do well; I *wanted* him to think well of me. I was a writer. I should be able to be objective. Thus vanity attacks at incongruous moments and saves us.

Finally he thanked me and said, "Excuse me," to Chad for dislodging his chin. It's perfectly all right, Chad assured him, all of a wriggle. My pleasure!

"Is there any news about Sonny Neville and Janine?" I asked him at the door.

"Not yet," he said.

"Janine worshipped them," I said, "and Sonny was never violent. I can see them running away together, maybe just for a few hours, and then coming back and finding the police there and being too terrified to show themselves."

"That possibility's been taken into consideration."

"They could be hiding not very far from here," I said. "Janine must be in a terrible state, and he wouldn't leave her like that. Somebody could have come by water." I was remembering Toby's alien clammers hanging around the Fox Point shore. *If Toby didn't make them up.* I squelched that.

"That possibility is under consideration, too," he said kindly. "Unfortunately the wind and high tide at midnight loaded the beach with rockweed, hiding any marks."

"Ninety-nine percent of the clammers are honest people, working hard for a living," I said. "You just can't tell about the other one percent."

"Speaking of clammers, where do the Barrys live?" he asked. I couldn't see them as first and second murderers, and I wondered who'd brought them up this soon. "They're your tenants, I believe."

"Right across the parking lot," I said. "But I don't know if the boys are home." I went out on the deck and looked at their mooring. It was empty. "Nope. I don't know where they'd be. The tide's pretty high." Across the river checking out their alibis, that's where they'd be.

"Well, they'll keep," he said pleasantly. "Thank you again, Miss Winter. My wife likes your books, by the way. So long, Chad." Chad's eyes were eloquent. *Must* you go? Won't I ever see you again?

My grandparents were driving in as Lieutenant Jensen drove out, and at the sight of their car, Chad forgot his newest love object and went mad with joy. I knew in my first glimpse of them through the windshield that they'd been told. They looked bleached and old and tired as they got out. They ignored Chad and stared straight at me, and I found myself speechless, wanting to escape from seeing them like this.

"Whose car was that?" Grampa asked gruffly.

"Lieutenant Jensen, C.I.D., State Police," I said. "Speak to Chad before he bursts."

He put his hand on the dog's head, but his dark blue eyes pinned me. "How are *you?*"

"I'm OK. Honest, Grampa."

"I'm going down to the wharf before I change my clothes," he said in an angry growl and tramped off. Chad gave Gram's hand a fast lick, then went with Grampa, throwing his favorite stick of firewood ahead of him and then jumping on it.

Gram blew her nose. "The older you grow, the easier it is to cry," she said tremulously. "Something sweet or something awful—anything can do it to you."

"I wouldn't mind crying myself," I admitted, "but it's as if all the springs have dried up." I carried their things into the house; there was a carton of corn on the cob, fresh tomatoes, and green peppers.

"Picked this morning," Gram said. "The dew was still on everything, and it was a real happy time. Peg and I were planning their visit here, while we picked. Then we went into the house, and Hank and your grandfather, they had this *look*—" Her tears overflowed, and she sat down abruptly and put her face in her hands. Automatically I put the teakettle on. A child is awed and frightened when a parent weeps; I understood Uncle Early's despair when he said this could make an old woman out of her. I had never before thought of Gram as old, and I wanted to run and hide from it, but the child was in an adult's body and knew how an adult should behave.

I got her a handful of the man-sized tissues she keeps on the counter and pulled a chair close to her and put my arm around her. Her shoulders felt reassuringly sturdy. She kept on weeping into her hands and talking at the same time.

"I keep seeing her coming in that door. I keep hearing her voice. I've heard it all the way home from Hiram. The way she laughed. She sounded just the way she always did. So *young.* And we had plans. We were going to take some trips around Maine when the leaves began to turn." She buried her face in the tissues and cried into them, "Oh, Eden, I can't take this!"

Sitting there with my arm around her, I felt my own tears for the first time. I didn't fight them. I just let them well up and over and run down my face. In a few minutes she said in a clogged voice, "Turn off that fool teakettle. I don't want anything to drink. There's a flat of blueberries in the trunk, and I'm going to start picking them over. You go get them while I wash my face."

She didn't want me to see her just yet, and I hoped nobody would see me when I went out to get the blueberries. Vanity again. When I brought the flat in, she was already in a housedress and tying on her apron. Her eyelids and nose were pink, but her voice was strong. "No, I don't want help. Your eyes look like two burnt holes in a blanket. Go and get some sleep. Try some warm milk."

"Yuck," I said.

"That's what you always said. Scoot now."

"Mother's bringing down supper for everybody tonight," I said.

"*Good.* Now will you *git?*"

She wanted to be alone, and I was now aching in every bone and longing to collapse. A good case of the genuine flu would have come in handy, but unfortunately it wasn't around in August. I put on my pajamas and went to bed in my darkened bedroom.

I slept without dreams and woke up suddenly; someone was moving around in the kitchen. The murderer? I questioned in my fog. I staggered out, foolhardy, bleary-eyed and wobbly of limb, and found Glen trying to prop a note against the sugar bowl. He put his arms around me and rocked me gently, his chin on my head.

"How are you?"

"All right." I yawned against his shoulder. "Actually I feel horrible, the way I always feel after I sleep in the daytime, even when everything's all right. How was Fee?"

"I'll tell you when you're conscious. I'm going home and clean up."

"Everybody's coming to supper tonight, so will you?"

"Yep." He sat me down in a chair, where I sagged like a rag doll. "You'd better come up slow so you won't get the bends."

Even my seiner cousin was there for supper that night, which marked it as a special occasion. It was a family joke that you'd have to rope and hog-tie Jon to get him ashore when there were herring out there. He and his crew would be going out again that night, so I gave him the eclairs meant for me and Fee.

There'd be many such gatherings in the town that night. This crime could rock everything familiar off its foundations as surely as if an earthquake had split the ground under our feet, broken every dish and window, and toppled every chimney in the town. Who'd want to be alone? I even hoped Nick was with someone, the Bains, perhaps. To clothe him in the murderer's skin was ridiculous.

At our house the crimes were not discussed, and the clan performed superbly; we kept the talk going from one safe subject to another without any of those helpless lapses into panic-stricken silence when everyone's mind goes blank.

My mother and aunt sent Glen and me out as soon as the table was cleared, and Chad went with us. I'd forgotten my wash when Lieutenant Jensen came, and now the dew had gotten to it; everything was too damp to take in. We went down to the wharf and saw Jon and his crew off for their night's work and then sat on a crate on the lobster car in the last light of the sunset. The wind had dropped. Sky and water were the same over and around us, all transient melting pinks and blues. It was like being inside a soap bubble. Chad wanted to bark at the sea pigeons, but I made him lie down and shut up, keeping my foot on his back.

"Fee was a wreck," Glen said. "I'm glad you didn't go out there; it wouldn't have done you any good. She never took on this way when Dad died. But then he did it himself, didn't he?"

"It's the horror," I said, stupidly; how could a six-letter word describe it?

"Julian's so damn' helpless. He doesn't know what to do with her, but I didn't know, either. I told him she'd howl herself out. Well, I had to say something to the poor dumb bastard. He's going to take her ashore with him when he works on the boat, whether she wants to or not. He'll lug her aboard bodily if she puts up a fight."

I was ashamed of my relief. Fee and I had sustained each other through many an adolescent crisis. But all they'd needed was talk by the night and the mile, and most of them either dissolved or were exorcised.

Glen yawned suddenly. "Go home tonight and get some sleep," I said.

"Why? We're legitimate now. Your folks thanked me for being here last night. So let's take advantage of the blessing."

"I slept all afternoon," I said, "which means I'll be restless all night. You've been working hard, and you didn't get much sleep last night because you came when I called. And that's what counts."

He was watching me as if for signs of a nervous breakdown bravely hidden, and I gave him a rough nudge in the ribs. "Did I interrupt anything when I called, by the way?"

He grinned. "Do you think I'd tell you?"

"How about the brainy lady who's in the numbers racket?"

"How about her?" he responded agreeably.

"Does she have a built-in abacus?"

"Don't talk nasty in front of this young dog," he said.

Our walk back to the house was diverted off course when Chad made a dash for the apple trees. Chasing him gave us a good cardiovascular workout. The porcupine had climbed out of Chad's reach and sat in the crotch of a tree looking down at us while we kissed good night. Chad stood with his forepaws on the trunk, whining and growling up and down the scale and making feckless little leaps.

We took him back between us, each holding onto his collar. Glen said thanks and good night to everyone, and I walked him to his truck. "You sure you'll be all right?" he asked me. "Who's going to hold you if you have nightmares?"

"I've got to meet them face to face, Glen." I didn't have to be asleep to hear the footsteps.

"Pride's a great thing, but hell, woman, it hasn't been twenty-four hours yet!"

"It's felt more like twenty-four years. Most of my lifetime." I pulled his face down and kissed him. "Go home."

25

Maybe the plaguey little dread of being too dependent is another component of vanity, but I'm glad of it. In spite of the long afternoon sleep, I dropped off quickly, while it was not yet twilight, before my parents' car left the yard. I slept through the first anniversary of the murders, and the telephone woke me up. Sunlight blinded me in the kitchen, and I squeezed my eyes shut against it while I groped my way to the telephone. It was my agent, with the happy news that she'd stayed up all last night reading my book. She loved it and was sure my editor would, too. "I'm going to ask her to double your advance."

"Fine," I said.

"You sound strange. Have you got one of those hellish summer colds?"

"No, I just woke up."

"No kidding! I thought you were always up with the birds and the fishermen."

"But I don't go to bed with the birds or the fishermen," I said, and we both laughed. I was surprised at how easily I could go on stage. "I had a late night, but it's time I was up, and what a way to begin the day!"

"I'm sending the manuscript to Marcia this morning. She'll probably read it over the weekend."

"Thanks. I'll try not to spend the money before I'm sure of it." We had a little social chat, inquiring about each other's health, families, and activities, and said goodbye.

It was after eight, and the boats were all out. There was a note on the table from Glen, with a bluejay's feather lying across it. He'd torn yesterday's leaf off my word-a-day calendar and written on the back of it, "You need the sleep more than you need me to wake you up. See you when I come in. See today's word."

The word for today was "fortitude."

I smiled wanly, touched by his noticing and saving the sleek blue feather. Only nature could produce such purity and brilliance of color. I thought about that while I fixed a breakfast of sorts. I'd seize on any subject to dissect, so as not to see and hear what was always there in my head, where the killer walked and left bloody footprints.

Gram came in while I was eating an English muffin. She was dressed for town; her eyes looked tired and strained behind her glasses, but her shoulders were unbent.

"I'm going to Tenby with your mother and Eleanor," she announced. "We've all got errands to do up there, and then we'll have a bite to eat and go to the museum to get a look at the Sim Trescott pictures before the Labor Day crowds swamp the place. When are *you* going up to see them?"

"I've been waiting for the summer complaints to clear out," I said mendaciously. I'd completely forgotten Sim's show. "Sim won't mind if I haven't rushed right up. He probably hasn't read any of my books yet, either."

"You'd better come along with us today," Gram said. "Your mother and aunt dreamed it up to distract this old woman, so you might as well take advantage."

I smiled and shook my head. "I'd rather not, Gram, but I've got a little pleasant news to think about." I told her about the book. "It's not sure yet, but it's *pretty* sure. Just don't tell anyone until we know, huh?"

"Well, I'm glad to hear something positively good instead of positively awful," she said austerely.

I was left alone with time in which to sort myself out, or try to. Chad was down in the store with Grampa. I wanted to be outdoors; I could have gone rowing, but I'd be likely to meet someone, if only the kids who played around the harbor, in and out of their skiffs like seals.

I went into the barn and wiped the dust off my bicycle. I knew I had to go up the road again, and this was the time for it. It would not be the same road. The two worlds of day and night orbit each other like twin stars, and we are transported from one to the other in our sleep. The birds were all awake now, and the road was splashed with cool blue shadow and sunlight that warmly caressed my cheek and shoulder. In the sunshine monarch butterflies dipped over the goldenrod; in the shade the asters gave off an almost fluorescent blue-lavender glow. At the Beaver Dam a couple of little swamp maples had turned crimson early, another of those pure vibrant hues.

And then the color slapped me like a sponge full of blood. I could almost taste it on my lips, smell it, see it spattered on my hands and splotching my white shirt. I nearly lost control of my bike, and if there'd been a car coming around the curve, I'd have been hit. I steered back to the side to dismount and stood there breathing hard, gripping the handlebars so tight my hands hurt. I'd read about anxiety attacks, but I had never expected I'd be having one, and on this familiar roadside. Don't hyperventilate, Winner Winter commanded me. Stop panting. Breathe deeply and slowly. You'll never forget all that blood until the day you die, but if you don't look out you'll be swooning at the sight of a cut finger. And don't you *dare* turn around and run for home.

I was going all the way to the Fox Point mailbox, and I hoped I wouldn't meet anyone who knew me. The road climbed slightly, and I was glad of the extra effort. When I reached the driveway, I thought I heard a car out of sight above Sunday Hill, so I hurried in and hid the bike in a patch of wet bracken as tall as I was, and waited. The car went on by.

Everything was quiet except for the birds, and the long emphatic buzz of a red squirrel. When I was about to see the house I almost lost my courage, but I wouldn't let my feet stop moving. I took my fists out of my pockets and unclenched them and breathed carefully. This side of the house was shady in the mornings, and the nicotiana still gave out the fragrance that went with dimness and dampness. I expected to see a cruiser and maybe Jensen's car, but no vehicle was there except a bicycle leaning against one of the big boulders that rose like volcanic peaks from a sea of lawn.

Tracy Hearne stood beside it staring at the house, with her hands shoved into the hip pockets of her tight jeans. A bluejay shrieked an alarm over my head, making us both jump, and then she saw me.

Silently we confronted each other across the driveway. Her face seemed to have thinned just since Sunday, and she had been crying. The wet still glistened on her cheeks, and she wiped them with the back of her hand. She looked more forlorn than defiant.

"Hello, Tracy," I said. My voice came out husky, just above a whisper. "Are the police here?"

"They're parked around back, and the Thatchers are in there. With that Jensen. I don't know why I came. It feels awful."

"I had to come alone and face the place," I said.

My honesty helped to break down any reserve between us. "So did I," she said hoarsely. "I know it's not the same for *me.* I mean, I didn't *see* anything, and they never asked me to go in there." She nodded toward the living room windows. "They had the doors shut. But it was terrible enough, just knowing."

"When was this?" I asked.

"Yesterday they drove me down here to look at Janine's room and see if she took anything." Her eyes overflowed, and she hunted for something to wipe them with. I gave her a tissue.

"You must be worried about Janine."

"Yes, but it's not just that. It's *them.*" She pointed at the house. "How can it look just the same after something like that's happened to it? Why doesn't it *show?* It's as if nobody cared. As if *God* didn't care! I mean, it ought to look *different,*" she said fiercely. "Marked, somehow. And how can something like that happen to people like them? I just can't understand it!"

"Neither can I, Tracy," I said. "It couldn't, it shouldn't, but it did." The words tolled in my head.

"I know when Aunt Marianne was young everybody thought she was immoral, and I know about the money *he* stole, but that was a long time ago. Who'd hate her now? And what did Aunt Emma ever do wrong? And I *am* scared about Janine!" she blurted.

"Don't you think she's safe with Sonny somewhere?"

She kept biting at her lower lip; already it looked raw. "Mr. Jensen asked me what I knew, so I told him, because I was so scared for her, specially after I saw she hadn't taken *one* thing, not even a jacket or her pocketbook. Do you think I was disloyal to her, to tell?"

She was pathetically eager for some kind of comfort. "What could you tell that could hurt her, the way things are?" I patted the rock beside me. "Sit down."

She sat hunched over, her arms folded tightly across her belly. "I'd been asked down to have supper and spend the night with Janine, because they were going out to dinner at the Carvers', and they didn't want to leave her alone on account of Lucas, right? Well, she *knew* Sonny was coming that night if he could make it. Some boy who just got out called and told her. Sonny asked him to. Do you think they'll arrest her for not telling?"

"No," I said. "It's nothing, compared to everything else. Besides, the Cruikshanks wouldn't allow it." Their name convinced her.

"So after the boy called her, she called me, when they were practicing and Mrs. Thatcher was outside, and she asked me to make up some excuse to stay home. I mean, my parents *wanted* me to go, right? Like I'd be the heiress if I did everything right," she said sarcastically. "But she wanted to be alone when Sonny came, so she could talk him into going back. She wanted to do that more than she was afraid of Lucas, and she said she'd keep everything locked up and stuff. Sonny would've listened to her, Eden. Like he just wanted to see for himself she was OK—so where are they now?"

She looked sick, and I felt pretty sick myself, but you instinctively try to hide this from children. "I think you were right to tell Lieutenant Jensen, and it can't make any difference to Sonny and Janine now. It wouldn't change anything."

"You mean if they're dead," she said starkly.

"No, I wasn't thinking that, and don't you dare think it, either. But what you told about them is past history. What excuse did you give your mother that night?"

"I said I had this summer complaint that's going around," she said. "Of course it meant I had to spend all the time in bed from when she called me and pretend I was running to the bathroom all the time. I had to take Kaopectate and not eat, but it was for a good cause. I guess." Her sigh seemed to come up from her toes. "I think something's happened to them," she said in despair. "I don't think they ran away."

"The police think they're alive somewhere," I told her. "Sonny may have stolen a car or been lent one, and they've taken off in that. They'll turn up, or they'll call when they get their breath. You can't tell. Janine might be in such a state of shock Sonny's got his hands taking care of her."

"They must be some scared," she said. "Maybe they saw who did it." But she brightened with the comfort of imagining them holed up somewhere, terrified but alive. "You know, I liked coming here after a while. I mean, I used to think, oh, yuck, who wants to sit around with a couple of old women and listen to old dead music, just in case they might leave you a few dollars? And it turned my stomach to hear Dad and Esmond going on and on about what they'd do with Fox Point. Tear down this place, to start with." She gazed at the house. "It's like an animal, isn't it? I mean, it doesn't *know.* But it must miss the music."

She wiped her eyes again. "When they first came home, and Dad and Esmond talked about the place, it was like they had them already put in their coffins. It grossed me out. Well, *I* wasn't going to go smarming around. Then that happened to Janine, and they were so *nice* to her—"

"You figured you could honestly like them without wanting anything from them."

"But it was too late. There wasn't any time left, but we didn't know it." She gave me a shamefaced and watery grin. "I was even practicing to call them *Aunt* to their faces. Just the little while Janine was here before it happened, I was getting to know them. Aunt Emma was so sweet, but she could be funny, too. It was like she was still a girl inside. The one who played the violin was another person." She blushed. "Does this make sense?"

"Plenty of sense," I said, "and I hope this is doing you good, Tracy, because I think it's helping me. What about your other aunt?" I was actually saying it, actually conjuring Marianne up before me, as if she were listening with that ironic and yet indulgent little smile.

"Well, before Janine, she could make me feel like a fat dumb brat just by being in the same room. She was so straight and so handsome and kind of regal. I thought, I'll always be be a mess, no sense trying to be anything different. Then *after* Janine, she was somebody different. I'd have run my legs off for her. And it wasn't dead music they played. I was getting not to mind it." I gave her another tissue, and she blew her nose. "I'd have been bragging about my aunts by the time I started school, you know? Oh, *God!*" she cried. "Three days ago it was Sunday, and they were alive, and Janine was safe!"

I patted her. It wasn't much, but I've always appreciated a friendly pat (like Chad), and I could have used one right now. "You're going to look like her, Tracy," I said.

"I am?" she said incredulously through her tears. "Like Aunt Marianne? I never can!"

"Today I could see it for the first time," I lied. "It comes and goes, but it's there."

"I've got blue eyes, that's all."

"Yes, and you shouldn't hide them all the time. But it's also in the cheekbones and the line of your jaw. It shows when you put your shoulders back and lift your chin. It'll come with a little help from you."

"Losing about twenty-five pounds, you mean." But she was mournfully pleased. "Thanks, Eden, I needed somebody to talk to today, so I owe you one."

"I know, you're going to promise to read my books."

She said seriously, "I've read them, and they're neat. Nope, it's something else, and don't tell it. Wait till you hear it from somewhere else, because it's going to get around some fast. Oh, boy, will it *ever* spread fast!" She was grimly triumphant.

"Should you be telling it?" I asked, for conscience' sake. But the writer was still alive somewhere in the smog.

"I don't know and I don't care!" Tracy said. "My brother's an arsehole and always has been. Excuse me, but that's just what he is. They've always treated him like the crown prince to the Hearne Empire or something. If I ever told them how many times I had to lock myself in the bathroom to get away from him when he was supposed to be taking care of me, I guess the you-know-what would hit the fan all right."

Somehow I wasn't surprised. "Just out of curiosity, why didn't you ever tell?"

"Because my mother would cry, and if my father believed me—he's got a temper you wouldn't believe—he might have beaten Esmond up. And Mum would cry even more, and everybody would know there was a dirty mess at the Hearnes'. Anyway, I learned young never to let him sneak up on me, and I could kick and bite like mad, you know? The last time, I was twelve. They went out, and he was supposed to be right home to have supper with me, right?" She was taking a black satisfaction in this. "I had just enough time to get ready. When he came in the door, I met him with his own shotgun. It wasn't loaded, because I didn't know how, but I told him it was. I drove him out of the house, and I told him if he came back before they did I'd shoot him for sure and tell everybody he tried to rape me."

"My God, Tracy," I said faintly. And then I saw, in the arrogant lift and turn of her head and the quirk of her mouth, a genuine resemblance to Marianne. It was quickly gone, but I had seen it.

"That isn't what I meant when I started to talk," she said. "Yesterday Dad calls the Cruikshanks as soon as he's over the first shock and says that as the nearest relative he'll be making the arrangements for the funerals as soon as the police give him the green light. That's what he actually said. As if funerals aren't gross enough. And how could he stand to be talking about *theirs?*" she appealed to me. "Well, anyway, Mr. C. Sr. talks then, and Dad turns white as a codfish, and his mouth keeps opening and closing like one. After a while he hangs up without a word, right? My mother's flopped in a chair with her hand on her heart—she gets palpitation under stress—and he goes, 'They made their own arrangements! They're going to be cremated! Without any services!' And he falls into the nearest chair and sits there staring into space."

"Of course they'd have everything taken care of," I said. "It was the way they were."

"My mother goes in this weak voice, 'It's just as well, I couldn't bear to go through it,' and 'Did they say what they wanted done with the ashes?' Well, this was getting too much for me. I wanted to cover my ears and run, but still I didn't, you know? I mean, I wasn't even used to their being dead. I just found out, and he was already *burying* them!"

I nodded. I couldn't have spoken.

"Now this is what really slammed Daddy in the gut. Mr. C. Jr. and *Kenneth Rigby* are in charge. You know what that means? *Kenneth?* No wonder Dad turned white, and Esmond's bracing himself with booze, you can smell it on him all the time. They've always said such cheap things about him, and now they're scared foolish that he's the heir. Dad knows already *he* isn't the executor, so he hasn't seen their wills yet, but he and Esmond are some sick. They were so sure, because Dad's mother was their sister. And I'm laughing." It was more of a gulping sob.

26

After that Tracy had nothing to say. The reaction set in, and she looked sulky and dull. "I'd better start back," she said.

She walked her bicycle down the driveway with me to where I'd left mine, which was cold and wet from the bracken. I thought she was repenting her confidences and now couldn't stand the sight of me, but she said suddenly, "If I make it all the way down to the harbor some day, can I come in?"

"I'll be mad if you don't," I said. "And don't worry about anything you told me. I'm a good keeper of secrets."

"I know you're honorable," she said, surprisingly. "Your father is Mr. Winter." She set off up Sunday Hill, working hard, standing up on the pedals. I went the other way, focusing on what I'd just heard, trying to keep everything straight so I could write it all down as soon as I got home. For what good I didn't know, except that by taking any kind of action I felt less at the mercy of events. It was like steering in the direction of a dangerous skid.

I was coasting along, all alone in the world, when from the corner of my right eye I saw a tree move. It was Gideon Wilkes. He stood by his mailbox, his fatigues blending into his background. A grey and white cat leaned against his legs. His gaunt, bearded face was shadowed under the broad brim of his Allegash hat, which is like an Australian bush hat; usually he wore it with one side of the brim rakishly turned up, but not today. From its shadow his eyes were like distant points of light.

"I thought you were a tree," I said.

"Birnam wood on the march, eh?" His voice was colorless. Here was another one who had been gravely wounded. He picked up the cat, which put white forelegs around his neck and sniffed at his beard.

"Well, see you, Gideon," I said. He nodded, and I rode away. Meeting him and Tracy had nudged me off self-center, so I was forced to remember the others besides Gram, Fee, and myself for whom this was an intimate tragedy. For the much older ones, like Clem Sr. and the Carvers, it could shatter what was left of their lives. Gram hadn't bragged yesterday about how tough they were; she had cried out, "I can't take this!"

I wasn't alone on the road for long. The Temple boys came racing toward me below the Beaver Dam, neck and neck on either side of the yellow line. They yelled at me as they passed me, did some fancy figures in the middle of the road behind me, and then fell in with me like an escort. After the exhilarated shouts they were now stuck fast in a torturous silence. Their young faces were severe as they tried to think of something to say within safe limits. I knew they'd been told by their parents not to hang around me making pests of themselves by asking questions. Now they'd caught me by accident, which made them blameless, but they didn't know what to do with their luck. They were consumed with horrified curiosity, but they had an innocent delicacy about saying so.

They were my silent outriders until we reached their mailbox, and I stopped. So did they, gazing at me with those yearning eyes. "Listen, kids," I said. "They were my friends, and I don't want to talk about it. I don't talk about it even with my own family. OK?"

"OK!" The quick sympathy lighting their faces almost did me in. "Can we say we're sorry?" Ben asked gruffly.

"Yes, and thank you."

Sternly they gave me identical choppy nods and spun their bikes around. "So long, Eden!" they shouted as they sped off. I went down our road where the scent from the ever-blooming rose hedge flowed out to surround me, and with it another of those damned scraps that make my brain a ragbag.

I shall never be friends again with roses,
I shall hate sweet music my whole life long.

This time it could be the truth.

* * *

Chad was busy down on the wharf where Jon's boat was in. The men were hoisting baskets of pogies up to the bait shed, and the acrid deep-sea tang undercut the scent of roses. I made coffee and warmed two doughnuts. While I had my mug-up I wrote my account of the morning, including Tracy's earthy opinion and indictment of Esmond. I used to wonder if I was being unfair to him simply because he was unattractive, but now I knew that Fee and I had always been right about him. There was also a small satisfaction in seeing that pompous, chauvinistic Morrie Hearne brought up with a round turn by the quiet existence of Kenneth Rigby.

Afterwards I burned everything in my Franklin stove. Filling all those lined pages by hand had taken me back to the days when I stuffed notebooks with long Gothic novels set in the Maine equivalent of moors and haunted countrysides full of evil or psychic or golden-hearted peasants. I would write a chapter in bed every night, and at the end of the week Fee greedily read them. "I don't know how you do it!" she'd keep saying. I didn't know, either. With the help of the Ouija board we were convinced that the Brontës were dictating to me. I think we assisted the board to reach its conclusions, but we would never admit it; I did think the Brontës might have picked me to carry the torch, if they could have. But whenever I read the stuff over a few months later, I knew I wasn't their nominee.

But it had been wondrously exciting to settle down with a thick new notebook and a mugful of ballpoint pens, think up a provocative first sentence, and then let 'er rip. It had also been a superb escape from my troubles. Today I had a couple of thick new notebooks and plenty of pens. I arranged myself at the table, shut my eyes, and saw a female figure, minute with distance, walking along a surf-lashed beach at the foot of stark red cliffs. Sometimes she stopped and picked something up. Sometimes she shaded her eyes and looked out over the turbulent waters.

As I began to write, I knew this was how the alcoholic or drug addict feels when he finally gets his drink or his fix. Who'd want to give up that marvelous moment when your life shudders back into your own hands? The difference was that my addiction earned my living; whatever filled this notebook just might end up as a best-seller and a sensational television mini-series. Just might, and probably wouldn't. I didn't care as I plunged in. I wasn't writing to sell.

I was roused by Chad's paean of joy, car doors, and voices. I wouldn't have heard them if I hadn't reached the point where my cramped hand didn't want to move. Someone had built a bonfire on the back of my neck, and my feet had gone to sleep hooked around the legs of my chair.

Aunt Eleanor was bringing Gram home, and it was almost three in the afternoon. I was written out, but now I had something to which I could return. I wandered through the house, rubbing my neck and wriggling my shoulders. Gram had the teakettle on and was sitting at the table sorting the mail.

"We went to that Chinese restaurant for lunch," she said without looking up. "I'm drier than a cork leg and dying for a good cup of real tea."

"How was the museum show?" I asked, putting tea bags in two cups.

"How would it be, if it's Sim Trescott? That's all I'm going to say because I couldn't do it justice anyway." She gave me a pawky look over her glasses, and I felt a little spark of pleasure—it was so typical. "You get on your horse and go up and see it yourself."

"Yes, Gram," I said meekly.

"And you can take these papers and read them if you've got the stomach for it. Just bring them back later for your grandfather. *I'm* having nothing to do with them." She shoved them across at me. "Get them out of my sight."

I put them on the back stairs. "I don't know if I want to read them, either," I said. I poured boiling water in the cups, judged the color, and took out the bags. She watched me as I carried the tea to the table, concentrating on not slopping.

"I'm all right," I said. "Are you?"

"I'm not thinking about us. Eden, guess what?"

"What?" I asked. She had undeniably changed since this morning. There was color in her face, and her glance was full of spirit.

"I made a scene on Maddox Main Street! Yes, I did, and I don't care who knows it! It's been something I've been aching to do for years, and now I wish I'd done it earlier."

"Make a scene on Main Street?" I said. "What an ambition!"

"*No!*" She flapped a hand at me. "Shoot down the Harpies!" She shone with unholy joy.

"Tell me, tell me!"

"Well, when we came back to Maddox from Tenby, I had Eleanor drop me off on Main Street so I could go into the drugstore while she was taking your mother home. And when I came out, who was holding a convocation on the sidewalk right outside, but the Three and a couple of their hangers-on. I spoke civilly and was going right along, but Clara Fitton sounds off like the noon whistle. 'Well, Vinca, you've had some excitement down your way, haven't you?' Sometime I'm going to tell her that her dentures *look* like dentures from half a mile away. 'What excitement?' says I, looking vacant."

She showed me how vacant. "'Come on, Vinca dear,' Dora Sayers says. 'You know all about the ax murders. Didn't Eden just miss him?' And Sarita Barron chimes in with, 'It was a crazy idea, those two taking that girl to live with them. They should've known what she'd bring there.' 'You mean like bedbugs?' I asked, still trying to get away. But Clara had me right *here.*" Gram rubbed her forearm.

"Ungodly cold fingers, she's got, too. 'Now you know what we're talking about, Vinca,' she says. 'Mary Ann Esmond never did think about consequences. She always went her own way, never mind whose face she walked on or whose home she wrecked. Well, now she's got hers, hasn't she? Too bad Emma hadn't the sense to stay away from her.'" Gram sat back and took a long breath. "What do you think of that?"

"All this was actually being said out loud, on Main Street?"

"*Loud* is right," she nodded violently. "Spang in front of the drugstore, and never mind who's sitting on the bench waiting for Greyhound, and all the people going along the sidewalk. Those three were wound up and spitting acid. The fringe began to fade away; they'd have run like rabbits if they weren't all past it. I couldn't believe my ears, I didn't think even those three would sink so low. Sarita says with that sighing, sticky way of hers, 'I'm surprised she's lived this long. Sometimes you wonder if there's any justice or even a God, the way we were brought up to believe.' Clara's waggling her head like one of those idiotic dolls you see in the back windows of cars. Then Dora says in a mincy little voice with her mouth puckered up as if she'd been eating sour pickles, 'But it comes at last, doesn't it? As ye sow, so shall ye reap.'"

"I'm surprised you didn't take a swing at her with your pocketbook," I said.

"I wouldn't lower myself to brawling in public," Gram said seriously. "I don't hold with physical violence among the elderly. It's undignified. But I told *her,* I told all three. Very clearly. Giving each word its due importance. I said I was looking forward to the harvest *they* were going to reap from all the rotten seed they'd been sowing for years. If there was any of this justice they'd been blatting about, something would reap *them* with a big scythe, and there wouldn't be enough left of them to bury, and that wouldn't be fit to use for fertilizer."

She took a long swig of tea. "Ah, good," she murmured. "And you know what? I got a round of applause from somewhere! I don't know where, but I heard it all right. And I just walked off and left them there gaping, and I felt *good!*"

"I would have felt good, too," I said. "But better if I could have given them all a few hard kicks in the shins before I left."

"Eleanor was parked farther along, waiting for me. She didn't know what was going on, but I had to tell her because she could see I was different, just the way I walked. She congratulated me. And now I'm some tired," she said with a catch in her voice. "I'm going to change my dress and lie down."

"Gram, I congratulate you, too," I said. I leaned over her chair and kissed her.

"Get out before I overflow," she ordered me.

I read the pertinent pieces in Grampa's Bangor paper and the midweek *Tenby Journal* for the same reason I had forced myself to go to Fox Point this morning. You keep hoping that if you look the monster in the eye long enough it will go away, or at least grow small enough to manage.

The two stories were substantially the same, with differences in the phrasing and emphasis. The Bangor paper went into more details about the sisters' musical careers. The murder weapon had been determined to be an ax, not found; the police had no definite suspect yet, but many useful leads. Robbery might or might not have been the motive. It was possible that the women had returned home from a dinner engagement and surprised the intruders before they could thoroughly ransack the house. Mrs. Rigby's piano hadn't been vandalized, but a violin was smashed; however this was not Miss Emma Esmond's Amati, which was upstairs with several other valuable instruments. The housekeeper was expected to tell the police whether anything had been stolen or not.

A search was being conducted for a young girl whom the sisters had taken into their home and a local youth who was an escapee from the Maine Youth Center.

The Tenby article was more personal. The writer said that everyone who knew the missing boy swore that he couldn't have committed such a crime. His parents were distraught and suspected foul play. The girl's father, in jail awaiting trial on an alleged assault and battery charge, was pleading to be released so he could join the search for her.

Both stories named me as the discoverer, calling me a well-known Maine novelist. It was a nice puff, that, but I wasn't able to appreciate it. When I finished reading, I slumped with fatigue and that one big ache which is worse than actual pain, because it is an ache of the mind and spirit, and there is nothing you can take for it. It had already become a constant in my life.

I lay down on my bed and fell asleep without a struggle. I dreamed that the murderer was somewhere in the vicinity, but out of sight. The other people and the setting were known to me with the familiarity you experience in dreams, even when they don't exist in your waking life. Everything was well lit, spacious, ordinary. Even my anxiety about the murderer was not acute, though I kept wanting to know where he was.

"He's out on his coffee break," an invisible companion told me.

"Oh, well!" I answered blithely. "As long as he can't see me, he doesn't worry me." Then I thought I'd better wake up before he came back.

I was too hot from the afternoon sun coming in on me. There was a terrible taste in my mouth, and I was stiff from lying like a log for hours. *Coffee break.* Nick had called me on his coffee break. So what? I wasn't psychic. The murderer was a transient maniac. A chair creaked out in the kitchen; I nearly fell off the bed, stifling my groans, and went out there trembling.

Glen sat in my rocker with his feet on the windowsill, reading the papers. "Wash your face and comb your hair," he said without looking around. "I brought in a mess of lobsters, and we're going over to my place. You need a change of scenery."

"Yup," I said. "Will you take those papers back to the house?" I got clean clothes and tottered into the bathroom. A tepid shower and a shampoo returned me to full consciousness and mobility once more.

We sat on the cabin's deck looking out at Bugle Bay and cracking hot lobsters. When we were full, we gathered up the mess and took the shells down to the rocks to leave for whatever found them first, the raccoons tonight or the gulls and crows in the morning; it would probably be the raccoons. We ate peaches afterwards, dead ripe and running with juice. The twilight came on clear as liquid amethyst, and then the boundaries of day disappeared. We had long, restful patches of silence except for the crickets, and miraculously unspoiled by mosquitoes.

"I saw Fee today," Glen said all at once. "I was hauling to the south'ard of Tamarack, and she came rowing the dory around the Noggin Rocks. Surprised hell out of me. I thought she was on the mainland with Julian."

"How was she?" I asked. "Did you talk?"

"Oh, sure, we talked," he said sourly. "She whistled and waved and came up alongside all smiling. She'd been fishing."

"She was *smiling?*"

"Smiling," he repeated. "And inside of five minutes I felt like slapping her arse. I'd have done it if I could have hauled her out of that dory and across the washboard. You know what she's up to?"

"No," I said faintly. "Why was she smiling?" Lobster had never made me queasy before.

"Remember that Ouija board you two used to play with? Well, she's trying to raise *them* on it, to find out who did it. That's all she could talk about. She'll be through to them anytime, she says, because she's got *contacts.*" He sounded the way I felt. "I wanted to shake her till her teeth rattled. It's not decent."

I hadn't seen him so upset since the day of his father's funeral. I was badly disturbed myself, but I could understand Fee.

"She was so crazy about them, Glen," I said. "She just can't give them up. She has to find comfort in her own way. Julian's nice to cry on, I suppose, but I'd rather have you than a man-sized teddy bear, because I know you're hearing what I say." I put my arms about him, but he was unyielding in my embrace. "This is hitting everybody in a different way because they mean—meant—something different to everyone. Maybe for Fee it's like this because she hardly knew her mother and never a grandmother."

"I never knew them, either," he said.

"We're talking about Fee. I knew she missed them when we were kids. She always acted so tough when I was as easily frightened as a baby chick, but I soon found out she was just as easily bruised. It didn't show on her, that's all."

"Scares me," Glen said abruptly. "The old man never could stand on a straight course. And when I can get so mad at her, *I* scare me."

"It's only because you love her. It's natural for you to be upset, and then you feel like slapping her. Besides, you ought to fly off the handle once in a while just to show us weaker critters that you're human." I squeezed him around the middle as hard as I could, and finally he returned the embrace. We settled comfortably against the warm logs. The raccoons were out in the dusk, rattling the lobster shells, occasionally growling.

"I can't dislike Julian," he said after a while. "It would be like not liking Chad. But something you said back there about my hearing you—who's going to hear *her?* Do you realize he'll be as helpless as this in any crisis not connected with carpentry or a boat? As long as she stays with him, she'll have to face everything all soul alone, because she's too damn proud to ever come to one of us for comfort."

"She chose him," I said. "There wasn't a thing you could do about it."

"Yep. And in time she'll choose the bottle and her spooks. Can you see them out on that island fifteen, twenty years from now? In the words of that great thinker Sprig Newsome, don't that gag a maggot?"

"How'd Sprig get into this?" I said, to redeem the moment. Glen's vision was a nasty one, and I refused to believe in it. I'd been forced to believe in too much nastiness this week. "Look, things can change all at once. Any time now she can really fall for someone who's as bright as she is."

"She'll feel responsible for Julian forever," he said. "I'm hoping like hell that she isn't pregnant."

"Can't we go out there Sunday?" I asked. "Maybe all she needs is a chance to talk it out, and then I can get her to ease up with the Ouija board. We won't let her isolate herself with it, Glen. I can be a worst pest than a whole swarm of black flies."

While I spoke with such energetic resolve, it had me worn out before I'd even begun. But Glen's cautious elevation from depression to hope gave me a large infusion of courage. I couldn't let him or Fee down. "Fortitude," I said aloud. "That was the word on the calendar. Remember?"

27

Glen walked back to the harbor with me around midnight. Our footsteps on the road were the only sounds until a fox barked in Uncle Early's woods and was answered. Then a rustling and scratching meant that a porcupine was climbing a tree. Turning down the driveway toward the harbor, we could hear the far-off noise of gulls. The herring were thick this year, and we could smell them on the damp southerly breeze stirring the poplar leaves, as it had done at Fox Point on that night. Suddenly the fog horn began over at St. David's; there was fog out there, or at least enough moisture in the air to trigger the automated signal.

We kissed good night inside the Hayloft. "Thank you for everything, Glen," I said. "Thank you for being."

"Ayuh," he said.

"I know women are forever trying to climb aboard you because they crave your body, but you don't have to sound so blasé."

He laughed and gave me a companionable slap on the rump. "Get into bed before you wake up too much, and thanks for letting me rave about Fee."

"We both love her, don't we?"

He didn't speak but wrapped his arms around me again and put his face in my hair. "Be sure you lock up. He's probably long gone, but I'd feel better about you."

I promised, and when I was bolting the door behind him I found the folded note on the floor. It was from Nick, written on a leaf from a pocket diary. "Sorry I missed you, but I talked with your folks and they say you're holding up like a champion. I'm not surprised. See you soon, I hope.—Yours, Nick."

I was touched, but dammit, the man was a stranger, and could have as many facets as a diamond. Angry but not sure why, I got into bed and wrote until I could hardly hold the pen and dozed every time I closed my eyes for a moment. Then I put out my light and slept.

The promised fog was there in the morning when I woke up around five. I went back to work on the notebook along with my coffee and muffin. I felt safe in the fog; time hadn't really come to a stop, but it felt that way. Gram came in the late morning to invite me to fish chowder at noon. She didn't mention current events, and neither did I; I was pretty well written out and ready for chowder. The story was developing so many tantalizing characters and far-out twists that I was tempted to keep thinking about it after I stopped, but that was against the rules. The notebook would lose its power if I broke them. The important thing was to know it was there within reach.

I was selfishly disappointed when the fog burned off and the day cleared to a breezy, bespangled, blue afternoon. I hated it because *they* weren't alive in it; it was the third day they hadn't been alive, and the fact had not yet begun, even slightly, to lose its edge. At regular intervals, except when I was safe in the notebook, an iron boot kicked me in the belly, and I walked into that living room again and saw them. It was for only a flashing instant, like a Hitchcock trick, but it was enough.

It happened when I was going through the open chamber on the way to the Hayloft after the meal, and it immobilized me for that glaring moment. When it released me I didn't take time to think. I went back downstairs to the kitchen. Grampa had already returned to the wharf, but Gram sat at the table, sadly sorting out recipes, the way I'd tried to tidy my bureau drawers that day.

"Come on, Gram," I said. "Let's go somewhere. You choose. We'll go north, south, east, or west, wherever you say."

"Let's go inland," she said at once. "There's a fair at Barlow Mills, and they're having a big quilt show. I saw a poster for it in Maddox." She shoveled everything back into the English biscuit tin. "Are you going dressed like that?"

"No, I am not going dressed like that. I'll meet you at my car."

"Run down and tell your grandfather, will you?" She was on her way up to the bedroom.

It was a long and pretty drive inland, and when we got there, we didn't miss anything from the livestock to the quilt exhibit. It was a big fair, and we kept charged up by stops at every booth that offered food and drink. Gram doesn't care for canned soft drinks except ginger ale, and neither do I, but the Girl Scouts had a lemonade stand, and the ladies running the quilt exhibit were dispensing tea in real cups, not Styrofoam. There was also a place to sit and admire; the quilts were worth the whole expedition. Gram got into conversation with some of the designers and makers, and I was happy to see her having a happy time.

We didn't get home until it was time to put supper on the table, and Grampa had it ready. Gram and I didn't need much after eating our way through the fair.

I slept well until the boats began going out at dawn on Saturday, and then I got up and worked in my notebook. As soon as the sun was high enough to dry the dew on the deck, I went out there to work during the quiet time before people began coming by car or boat to buy lobsters for the Labor Day weekend. I was briefly distracted when the Barry outboard motor blasted into action; Toby waved to me as they started out. I wondered if they had after-holiday plans for certain isolated summer cottages, but I didn't wonder for long; I saw them as through a glass, darkly, which was only natural because I was wearing dark glasses. I had forgotten them before the awful clatter of their engine died away outside Fort Point.

Because Chad was down in the store with Grampa, I didn't know Nick was here until he was coming up the steps; he hadn't slammed his car door. He was wearing dark glasses, too.

I closed my notebook. "Are we in disguise?" I inquired.

"Yeah. We are playing a Mafia prince named Niccolo Machiavelli."

"Good old Nicco," I said sentimentally. "Thank you for the note." I realized I wasn't feeling any instant shock of revulsion.

He sat on the railing and looked out at the harbor. "I guess a few folks do think I'm a Mafia prince under another name, working my way up the ladder by getting experiences in the field. Setting up a new arrival-and-distribution point for drugs." He gave me a savage grin, as if he held a knife in his teeth.

"Well, it wouldn't be all that farfetched," I said. "Not necessarily you doing it, but the drug-runners are finding the Maine coast pretty irresistible, especially when they can get the natives in on it, people whose names have been here since before we were a state. Their forefathers worked their guts out and went to war to hold onto the land so their descendants can prostitute it. And how they love pimping for the crime lords!" This is a favorite hate of mine. "I think some of them would sell their daughters or sisters for the right price."

"Why don't you write a book about it?"

"I guess I will, damn it. I loathe them more than I loathe their bosses." I subsided. "Sorry. I guess it's a relief to have something I can legitimately howl about; everything else is too enormous for mere screams."

He nodded absently and returned to his study of the harbor. "Hey, wait a minute," I said. "Is somebody actually giving you a hard time?"

He shrugged. "Just straws in the wind so far. Nothing official yet. My landlords haven't given me notice, and I'm still on the Glenroy payroll. What I feel is only the natural suspicion directed toward the undocumented outsider, I guess, and it doesn't come from everybody."

"What about the police?"

"They haven't got to me yet, but they will. They aren't just sitting around waiting for those two kids to be discovered. They'll be putting all the dark horses over the high jumps, and I may be the darkest. I don't mean *this.*" He shoved his fingers through his black hair. "That night I was out of sight of anybody who can identify me—from the time the Tenby cop and I put Gilly into my car until I talked with the deputy by the Fox Point mailbox. Gilly won't remember a thing, and I have no other witnesses except the kids in the station wagon." His mouth was sardonic; I couldn't see his eyes. "I could take out an ad in the paper, begging them to come forward, but they probably won't. It'll turn out that none of them were supposed to be up on the mountain that night. Go on, admit the whole story sounds insane."

"Oh, for heaven's sake, Nick!" I flared out. "Don't go hanging yourself before the police have even thought of it! And they may never get to you!" I had called it insane, and now I was perversely defending him to himself, still not knowing what he was.

"What do you bet? I'm not slopping around in self-pity, my sweet Eden. I'm in a cold shower called reality. If I can't prove I was where I said I was, and that I am what I am, Chad will be an albino compared to this dark horse."

"And just what are you, Nick?"

He stood up, smiling, and opened his arms wide like a performer embracing his audience. "Just what you see! A ship carpenter with a gold ring in one ear as a charm against drowning. A caul is better, but they're hard to find.... You're trying, but you're not quite sure, are you?"

"What I see is all I know of you. So as far as I'm concerned it *is* what you are. Fee calls you Young Frobisher, by the way."

He bowed. "I'm honored."

"Nick, getting back to what you said about drugs, is it possible that they could have—I mean—" I was stumbling all over myself, and he took it away from me.

"People running drugs want to be invisible. They don't go in for vandalism and spectacular forms of murder. And that cove's no good for a drop, unless another boat does the pickup, because there's no way for a vehicle to get to it. I sound suspiciously knowledgeable, don't I? But it's just common sense."

"I don't know whether you're reassuring or not," I said as my stomach began that slow, disgusting heave again.

"You want it to be someone from away," he said. "But you know that the use of drugs is a fact of life even in Maine, and somebody spaced out on speed or angel dust, looking for stuff they can steal to support their habit—yes, that's crossed my mind. And I'm sure Jensen's thinking about it, too."

"But nobody in Whittier—" I began instinctively and then was angry with myself. "Oh, damn it, I don't *know* about everybody in Whittier! I don't pick up kids along the Whittier road the way I used to. I'm wary of the ones I haven't known practically from birth."

Nick walked restlessly around the deck with his hands in his pockets. "Jensen's not sitting there with his feet on the desk, drinking coffee while they're looking for Sonny and Janine. He's working his way down a list. He'll get to everybody sooner or later, and in the meantime you can bet he's talking to a lot of people on the outer edges, hoping for names."

"You're sure you're not a crime writer?"

He stopped with his back to me and appeared to be watching something in the sky. I looked up, too. Three shags flew low and fast over the house on their way from the harbor to Bugle Bay. Above them gulls glided on currents of air we couldn't feel down here; and above the gulls, so high that if you tried too hard to see him you kept losing him, an eagle rode the wind.

"Ah, look at that," I whispered.

Silently we watched, our heads strained back. My neck hurt and my eyes kept blurring, but I hated to blink for fear he would disappear. It seemed imperative that I should not lose him until he was ready to go.

"What I really came down here to tell you," Nick said, still staring upward, "is that they've been cremated, and yesterday afternoon Marianne Rigby's ashes were scattered, with her husband's, on the waters off Fox Point."

I shut my eyes and let the eagle go. How could this be? How could they have ended and disappeared in four days as the bird had gone in the blink of an eye?

"*Eden.*" Nick was holding both my hands. I squinted at him until he became clear.

"Where is Miss Emma?" I asked in a croaky voice.

"In the family cemetery." He released my hands and sat on the railing opposite me. "You know Bourne, the funeral director in Maddox? His son works at the yard. He told us his father and older brother had to drive inland in the morning to the crematory. I don't think he's supposed to talk about these things, but it was making him important for once in his life. Everybody's had something to say about what's happened, and that's his bit. He managed to convey just who the clients were, or whatever they call them, without saying the names right out."

"Nick, I *hate* this!" I burst out. I started to get up, but he reached across and took my hands again, so strongly that I couldn't even wiggle them.

"No, listen, Eden. We're friends, aren't we? God, I hope so! I could use one." I slumped back into the chair. "I keep my mouth shut everywhere. Nobody at the yard knows I ever went to Fox Point; the Bains don't know it. It's a part of my life I wanted to keep separate. But I have to talk to someone about this, can't you see?" Tremors ran from his hands into mine. "Somebody who can understand, just a little bit, what they meant to me."

It shamed me. "But will you just unsqueeze? My hands are going numb."

"I'm sorry." He let them go and began rubbing first one and then the other. "The Cruikshanks went to Augusta, too, and Kenneth Rigby. So they weren't alone." He cleared his throat. "I mean, there must have been something, a few words, maybe a prayer. Music. There'd have to be music for them, wouldn't there?"

I nodded mutely. He stopped rubbing my hands and held them again. "In the afternoon we saw Kenneth Rigby's Friendship sloop coming down river, all winged out. You know one of the most beautiful lines ever written? 'Speed, bonnie boat, like a bird on the wing.' And that's what she looked like. Rigby was at the tiller, and the younger Cruikshank was with him. 'See, there they go!' the Bourne kid yelled. 'On the way to Fox Point!'"

He released my hands and began pacing the deck like a prisoner in a small cell. "They've got to be *somewhere,*" he said. "They couldn't have ended just like *that.* The sight and the sounds of them are still in my eyes and ears, for God's sake! I can't believe some lunatic came in with an ax and destroyed it all!"

"*Don't!*" I implored. He was back at the railing, gripping it, but not seeing the harbor below us. His eyes were squeezed shut, his mouth set in a grimace, and tears were running down the brown cheek nearest me and glinting in his beard. I took his arm. "Come inside," I said. He came, and I shut the door behind us.

"It wasn't all blarney, you know," he said. His chest was rising and falling quickly with his effort to calm himself. "You thought it was, but I really worshipped those two. I'd never known anyone like them." He wiped his face with his hand as clumsily as Tracy had done. "Just to be allowed to come freely into their house was such a privilege. God, I'd have done anything for them! But I couldn't save their lives, and I'll never get over that."

We reached out simultaneously and hung on to each other with all our might while we wept. It was a short but intense storm. Then we stood apart, grinning weakly at each other and snuffling. I got us a handful of tissues, and we blew our noses. "I don't know if I could have done that with anybody else," I said. "Gone at it so hard, I mean, except maybe with Fee, but she's out of reach right now. I hope you're not ashamed of letting go."

"Why should I be?" he asked simply. "The last time I did that was when my mother died, and I felt the same outraged disbelief. I was fifteen, and I thought she was the only friend I had in the world."

"And was she?"

"I had my kid sister, who was just as sunk and who needed me. And our stepfather turned out to be a pretty decent guy, considering that he'd been left the care of two kids who'd resented him from the start."

"Yesterday was a perfect day for sailing," I said. While Gram and I had visited the fair, it had been happening. "She'd have liked that. We have to believe she knew, she and Guy. They were—*are*—more than a handful of ashes."

"I wonder whom Miss Emma went to," he said. I wished I could imagine her young as an apple blossom and running to meet a lover, instead of remembering that less than two weeks ago she'd been setting out plants in the family cemetery.

"There was someone, I'm sure," I said. "Have some tea or coffee? Sorry I don't have any of the hard stuff."

"Thanks, but I'm leaving. It doesn't do to prolong some things." He took me into his arms and kissed me. "Some time, if I can avoid entanglement with a drunk, will you go out with me?"

"Sure. Just don't go near the Brookside Bakery first."

"That place is permanently in quarantine for me. Look, right now I don't know what's going to happen from one day to the next, I haven't a lucid idea in my head, but when I get one I'll call you. All right?"

"All right," I repeated. When I said it, I had the first fragile intimation that some day time would begin to move at its usual pace again instead of inching through dreadful hours, and that the pictures which lived day and night with me would fade, even if they never disappeared, just as my uncle had promised me.

28

Sunday was the last day for those out-of-state summer people who had to leave to put their children in school the day after Labor Day. This one was raw and cloudy, with a mean little northeast breeze that whistled around the Hayloft door in a wintery key. Even with the inside door shut, I could hear the sad song through the screen. Those who left today to avoid the Labor Day traffic would get some satisfaction from the weather; when the last day was beautiful, the departure was especially wrenching.

The anchorage cove at Heriot Island was sheltered by the larger island of Tamarack to the northeast of it. Only random cat's-paws touched down on the gull-grey water. *Island Magic* was back on her mooring in a new dark red coat, all her letters, numbers, deck, and other trim a virginal white; the dory had been painted to match. Fee and Julian were down on the wharf to meet us. Fee was in jeans and an outsize Norwegian fisherman sweater. She was doing a kind of war dance and laughing while Julian leaned on a stack of traps watching her.

"She looks skinny as a broomstick," I said, as *Little Emily* went slowly across the cove.

"You're getting there yourself," Glen said. "I'll be having to shake the sheets to find you."

"I can stand to lose it better than she can."

"I don't like the way she's hopping around," he said. "If she meets us with some damn message from the Ouija board, I'm turning around and going right out again."

"No, you aren't," I said. "You and Julian just leave us alone. Right now she's jumping around because she's so glad to see us—it can all turn to tears in a twinkling." I hugged his arm against my side, and he gave me a little sidewise grin.

I went up the ladder to Fee's waiting arms while the men were making fast the bow and stern lines. "Oh, God, there's so much I want to talk about!" she said when we hugged. "I don't know where to begin." Her embrace was so frantic it hurt, and she looked desperately into my eyes. "I love Julian, but he doesn't even begin to understand. Eden, I—"

"Don't talk now," I calmed her in whispers. "We've got all day."

"Well, Julian," Glen said brusquely, "what jobs need a couple of extra hands around here? Good day to work in the woods, isn't it?" He was so jumpy it would have been funny in other circumstances. But he couldn't move Julian, who stood watching Fee as if there were nothing else in the world.

"What'll I do with *this?*" Glen asked, sounding very close to either despair or rage as he picked up my basket.

"I'll take care of it," I said soothingly, trying to reassure him with eye signals past Fee's blowing hair and not knowing if I was getting through. "Fee, you're breaking my ribs."

"Oh, hell, you're tougher than that," she said, releasing me. "Doesn't Glen ever squeeze you? Or is he past it?"

"I'm glad you came, Eden," Julian said in the deep voice which always startled. He used to sing bass in the choir of the First Baptist Church at St. David until he moved in with Fee. His family said it was her idea, and it probably was. Seeing the pair come up our wharf one day, Sim Trescott had described the two as a handsome Clydesdale being led by a child. With the noble auburn head and the classic mold of features, when Julian turned those beautiful amber eyes on you and that slight, tranquil smile, the reaction was pure pleasure. Fee owned a genuine *objet d'art,* and I hoped for her sake that he would be as beautiful an old man as he was a young one.

"You guys leave us alone for a while," she commanded. "Come on, Eden." She took the basket. "What'd you bring?"

"Makings for pizzas, with plenty of mushrooms for you—" But she was far ahead of me, leaping up the path to the old house. It cuddled like a lamb with its mother into the green ridge that ran the north and south of the island. Smoke blew fragrantly and erratically round the chimney of the ell kitchen. There were swallow houses nailed high to the gable at either end of the dwelling, but they were empty now; the swallows came early and left early.

A border of marigolds and zinnias burned against the weather-dark shingles; the front and ell doors had been newly painted white and so had the trim around the windows. We went into the kitchen. Two pies were cooling on racks on the table by the windows looking down on the cove.

"Blueberry," said Fee. "I must have been psychic. I *knew* you and Glen would be out here to help eat them.... God must have known how I needed this!" Her eyes shone with imminent tears, but she angrily wiped at them with her sleeve. "Listen to me running on, and you're the one who found them. I won't ask you about it." She ripped her sweater off over her head and reappeared rumpled but resolute. "I'm not going to cry. I've had enough of that, and we've a lot to get through before the boys come in. Take off that jacket, for heaven's sake. It's hot in here."

She put more wood in the stove and took the teakettle into the pantry to fill it from one of the white enamel pails on the shelf beside the black iron sink, which she kept scrubbed and oiled to the sheen of black satin. "How about some herb tea? It's my own mix, guaranteed not to kill. I've been drinking it for weeks."

"I know your mixes," I said. "If you don't have a nice dull safe commercial teabag, forget it."

"You and my nice dull safe Julian," she said, returning to the kitchen. She removed a stove lid, added more wood, and set the teakettle over the open flames. "No spirit of adventure. I can't say that about my twinnie. He might not like my mixes, but you can't say he's not adventurous." She squinted an eye at me.

"Let's not get into that," I said.

"OK, I'll see what I can dredge up for you to drink." She went back to the pantry and began clattering among tins and mugs. I held my hands to the stove and looked around me with pleasure; she had kept this the sort of old-fashioned kitchen room seen nowadays only on calendars and greeting cards. Nothing was there simply for a cozy period effect, everything was in daily use; the big well-blacked range with its polished brightwork and the large copper-bottomed teakettle; the lamps lined up on the mantel shelf behind it, their clean chimneys shining like soap bubbles. The radio on a shelf between the two front windows was the only modern thing in the room. Julian knit his trapheads by these windows, and a half-finished head hung from a large cuphook in one sill. The tide calendar was tacked above it. There was another calendar above the mantel, with a painting of a lobster boat working in rough seas.

Two bowls on a newspaper below the back window reminded me; I looked behind the stove for the basket, and the small silver-striped tabby gazed up at me, drowsily shutting and opening green eyes while the kittens fed. One was marked like her; the other three were black.

"Hello, Polly," I said. "Who was your gentleman friend over on the mainland?" Her purr rose in volume until I could hear it above the teakettle's rumbling. I knelt to smooth her head and to touch with a finger the oblivious little heads of the kittens. She'd been a stray on the mainland. Julian had brought her home one day and was enchanted when her pregnancy began to show. I asked when Fee came out with a tray.

"Three boys and a girl. The boys are the black ones. You thought up any names yet?"

"I forgot," I said guiltily. "I'll make a list for Julian to choose from."

"Who could think?" she said. "After everything... come and eat. The sight of you improved my appetite. Would you have believed anything could make me lose it?" She had buttered thick slices of bread. "This is great stuff. We made it together. Julian kneads yeast dough as if to the manner born."

Suddenly she broke into a wild noisy crying, like a child. I took the tray from her, and she ran into the pantry and ladled cold water into the basin, leaned over, and splashed handfuls over her cheeks and eyes; then she blindly took a towel off the rack and held it to her face. She was shaking, but in a few minutes she conquered that; she tossed the towel at the rack and returned to the kitchen.

"All right," she said quietly. "I said I wouldn't, and I mean it. It's not going to do anything for *them.* But there is something we can do." She took the teakettle off the flames and replaced the stove lid. "Come on in here."

I followed her into the bedroom across the hall. It was papered with a delicate flowery design, and there were ruffled white curtains. The sleigh bed (one of her father's antiques) was made up with a quilt in the log-cabin pattern, and there was a sheep's fleece on either side of the bed to step out on, rather than onto the bare floor of wide pine boards, painted soft green. There were three Hitchcock chairs and two chests of drawers beautifully refinished. Over one of them was a mirror with a mahogany frame carved with acorns and oak leaves. That had always been in the parlor of the Heriot house. On the mantel above an open fireplace *Sea Swallow* forever sailed into a wind that filled her sails.

"I was going to give that to her," Fee said matter-of-factly. She opened the bottom drawer of one of the chests and took the Ouija board from under a pile of blouses. The planchette was wrapped in a scarf in a corner of the same drawer.

"I've done quite a bit on my own," she said, polishing the board with her sleeve. "I've been trying to locate Sonny and Janine; they must know *something.* I get a yes every time I ask if they're close by, but can you imagine how the police would look at me if I told them that?" She moved a chair close to the bed. "There, you can sit on that or on the bed, whichever you want."

Supposing I don't want? I said to myself. I was trying to think of a way to refuse gracefully when she said, "It needs energy from both of us. Together we always did make quite a power source, didn't we? We always got results."

"By fair means or foul," I said. "Now that I think back, I think there were more foul than fair."

"*I* never cheated." She attempted to stare me down, then shrugged, "Oh, well. We were just romantic kids then. But I don't cheat now. This isn't for fun. Sit down, Eden. Between the two of us we ought to get them, person to person."

I took the bed, and we sat with our knees just touching and the board balanced on them. We placed our fingers lightly on the planchette. Speaking of foul means, I intended to see that nothing worked. Fee's thin face was drained of expression and brilliancy; her gaze went blankly past my ear. A little breeze whined around a window, and fine chills ran over my skin; my hands and feet were cold. She was trying to take our old game far beyond mildly spooky fun.

We had never once tried to talk with anyone recently dead or, for instance, Fee's mother. We had been instinctively cautious; whenever we "got" someone, it was always a figure from the distant past, occasionally a celebrity, like Byron or a Brontë. More often it was someone of whom we'd never heard but who was a mine of misinformation on practically everything.

The life histories varied from the spectacular to the commonplace, but we loved it all. I found my best Gothic ideas up in the Heriot attic with the rain beating on the roof and dripping noisily in the pans under the leaks. The rain was a disadvantage because we couldn't hear Glen coming; he crassly broke up the séances and had more than once been slammed over the head with the board.

At other times, as we crouched tensely in the dim light with our fingertips tingling on the planchette, we heard her father moving drunkenly down below. A crash would bring me up all standing, sure he had fallen downstairs and broken his neck, but Fee didn't even jump, she would be concentrating so hard.

Then we would hear him talking to himself. He never cursed or raved. Coming or going, I tried to avoid him because there was something about his boyish smile and his meticulous courtesy that made me sad even when I was still a child.

"Damn it, Eden!" Fee's angry voice slapped me. "You're holding the planchette down while you're off in never-never land!"

"I was putting myself into a state of freedom from my mind," I said coldly. "If anything's holding it up, it's you, trying to force it to say what you want it to say."

She slitted her eyes at me. "*Miss Emma!*" she called defiantly. "Marianne! Are you out there?"

The skin tightened from the nape of my neck to my eyebrows. I took my fingertips off the planchette and got up from the bed. "I don't want any part of this, Fee," I said.

"What are you afraid of?" Her sharp cheekbones were geranium red. "Ghosts? They'd never hurt you! How can you give up any chance at all to keep them alive?"

"They're alive in our hearts and minds," I protested. "They always will be. But they're gone from us, Fee. If you don't believe in God, they'll live in other ways, as long as anyone remembers them. But they're not spirits floating around *out there,* wherever that is, waiting for a phone call."

"But that's just what it is!" she cried. "They need to make contact! They need to know what happened!"

"I thought they were going to tell *you* that."

She ignored me. "When people die suddenly, violently, no matter how, they're confused. They don't really know what happened. Sometimes they don't even know they're dead. They'd give anything for contact with someone they know. Eden, listen," she pleaded. "Imagine waking up some morning and finding yourself all soul alone in a place like the moon or with everything around you destroyed by some mysterious catastrophe while you slept. Imagine what it would be like if suddenly the telephone rang, and someone alive was at the other end, who could tell you what happened."

She was so unexpectedly eloquent that I listened in spite of myself and was more disturbed than before. The grey eyes were cannily watching me for signs of weakening. "Come on," she urged. "Be a sport. You're the only one who can help. It always ran all over the board for us."

"*No,*" I said. "I can't go along with you because deep down I don't believe it. Even if I tried to be loose, I'd be unconsciously opposing you." I wished the men would come in; for the first time in my life I was in a hurry to leave the island, and the Hayloft looked better to me than at any other time since the deaths. So much for my promise to straighten her out.

Her head went lower and lower over the board, and her loose hair fell past her face. I was sad because I loved Fee and shouldn't want to rush away from her; that I did disturbed me as much as anything. There was something so defenseless about the shoulder blades showing through her gingham shirt, the drooping head, and the way she sat there with both sets of fingertips on the heart-shaped planchette, sliding it gently back and forth across the board.

"Damn it, Fee!" I said.

Her head came up, and she winked at me. "Had you going there, didn't I?" Moving briskly, she put the board away in the drawer again. "I wonder what the guys are doing."

"Were you just making up all that stuff?" I asked. "About milling around trying to find out what's happened to them?"

"Nope, I read it. That's what the ghost-hunters believe, and who's to say they're wrong? If you can't prove it's true, you can't prove it's untrue, either."

"No," I said reasonably. I was so relieved that I was willing to discuss it. We went out to the kitchen and had our tea and bread and butter.

"I keep the lines open," she said. "If it moves for me alone sometimes, why not at other times? I've been experimenting with automatic writing, too."

"Any success?"

"Not yet," she said. "But I'm not giving it up. I wake up a lot in the middle of the night since it happened, so I come out here and light a candle and stare into it and wait, with my pen in my hand. Usually I just itch or start yawning. But sometimes I could swear it's coming. So I know it will, if I'm patient enough."

"I can go along with automatic writing," I said. "Only I don't think anything's guiding your hand but your own unconscious mind. I'll be interested to see what you dredge up."

"You'll be surprised some day," she said soberly.

"I know. You'll probably come out with a blockbuster, and clean up."

After our mug-up we went out to find the men; the cat left her nest of fed and sleeping kittens and came with us. We followed a narrow track along the side of the ridge through bayberry, brown-eyed Susans, patches of blueberry, and tall elegantly curling fern. The world roared like a conch shell with the voice of rough water; puffs of wind brought intermittently the agitated shrieking of gulls and crows. Where the branch forked, one path leading into the woods, we took the left-hand one onto the broad southern slope where Fee and Julian had their garden. Now we saw the gulls and crows rising, diving, and calling over High Ledge Cove which lay at the foot of the field, named for the rock formation that arose steeply from the sea just out side the cove's mouth. Glen and Julian stood by the garden watching the birds. At sight of the men the cat ran ahead of us down the path, her tail straight up, uttering glad little cries.

"Daddy's girl," said Fee. "Hi, guys!" she shouted.

They looked around and up at us with flattering smiles of welcome (or relief). Julian picked up the cat. When we reached them, Fee said, "What's going on down there? Aren't you two even curious enough to go and see?"

"If they're not yelling their guts out about something we can use, we aren't interested," said Glen. "Are we, Julian?"

Julian, cradling Polly, smiled and shook his head.

"Well, *I'm* going down," said Fee, "Come on, Eden, and see the new fireplace. And if I find something good in all that fresh rockweed, like a brand-new skiff, it's *mine,* you two lazy male critters."

"You can have the dead seal, too," said Glen. That stopped her.

"*Is* there one?"

He shrugged. "I dunno. I haven't looked."

"Smart-arse," she said. She started down the steepening path, and Julian walked behind her, with Polly under his chin. We followed.

"What did you and Julian talk about?" I asked Glen.

"Well, we didn't talk much when he was chain sawing up a couple of blowdowns. After that, we said all that could be said about fall fishing. After that we inspected the garden, and then we just *were.* It's like being with a friendly rock. You get anywhere with Fee?"

"I don't know. I'll tell you about it later."

The other two had already reached the beach of popple rocks worn round and smooth by years of the sea's rough handling. The crows retreated, the gulls flew up in a clamorous crowd and circled over us. Some came down to perch in a white row on High Ledge, watching us. The fresh rockweed was scattered with the usual plastic detritus and a few pot bouys painted in blindingly bright colors.

Julian had set the cat down, and she prowled stealthily along the brow of the beach among the beach peas, pink bindweed, and thistles going to seed. Glen stood with his hands in his pockets watching the rest of us skidding through the wet rockweed. While watching for useful loot like good oars, boat cushions, whole crates, and lumber, we conscientiously tossed plastic containers up the beach to be collected for burning and stuffed our pockets with the plastic collars for six-packs. "I'd like to wrap these around some necks and pull tight!" Fee said. "Or push them down some throats and leave the bastards to strangle!"

"*Fiona!*" Julian stopped and looked back at her. He objected to her using strong language.

"All right, lover," she said. "I know. And on Sunday, too."

He turned and went on. Then he stopped so suddenly that she almost walked into his back. He was looking down at a thick rolled-up mass of rockweed, and the side of his face visible to me had changed to a greyish yellow. Fee followed the direction of his gaze; I saw the convulsive motion when both her hands dug into his arm, as if she were trying to save herself from an abyss.

A crow went sailing over, banking to cock an eye at us. There was a fresh outcry from the white ranks out on High Ledge. It's a body, I thought. Someone drowned. After a lifetime of wondering, whenever I walked a shore, how I'd react if ever I found a human body, now I knew. Having found two bodies in a living room, I wanted to run from this one. To find a seal or a porpoise would have been bad enough, but bearable. Not a human being, though. I turned around and slogged up through the slippery weed, skidded on kelp, and almost fell down. Glen nearly skidded off his feet as he came down past me. I stopped where I was, breathing the cold, invigorating, deep-sea scent of the stuff I was standing in, and thinking, incongruously, now it will be like the roses. I'll hate it.

I couldn't see Julian's and Fee's faces, their backs were toward me, but I could see Glen's, pale and stern as he dropped to his heels and pulled at the rockweed. Then I thought that as a writer I owed it to myself to join them, but I seemed to be held fast in tar; I'd heard all my life about how they looked after days in the water with the crabs and the fish feeding off them. I set one foot ahead of the other, but before I could take the next step Fee screamed, "It's Sonny, I know it is! Oh, God!"

She drove her face into Julian's chest, and he embraced her like an automaton, staring down past her head at what was in the rockweed. Her cries were only half-stifled, and her hands twisted fistfuls of his sweater as if they could rip the strong yarn to shreds. With the objectivity that keeps operating even at terrible moments, I saw and heard all this with mild awe. I'd never known Fee to go to pieces so completely, but then I didn't know how I'd react, either, and I wasn't about to find out. I stayed where I was.

Glen stood up fast and said in a loud, hectoring voice, "Shut up, Fee! Get hold of yourself! Sonny's hiding out in Canada by now, for Christ's sake!"

With her face pressed against Julian's chest, her answer came out with muffled hiccups, "The description said h-h-he was wearing a T-T-T-shirt saying 'Maine Secedes.'"

"Half the state wears those." This poor guy fell overboard somehow, somewhere, and not just yesterday by the looks of him. Nobody's been reported missing off a boat anywhere around here, so he must have come a long way, the poor son of a bitch."

"Sonny's been reported missing for a week," she persisted and broke into new hysteria. "Julian, hold me, hold me—"

"Get her away from here," Glen said harshly. Julian hadn't changed expression since the discovery; he seemed unable to stop looking. Glen had to speak to him twice before he picked Fee up and carried her to the top of the beach. She was alternately sobbing and wailing, "Where's *Janine?*"

Glen stayed where he was, gazing out past High Ledge and the gulls at the grey and white sea. I went to him and put my hand in his pocket and held his. His fingers nearly crushed mine. I made myself look so I could be with him in all ways; I saw that what was half rolled up in the weed and kelp had no face and very little scalp. What could have been recognized as remaining flesh was bloodless and swollen. An exposed arm was half-nibbled away. The stained red and blue design on the T-shirt was blatantly incongruous.

Suddenly Glen said angrily, "Get out of this, Eden! You shouldn't be here!"

"Why? So you can throw up without a witness?"

He ripped my hand out of his pocket as if it were a disgusting object and took my shoulder in a punishing hold and tried to turn me around. "Go on, get out of here! Damn the women anyway, always squealing and fainting."

"I'm doing neither," I protested, "and you're breaking my shoulder, after nearly twisting my hand off the wrist."

The fire went out of him. "I'm sorry." He barely moved his lips. "I just didn't want you to see, after everything else you've been through. And maybe I do want to heave. I never saw a drowned one before. So get out of here, will you?"

Meanwhile the drowned one lay at our feet, less now than one of the cruising gulls. The inevitable second reaction washed over me in wavelets like these washing over the popple rocks. I leaned forward and kissed Glen's cold cheek and then went up the beach. I met Julian coming down, impassive, nearly glazed of eye. Fee was sitting on a log at the top, blowing her nose.

"I sent him back," she said thickly. "Let's go to the house and leave the macho males to make their momentous decisions." She got up. "God, you're white. You aren't going to faint, are you?"

"That's great, coming from old Hysterical Hattie. You look as if you've just come off a ten-day drunk."

"I couldn't believe I was making that noise, but I couldn't stop myself. It hit me all at once that it had to be Sonny, but where's Janine? Is *she* somewhere in the rockweed or rolling around out there?" She nodded at the sea outside High Ledge.

"Stop that!" I ordered, unable to cope with the image of Janine as a mutilated and hideous thing like what I'd just seen. "Come on."

We went up the path without looking back, Fee behind me. "The Ouija board said they were somewhere near, but I didn't think it meant anything like this."

I stopped and turned around. "Listen, don't go telling the Coast Guard and the police about that Ouija board. You'll get some really funny looks."

"Don't you think I know that? Everybody thinks I'm flaky enough now. Besides, Julian doesn't know I've got it. He's scared to death of it."

"I don't blame him," I said.

The men caught up with us in a few minutes. Glen overtook and went by without a word; we knew he was going to his boat to call the Coast Guard. Julian stopped beside us and looked wordlessly at Fee. She reached up and took his face in her hands and kissed him.

"All right now, love," she said. He smiled, somewhat weakly, and loped after Glen.

"He'd have thrown up like a geyser if he'd found it all by himself," she said. "Good thing the tide's going, otherwise they'd have to take hold and secure it somehow. Hurry up. This calls for the Napoleon brandy."

"Honest?" It would be just like Fee to have some tucked away under the black sink.

She gave me a feeble grin. "Don't I wish! But we can't even have the medicinal kind in the same house with my teetotal Julian. It'll have to be tea."

Polly was waiting for us on the doorstep. Fee picked her up and rubbed her chin on the cat's head. "You didn't get to see the fireplace," she said sadly. "I'll never want to use it now."

29

Glen, Julian, and the Coast Guardsmen made a complete circuit of the island in case another body had come in, but there was nothing except a dead gull. When they went away with the body, we all sank into the dead waters of fatigue. I began to yawn and couldn't stop. Fee leaned against Julian as if he were a convenient tree or a wall; his eyes still gazed on something he couldn't forget. Glen kept an arm around me, for his own sake as well as mine.

"You two coming ashore for the night?" he asked. "Bring your sleeping bags, and you can bunk on my floor."

"Or mine," I said.

They didn't want to. "I couldn't sleep anywhere but in my own bed," said Fee. "If I sleep at all."

"Nothing to be afraid of," Julian said in his bass voice, but his eyes belied his words. "He's gone, poor bastard, and there's nobody else."

"Besides," Fee said, picking up Polly. "We've got this sweetheart and the babies for company. You drive away the bad things, don't you, darling?"

Julian's eyes changed; his face was illuminated by a fatherly tenderness. His big hand fondled the cat's head, and she leaned into his palm, eyes shut, her paws kneading Fee's shoulder, her purr sonorous.

We made the pizzas and ate the blueberry pie, and then Glen and I left. It was nearly seven. The dark was coming faster than usual; the security light was already on in the deserted harbor, which looked as if summer had left it for good. The only human being in sight was Toby Barry, who was coming down the company wharf to meet us where we rowed ashore from the mooring. He held out his hand to assist me from the skiff to the car. I'm not used to such courtesies, having been in and out of skiffs since I was three or so, but I never wave them away.

"Hey, what's going on out there?" he asked. "I heard the ambulance call on the scanner. Hey, it wasn't—" He rolled his eyes toward Glen, whose head was bent as he slid the oars under the seats.

"Fee and Julian are OK," I said. "But we found a body in High Ledge Cove."

"*Jeest,*" said Toby. "How'd he look?"

"Not rugged," said Glen, stepping onto the car with the painter in his hand. "You a ghoul or something?"

Toby grinned sheepishly. "Sorry. I guess you could call it morbid curiosity. Every time I head out to those islands to go clamming, I think about it, but it never happens. I guess I'm glad."

He walked up the wharf with us and left us with a fatherly admonition to take care of each other. Chad was locked in the house, and Grampa's car was gone. I remembered as if over a space of years that they were going to supper somewhere. "Shall I stay?" Glen asked. He looked as tired as I felt.

"No, you go on home and flop. The folks will be back soon, and I'll keep Chad with me till then. In the meantime I'm going to take a long hot bath and go to bed."

"If I can't sleep, I'll be back and crawl in with you," he warned me.

"Great, if you don't wake me up," I said with insipid humor.

Chad had to be given a run, but I put a leash on him to forestall any enthusiastic pursuit of a porcupine. We walked in the chilly dusk out to Winter Head, meeting no one on the way out or back. Then he convinced me he hadn't had any supper, so I gave him a small one, though I knew they must have fed him before they left.

Running the water for my bath, I knew my notebook wouldn't help tonight. I longed for the solace of a new book to read in bed afterward and a half-dozen Hershey bars. This remedy used to work once, but then the ailments had been minor. I was just starting to undress when Chad broke into his warning uproar. Somebody pounded on my door, and Toby yelled through it, "Eden, you there? She's having it!"

I ran to the door, buttoning my shirt on the way. Mercifully Chad shut up at the sight of a friend. Toby was so white his freckles looked dark, and his eyes were wild. "She's having it!" he repeated. "And that shit Richie's off to hell and gone with the truck, and the ambulances—"

He was so out of breath I thought he was going to pass out at my feet. "Jesus, they've got heart attacks and accidents, and—" He sagged over the back of a chair. "Will you drive us?"

I had the presence of mind to turn off the water in the bathroom and to leave a note on the table. I told Chad to *stay;* he'd raise the roof when the family came home, and whoever came up to get him would find the mate. I took the Hudson's Bay blanket and my billfold. Going down the steps behind Toby, I reflected that I seemed to have reached some plateau of tranquility simply because I was too tired to be astonished, excited, or horrified by anything else.

"What about Derek?" I called after Toby, and he stopped short halfway across the parking lot, speechless. "If the Temples are home, get them," I said, praying, *Let them be home, dear Lord.* And what do we do if she starts to have it in the car? I was growing less dispassionate by the second.

Toby brought Shasta across to the car. She was very quiet, and I was relieved. I didn't want to start off with her in a panic. Two of us were already in tough shape. "Amy Temple's coming over to sit," Toby said. He hoisted her into the back seat and tucked the blanket around her, saying, "Everything'll be all right, Shas." He put her bag in after her.

"I'm scared," she whimpered. "I don't want to have it without a doctor."

"We don't want you to, either, Shasta," I said.

"You sit with her, and I'll drive." Toby ran around to the driver's door.

"Nope! You get in and hold her steady." I'd met the Barry truck nearly head-on several times, coming around some of those turns for which the Whittier road is famous.

I went as fast as I dared, keeping in mind the local riders of the yellow line. I heard Shasta's gasps now and then, sometimes a whimper. Toby kept up a stream of reassurances as if he hoped to hold the baby back by a dam of words. I didn't want to hear any screams; every time a car came toward us I wondered if anyone in it would be of help if we suddenly had to stop so Shasta could give birth on my Hudson's Bay blanket.

As the lights of Maddox began to show in the distance, Shasta wailed, "My water broke!"

"What's that mean?" Toby yelped.

"It's perfectly natural," I said with false bravado. There were doctors in Maddox; should I turn into Dr. Frost's driveway on Quarry Lane instead of chancing the long stretch between Maddox and the hospital on the far side of Tenby? Dammit, he could be away for the holiday weekend. . . . A cruiser shot out of a driveway behind us and overtook, blue lights flashing.

"Goddam the bastard to hell," Toby groaned. "If that's Rance Carver, he's out to get me."

"They take courses in delivering babies," I said lightheartedly, pulling over.

"They're all out to get me," Toby said.

"Oh, shut up," I said. "I'm doing the driving so I get the ticket." I had my head out the window when the deputy came back to us. "Thank God," I said to the round young face under the broad brim. "Can *you* deliver a baby?"

He was still too new at the job not to look aghast. "*What?*"

"I'm trying to get this woman to the hospital. She's in labor."

He flashed his light into the back seat; Shasta, face vacant with fear, stared back at him from Toby's arms and started to cry.

"Hello, Toby." The deputy snapped off his light. "Just keep behind me," he said efficiently. "I'll get you there slick as a whistle, and I'll let them know you're coming. What's her name?"

"Shasta Barry," I said.

"Dr. Ames is my doctor," Shasta blubbered.

"Don't you worry, ma'am," the deputy said and left us at a run.

After that I had the exhilarating experience of driving out around Tenby at seventy miles an hour behind a cruiser with the siren warning everything else out of our way. Toby was still swearing but reverently, and I even heard a faint giggle from Shasta. But by the time we swung into the hospital grounds, she was not able to hold back a cry.

They took her out of the car, and Toby followed the wheelchair through the emergency entrance. I thanked the deputy, who was very hearty in his relief; we both were. "I guess I might have made a fetch of it," he admitted, "but I'm sure glad I didn't have to try."

"Me, too," I said. "Anything that calls for more than a Band-Aid or an Ace bandage is beyond me."

After he drove away I folded my arms on my wheel and leaned my head against them. My body was still vibrating, and the comparative peace of the parking lot seeped around me like the water welling back slowly into a spring that has been bailed out. I felt as if I'd been in frenzied motion ever since we found the body in the rockweed.

"You all right, Eden?" Toby said anxiously in my ear. I sat up. "I came back for her bag. Jesus, she disappeared some fast. I don't know what the hell's going on."

"A baby's going on, that's what," I said.

"You're coming in, aren't you? It's some bleak in there when you're all alone. There's a lot of people, but I don't know any of them."

I couldn't say *no* to that frightened entreaty, so I rolled up the windows and got out. "You'd better lock your car," he said. "There's an awful lot of crooks around this place. I'm glad we live out in the country."

Some day, I promised myself, I'm going to laugh at that. When we were inside in the light, I saw how pale and wet his face was. "I never ran into anything like this before," he said. "Her sister took her in when Derek was due. I wasn't living with them."

"Did Richie run out then, too?"

"Yep." His lips were so thin and tight they almost disappeared. "They were living in a camp down on Mokinic Point, no telephone, no nothing. She woke up feeling funny that morning, and when he drove out to work—he was lobstering with another guy then—she asked him to tell her sister. Well, he never did. After a while, when nobody came for her and she was starting to hurt bad, she set out to walk it to the town road and couldn't. A feller came in there to cut Christmas trees, and he picked her up." His chuckle scraped from a dry throat. "If he'd a been an honest man, he wouldn't have been there. He was stealing them trees off somebody else's land."

"I hope he did well on them," I said. "Stolen or not."

"When he went back to get what he'd already cut, the owner was there and claiming them." Toby shrugged. "The wind blows the way it wants to. Sometimes *for* you, sometimes against." He stared distractedly at one of the watercolors decorating the corridor, as if his life depended on his making some sense of a rocky cove, a wind-tortured spruce, and an old house. I touched his arm, and he jumped.

"Let's go to the cafeteria," I said. I didn't know whether there were a normal or abnormal number of emergencies that night, but the busyness of the cafeteria was a relief after the silence of the waiting areas. We got roast beef sandwiches and ginger ale, and Toby gallantly paid. "Anything more you want, you just help yourself," he urged. He ran back and seized two servings of chocolate cake. "Let's live it up."

We went to a quiet corner. "Don't you have any idea where to reach Richie?" I asked. Toby shook his head because his mouth was full. He acted starved. "Well, what about her sister?"

His eyes went wide, and he swallowed so much at once, I was alarmed for a moment. "Oh, my God, I have to call her. Well, I will as soon as I eat this. Rich and I had one old baister of a row and that's when he took off." He looked around him and then leaned toward me, lowering his voice. "And he won't be back."

"How do you know?"

"He knocked her down, bunted her in the belly with his head. That's so he can say he never laid a hand on her. I'd have broken every bone in his body, except she was so upset, and Derek was screaming his head off. So I told him to clear out and stay out. And I said something to make sure of that." A sly triumph barely curved his pale lips but gleamed in his eyes. "I told him this one wasn't his. It's mine, I said. And Shas, she just crouched there listening, never said a word."

People in my books did things like this, and I knew personally one man who'd raised another man's child as his own when his wife came back forlorn and pregnant. But this kid astounded me. "Toby, did you just say that to infuriate him, or are you willing to take Shasta and Derek on?"

He braced back, proudly indignant. "Of course I am! And I can do it, too. Don't you believe it? She's willing. We sat there and talked it over. It calmed her down, and she went to sleep. I fed Derek and put him to bed. Then when she woke up, she had the pains." He rubbed his big-knuckled hands nervously; his teeth chattered with chills. "I *feel* like it's my kid she's having, you know?"

"It really isn't yours?"

"Shas was a *good* wife," he said. "'Course it isn't mine. But we'll register it as mine, so don't you tell anyone the difference. She'll stay with her sister awhile—I'll pay her board if Fern makes a stink about it—until she can get a divorce. Then we'll get married." He pushed back his chair. "I got to call that lady, or she'll hate me worse than she already does." He gave me his old cocky grin and went looking for a telephone.

A passing nurse stopped to speak; she'd been in school with me. "Moving in exalted circles, aren't you?" she asked mischievously.

"We brought Shasta in to have her baby," I said. "And don't knock Toby. He's treating me to this sumptuous repast. Tom Selleck couldn't do better." When Toby came back he said, "Well, the Dragon Lady's on her way in. My ear's practically frostbitten. And I don't know who to ask about Shas." He sounded frightened again.

"I'll see what I can find out," Lynn said kindly.

"Gosh, you're nice," Toby said with such feeling that she was taken aback. She smiled at him and went away.

"This is something like," Toby said with satisfaction. "Talking to somebody who knows something around here." He moved his soda can in circles on the table and frowned at it. "I've been so hawsed up about Shas I forgot all about that body out on Heriot. You think it's Sonny?"

"I hope it's not," I said.

"Me, too. But I keep wondering where he and Janine are. They must be some scared. I know one thing; if those old women were taking care of Janine, Sonny Neville wouldn't so much as steal an ashtray from them."

"Do you have a favorite suspect?" I asked.

"Nope," Toby said. "I don't know anybody who'd do a murder if he got caught. All they have to do is wear ski masks. Oh, they might knock somebody out of the way when they ran, but use a gun? Or an *ax?*" I winced; the word triggered one of those brilliantly lighted photographic flashes of the scarlet-splattered room and the eye like glass gazing out from the bloody hair.

"I'm sorry," Toby was half-whispering. "I forgot."

"It's all right," I said. "Toby, was your family affected by the embezzlement way back then?"

"Would you believe that on both sides we're shirttail cousins to half the folks in the big white houses in Maddox? Even if they'd never admit it?" He grinned. "I bet some of 'em would like to rewrite their family histories to get the Barrys out, but they had plenty of reprobates who could put us in the shade when it comes to raising hell."

"I know it," I said. "I have to be pretty careful with my villains, so I don't accidentally come up with something that really happened in a family with a lot of living descendants who'll go for my scalp."

"Gosh, I never thought of that. Well, you asked about us and the bank. My old man says he remembers his grandfather saying *he'd* rob a bank if he could elope with a good-looking girl like Mary Ann Esmond. But we didn't have much in the bank, so it didn't ruin us like it did some of our upper-crust cousins in Maddox. We'd kept our land free and clear ever since we got it from the General; old Simeon Barry was one of his veterans, and it was the family religion never to mortgage the land or the house. The old man always said he'd mortgage one of his kids before he'd put the house in hock." Toby laughed. "Time came when he said he wished he *had* put Rich and me in hock and let the bank take us."

A thick-set male nurse with heavy-rimmed glasses stopped at our table. "Mr. Barry?" he said to Toby, who was clearly flattered by the title. "I was asked to tell you you've got a nice little girl, and she and her mother are both fine."

I thought Toby was going to faint. "Thank you," I said to the nurse, who smiled and went on to the counter. I reached over and gripped Toby's trembling hand. "Come on, Toby, you've just become a father in word if not in deed. Let's find out when we can see her."

Dazed and shaky, he got to his feet. "A g-girl?" he said foolishly.

"Are you disappointed?"

He shook his head and took a deep breath. "Let's go," he said. We headed for the door, and that's where we met the deputy who'd escorted us to the hospital.

I was ready to greet him with a quip about another baby, but his expression stopped me. He was too unmistakably on business, and his business was Toby.

"Tobias Michael Barry," he said rapidly, "I have a warrant for your arrest." He read Toby's rights to him from a small card while Toby stood transfixed with his mouth open; he looked as incredulous as I had felt a little while ago. When the deputy finished, Toby said plaintively, "Oh shit, Rance. Where'd you get all this foolishness from?"

"A little while ago Richie fell into the police station in Maddox drunk as a skunk and spilled his guts in more ways than one," said Rance. "Seems he was mad at you, and this was the only way he could get even. Since none of your and his alleged actions took place in Maddox, the chief called the sheriff. Hands against the wall, please." Fortunately, we were alone for the moment.

Toby, moving like a sleepwalker, obeyed and was quickly frisked. Handcuffs jingled, and Toby wet his lips. "Can't he stop at the nursery first and see his baby?" I asked.

"And without handcuffs," said Toby. "I don't want to be in irons when she and I get our first looks at each other."

"Well," said Rance.

"You won't be sorry," Toby promised ardently. "I won't try anything. I'm not running out on my daughter the minute she's born. Or any time."

All three of us stood outside the nursery window. There is something so marvelous about them with their squashed small faces and their bedraggled hair and tiny fingernails. After Shasta's long months of mostly mute misery, Richie's stupid cruelties, the panic in the car, *she* was here, a real little person with long black eyelashes.

Without opening her eyes, she stretched and yawned. "Look at that fist," Toby whispered. We stood there holding hands while we looked, and all at once I had another of those flashing images, but it was not of the living room at Fox Point. I saw myself standing here looking at a sleeping new baby in a nurse's arms, knowing its mother was dead, and that I would soon receive this baby into *my* arms.... *Fee,* dead in childbirth? What had all these deaths done to me, to cause such an evil vision?

"She's a pretty little girl, Toby," the deputy said. "Congratulations. Now come along. If you behave yourself, I won't put these on till we get to the door. But if you cost me my job, I'll have your hide."

"I told you you wouldn't be sorry," said Toby. "Eden, will you tell Shas I'll be in as soon as I can make bail?"

"They wouldn't let me see her now," I said, "but I'll leave a note for her to get in the morning. Good luck, Toby."

"Thanks for everything, Eden." He looked yearningly back at the window. "She's not just pretty—she's beautiful."

When they'd gone, I asked for paper at the desk. Someone tore a slip from a memo pad and loaned me a pen. Lynn had gone off duty, but a sympathetic woman at the desk, who'd seen Toby leave with the police, said she'd be sure Shasta got the note. "Poor thing," she said. "Her husband going to jail the night the baby's born. But I suppose she loves him. These girls!" She sighed.

30

I was glad to get away before the in-laws arrived. It was almost midnight, and there was very little traffic. I had to concentrate on my driving; traveling alone through the night, I had a tendency to speed. I'd reached that state beyond the first fatigue when one thinks one can go on forever. Once over the lighted bridge I concentrated on the serpentine curves and sudden little hills of the unlighted Whittier road, but I had passed Fox Point before I realized it.

I coasted quietly into the yard. The house across the parking lot was dark; Amy would be sleeping on the sitting room couch. I took out the soaked Hudson's Bay blanket and threw it over the clothesline. The northeast wind had stopped, and everything was quiet except for the crickets and the small sounds of water around the spilings and leisurely creaking from somewhere along the wharves.

Glen was sleeping on my couch, and he didn't wake up while I was in and out of the bathroom and getting into my pajamas. I put a blanket over him, and he stirred and said clearly, "What is it?"

"Sleep in peace, love," I said. "The harbor will now be safe from crime except by amateurs. The Barry boys are in jail."

"Is it a boy or a girl?" he said irritably.

"Oh. Girl."

He turned his back on me and pulled the blanket up to his ear. His drowsy voice came slowly. "What are they calling her, Bonnie or Clyde?"

"You should be ashamed to talk so about that innocent little flower."

I went to my own bed, calling back to him, "And they might just get another suspended sentence. How do you like *them* apples?"

No answer.

The murderer didn't appear, but I dreamed for the first time of Janine, and I knew I was dreaming. "Is it because she is dead?" I asked somebody. This was the familiar presence whom I knew but could not see; however, the invisibility was perfectly natural. It answered my question by saying, "Go next door and see."

I went across the parking lot in that transparent darkness possible only in dreams and walked from night into a day-bright kitchen, and Janine turned from the sink, not Shasta. Under the thick yellow bangs her face was transfigured by an almost frightening joy; frightening because it exposed her absolute vulnerability.

"Janine, you're alive!" I cried. "You're safe!"

"Of course I'm safe!" She was laughing. "I've been safe all the time. Sonny didn't do it, you know."

"Where is he?"

"He's just gone to the wharf." I ran to the window and looked out. A lean boy was walking down the slope, his longish brown hair blowing in the wind. He wore jeans and rubber boots with the tops turned down into loose flapping cuffs below his knees and a sweatshirt with the sleeves chopped off above the elbows.

"Are you sure that's Sonny?" I asked.

"I'll call to him and you can see!" She was still laughing.

But I didn't want him to turn around. I was afraid to see his face, so I woke myself up, and it was daylight. My rapid heartbeat reverberated through my body, and my pajamas were damp with sweat. I sat up shuddering in my deliverance from the dream. Glen was gone from the couch, and when the drumming ended in my ears, I heard *Little Emily* leaving the harbor.

His coming back last night was the nearest he'd ever come to admitting that he needed someone since his breakdown at his father's funeral. He'd torn yesterday's leaf off the calendar and written a note on the back of it. "I'll be in by noon for N. and S. game. You going?"

The baseball game between North and South Whittier was a Labor Day tradition, and it didn't look as if this one would be rained out. The sky had a milky luminescence; the sunrise was tender rather than fierce; and the air was distinctly warmer. I dressed and went through the house to have breakfast with my grandparents and tell them what had happened yesterday. Uncle Early had heard about the body on the late news last night, so they knew about that. The baby took the curse off it, so to speak. I made a good spirited story out of the trip to the hospital and Toby's arrest.

"They'll really go to jail now," Grampa said. "I hope they don't come out worse than when they went in. Toby's a likable boy. Trouble is, he hasn't got a moral to his name."

"I think he has," I said. "In ways that would surprise you. At least he feels much more responsibility for Shasta and the babies than Richie does." I didn't tell them anything else that Toby had confided in me.

"I must start piecing a quilt for that baby," Gram said. "Lord, it'll be good to concentrate on something young and growing for a change."

I returned to put the Hayloft in order. I had barely looked at it for days, just ate and slept in it or walked through it, and there are times when a little housecleaning will give a sense of accomplishment, even virtue, if not release. Janine was with me constantly; the dream was remembered now as a nightmare because of that dazzling happiness. Supposing that *was* Sonny we found, and Fee had been right about the T-shirt, never mind how many people wore them? Where was Janine? Until now we'd all assumed they were together. Supposing they still were, but not in the way we wanted to believe?

The Temple boys at the door must have been surprised by their welcome. They said they had something to tell me. Ben got it out first. "A lady came for Derek this morning, and she said Shas has a new baby girl."

"Of course it's a *baby*," Will drawled. "It couldn't be anything else but a baby. And it can't be a *new* baby girl because she hasn't got an *old* baby girl."

"Oh, put a sock in it," said Ben. "And hey, Eden, somebody's got a truck backed up to the door, and they're moving things out."

"That's right," I said. "They're moving. It'll be done while Shasta's in the hospital."

"Gosh." Ben looked disappointed.

Will balanced himself on the railing and quipped, "Well, that's the way the cookie bounces." Adolescence was advancing fast on him. To cheer Ben up I told about the ride behind the cruiser, and in his envy Will forgot to be sophisticated.

"OK, boys," I said. "See you at the game. Make sure nobody lugs off my stove and refrigerator, will you?"

"Sure!" They hurried back across the parking lot to supervise the moving. I'd gotten rid of them before they could ask me about the body.

On Tuesday the sun rose in a clear sky. The day would be one of

September's jewels, the kind that made Grampa say we saved the best weather for ourselves to enjoy after the summer people left. It didn't hold, now that summer people often became autumn people; but we were all ravished by those days.

I'd have gone out with Glen this morning if he and the other town officers hadn't gone to an all-day seminar at Augusta. I began to put a lunch together while trying to decide what I'd do to keep out-of-doors, when Jean Whittier called from the Cruikshanks' office.

"Could you possibly come up, Eden?" she asked. "Today, tomorrow, soon? We're sending letters only to people we can't call."

"What for?" I asked blankly.

"Mrs. Rigby's will," she said. For a moment, stupid with surprise, I thought she meant Kenneth's mother.

"Are you still there, Eden?" Jean asked. She was a direct descendant of our Captain Whittier. She had been with the Cruikshanks ever since she'd had to give up law school when her father died. There'd been plenty of money for her to continue, but her mother decided she couldn't spare her. I remember my parents' indignation at the time.

"I'm here," I said, "but—"

"Just come up when you can, Eden. All right?"

"All right, I'll be there shortly," I said. "Thanks, Jean." I hung up and said to the room, "When is this going to end?" I still had no idea why I was being summoned. I didn't want even to think about the will, let alone be in the same room with it. All I knew was that this was another chore to be done and put behind me.

I didn't tell Gram about the call; I dressed for town and went out, stopping on the deck for my usual scan of the harbor. There were no yachts, and all the lobster boats had gone out, leaving skiffs on the moorings. Grampa and Uncle Early weren't in sight on the company wharf. Chad lay sleeping in the shade of the store, and the gulls on roofs and spilings seemed to be engaging in mass meditation. The sea pigeons strung themselves out in a line across the water like a row of toy birds.

"Hey, Eden!" The shout brought Chad to his feet barking until he recognized Toby Barry out beyond the wharf, standing up in his drifting aluminum boat.

"What are you doing around here?" I called back.

"I made bail!" he said triumphantly.

"Good!" I heard myself answering. What was the etiquette in our case? Something more than an "Oh" was called for after our hours of camaraderie. "How are Shasta and the baby?"

"Great! They're going home to her sister's tomorrow."

"Where's Richie? Did he make bail, too?" I wondered if Grampa and Uncle Early were listening from inside the store.

"Ayuh, the old man got us out. He's taking Rich dragging with him. Jeest, it'll be some good to work by myself without that one. He was never what you'd call inspiring company."

"Well, good luck," I said.

"I need it. Got me a family to take care of now," he said happily, just as if a jail term weren't in his immediate future. He gave the starting cord a powerful yank, and the engine came alive with the impact of a sledge hammer shattering a plate glass window.

Clem Sr. wasn't in this morning, and Clem Jr. was gently businesslike. We sat in the big sunny front office overlooking Main Street, and he explained that by the terms of Mrs. Rigby's will I was to choose five albums from her collection, subject to Miss Emma's approval. Of course there was no such restriction now. I had also a choice of ten books from the shelves. She had made many other gifts and bequests, Clem said. I hoped Fee was remembered and asked him outright. He nodded. "She'll have the same freedom of choice as you have. I don't know how often they pick up their mail, but we've written to her."

I didn't ask any more questions. I didn't want to know anything more. I wanted only to be out of there before I suffocated. Fortunately he was interrupted by a telephone call and went into his office to take it behind a closed door. I let go a long breath.

"Wouldn't you like a cup of coffee, Eden?" Jean asked.

"No, thanks. My stomach is in an uproar." I didn't mind telling her; she has a manner that is a blessing for many a frightened or furious or heartsore client.

"You've had a rough time of it," she said. "The experience would have put some women under a doctor's care. But you're one of those tough-as-tripe Winters."

"Thanks," I said. "You make me sound absolutely gorgeous." We both laughed. Jean is big and good looking in a rich and spacious way; her warm Latin coloring makes her a throwback to the handsome Cuban woman her Whittier great-grandfather brought home from Santiago. She walks with a proud carriage, immaculate black head always high; she wears uncomplicated and elegant tailored clothes. Her car and her brief shopping trips to Portland and Boston each year seemed to be her only extravagance in a life given over to her employers and her mother. It was a general belief that Jean was devoted to Clem Jr. above and beyond the call of duty, and that he was a fool for not seeing it.

It was a pleasant relief to think about that now while Jean read something at her desk; I imagined a really hokey scene when Clem Jr. suddenly saw her as she was for the first time in his life, and the sound track burst out with Beethoven's "Ode to Joy."

Clem Jr. came back, without Beethoven. "Kenneth will let you know when it's a good time for you to go to the house," he said. "Kenneth is the executor, or personal representative as we call them these days," he explained. "Don't be too upset, Eden, the room won't look the same as when you last saw it."

I couldn't answer that I wouldn't ever in my life go back to that room again, so I said thank you and goodbye and managed to get downstairs on my feet instead of head first. My hands were so shaky, I left the car where it was and walked down to my parents' house.

It did me good, so that by the time I arrived I'd gotten over my shakiness and was able to tell my mother about the gift. I sounded matter-of-fact, and I'm sure my mother knew I was anything *but;* however, she was equally dispassionate.

"Now let me tell you about Kenneth," she said across the kitchen table where all these life-shaking conferences take place. "I found out by luck, if you want to call it that. I didn't tell you before, because you were having enough to contend with without my clattering gossip into your ears."

Two days after the murders, she'd met Morrie and Annie Hearne coming away from the Cruikshanks' office, Morrie black and Annie's face contorted as she tried not to cry. My mother stopped to offer condolences on their loss, and Annie wailed, "Oh, Jess!" in the hearing of everyone on the sidewalk for half a block.

My mother instinctively reached out, and Annie had fallen into her arms, almost knocking her down; my mother is quite a bit smaller. Morrie swore under his breath and strode across the street to his office. Mother pushed the sobbing Annie into Annie's own car, drove her to our house for a cup of tea, and heard the whole story. (This is where my writer's instinct comes from.)

It seems that the sisters had unforgivably snubbed Morrie by not allowing him to bury them. "Why did they ever come back here?" she wept. "*He's* been hell on wheels ever since! He thought they'd be so frail and helpless, but they weren't, and he took that as an insult. He thought he could—you know—manage everything for them, the way a man can do."

Mother murmured and poured tea for her, surreptitiously adding a good dollop of brandy. "Then when he found out he wasn't executor for *either* of them—Jason Higham was for Miss Emma if Mary Ann died first—well, he knew we'd just get some piddling little gift. Everything else is left away from her own flesh and blood." She tossed the tea down and pushed back the cup for more.

"And Esmond had such *plans.* He's really gifted, you know, even if he doesn't have an architect's degree. He doesn't say anything, but a mother always knows when one of her children is suffering."

More tea, more brandy. "I think she knew about the brandy," my mother told me, "but she didn't let on."

"Fox Point is the big thing," Annie went on with embarrassing candor. "Aunt Emma didn't have so much to leave. It's a wonder her best violin wasn't the one smashed. He was trying to make it look as if a maniac did it all."

"Who?" asked my mother.

"Kenneth Rigby, of course," said Annie confidently. "Don't try to tell me Mary Ann Esmond hasn't left everything to that little queer."

It was of no use to try to defend Kenneth; my mother had only herself and the brandy to blame.

"Why Kenneth?" she asked. "Maybe he didn't even know he was the heir."

Annie squinted one eye at her and nodded portentously. "Oh, he knew all right! Turns out he was dropping in there, smarming around, the way that kind knows how to do. He probably talked her right into it, and looking like his grandfather helped out. Not that Guy Rigby was one of *those.* Far from it!" From the way she laughed, Mother thought she might have liberated a new personality in Annie, diametrically opposed to the one whom Morrie bullied. "Oh, no! He was a *man!* No wonder Beth worships him! If she had that portrait in *her* house, she'd make an altar of it!"

"But why would Kenneth want to harm Mary Ann?" My mother gently persisted in getting her back on course.

"Probably didn't want to wait for her to die before he could get his hands on the property. That's what *we* think. Or maybe she found out that he had plans for the land she wouldn't like, so he had to get rid of her before she could change her will."

"How would she find out anything like that?"

The shrewd squint again. "Maybe somebody warned her," she whispered. "Maybe somebody who had their suspicions and just wanted to be sure she thought everything out before she put her name to anything. But she always knew more than everybody else, or thought she did, from what I've heard."

"Morrie must have done some dropping in himself and found Kenneth there," I said. "I did, once. I'd laugh if it weren't so horrible. Morrie and Esmond with the place all chopped up between them and projecting it all on

Kenneth. No wonder Esmond's sick. I hope he chokes to death on it," I said viciously.

"I left the brandy out that time," Mother said. "I thought she'd had enough. She went on about how Beth had been dripping poison into Kenneth all these years, and he's probably been crazy for a long time without anybody's knowing it. He's a loner, and everybody knows loners are dangerous; look at Gideon Wilkes! I asked her if she thought Gideon could have done it, but she kept shaking her head. Kenneth is *it.* Then when she started to come down a bit from her high, she said, 'The Morleys will be fit to be tied. They didn't do any better than we did, even if Edith *is* a Rigby.'"

Then she had rambled on and on about the sisters' wish to be cremated. It was not Christian; it was like India. What about the day when we arose from our graves? How would all those ashes come together? Especially the ones scattered over the ocean? Marianne's and Guy's mingled ashes sounded particularly scandalous, as if they were still flaunting their adultery.

"*Annie,*" Mother said. "If God can flesh out all those bones that have been a-moldering in the earth for centuries, he'll certainly have no trouble reconstituting ashes. Where is your belief in the immortality of the soul?"

"You're right, Jess!" said Annie, ready to weep again, but this time quietly. Mother got her out and into the car before she could fall asleep and drove her home. She took the long way to walk back to her own home.

"I needed a few miles to compose myself," she said. "Still, I wasn't as ashamed of myself as I should've been." She did not look penitent now.

"Have you seen Jake and Edith?" I asked her.

"Oh, Edith's been in and out next door, and I run into Jake now and then. He's the same as usual. A realist. He's not the kind of man to stand around hoping for a handout. I think he'd gotten very fond of them and sincerely mourns them. Edith never did have much expression, so you can't tell whether she's glad or sorry. And Beth has gone into black."

"You're kidding."

"No. Sheer black, with crisp touches of white. Very tasteful. Well, if Kenneth is heir to a million dollars' worth of property, the donor is entitled to a decent show of respect, don't you think?"

"It beats running up and down Main Street shouting 'Wow, we're rich!'" I agreed. I left, feeling better than when I'd arrived, but I knew I was never going to Fox Point to pick out my gifts. I would never again set foot inside that house.

31

By the evening of that day, we knew that we had found Sonny. He hadn't drowned; he had died when an ax crashed down through his skull. His parents were restrained by their other children from seeing what was left of him. He was no longer a suspect, and Janine could also be dead, or else she had somehow escaped; but *when* and *how* could only be conjectured.

The day after the news release, Whittier made all the papers, radio stations, and TV channels again. Janine-sightings commenced in all parts of the state, and out of it, but for all of us at home Janine was dead, too. I wasn't the only one with bad dreams, though I might have been the only one who saw the murderer. He came back, and I thought I'd know him if he came close enough, but I always woke myself up before he could reach me.

No one wanted to find Janine wrapped up in kelp and rockweed. Better to believe that what remained of that young body had been carried out by the currents to be lost in the ocean. Lucas Wolcott went berserk in his cell and was taken to the psychiatric wing of the Tenby hospital for treatment.

On that next day Jensen was seen here and there, but he never seemed to light, at least not where anyone could be sure of it and report it to the grapevine. He has a list, Nick had said, and he'll work his way down it. He'll get to everyone sooner or later.... If that's what Jensen was doing, where was he doing it?

Judging from the conversation around the wharf and in the store, everyone preferred to believe in a drug-crazed transient, or a pair of them, who'd probably murder again, but at a good distance from here. There was no open panic in the town, but more doors were locked. Most people knew that Gideon had been in a mental institution long ago, but we were all so used to him that he was part of the landscape.

Glen and I didn't talk about it; neither did my family and I. When I wasn't trying to keep my mind occupied with the notebook (and that wasn't working well, Janine was always between the page and me), I thought about Nick, the stranger in our midst, and Robbie. Both had stopped in at Fox Point at odd times. Robbie could have been a time bomb ticking away until that night. "I am what you see," Nick had proclaimed, but how many people have spoken the same words from behind a mask?

Sonny's funeral was on Thursday. The Nevilles had decided on a short service at the graveside rather than an indoor one. My family were all going, but I was tempted to run away to haul with Glen that day; he had managed never to go to a funeral since his father's. Finally I stopped whiffling and decided I would go, but only because it would be outdoors, which would make the occasion just bearable; it was going to be a warm, bright day.

It was already hot when Toby came up my steps in mid-morning. "I just wanted to tell you I'd be down to move out our stuff next weekend. Shasta's brother-in-law is helping me, and he's got a good big truck. I can't stand *her,* but Tommy's a hell of a nice guy."

He sat on the railing. "Her folks've been over to Fern's and talked sweet to the baby and made a fuss over Derek, so I guess she's forgiven. I don't dare stick my nose inside the door for fear Fern'll slice it off with a cleaver, but Shas is doing fine and that's what counts. Tommy sneaks messages to her." Out on bail, facing prison, he was so insouciant he made me feel old.

"Eden Michelle Barry," he said. "How's that?" "Beautiful," I said. "Almost as beautiful as she is." I was so surprised I was flustered. "Nobody's ever been named after me before! Thank you, and Shasta."

"It was the least we could do," he said solemnly.

"Her middle name's for mine, Michael. Nobody knows that yet but you."

"And I won't tell."

We both laughed. It was a moment of pure happiness, untainted by everything that had gone before and all that would follow. But we knew how evanescent it was. The next moment he was staring down at his swinging foot and saying, "So it was Sonny. You going to the cemetery?"

"Yes," I said. "Not that I want to, but—" There was no way to finish it.

He was silent for a few moments, head bent, watching the swinging boot, and then he sighed and stood up. "The old man has this saying, when he's just sitting around and then decides to get moving: 'Well, this won't buy shoes for the baby, nor pay for the ones he's wearing.' I used to ask him whose baby, we didn't have one, and he'd just laugh. Well, I'm thinking it now and it's no joke—I don't know as I ever said thank you right out, Eden."

"You didn't have time, did you?"

He leaned forward and kissed me quickly on the cheek, then ran down the steps. Crossing the yard, he waved without looking back. A few moments later he was pushing off in the old aluminum skiff.

All the men except Glen began returning to the harbor before noon; they would be going to the service at the cemetery. Fee and Julian came in from the island. Fee had trimmed Julian's hair, and he wore good slacks, a shirt and tie, and a sports jacket; he looked handsome but unhappy. Fee had brought along a lavender cotton shirtwaist dress she'd had for years. She never wore out her dresses because she hardly ever wore them. She changed her clothes in my room.

"I don't think women should wear slacks to a funeral," she said primly. "What are you wearing?"

"Not slacks," I said. "If I had an island to hide out on, I wouldn't have come off it today, even for money. . . . Poor Julian." He slumped deep in a chair out on the deck, and his depression seeped into the Hayloft like fog.

"He'll survive." This was as out of character as the sudden sense of propriety. "I know we didn't *have* to come. The Nevilles won't care; they probably won't see anybody who's there." She swung shut the inside door to the deck and stood against it. Her eyes were glistening but, not with tears.

"Guess what Milton told me last night," she said like a conspirator.

"*Who?*" Too late I realized. "Oh, my God! I love you, Fee, but if you mention that board today, so help me I'll stuff your mouth full of old socks. Some of those Chad's been carrying around," I added. "All dirt and dog-spit."

"*Shush!*" she hissed, waving her hands at me. "*He* doesn't know. I shouldn't laugh," she whispered, "but it's either laugh or cry, and you looked so outraged, it was hilarious."

"I *am* outraged," I whispered back. "And *you* should be ashamed of yourself."

"I'm not," she answered calmly, "because I believe Milton. At least admit I'm doing as well as the police. At least I've got a trustworthy contact."

"If you tell me it's John Milton, the poet—" Don't sputter, I told myself.

"It's Milton Whittier, the one who was in the Twentieth Maine Regiment under Joshua Chamberlain and died at Gettysburg. He's going to put me in touch with Sonny as soon as he can, and the cemetery is a good place for it, because Sonny will be there. Not just his poor body, but the real Sonny."

I cut this off. "We'd better eat something. Maybe that will brighten poor Julian up."

We had a lunch of chicken sandwiches and milk. Julian ate three times as much as Fee and I did, but without any perceptible change in his outlook. My aunt and uncle called for my grandparents, and we three went in my car.

The cemetery in North Whittier lay beyond a wall of woods at the end of a right-of-way through an orchard. Everyone parked along the road and in the nearest driveways and walked in through the warm cidery scent of windfalls rotting in the orchard grass. There wasn't a cupful of wind, and the old apple trees made me think of Chinese carvings; the leaves against the sky were as translucent and motionless as leaves of jade; the apples were porcelain.

My family stood close to the Nevilles, but Fee, Julian, and I stayed as far back as we could on the western bounds of the cemetery, against the woods. The crowd was silent while we waited for the last comers to emerge through the gate from the right-of-way; there was some nervous coughing and throat clearing, but we were too far from the grave to hear the Neville women sobbing. A boisterous family of crows flew overhead, and almost everyone stared eagerly upward, as if crows were seen here only once a century and mustn't be missed.

When the minister began to speak, I didn't try too hard to hear him. Fee stood with her arm through Julian's and kept staring skyward long after the crows had gone; she'd told me once that to keep looking up would hold tears back. Julian stood like a stone pillar, and just as expressionless.

There was a tight cluster of high-schoolers let out of classes for the occasion, mostly boys, with a few quietly sobbing girls clinging together. Tracy was with them but seemed proudly isolated. Robbie Mackenzie was another solitary, made even more so by his dark glasses. I wondered, without much conviction, if this slight, innocuous figure could be the prowler of my dreams.

Gideon Wilkes had materialized not twenty-five feet from us, sitting on the low stone wall with his Allegash hat beside him. He had trimmed his hair and beard and wore a clean blue shirt open at the neck, corduroys, and an old but respectable tweed jacket. Through a gap between groups I saw Nick Raintree leaning against one of the granite gateposts, his arms folded. When he turned his head to watch the low flight of a red-shouldered hawk over the far side of the cemetery, the gold earring caught the sun. If he was the darkest of the dark horses, it could be for the best of reasons.

A little breeze began stirring the oak leaves and white-pine needles. The scamper and chitter of a red squirrel were so close to my back that I twisted my head around to look, grabbing at any diversion. I saw the squirrel jump from a shadbush to a black alder and then to a poplar, and run up that to the top, making it shake. It leaped from there to a landing out of my sight. I wished I were free in the woods like him, going farther away all the time.

Fee was groping for my hand, and I turned reluctantly; but in the very instant of twisting my head back, I thought I saw Janine. It was like the first few seconds after you turn off a lamp, and the dark room still seems to hold light. I swung my head around again so fast that it hurt my neck. Nothing was there that hadn't been there before: shadows, leaves, spots of sunlight quaking in the freshening breeze. The squirrel chirred from deeper in the woods. But the image persisted, and sweat ran down my back like an insect. I wondered with a sickening excitement if I were having a genuine experience, if I'd just seen Janine's ghost.

Janine must have been very much with everyone here; a psychic might claim that all the concentrated energies could produce the image, helped by a certain formation of branches and the movement of light and shadow. Who could disprove it?

But I had met her eyes.

I touched Fee's shoulder with my free hand, and she jumped. "I have to go, or burst," I whispered. "I'll duck into the woods for a minute."

She nodded and released me. I sat on the wall and swung my feet to the outside, walked through a band of ferns, past the shadbush over moss-capped ledge, and pushed in among the black alders. These of course resisted me; twigs pulled at my hair and scratched my bare arms. The instant the cemetery became invisible to me behind the screen of leaves and low-swinging spruce boughs, I had a great sense of release.

I went around a stand of young spruces growing thickly together and came into a little clearing. Across a patch of green moss and silver lichens and a few reddening blueberry plants, Janine stood braced against a big birch. She was wearing blue slacks and the checked blouse I'd seen on her once before. This was no hallucination; she rushed at me and into my arms, and I held her while she cried.

"You're alive, you're alive," I kept saying inanely. Primitive instinct kept my voice down. "Come on, you have to show yourself. Everybody thinks you're dead! Tracy's out there right now—"

She fought free of me as if I were trying to wrestle her into a pit of alligators. "I can't! It's not safe! They may still be around!"

"Who?" I kept a good grip on her shoulders. "If you know who did it, you have to tell, and then you'll be safe."

"I don't *know!*" She was still terrified. "It was just this dark figure all of a sudden rising up over us. Sonny yelled at me to run, and he shoved me, and I ran, and I ran, and—" Her voice caught in her throat and then came out small and keening. "And I kept on running. I *left* him." She sagged, and I couldn't hold onto her. She dropped to her knees on the moss and covered her face with her hands and wept into them. I knelt beside her and took her head against my breast.

"He wanted you to go," I said. "If you hadn't, you'd have been killed, too." My own voice was quaking. "Where have you been staying? Not in a hollow tree, that's clear." Both she and her clothes looked and smelled clean.

"With Gideon," she said, almost inaudibly. "In his camp."

"How did that happen?" I asked. "Was he there?"

"*No!*" Her head came up so fast it almost clipped my jaw. "I was on the road—I don't even remember getting there, but I remember how it looked, with the clouds blowing over the stars, and I was so cold, and it was like being stuck in this nightmare." She shivered, and I wrapped my arms tightly around her. "I kept wanting a car to come but none did, and all of a sudden Gideon was there on his bike. I kind of rushed at him and grabbed hold of his arms, and he sat me down on a rock just inside the woods, parked the bike with me, and went off. I didn't dare move, I didn't hardly breathe, and I was so *cold.*" There was a new crescendo of shivering. "Then he came back. He didn't tell me anything, and I was afraid to ask him. He said, 'Come on,' and he took me on the handlebars of his bike. Once we heard a car coming, and we went off the side of the road into the bushes till it went by. He watched and said he thought it turned in *there,* and that meant someone would call the police."

"It must have been me," I said. Now *I* was shivering.

"He took me down to his camp, and then he told me. He made me promise I wouldn't kill myself, because that's what I felt like when he told me about *them* and Sonny." She sat up. "Don't you tell anybody where I am, or I'll run away from there. Gideon promised *he* wouldn't tell."

"I won't, Scout's honor!" I held up my hand. "Do you need anything?"

"Could you get me—but how can you remember everything?"

"I'll come around tomorrow, and you have your list ready."

"I can't let you come down without asking Gideon about it first, but I can leave a list in his mailbox, tomorrow morning early."

"All right," I said. "What are you doing here now? It's a long way from Gideon's camp."

"I wanted to be somewhere near Sonny." The tears were quiet now, simply welling up and slipping over. "We walked a long way through the woods, along a trail the hunters use in the fall. I saw when they drove in with him, before anybody else came. I couldn't make it true that Sonny was in that box."

"Oh, Janine," I said sadly. "It's all so terrible. But we have to do the best we can. *They* wouldn't want us to go under. Keep thinking that. And I have to go back now, or Fee will be charging in here thinking I've fainted or something." I took her face in my hands. "Be brave. I'll get your things, and maybe I'll see you tomorrow. OK?"

She nodded, with a wan little smile, and I left her there by the big birch. When I reached the cemetery, I looked first for Gideon, but he was no longer on the wall. The service was over, and a tide of people was moving very slowly toward the way out. Fee was where I left her, mopping her face on a large handkerchief while Julian watched her, one big hand on her back.

She gave me a wobbly grin. "What happened to *you?*"

"I lost my lunch, and then I had to rest a bit, my legs felt so weak."

"All right now?"

"Yep. How about you?"

"I may just melt into a flood of salt water and raise the sea level by an inch."

Nick Raintree came toward us. He stopped and spoke briefly to Robbie Mackenzie, who then went on out the gate with his head lowered as if he were pushing into a gale. Nick's tough, swarthy face was gentle and his voice soft, but he wouldn't be the first killer to attend his victim's funeral and even shed a few tears.

"Where are you, Eden?" He was waving his hand before my eyes. I had the sensation that he was reading my mind, and that this was a threat disguised by ordinary words. "Come back," he said. "We need you."

"Oh, Lord, I'm no good even to myself. I think I'm coming down with something," I lied glibly. "Summer complaint. I'm going home and go to bed. Don't anyone come near enough for me to breathe on him."

32

It was a good way to get rid of all of them. If Nick didn't believe me, he couldn't very well say so, and Julian's mother had raised him to fear other people's germs, so for him one sneeze was the equivalent of the Four Minute Warning. He wasn't disposed to let Fee linger in the Hayloft to tell me if Milton had shown at the service.

I played out the charade for the family, too, because I didn't know how I could otherwise keep Janine to myself. There's always one of these twenty-four-hour things going around, so nobody would think it peculiar if I laid low overnight but recovered and was on my way uptown early in the morning. I told Gram from a hygienic distance that I didn't need any attention, and she said, "That's good, because I'm a hundred and ten years old today. Don't drink anything but weak tea." She waved me away. "Get to bed now."

I was in bed when Glen came in from hauling; I was meek, and drowsy, and allowed only a kiss on my forehead. "You know how these things can knock you down," I warned him. "And the way the lobsters are coming, you don't want to miss even one day."

By now I could lie with hardly a trace of shame, perhaps because I had no choice. When the harbor had quieted for the night, I made myself a meal and read myself to sleep with an old Ngaio Marsh favorite. Surprisingly, I slept well, perhaps because I was anticipating action in the morning instead of trying not to think of the day just passed. The murderer didn't come, and I was glad, because I wouldn't have wanted to see a gold ring in his ear, or Robbie's knobby chin under the mask.

Glen went by in early morning without stopping in, no doubt afraid of waking me. Shortly before the stores would be open in Maddox, I went through the house and told Gram I was fine again, going to Maddox for a new typewriter ribbon. She looked rested and said she had slept eleven hours, and she didn't want anything from Maddox, but I could pick up something at Whittier's on the way home. She'd call in her order.

When all the pickups have come down to the harbor, and the schoolbus has been and gone, the road is empty for long intervals. In solitude I opened Gideon's mailbox and found an envelope that had once been addressed to Box Holder, but that had been crossed off, and my name was written above it in a round, careful hand all young girls seem to use nowadays. I put it in my pocket without opening it and drove on.

Main Street in Maddox was also pretty empty. I parked outside the hardware store and read Janine's list. At the end she had written, "It's OK to come down to the camp, but don't try to drive in. There's room to park out of sight off the road. Please put down the price of *everything.* Thank you."

I was early enough to meet no one I knew well in the drugstore or anywhere else, but I was still driven by guilty haste. After I collected her necessities, I bought her a gift of a pink sweatshirt that said, "Hang in there!"

When I was getting into the car, Esmond Hearne came across the street from the office. He went into the drugstore without seeing me. The lunch counter there is an unofficial men's club for the first hour or so of the working day; not that a woman would actually be elbowed off her stool if she climbed onto one and ordered a hot muffin and coffee, but you always feel it could happen. I got away before he could look out and see me leaving.

On the way home I met a few more vehicles, and there were two pickups along Gideon's stretch of road. I smiled and waved and drove on to the Beaver Dam, where I made a U-turn and went back up to Gideon's mailbox. Feeling exceedingly furtive, I lurched off the black road onto the wood road. I thought for a moment that everything had been scraped off the underside of the car, but I persevered. There was a deep curve almost at once, and when I'd gone around it, I knew the car couldn't be seen from the road.

I walked down the steep track into the sunny clearing where Gideon lived in a one-room cabin of board-and-batten construction, agreeably weathered. A small washing, still steaming, hung on a line strung between birches, and hens ran under it away from me, squawking. The big grey and white cat lay atop the woodpile, blinking cordially at me. I'd never been to Gideon's place before and would have felt as if I were trespassing if he hadn't ostensibly given permission.

The cabin looked as if it had grown there. Flowers bloomed in haphazard luxuriant patches, and so did his corn, tomatoes, and other vegetables; but the lines of the cabin, the placement of its small windows, the pitch of the roof, and the symmetry of the woodpile all expressed a sense of artistic order.

There was no sign of Janine. I could hear boats working in Bugle Bay and saw the start of a path on the far side of the clearing. I was sure she wouldn't have gone to the shore, where she could be seen from the water or through some bird-watcher's binoculars across the bay. Then she spoke to me from behind the cabin's homemade screen door and came out, smiling diffidently. She thanked me and insisted on keeping a record of what I'd spent. She would pay me back eventually, somehow.

"I've just made us a gingerbread," she said. "Do you want tea or coffee?"

"I'd like cold water from Gideon's spring," I said. "I hear he's always bragging about it."

She'd baked the gingerbread in a camp oven set over two burners of an old-fashioned oil stove, and we ate it on a bench outdoors. She showed me the little window in the eastern gable end. "That's where I sleep. There's a raccoon who climbs up the pine tree and looks in at me. He can't figure me out."

She looked slightly less devastated than she had yesterday. "Sonny's gone," she said. "Gideon and I talked about it last night. He knows about beginning again, too. Sonny's gone," she repeated. "I can't change that, nobody can. Even God couldn't. I have to face facts and begin to live, when I can figure out how." There was a tremor in her voice, but she fought it down. "Gideon didn't know how he could begin again, but he did. . . . Did you hear anything about my father?"

"Only that he's in the hospital at Tenby. They're drying him out. Maybe when he knows you're still alive, he'll have a new lease on life and be a different person."

"I hope so," she said. She sounded much older than fifteen. "For his sake. I don't ever want to live with him again, he's too young to be a bum. . . ." She put her hands to her face and doubled over. "It was heaven in that house," she choked. "They were so good to me."

"I know," I said. "I know." She battled the tears and then said more strongly, "I saw Tracy yesterday. She looked so sad."

"For you," I said. "She thinks you're dead. Everybody does."

"Everybody but *him.*" She lifted her wet face from her hands. "I'd like her to know I'm alive, but she couldn't hide it, and then *he* might find out."

"I'm having a hard time hiding it myself," I said, "but I think I can do better than Tracy."

"Can I tell you how it happened?" she asked timidly. "You should know, and if I say it all to you the way I said it all to Gideon, it'll be that much easier when I have to tell someone else."

I didn't want to hear, but I didn't say so. "I know you were expecting Sonny," I said, "and you wanted to make him go back to the Youth Center. So you asked Tracy not to come, and she pretended she had a bug. Which is what I did last night," I said wryly, "so I could hide my guilty secret. These little bugs come in very handy.... All right, tell me."

The sisters had left around six, and Sonny came when it was getting dark; he'd been hiding out in the woods nearby. They'd both cried, she said with a touching dignity; they had wanted the baby so much. She convinced him she was well and safe and was pretty sure she'd never have to go back to her father again. Then she gave him a good meal and tried to persuade him to call his parents and have his father drive him to the Youth Center. They argued about this and about what his life would be if he had to keep running and hiding.

"He really knew it would be no good," she said. "He just hated to leave me again, and I hated it too. We'd taken our food out to this old picnic table in the woods beyond the garage and stayed there after the stars came out. We didn't argue real loud, because even if we thought nobody was around we didn't take chances."

Finally, after a couple of hours of their being together—I guessed there'd been interludes of cuddling between the arguments—he gave in, and they walked back to the house for him to call his father. When they came out by the garage, the Thunderbird was there. Sonny was jumpy, but she persuaded him to come into the kitchen. They could hear music from the living room, and she wanted him to meet the sisters; she couldn't keep this important secret from them. It would have been the worst thing she ever did in her life, she told him.

She walked through the house toward the living room, Sonny behind her, unwilling, but wanting to please her. "If I hadn't insisted," she said bleakly, "he would still be alive. But Gideon says I don't know that for sure, maybe we'd both be dead." The grey and white cat got into her lap, and she stroked him absently.

There hadn't been any light in the hall, just the lamplight coming out with the music from the living room. They stood there to listen, and she realized that it was a recording. "They liked to stack the stereo and have a concert," she said. Then she heard or sensed something behind her—she could not yet remember what it was, only the way she'd jumped and looked around and saw the black shape on the stairs. Until death closed her ears she would hear Sonny's shout. *Run, Run, Run!*

She was not sure now whether she had seen or imagined the reflected lamplight flashing off the ax blade as it rose and fell or the sound it made when it hit Sonny's head. Gideon said she couldn't have heard the sound, because she was running.

She went out the front door and down the drive, falling down twice—she lifted her hands from the cat and looked at her palms—before she reached the road. She started down the hill for the harbor and almost ran headlong into Gideon on his bicycle at the turn by the Beaver Dam.

"Poor Gideon, I nearly strangled him," she said, "and he couldn't make any sense of what I was saying. I was pretty crazy when we got down here, and I don't remember anything *about* getting here, except that road with the clouds blowing over and the wind in the trees. I still have dreams that I'm on the road—it goes on and on, and I can't get off it." She made fists of her hands and pressed them against her eyelids. "Gideon says the nightmares will go away some time if you live long enough. He thought he was having a nightmare when he killed his mother." She said it almost casually. "Then he woke up and began living all the time in a nightmare. But not now." She sighed like a small child worn out by a passion of weeping.

I don't know how I looked to her, but my face felt cold and bloodless. "You found them, didn't you?" she whispered. "And then you and those others found Sonny. Eden, if I could have just gone out of my head forever, then and there, I'd have been thankful. If I knew enough to be thankful, I mean. Poor Gideon had his hands full. And then I kind of came to, and I knew I wasn't going crazy, and I wanted to go to the cemetery, just to be there when they put him in the ground. Maybe it was meant, so you could see me," she said. "I'm glad somebody else knows about me, somebody I can trust, I mean. Besides Gideon. I don't care what he did once—I trust him as if he were God, and I wish he was my father." She stiffened her jaw defiantly, and I smiled.

"Well, I think he's pretty good myself, Janine, now that I know what he's done for you. But I want to warn you of something. The police are asking a lot of questions of a lot of people, and they will come here to talk to Gideon, if they don't find him on the road somewhere or tuning a piano in somebody's house."

She put her fingers to her mouth, her eyes rounded to those of a horrified child. "But Gideon never did it! I know he didn't!"

"But when they come down here looking for him—"

"Only a cat, or Gideon, can come quietly down that path," she said. "I'd have plenty of chance to hide." I thought I wouldn't mention her clothes and toilet articles, she was so confident. "But if they *do* accuse Gideon, then I'll come out and let them know I'm alive," she went fiercely on, "even if I'm scared out of my mind. And I don't believe even the police can save me from *him* as long as he thinks I saw his face."

33

Her bravery and her terror stayed with me. I didn't know what to do; I wanted advice, but I didn't know whom to ask. I was sure I was withholding evidence or committing some other related crime. Besides the police, her father should know she was alive, and Clem Jr. should know; he was her guardian. I wanted to dump it all into Glen's hands, like a tubful of snarled trawl and hooks, but I knew what he would say. Hand it over to the police; they'll know how to protect her.

But Janine would know then that she had been betrayed, and if something should happen to her, I would believe for the rest of my life that I'd helped to murder her. It never occurred to me that she might be in danger where she was; if Gideon had taken her home to murder her, he'd have done it already.

I kept up a good front for the family, but I couldn't keep going to bed and saying I was sick; somebody would have insisted on the doctor. I wouldn't let Glen stay with me that night, and I woke up nauseated and soaked with sweat as usual now, wondering if at that moment Janine was being killed or if already she lay dead in a pool of blood. If I thought of Gideon in that first sickening rush to full consciousness, it was only to wonder if he too were dead. The blood I'd seen at Fox Point was still splashed over my field of vision, whether I was waking or sleeping.

In the dawn I shook with dreadful anticipation. I even considered sneaking my bike out and riding to Gideon's lair right now to see if they were all right. But once I was vertical and out on my deck smelling and hearing the start of a warm September day, I realized that if the murderer had so far no clue to Janine's location, he wasn't likely to have picked one up in the last twenty-four hours.

Sprig Newsome's whistle was particularly shrill as he rowed, a moving silhouette, to the black cutout of his boat. The first gulls of the day were flying in, conversing softly. I decided to give myself another twenty-four hours and hoped the solution would come to me out of blue space, as the gulls came, or that something would happen to remove my burden of responsibility.

I made a list of twenty names for Julian's kittens and then started on my mail; I wrote a note to Shasta and a check for twenty-five dollars to spend for whatever the baby needed or to start a bank account for her. Every time I thought of Eden Michelle, an arrow of light shot through the black pall that lay over this most golden of Septembers. I saw her in the nurse's arms. No matter what they become, all babies are miracles, wanted or not; even the murderer had once been a yawning or squalling little thing created by the union of two infinitesimal particles in the true equality of creation.

Working on mail always makes me feel virtuous, and this was therapeutic. I was hungry by noon and made a large onion sandwich and ate it while I typed more answers to fan letters. When I had a good stack of envelopes all stamped and addressed, I put a rubber band around them and walked up to the mailbox. Chad came tearing after me, but I sent him back, though I had no conscious plan then to go any farther than the mailbox. I didn't look around to encourage any forlorn hopes; I knew how he stood in the driveway waiting for me to change my mind. I'd make it up to him later, I thought, as if he'd be disappointed for any longer than it took for the next promising sound to reach him.

I put my mail in the box and went on up the road. I met the driver at the Beaver Dam, and we yelled "Hi!" at each other in passing. Apart from him, there was no one else around in the mild September noon as I walked all the way to Fox Point. I stood for a while by the mailbox, listening to the eternal rustle of the poplar leaves among the spruces and a purple finch singing out of sight on a treetop.

I don't know why I looked down, but there, almost at my feet and just missing death by inches, the minute leaves of a maple seedling about two inches high had turned red. Each leaf was not more than a half-inch in itself, but they blazed up at me from the sandy soil in miniature scarlet perfection.

We are here! they proclaimed. *We are alive!*

"And you know just what to do," I said, kneeling beside them. "Tiny as you are, you know maple leaves are supposed to turn red in the fall, and you're a maple tree even if you're only two inches high. . . . And if anybody hears me talking to the ground, they'll know I've bounced off the wall once too often."

Tenderly I dug up the seedling with my fingers, carried it to a sheltered place at the edge of the woods, and replanted it.

Then I knew what *I* was going to do. I was going to walk up to the house as a dress rehearsal for the day when Kenneth would summon me to pick out my books and recordings. If Marianne wanted me to have them, I should take them instead of trying to wash it all out of my mind, as a flood tide in a gale sometimes makes a clean sweep of objects that should have been saved.

I'd already been there, with Tracy; I needed to confront the house and myself in solitude. But today Robbie Mackenzie stood motionless in the pool of midday heat, staring at the house across the herbaceous border alive with bees and butterflies. He didn't shift from one foot to another; his hands hung at his sides, and not a finger twitched that I could see. His sandy head was bent. It was exactly as if he were listening to music. The skin on the back of my neck tightened, and the disgusting tautness crawled up over my scalp. I could almost hear Marianne's mastery in one of Chopin's stormy polonaises, and I wondered what *he* was hearing. Involuntarily, and with horrid banality, I thought: Murderer Returns to Scene of Crime.

I tried to back off as I back off from the sight of a deer, with a soundless melting away so as not to make a sudden frightening move. But some peculiar acuteness of the senses alerted him, and he turned and saw me. My first thought was that I shouldn't have seen his eyes without his dark glasses.

I felt foolish and stupid, faced with his absolute wretchedness. He'd never been plump, but now he looked hollow-eyed and undernourished, much older than his years. His coveralls seemed to have nothing inside them but bones. We stood looking at each other, speechless, until I said feebly, "Hi, Robbie."

He had to clear his throat. "Hi, Eden." He pulled out a handkerchief and wiped his face, then blew his nose. I didn't want to raise my voice. Engage him in normal conversation, and don't turn your back. I walked toward him, saying, "What were you hearing?"

"How did you know?" He was frowning at me as if trying to peer into a dark cave.

"Because to me it feels as if the music is still there. As if it has to be.

It can't have gone all at once, forever. The walls should be permeated with it." It sounded uncomfortably like Fee's theories, but it worked. His face softened, and a few years left him.

"If she'd taken me as her pupil," he said, "she wouldn't be dead now."

This isn't happening, I insisted. I'm not standing here about to hear the confession of a murderer, who certainly isn't going to let me get away with it. I made a few futile attempts to ask how he could have prevented it, but I couldn't articulate a complete question; I had a picture of myself with my mouth opening and shutting like a fish's. I mustn't have looked that strange, though, because he was going on in a kind of winded, limping manner.

"I'd have been around here much more," he said. "I could have made myself useful. They wouldn't have known, but I could have sacked out in my sleeping bag outside the back door every night, after they'd gone to bed." He ran his hand through his hair, lifting it off his wet forehead. "It wasn't fit for two old women not to have somebody around at night! One of 'em could have fallen. Broken a hip, or had a stroke. All their relatives wanted was what they could get out of them, not to keep 'em alive. If only she'd taken me on—oh, goddam it all to hell!" He pulled out the handkerchief again. "I should have done it anyway. I'm just as bad as those stinking Hearnes!" His voice broke, and he blew his nose mightily. "If I'd only done it, nobody could have killed them."

It was a perfectly natural explanation, and he sounded perfectly sane in his frustration and grief. "Robbie, you might have been killed yourself," I said. "Like Sonny."

"And Janine," he said gloomily. "But I'm older than those kids. I'd have been there on purpose to watch out for something, you see. I could have stopped him, held him up a dite anyway, and made enough noise to warn them, so they could telephone or lock themselves in the cellar or something. Now they're gone, and my goddam life is nothing but what it always has been. A rotten shitty mess." He put on his dark glasses with shaking hands. "I wish *I* were dead."

I kept myself from saying, "No, you don't," which is never helpful, only infuriating. Too many teenagers have not only wished themselves dead but killed themselves to prove it. "I feel pretty rotten myself," I said.

"Oh gosh, I forgot." He was pitifully embarrassed. "You found them, and you saw Sonny, too. Hey, what are you *doing* around here? I should think it would make you puke your guts out."

"It's feeling that way," I said. "I'm getting out of here. You coming?"

"Yep. I'm parked around at the kitchen. I had to leave some gas." He tramped rapidly away with his head down. I began walking down the drive.

I felt that fine inward shaking as I turned my back on the house, recalling Fee's maddening assertion that They were waiting anxiously at the place of their murders, crying out for someone to notice them.

Robbie's truck caught up with me. "I'm not supposed to give anybody a ride, but I guess we aren't likely to meet anyone from the office or the insurance company way down here. Get in." He leaned over and opened the door for me.

I didn't want to ride with him, or with anybody, but he needed company, and it was only common sense to give him a chance to talk more instead of letting him go blindly driving up the road with his tank of propane.

"The hell of it is," he said glumly, "Jensen will probably nail me next." I was glad to see that in spite of his state of mind he was careful about leaving the driveway for the black road, even though nobody was in sight.

"Don't you have an alibi?" I asked.

"*No!*" he said vehemently. "And she left me something. Five hundred dollars to spend on lessons with this guy in Portland she knows. They could say I did it for that." When I didn't answer he said slowly, "*Couldn't they?* As much as they could say Kenneth Rigby did it because he couldn't wait for what he was getting?"

"Who cares what 'they' say? Are you going to use your legacy the way she wanted you to?"

"I don't know. I don't deserve it, after the last time I slatted out of there like a snotty little spoiled bastard. Oh, God, when I *think* of it!"

"Don't break down here, Robbie," I yipped, "unless you want to blow us both up!... Just keep your eyes on the road and your hands on the wheel. Robbie, she *understood.* But it was just as she told you—she wanted to save all her energy for herself, for the time she had left."

"And how long was that? A couple of weeks?" His fist pounded the rim of the wheel. "How the hell does anybody ever stop thinking about it?"

"We have to keep giving each other moral support," I said. "I can start by giving you a cup of coffee or a can of soda. You don't get anything stronger from me." I saw the corner of his mouth turn up at that.

"And you'd better start practicing again," I said. "She'd want you to."

When we drove into the yard, Chad came galloping to meet us, carrying a flat plastic bucket cover which must have come ashore at high tide. Robbie grabbed it from him and scaled it across the yard; playing with the dog, he was any boy for a moment. I blessed Chad's relentless enthusiasm.

"Hey, Robbie!" Sprig Newsome yelled from the parking lot. "You taking Eden out now in that luxury vehicle of yours? Gorry, if I'd known she and Glen busted up, I'd have got there first."

"You haven't got a prayer, Sprig!" Robbie sang out, with the first natural grin I'd seen on his face for weeks. Glen came out onto my deck.

"What was that, Skipper?" he called over to Sprig.

"No offense, Cap'n, *sir.*" Sprig, laughing, climbed into his truck. "I'd better cast off quick and head out of here before I get tide nipped."

"Ayuh, and in places that'd surprise you," Glen said.

Sprig waved his arm out the window and tore out of the parking lot like a juvenile intent on burning rubber. "Come on, Robbie," I said. "The bar's open."

34

I woke up before daylight to a heavy rain without wind, the kind that usually acts as a sedative, but not when you're beset with guilty secrets and the kind of memories you'd like to throw out into that rain to be washed away. Some people reach for Valium, but I'm as deeply addicted to pen and paper beside my coffee cup. I don't want to talk to anyone in the morning, but I talk to the paper. When I realized I'd been staring vacuously at the raindrops on the window this morning for all of ten minutes, with no physical or mental motion whatever except an occasional blink, I was a little frightened. I drew the curtains against that sodden dawn, turned on a lamp, and took out the notebook. I read over the last few paragraphs to see if they'd be a springboard for something new and then plunged.

I wrote for almost an hour without stopping to think ahead and only halted then because my hand was cramped and my neck hurt. Someone was coming up the steps. I opened the door to full streaming daylight and Glen in streaming oilclothes.

"Just saying good morning," he said. "Want to be my sternman today?" He laughed and poked his face forward, and we kissed under the dripping sou'wester. "Finest kind of a day. No glare on the water, flat-arse calm. The buoys will show up pretty as posies in a garden."

"I'll go!" I said at once. He shook his head.

"No, you won't. After the first ten traps, you'd be damned tired of standing out there in the rain, while I'm snug under the canopy. Are you all right?"

"I woke up too early, that's all."

"You need your bunkie."

"No point in us both losing sleep. I can get a nap, but you can't. Go along. I'll be here when you get in."

"Marry me, and we'll move in next door."

"This afternoon?" I said. "I'll never be able to pick out six bridesmaids and a ring-bearer and two flower girls and get my wedding gown made in time, with a train and all; to say nothing of a four-story wedding cake. And what about your best man and ushers?

He kissed me again. "You've just put the idea permanently on hold. See you."

I went back in and watched him go down the wet wharf. At least I was alive now. I scrambled a couple of eggs and toasted a muffin and sat down to read what I had written in the past hour, breaking my own rules.

It wasn't bad. In fact it was damned good for what it was. My God, I thought in awe, maybe I'm working too hard to be a serious writer. Maybe I'll become one of those women who write bodice-rippers at the kitchen table, after the kids go to school, and make millions. I could even imagine an infant standing in the playpen meditatively chewing on the rim while watching Mummie's ancient typewriter send up clouds of steam like Old Faithful, just before the machine fell apart from pure shame at what it was producing.

If I went on with this—supposing all those first and as-yet-unread pages held up—I could imagine my agent's face; and she'd probably have to find me another publisher. But should I care, if I made ten times what I was making now? Yes, I would care, because I couldn't exist as a writer consciously reworking the same plot over and over, only changing the names and costumes and mansions.

And if I gave the stuff in the notebook any more serious attention, as if it really had potential, it would lose its value as a therapeutic narcotic to be taken only at prescribed times and forgotten in between. I put it away and turned my mind toward a productive use of the day.

I never had gotten to the library that day—I winced away from the reason—so why not today? Life began to flow again. I even knew what to do about Janine and Gideon: simply pretend I didn't know anything about it. That was preferable to hauling her out into the light of day and exposing her to God knew what; her own fear would be bad enough.

The telephone rang, and it was Kenneth.

"Tillie Higham and Mrs. Carver are going to Fox Point this morning to pack up clothing and other personal belongings," he said. "Would you be interested," he asked diffidently, "in making your choices today? Of course you don't have to. I know how you must feel about going there."

"I know I must do it sometime," I said. "It might as well be today. When will they all get there?"

"Around ten," he said gratefully. "Of course Mrs. Thatcher's been there right along, I've asked her to pack Janine's things."

My conscience, not quite deadened, flinched at Janine's name.

"Fee can come whenever she's in from the island," he was saying. "I have no plans to strip the house bare."

I felt like asking, "Will you let her bring her Ouija board?" but restrained myself.

I told Gram where I was going, in case anyone needed to know. She was alone in the house; the bait truck had arrived, and Grampa and Uncle Early were down on the wharf in their bright orange foul-weather gear. Chad was shut up in the store while the big truck backed by inches down the incline from the parking lot. Gram was starting Eden Michelle's quilt and listening to a talk show from Boston.

"You'll be glad to get the business over with," she said to me. "Take something to wrap your things up in. There's an old poncho in the entry."

She took it for granted I wouldn't turn down the bequest, but even as I left I didn't know what I would do when I actually walked into the house at Fox Point; I might turn tail and run before I could step over the threshold.

Nick Raintree's car was there, and Tillie Higham's. Why Nick? I got out before I could have second thoughts; I didn't want Kenneth to think I was a coward. There was no wind, just a steady rain splashing down, making puddles in the driveway. The herbaceous border was drenched and beaten down. The scent of burning applewood cut sharp as spice through the blended essences of bruised flowers, earth and grass, wet woods and the sea. Dear God, it was desolate! It was really the end of things. But I preferred it to that rich, hot, perfumed, brilliant weather full of bees and hummingbirds, everything so profligate with life, and those two dead. No, those three.

When I let myself into the hall a pleasant warmth met me, distant voices in the kitchen and others near at hand. But not *their* voices, I thought. Never theirs again. I left the poncho and my raincoat in the hall, relieved their coats and jackets were gone. The hall and stairs were immaculate; there must have been much blood here, when the murderer struck Sonny from the stairs. But the carpet had been removed, and the hardwood floor gleamed under my feet.

The living room floor was also bare and shining. The slashed portrait and the shattered violin had been taken away, the piano keys washed. Familiar lamps, slip covers, ornaments, and books were no longer there. I took a good breath, fixed my eyes on the double casement at the far end, and walked straight toward it.

Lydia Carver and Nick were in the book alcove. Before Lydia retired from medicine at seventy-five, she was considered, in Grampa's term, a crackerjack. Nick and she were taking Scott Fitzgerald apart, and I heard a bit of it before they both looked around at me in a friendly and rather concerned way, as if I were a special case. My vanity vitalized me, as usual.

"Hi, guys!" I said brightly, if inanely, and couldn't think how to go on from there.

"Good to see you, Eden." Lydia squeezed my forearm. "I've picked out what Sydney and I want; now I'll see if I can help the others.... Confidentially, you two, I was glad Kenneth didn't give his mother or Edith or the Hearnes a chance to paw around in Marianne's and Emma's things. He brought me a dozen fresh doughnuts this morning for us to have with coffee—he'd driven to Maddox for them. But he wouldn't come down here. I don't believe he's been in the house since the police called him that night." She gave my arm another little squeeze. "It was terrible for you, Eden. You're braver than he is."

"You know men are the real weak sisters, don't you?" Nick said.

"Don't I just!" She grinned at us and went away, stopping to replenish the fire in the main room.

"Surprised to see me here?" Nick asked.

"I'm surprised to see me here. I expected to bolt like a rabbit."

"I had to screw my courage to the sticking point to get myself inside the door," Nick said. "It was just my macho pride and Mrs. Carver that kept me here. Of course she was having all she could do to manage herself, but she did it. She's a tough lady."

"They all are, my grandmother keeps telling me. But—" I looked around me for something, I didn't know what. I hugged myself, and Nick said, "I could do better than that."

It was no surprise for us to be in each other's arms. I pushed my face into his chest and felt his cheek against my head. I appreciated it and could have snuggled right into it, but the oddest things always interrupt; I didn't want my nose to run all over his sweater. I backed off, having to use a little strength to get free, and groped in my pocket for some crumpled tissues.

"I'm not safe these days," I said thickly. "But thanks for the hug. I appreciated it."

"So did I." We sat down on the sofa. "You know, it's not so terrible here. You could think they were with us, wondering what we'll pick. If you want to believe that, you could be almost comfortable."

"That's not the way Fee imagines it," I said without thinking.

"How does she?"

"She's read this theory people who die suddenly and violently are so confused they don't realize what's happened, and they keep milling around the place where they died, trying to find someone who'll notice them because they don't feel dead. I *wish* they were here!" I said. "I wish I could be the one to explain, even if I couldn't help them that night!"

I heard my voice go up, and I was afraid of dissolving again, so I got up and began looking blindly at the shelves. "If they are here," I said, "they don't know how to make themselves felt. They might need a medium, and you can't be sure she wouldn't be faking it, making it come out the way she wanted it to."

He came and stood beside me, running his fingers over titles. "The most convincing medium I ever met was a man. He almost made a believer out of me."

"Where and how?"

"In a place where I worked once," he said. "It's too long a story for now." He laid a book down on two he had chosen earlier.

"Can I hear sometime?" I asked. "I'm interested in these things, apart from what's too painful."

"When we know each other well enough. And do you think that can ever be?" He gave me that satirical grin over his shoulder, and it turned him into the Nick Raintree of the first Afternoon; the one who'd come to laugh at the rest of us.

"Come on, start choosing," he urged. "Don't be shy."

"I don't know where to begin," I said. I shut my eyes and put out a tentative finger. I'll never know why it went where it did, straight to a thin book of Shakespeare's sonnets tucked in between Michael Arlen and Gertrude Stein. The sonnets didn't need the enhancement of the ornate typeface and handsomely illuminated capitals, on thick handmade paper; they read just as well in my bargain "Complete Shakespeare." But when I opened to the inscription written on the flyleaf, the whole long story of the Rigbys' life together for over half a century blossomed out at me in petals of flame.

Nick stood with his back toward me, reading; I felt behind me for the arm of the sofa and sat down on it without looking away from the page. The penmanship was loose, but clear and self-confident, giving the lie to the words.

That time of year thou mayst in me behold.
When yellow leaves, or none, or few do hang
Upon those boughs which shake against the cold,
Bare ruin'd choirs where late the sweet birds sang.

Then he had gone to another sonnet.

But thy eternal summer shall not fade,
Nor lose possession of that fair thou ow'st,
Nor shall death brag thou wander'st in his shade,
When in eternal lines to time thou grow'st;
So long as men can breathe, or eyes can see,
So long lives this, and it gives life to thee.

With all my love, forever—Guy

Nick was returning his book to the shelves and taking another. I laid the sonnets down on the sofa behind me and reached sightlessly for something else. It was autographed "To Guy and Marianne, with many happy memories." Nick leaned over my shoulder, saw the signature, and whistled.

"I don't think Kenneth's ever looked at these books," I said. "There must be a lot more autographed first editions, and they'll be valuable. I guess I'll check with him about my choices. Except for something like the sonnets there," I nodded offhandedly at the book on the sofa. "No way *that's* a first edition."

"If you're going to be so damn' honest, you've put me on the spot," said Nick. Then he added in an entirely different tone, "Jensen's been talking to me. Took fingerprints and all."

At his expression my stomach seemed to heave up convulsively and then drop back with a nauseating thud. He nodded. "Yep. Remember when I told you I'm the darkest horse? That I'd never have an alibi? Well, the cop remembered my taking Gilly away, and *Gilly* remembers, though I had a hard time convincing him he didn't dream it. After that, we were both lifted off the planet by a flying saucer as far as he's concerned. He woke up in his own house the next day, and that's all he knows."

Dry lips are a cliché, but they are a reality. Another reality is that sometimes you don't have the spit to wet them with. "There are those kids—" I began.

"Jensen says if we need to, we'll see if we can locate them. With a smile that says 'We won't need them, you'll sweat out the truth before that.' " When swarthy people go pale, their color is strange. "I can't sweat out what isn't true. But what if we can't find those kids? What if they were out-of-staters, with summer jobs here? What's that expression? 'zero at the bone.'"

"Emily Dickinson," I stumbled over the D. He laid down the books he was holding as if he was afraid of dropping them and wiped his palms on his corduroys.

"I'll tell you something," he said. "I can see it. I can feel it in my gut. I'll be the one. I'm the convenient stranger."

"Stop it, Nick!" He could be the one, common sense said so, but at the same time I was dismayed by his hopelessness, which was contagious. "You're not the only one who can't prove where he was that night. I know about two of them for sure. Robbie can't, and he's had trouble in this house. Gideon can't, because he'd always out roaming around unseen at night after most people are in bed. And Gideon was put away once for killing his mother. So what makes you think you'll be picked for the lead? You think you've got more star quality than the rest of them?"

"Good try, old buddy. Jensen's looked me up. I do come from New Jersey, and I've got a record. No, Virginia, he didn't find out that I was a Mafia prince or even a foot soldier. And even he conceded that it's not the kind of record that suggests an axe murderer."

"Then what did you do on the Sinister Dark Planet of New Jersey? Were you a juvenile delinquent? Playing hooky, breaking windows, shoplifting?"

"No, I made it past eighteen. In the Raintree clan you could look forward to having your nose and both ears cut off if you got into trouble with the law." He was relaxed now, at least more so than he'd been a few minutes ago. He sat down on the sofa and took out his pipe. "If you're going to hear all, you might as well know the worst. My name isn't Nicholas, it's Nicodemus."

"Gosh, I like that!" I said. "It's exotic, sort of."

"Tell me about it," he said. "Nicodemus Raintree spent his tender formative years praying for a miracle to happen overnight so he'd wake up Tom Jones, Bill Smith, or Spike Larsen."

"Is that what drove you into crime? Being Nicodemus Raintree?"

"No, it was a *she,*" he said, around puffs to get his pipe drawing. It was either the smoke or his memories that narrowed and softened his eyes. "A lovely *she.* Still the love of my heart."

It was a simple story. He had worked at a marina during the summer after his first year at college, and he had fallen in love with a Down East pinky called *Halcyon.*

"The sea-blue bird of March," I said. "I tried to get Glen to name his boat *Halcyon*, back when we were kids and I found the word in a poem."

"Well, she was my sea-blue bird; they'd painted her blue to match the name. I repainted her for them that summer, and I loved every sweet line of her. But they had no time for her. All through those beautiful summer days, when the wind would be perfect for sailing, she was tied up, a prisoner straining to get free. It was like watching an animal in a trap. So one morning I came down early, before the boss, and I took her out. It was to be just a little treat for both of us. She hadn't been out all summer, and I was going back to college. They might sell her, and I'd never see her again."

He wasn't with me, smoking his pipe in the living room at Fox Point; he was with *her*. "The instant she felt the wind, she wanted to go and to keep on going, and so did I. So we just went. As everything dropped out of sight behind us, New Jersey could have disappeared off the earth. I was high, but not on drugs."

I knew exactly what it had been like. I could taste the joy of it.

"Late in the day we stopped at an island for food and water. Nobody ever questioned me wherever I stopped. We sailed through the nights, and *nothing*, even a night with a woman I was in love with, could top that experience. I remember thinking, when the Coast Guard picked us up down off the Florida Keys, that at least we'd had those nights."

"I'm sorry," I said. "I mean, I'm sorry you didn't have a lot more time with her before they caught you. What kind of a sentence did you get?"

"Because of my age, and no previous record, and Hal's owner being surprisingly sympathetic, I drew a light sentence. That's where I knew the medium, by the way. He was in for fraud, making money off people who wanted to contact their dear departed. But I'd swear he wasn't all fraud. He had *something*. He had plenty of the inmates and some of the guards convinced. He could tell fortunes, too, with a deck of cards, and everything was free to the trade. Professional courtesy." He grinned, looking entirely normal once more. "It sure made life interesting in the old cell block."

"Thank you for being so honest with me, Nick," I said.

"How do you know I was honest? It could have all been stitched together out of the best sailcloth." Then he laughed. "Ah, my credulous young Eden. I'm a thoroughly depraved character, but then so were Benvenuto Cellini and Correggio. . . . You can tell by that I read a lot of books while I was in the slammer, and I worked on my college education by correspondence and finished it when I got out. I couldn't leave the state while I was on parole, so I concentrated on naval architecture. I'll have my own yard some day, when I'm through seeing what I want to see."

"What about your family? Were they supportive?"

He slashed his hand across his throat. "Forget it. My stepfather was all right. He's dead now, and I'm sorry. Young Sally's the only one of my blood kin who still recognizes me. Don't get that pitying look," he said swiftly. "I'm free of them. I'll always keep in touch with Sally, but the world's *mine.* I can go wherever my passport's valid."

Envy was as bitter as bile in my throat, or perhaps just the lust to run away from this particular time. "Where will you go next?"

"Islands," he said promptly. "The Hebrides. The Orkneys, the Shetlands. Scandinavian islands, Greek islands."

The envy *was* real. All my old longings surfaced, those I'd buried under promises that some day I'd have the money to go. Suddenly I saw myself like *Halcyon* tugging all summer at her lines. I'd have to cut my own lines before I could run before the wind for as long as it filled my sails.

It took more than money; it took courage. I looked distractedly around the book alcove, again for something I couldn't name, to be a touchstone; a charm against such fire storms. But I couldn't find it.

Tillie Higham called from the hall door, "We're going to have coffee and doughnuts in the kitchen. Can you two stand some?"

Nick put his head around the corner. "We're on our way." He came back to me and imprisoned my face in his two hands. I couldn't move. "'Sweet as Eden is the air, and Eden-sweet the ray.' Oh, the big eyes," he gibed. He pressed his fingers into my cheek and jaw bones firmly enough to hurt. Then he kissed me and released me.

"Come on," he said curtly and went on ahead.

35

After the mug-up in the kitchen, which turned out to be a fairly cheerful affair because of everyone's efforts, I didn't want to go back to the living room to finish choosing books; the sonnets were enough for me, and I was so determined to keep the inscription a secret that I felt as if I were trying to get away with an actual first edition under my arm. But escape was not easy; Tillie escorted Nick and me into the room across the hall from the living room. The sisters had made it into a music library. The first thing I saw was the record album Miss Emma had shown me: *Rigby Plays Chopin.* Emma must have propped it there herself, against the wall atop a bank of shelves; Marianne in a blue dress, at the piano.

I told Guy I was waiting for the roses.

I could hear her voice as if it were in the room; it stopped me on the threshold, and I turned to leave, but Nick was in my way. Tillie was oblivious, her back to us, talking about the final disposition of the collection, which included some valuable manuscripts. I could make no sense of it through the chaos in my head, but when Nick forcibly turned me back, I walked straight across the room and took down the Chopin album.

Marianne wouldn't expect me to be such a weepy sponge of a fool; not the woman who wanted to throw a hot teapot at Lucas. So while Tillie and Nick were going through tapes, and she was telling him what she and Jason had chosen, I picked out mine without hesitation, as if I'd known all along what I wanted. Sydney had also made his choices, so I didn't need to feel greedy about my selections. There was a recording of "The Four Seasons," with Miss Emma the soloist; I wanted that for the too-short, eloquently simple passage in the last part. I found a tape the sisters had made for their own pleasure, Beethoven's "Spring" Sonata. I took Miss Emma playing Saint-Saëns's Violin Concerto in B Minor, with that long, lovely, dreamy section that makes me think of gulls gliding on the wind like skaters on ice. Finally, I picked Marianne playing Debussy.

I wrapped my treasures in the poncho, and Nick took the bundle from me and walked out to the car with me in the rain. "Play those now," he commanded. "Don't put them at the back of the top shelf in your closet and refuse to think of them again. They don't deserve that."

"I'll play them," I promised. "Maybe not right off, but in time."

"Good girl." He kissed me on the tip of my nose as if I were a small child, and I was absurdly comforted when I should have felt patronized.

The rain was still falling heavily. Down at the Beaver Dam, the alder swamp was flooded, and the road was under a few inches of water; the brown brook was noisily pouring through its miniature rocky canyon through the woods to Bugle Bay. I was so tired that all I could think of was getting into bed and going to sleep to the sound of the rain on the roof; I wanted to stop thinking about a number of things until I felt competent to deal with them one at a time.

As if it hadn't been exhausting enough to spend three hours in that house, I'd had to keep adjusting my responses to Nick, and it seemed to me that the hinges of my jaw were tender from the pressure of his fingers. He had a gift for creating a variety of disturbances; perhaps his family had a point. Imagine what he could do if he felt malicious or vindictive.

He'd been neither when he had most upset me today, but innocent, and I was just now getting the reactions, all the worse for being delayed. It was what he'd said about his freedom. If I'd been envious then, envy now ate into me like an infection. I wanted to run away this instant, to leave everything behind without a backward look or thought; to gaze, unremembering, on foreign landscapes under foreign skies. And here I drove home in the rain, my emotional existence so poverty-stricken that all I could think of was going to bed. Alone. In fact, that was my only option for escape. I couldn't quietly run away, even to Portland, because I was not a castoff like Nick. Being loved and cherished deprived me of the freedom to move exactly how and when I chose.

Chad sloshed across the sodden grass to meet the car. I tooted at him to get out of the way and to let the grandparents know I was back. Gramp came to the kitchen door and called Chad in and waved to me. Behind my answering smile and wave, I knew I was no Mary Ann Esmond (for one thing, I lacked a handsome and adoring scoundrel who had to get out of town); but then I didn't want fifty-eight years away from home, I just wanted to be gone until *It* had gone.

I drove the car into the barn beside Gramp's, took my poncho-wrapped bundle, and ducked out into the rain and up the steps to the deck. Rain splashed on the boards, gurgled in the downspouts; the harbor was dimpled with it. Almost all the men were out, leaving only skiffs on the moorings. The sea pigeons were strung out in their even line.

I opened my two doors and ducked in, with my bundle held against my breast like a baby, and nearly dropped it at the sight of someone in the kitchen.

Fee stood in the middle of the floor, combing her hair. "Anybody'd think you just robbed a jewelry store and were rushing to hide the loot," she said. "What an expression! Utterly petrified. What've you got in the bundle? Somebody's head?"

"It would serve you right," I said. "I'd like to petrify *you.*"

I unwrapped the things and took the wet poncho and my raincoat into the bathroom. When I came out, she was looking over the music; she hadn't got to the book yet, and I managed to keep from making a lunge for it. I hated this reaction; it frightened me. This was *Fee,* for heaven's sake. What was happening to me? Nerves, I replied prosaically but removed the book while she was gazing at the photograph of Marianne at the piano.

Without looking away from the picture she said, "Gram told me where you'd gone and offered me the car to go up there, too, but I'm not ready yet." I could see the chill pass over her, washing away her color, even in her lips. She wore a fisherman-knit sweater and tartan wool slacks, but she still looked cold. I turned on the gas under the teakettle.

"We'll have some lunch, and I'll build us a fire," I said.

"Thanks." She hugged herself as I'd done at Fox Point, when Nick had offered to do better. "It must have been awful for you. That room is full of objects that saw and heard it all. God, I wish I had the courage!" She turned to me, glowing again. "Their energy must still be trapped there. I could take the Ouija board, give them a way to get through to us."

"Mm," I said. I took the book and music into my room and stood there for a moment with my eyes shut. Canada was only half a day away, and you didn't need a passport.

"Do you think Kenneth would let me take the board in?" she called. "If I get brave enough, that is?"

"I doubt it," I said, returning to the kitchen. "It would probably upset the Thatchers too much. I hate to sound heartless, but most people don't believe in those things."

"Oh, I know," she said with a sigh. "Plenty of them already think I've got only one oar in the water. Well, love, I'd better get going. I was going to say, 'Hi, I'm off!' but I was afraid you'd agree."

"Off where?" I said. "And in what? And how about that nice fire and some lunch?"

"I'm stuffed with Gram's mince turnovers, but I've got time for tea, I guess." She got out the mugs while I built a small fire in the Franklin stove. "I had Julian drop me off here so I could use Glen's pickup. My car's had something deadly happen to the transmission, and I refuse to borrow one of *his* family's vehicles, because his sister would decide to go with me and make a chummy occasion of it, and I don't want anybody to know where I'm going."

"Where *are* you going?"

"To see Dr. Derby for a checkup, that's all."

"What's wrong?" I asked sharply, thinking *Now what?*

She put on her demure act, eyes downcast as she carefully pleated a paper napkin. "Nothing, except I think I'm pregnant. I hope so."

"Oh, Fee, I hope so, too!" I sat back on my heels by the stove to look up at her. She couldn't know that some of my joyous reaction was due to relief because I could still be concerned for someone else besides myself. We grinned at each other the way we did when we were kids and had just pulled off something ahead of everyone else.

"I can't stop to drink tea," she said. "I'm so nervous. I'd have to go pee twice before I got to Maddox. As it is, I've been running all morning. Eden, I'm scared stiff, and I've been trying to keep Julian from noticing anything."

"I'll go with you," I said. She shook her head.

"You look beat. I'll be all right once I get moving. I *think* I'm prepared for whatever he says, but either way it's going to be a shock. Because if I'm not pregnant, where are my lost two periods?"

"I will go," I insisted.

"Thanks, honeybunch, but I'd rather be alone." She had been like this when her father died; meeting everything head on and alone until Glen got his sea legs under him. "But come what may, I'll want something to eat when I get back."

"I'll have it ready, and remind me to give you the list of names for Julian. And take my car."

"I was hoping you'd say that." She was pulling her rumpled trench coat out of the canvas tote bag.

"Greater love hath no woman, that she lends her car to her friend," I said. "But I'd better back her out for you."

"I'll bring you a present," she promised. "Do you want a little doll you can sew for? Or a new box of crayons and a coloring book?"

"I want a dump truck," I whined. "Yellow."

When she had gone, I felt a little more like myself, at least the self that didn't give me too much trouble. The tide of longing had retreated; I could only hope it wasn't being sucked out to a great distance to return as a tidal wave.

I read Guy's inscription again and my favorite sonnets. Then I put the book in between two of my larger ones, so it would be inconspicuous. I wasn't ready to play any of the music yet, but I found a place on my bookshelves rather than hide it away. I could hear Nick admonishing me, and I liked thinking of his eloping with *Halcyon,* how he called her "Hal," and how they'd sailed through the starry nights.

Glen came in from hauling, stood on the deck with the rain running off his sou'wester, and said, "Come on home with me. We'll go up in the loft and listen to the rain on the roof and the brook roaring by."

"Damn it, I can't," I groaned. "Fee's taken my car and gone to the doctor, and I've got to feed her when she comes back. I promised."

"What's the matter with her?" He began shedding on his way in, and I rushed his dripping gear to the bathroom. When I came back he repeated belligerently, "What's the matter with her?"

"She thinks she's pregnant," I said.

"Oh, Jesus." He dropped into a chair and dragged his hands over his face.

"Listen," I said, "there could be another reason why she's missed two periods. Something a hell of a lot more scary. So you'd better hope along with me that it *is* a baby, Uncle Glen." I leaned over and kissed the back of his head and then his neck. He twisted around in the chair, grabbed me, and pulled me across the arm and into his lap.

"You want me to have my way with you?"

"Pray, sir, have mercy! Or I'll *pinch.*" I did so. The consequent wrestling match was not in your classic Greco-Roman mode, and we stopped just short of the point of no return. Then we had something to eat, and he talked soberly about Fee.

"I just can't imagine her being mature enough to be a mother," he said. "That cat of theirs knows more about it than she does."

"Do *you* feel mature enough to be a father?"

He gave me a startled glance. "You trying to tell me something?"

"Nope. Don't faint with relief."

"Hey, you and I would make a great pair of parents."

"Easy to say, now that you know you're safe."

He reached over and gently fondled the back of my neck, fingered an earlobe. "If she's starting a family, I want it to be the real thing. God knows *our* family life wasn't much, but I always figured we'd have the chance to do better for ourselves."

"Fee thinks no life could be better than what she has."

"I guess you're right." Though still caressing me, he had become remote. That high sea of longing was rushing back in and would shortly be up to my ears.

"Glen, there's something I want to talk to you about," I began without giving myself a chance to haul back. "I mean, I'd *like* to talk *with* you about it, if you'll give me the time."

"You've got it." He let me go and folded his arms on the table and looked expectantly at me, exactly the way Fee would.

"I have to think this Fox Point business is all going to be over some day," I said. Now that I'd begun I was magically free of confusion or self-consciousness; I even felt slightly high. "But in the meantime I need something good to look forward to. Something to make plans for when I lie awake at night. Otherwise there are times when I feel like a haunted house, and it's nothing that you or anybody else can do anything about, much as you want to."

He nodded. "You got any ideas as to what you want to look forward to?"

"What I'm getting at—getting around to—well, next year, before the shedder season, will you take a trip with me?"

"Sure. Where to? New York, the Grand Canyon, the Great Smokies? Canada?"

This was better than I'd expected, but it was too soon to be sure of him. "You aren't just humoring me, are you?" I asked cagily.

He looked surprised. "No. You ought to have something different to look forward to, and I wouldn't mind it, either. We're too young to be stuck fast to our rocks like barnacles."

"Well, then, next May or so, what about Scotland? I'll put my advance away and not touch it; it'll make a lot of interest."

"Why Scotland?" He didn't sound appalled, only curious.

"Well, why not?" That was a clever comeback. "I always wanted to visit the Greek Islands, but considering what's going on in that part of Europe I think the Scottish ones are a lot safer, and they're beautiful, and everybody speaks English, some Gaelic, too, but—and your Glenroy ancestors came from Scotland. Did your mother know where? I'll bet Sandy Glenroy could tell you." I was talking too much, too fast, and Glen had that tolerant expression which could put me on the defensive, and then my own weakness always angered me.

"Got a map?" he asked. I forgave him at once and rushed to get out my atlas. I'd been studying the Greek Islands for years, and now, just because there was a better chance of seeing the Hebrides, I had become instantly unfaithful.

"Aren't the names beautiful?" I murmured as we studied the map. "Mull, Iona, Tiree... Barra, and Skye, and look, here's where your Harris tweed jacket came from."

"What else do you know about it, besides tweed?"

"There's a lot of fishing and lobstering. Look, if I collect a batch of material for you, will you read it?"

"Yep," he said agreeably. "I'll bet you never knew I was always crazy about bagpipes."

"Me, too!" I said in astonishment. "How'd we ever happen to keep that secret from each other?"

"I guess because pipers are a pretty scarce item around here, except when they can get a pipe band from Canada for a Fourth of July parade once in a while. But the way they made me feel, and still do, it's nothing I could talk about. I can't explain it. Must be in my genes."

"*If* we go," I said cautiously, "we'll be hearing Scottish pipers on their own turf. I can't believe we're really talking about it! I'm shaky, but this time it's with good vibes, not bad ones."

He pulled me into his lap again. Then Chad began barking outside, and through the rain on the roof, we heard Fee's hilarious voice.

"She must be all right," I said, "or she's putting on a good act. Listen, Glen." I put my arms around his neck. "Can we keep this all to ourselves? It's not that I don't want Fee to know—"

"But she'll wear it out. Let her buzz around with the bees in her own bonnet, not ours."

I poked up the fire again in the Franklin stove, put the teakettle on to heat, and opened the door. She came running up the steps. "Where's the food? I've got to eat enough lunch for two!" Damp trenchcoat and all, she seized me around the waist and danced me about the room singing, "Rock-a-bye Baby."

Glen slouched low in the captain's chair, watching her with neither disapproval nor joy. She let go of me and yanked his forelock. "What about you, Twinnie mine? Why aren't you thinking about *your* posterity? It's up to you and me to bring some more Heriots into the world, and I'm doing my bit. Come April I'll have an heir to the island, and I'm going to have more, and if they ever think of selling it, I'll be around to haunt them."

"So when are you getting married?" Glen asked flatly.

"I'm not. I want this child to be a Heriot." She was still euphoric and beautiful with it.

"You mean, just like that you decide to make your child a bastard?"

"Watch your language, sweetheart. It wouldn't be the first one in our family, would it? And it probably won't be the last. Dad was one, wasn't he?" She winked at me. "And he came legally by the name Heriot, and he prized it, and so do I. So the kids and I are hanging on to it."

"What about this kid's dad?" Glen asked. "Don't you think he'll want marriage? He's pretty conservative. Or what is he in this, just the stud?"

I could have kicked him, but Fee took it with joyous equanimity. "He'll agree with whatever I want. And I don't want his family in on this, if anything should happen to me. Nobody gets that island but a Heriot. If I didn't have kids, it would go to you and your kids."

"That makes good sense," I said judicially. Glen tented his fingers before his face and looked past the peak at us. Fee turned to me.

"If anything happens to me when it's born, will you be a guardian along with Glen? Julian's family would take it away from him, and I don't want them raising my child." She was not merry now, but touching in her appeal. "Say yes, please, Eden. And you, too, Glen."

"Sure, Fee," I said, almost too fast. "But nothing's going to happen." I was back in the hospital, standing beside Toby, seeing Eden Michelle for the first time. "Nothing's going to happen," I repeated for myself, not her.

"*Glen?*" There was the faintest quiver in her voice.

"Oh, come here," he said tiredly, holding out his arms.

She made a stifled little sound and clung to him. Over her head his grey eyes looked into mine without expression.

She let go of him in a minute and left his lap, rubbing her eyes. "I'll have Clem make out the proper papers in plenty of time," she said brusquely. "Not that I expect anything to go wrong, I'm so healthy, but it'll be like extra insurance. Nothing can happen if we're all ready for it."

"OK," I said. "Now how about food?"

"I thought you'd never ask. Why don't you just leave the refrigerator door open and leave me alone? I promise to leave the light and the racks."

Making an omelet for her, I thought, with an April birth we can still go in May. May and June; none of your three-week packages for us. And of course she'd be fine, never mind that idiot (me) at the nursery window. Fee was the type who could have the baby in the morning and go out and weed the garden in the afternoon.

Besides the omelet she ate a large tomato and three slices of bread and butter, with a glass of milk. She managed to keep on talking at the same time. Glen lay on the couch ostensibly reading, but I suspected he didn't know what he was looking at; he was beginning a very tense seven months.

By the time she finished eating, Julian and *Island Magic* were coming into the harbor. "Julian's always punctual," she said. "I told him four, and he's right on the dot. He won't want a mug-up; he can hardly wait to get home to the island, and neither can I. *We,*" she added with a grin.

I gave her the list of names for the kittens, and we walked down to the wharf with her. The rain had stopped, leaving us marooned in warm, heavy, moist air, odorous with aromatic wet earth, beaten flowers, and the wharf's special emanations. Chad was on the lobster car barking at sea pigeons; there were two boats in, and Uncle Early was buying their lobsters. Julian sat on the stern of *Island Magic.*

Fee stopped us by the store, taking each of us by the arm. "Listen, not a word to Julian about this," she said rapidly. "He doesn't know what I went to the doctor about, and I don't want him to know until I can't keep it a secret any longer. He'd be so excited he'd be bragging to his brother tomorrow, if he couldn't make it tonight, and then they'll all be on his neck about getting married. They're so crazy to get their greedy little paws on the island. All they can see is a half-million or so."

"I've already forgotten," I said. Glen nodded glumly. We resumed walking down the wet wharf. All at once she took my arm again and held me back.

"I forgot to ask you, Eden," she said. "Isn't there anything new on the grapevine about Janine? The *Journal* never says anything except 'The investigation is on-going.' Sounds as if they're expecting the answers to drop from the sky." The mood swing from giddiness to this intense solemnity was understandable; she was going back to the island where Sonny had turned up in the rockweed. I wished I could tell her the truth.

"What about your personal grapevine?" I asked.

"Oh, bull," said Glen, giving me a disgusted look, and walked off ahead of me.

"I don't get a thing," she said. "It's just as if Janine had never existed. The last time was the day of Sonny's funeral."

Down by the car Julian laughed, which diverted her attention from me. I didn't think I actually jumped, but I felt as if I did. I don't know why I think everyone else is so much smarter at reading faces than I am; I have to remind myself occasionally that I'm as bright as anyone, and brighter than some. But Fee and I had been too close for too long.

Recklessly I asked, "Just what did you get? A message *about* her or *from* her?"

"Oh, it wasn't through the board." She was hastening toward Julian. "It was during the service. A strong sense that she was there. It may have been because almost everybody was thinking about her. I'm surprised you didn't feel it."

When I'm going to lie I need plenty of time to prepare for it. However, I did all right. "Not that I remember," I said. She was so intent on Julian, I don't think she heard me.

36

I wanted to tell Glen about Janine when we came back to the Hayloft after *Island Magic* left. I thought it might take his mind off Fee, but I had promised on Scout's honor, and besides, I knew what I'd get—and which I doubtless deserved. Anyway, with our trip as sure as anything could be in these precarious days, I didn't want to chance an argument about whether or not I should have gone straight to the police.

We lay on the couch in each other's arms, not wanting to make love but just to be together. Then he went home to get ready for a selectmen's meeting, called especially to deal with a North Whittier resident's desire to have a junk yard in spite of his neighbor's protests.

I watched television with the grandparents that night and returned late to the Hayloft, yawning, falling over my own feet all the way through the open chamber. But the instant I was in bed I was jolted wide awake by remembering Fee's question on the wharf. Maybe she was really developing latent psychic powers; or maybe we knew each other so well she was mind reading without knowing it. That got me out of bed, and once I was on my feet I decided what I was actually nervous about was having Jensen discover I'd been witholding evidence.

I don't understand how people endure the strain of living a double life. The only way I could settle down again was to anticipate our trip, and that had me wakeful in a much happier way. I could hardly wait to drive to Maddox on Monday and see what I could collect about Scotland in the bookshop and the library. Trying to decide whether we'd take off from Boston or Halifax, I fell asleep.

In the morning everything steamed in the heat of the rising sun, and I took a chair and a tray onto the deck to eat my breakfast. No boats were out this Sunday on water the pale blue of forget-me-nots. It *felt* like Sunday; a day when, according to one of the favorite hymns of my childhood, the saints would be joyously casting down their golden crowns upon the glassy sea.

The Temple boys came over to mow the lawn before Sunday school, but it was still too wet, which I'm sure they had figured on. They sat on my railing, and I asked them the usual questions about school. Will had left Whittier for the Middle School in Maddox, and both boys seemed to enjoy the separation. Ben was free of an older brother pulling rank on him; Will was free of a younger brother who relentlessly watched and catalogued his every move, especially if he so much as spoke to a girl.

They were full of their own questions; it had been a long time since they'd cornered me. What about Shasta's baby? Was I scared in the car? Was it true the sheriff had arrested Toby right in the hospital? Did I think Richie and Toby would really go to jail?

"I don't know," I said. "They're likely to."

"Dad says it's high time," said Ben.

"Well, anyway," said Will, "now that the cops know what they were doing that night, nobody can say they killed those old ladies and Sonny. Toby wouldn't, anyway. You can't tell about Richie; he's so mean."

"I don't think he's *that* mean," Ben objected. "I don't think he'd take an ax to somebody like splitting open a pumpkin." He demonstrated graphically, with sound effects. His older brother was mortified.

"Hey, knock it off, you creep! She found them, remember!"

Ben blushed. "Gosh, Eden, I'm sorry. It's just I keep thinking about it. Not all the time, but it's there. And the kids at school talk about what happened to that girl. They said her father's up in the crazy house because he's lost his mind about it."

"He's upset," I said.

"It's only natural," Will said. We nodded sagaciously at each other. I was glad to hear the telephone ringing; I went in to pick it up, and they ran down the steps, yelling at Chad.

I didn't know the voice at first, it was so soft and spoke so quickly. My first thought; anonymous call, about to turn obscene. Second thought: some kind of bad joke.

"Eden, I'm at Fox Point, and I'm about to be arrested. I came to tune the piano, and they've called the police, and there's a lad standing here aiming a shotgun at me."

Recognition stupefied me even more than the first surprise. I thought I'd never get the name out.

"*Gideon?*"

"Yes. Will you go to my place and take my yellow kitten and look out for her, in case I don't get home tonight? The old cat's fine alone, but I don't want the kitten left outside after dark."

"Sure, Gideon, right away," I babbled. "And if you don't get home tomorrow, I'll go and feed the old cat. Don't worry about them."

He had already hung up. I drove a gull away from my breakfast tray and brought it in, took my car keys, and ran down the steps. Out on the front lawn the boys were tossing Chad's plastic lid back and forth, with Chad barking and bouncing between them. A truck door slammed in the parking lot, and Toby sang out, "Hi, Eden! Wait a minute, I got something for you!"

"Toby, I'm sorry," I called back. "It's an emergency, and I can't lose a minute!" I just caught his philosophic shrug as I ducked into the barn. When I backed out he was standing by the rose hedge. "It'll keep," he said. "Hey, I hope nobody's sick or hurt."

"I won't know till I get there," I said.

A lad with a shotgun. Who was *that?* It didn't sound like Thatcher kin or Thatcher conduct. If they were arresting Gideon right now, how soon would it be before they came to search the cabin? In all this, I'd never given Gideon a thought as the murderer, even though he had already strangled an elderly woman.

I left the car in the secret spot just off the road and went down the trail. Once I skidded on wet moss and restored my balance with a dramatic series of contortions no choreographer could have designed. It was a wonder I didn't rip some vital tendon. When I erupted, panting, into the clearing, Janine stood staring at me, white enough to faint.

"I didn't know what I was hearing," she whispered.

I dropped onto the chopping block. "Come on," I said between puffs. "Gideon called me from Fox Point. They've got the police coming, and I don't know why the Thatchers would do that." She looked dazed and frightened. "They'll probably come here next. So let's get cracking."

She looked wildly about her. "But they'll know I was here! I'll have to gather up every trace of me."

"No time," I said. "Anyway, we'll go to them ourselves. It'll be better than them finding you here." I hadn't known I was going to say that. But

I couldn't very well hide her out in the Hayloft, and the time for all that had suddenly ended. Everything was different now.

She was trembling so hard she couldn't snap the padlock on the door, and I had to do it. She dropped the key twice while she was trying to slide it under a certain shingle. In the meantime I kept expecting us to be suddenly confronted by uniforms, and when I tried to think what I'd say to the wearers, my brain was at a dead end.

"He never did it," she kept repeating the whole time we climbed the steep track. "They can't arrest him! Will they hurt him?" she asked fearfully. "To make him say he did it?"

"No, no," I promised, "and besides, they'll listen to you."

I bundled her into the back seat, and she crouched on the floor, covered by the old blanket I kept there for when Chad rides with me. I had the car out on the road, on the proper side for driving to Maddox, just before a pair of joggers came down over the hill. I waved and smiled.

"I hope that blanket isn't too doggy," I said. A nervous giggle emerged from under it.

The rest of the way I concentrated on relaxing, so I wouldn't arrive at the police barracks all in a lather and as incoherent as I felt. I kept talking to Janine about what we were passing and told her to answer now and then so I'd know she'd neither fainted nor suffocated.

"You'll be safe now," I told her as we crossed the bridge. "They'll be responsible for you."

"I'm not worried about me any more," she said. "I'm just thinking about Gideon."

I drove straight up Quarry Lane from the bridge, and at the top of the hill I turned left on Main Street. This was well away from the thickest part of town and heading out to the more rural outskirts to become simply Route 1. The state police barracks were on the left about a mile from Quarry Lane. Janine was out of the car before I'd turned off the ignition, and she was inside the building while I was still crossing the blacktop. With a heady sensation of having surrendered completely to fate, I followed her in.

The same trooper who'd come to Fox Point to answer my call that night was giving Gideon's face first aid.

"What did you do to him?" Janine demanded, giving the impression she was about to hurl the officer bodily away from Gideon. He gazed at her with awakening comprehension.

"Are you Janine Wolcott?" He sounded almost awestruck.

"Yes, I am," she said belligerently. He left us at once, and we were watched interestedly by the dispatcher.

Gideon sighed. "I'm all right, dear," he said. "I made it hard for them, that's all, so as to give Eden plenty of time. Why did you bring her here, Eden?" he asked me with exquisite courtesy.

"I wanted to come," Janine said. "Because I'm your witness. I know you didn't do it."

Lieutenant Jensen silently appeared. "So you're Janine Wolcott," he said in a mild voice. "And where have you been all this time, young lady?"

"I'll be waiting outside," I said to Janine, coward that I am.

"Thank you, Eden," Gideon said, looking resigned. "Janine, I haven't been arrested on suspicion of murder, you know. It's trespassing and resisting arrest."

"But we know what they *really* think," Janine said in a hard young voice. "Just because you're different, and they have to get *somebody*."

Outside I went to the public telephone and called Clem Jr.'s home.

When his son said he was there, I sagged against the shelf and shut my eyes. "Thank you, God," I murmured. Clem's measured voice spoke to me, and I said rapidly, "It's Eden Winter. I've just brought Janine to the State Police barracks. Gideon's been hiding her out all this time, and now he's been arrested."

"I'll be right there," he said.

In about ten minutes he was pulling in next to me. This morning he was in slacks and a hand-knit heathery pullover patched with leather at the elbows and his shirt open at the neck. I could not remember ever seeing him like this before; it was rather like seeing your teacher off duty when you were a third-grader.

With exemplary brevity I told him what had happened. He nodded, said, "Thanks," and went into the barracks.

It seemed as if I waited for hours. Waiting anywhere without something to read, or to write on, turns into torture for me at the end of fifteen minutes. I walked five times around the small parking area; I admired the view over descending ground and intervening roofs and trees to the river out beyond the bridge, where it broadened into the pool and then began its lustrous azure sweep toward the sea.

When I had given that all possible consideration and recalled that the barracks were on the site of the old muster ground, I returned to the car and cleaned out the glove compartment, but I couldn't see a place in which to deposit the odd bits and pieces, so I had to leave them there. The sun climbed toward noon, and I was becoming so painfully hungry I wondered if all this stress had started an ulcer.

Then suddenly Life struck. Church bells! And I knew them all. Traffic was sparse, but there'd be more by afternoon. Across Route 1 a cluster of quite new houses looked like so many model dwellings, yellow, white, pale green, blue, and unlived-in. With a positive upspringing of joy I spotted a cat on a windowsill. I watched avidly while a man opened a garage door and backed out a station wagon. Two families emerged bound for church and Sunday school. Somebody else put a dog out on a run, and he began immediately to bark at the unperturbed cat. While I was feasting on this, somebody tapped on my rear window. Clem Jr. came around between the cars, with Janine behind him.

She gave me a wet-eyed smile. "Hi, Eden. Thanks an awful lot. I'll make it up to you somehow, for all the things you've done. I'm going with Mr. Cruikshank now."

Clem Jr. towered over her like a benign heron over its small and downy chick. "Get into my car, Janine, you can talk through the window." He glanced warningly toward the highway.

"What about Gideon?" I asked.

"Well, the trespassing charge won't stick," Clem Jr. said, "because they called Kenneth, and he said he'd expected Gideon to go on keeping the piano in shape."

"Didn't the Thatchers know that?"

"It wasn't them," Janine broke in. "Mr. Thatcher had an ulcerated tooth just about killing him in the night, and Mrs. Thatcher had to take him to Tenby as soon as she could. The dentist opened up the office specially for him. She asked this niece of hers to come and watch the house a few hours, and she forgot to tell her about Gideon. The boy with the shotgun was her son."

"But still Gideon's been arrested," I said. "I don't understand this. If they know he wasn't doing anything wrong—"

"Don't worry," Clem said. "He hasn't been booked. It's not suspicion of murder yet. But they want to talk to him."

"I *told* them!" Janine expostulated. "I met him too soon after I ran out. And I swore that there was no blood on his clothes or his shoes or his hands. But just the same they'll go down there and collect all his stuff, I suppose. They still won't find anything, because he didn't do it!"

"We'd better be moving along, Janine," Clem said.

"Where? And what about my clothes?"

"I believe Mrs. Thatcher has packed them. I can get them to you tomorrow. Right now I'm taking you to friends of mine where you won't have to be afraid. Nobody but the police and myself will know where you are."

"Can't Eden know?"

"I don't want to know," I said hurriedly. "Does Gideon want me to feed the cat tonight?"

"Oh, yes, please. You saw where I put the key. The cat's food is on the shelf under the kitchen counter, and the can opener's in a mug of things on top of the counter." Clem started the car. "His name is James," she called to me, "and leave him in for the night."

Clem looked over her head at me with quizzical indulgence. "Eden, we'll be seeing you. Here, Janine, put this on." He handed her a gaudy bandanna. "My daughter left it in the car; she scatters her clothes like autumn leaves. You might as well hide that yellow hair of yours."

They drove out and turned west to leave Maddox. Nobody came to summon me in and accuse me of suppressing evidence, so I surmised that both Janine and Gideon had allowed Jensen to believe I didn't know where she was until Gideon called me this morning. I was so relieved to have her off my mind that I was almost happy as I drove home. For the first time since the murder I passed the Fox Point mailbox without a physical impact in the gut.

The lawn had been mowed. Chad was shut up in the house. The grandparents and the Temples had all gone to church at the old North Whittier meeting house on the crossroad to Amity. This side of the harbor belonged only to me for a little while, and I savored the opportunity just to sit and soak in my new freedom as if in a warm bath. And *eat!* I hadn't gotten far with my breakfast. I fixed a good brunch of French toast, maple syrup, and bacon, with cantaloupe on the side, and took it back out to the deck. I gave Chad the leftovers from my interrupted breakfast, and we crunched away in the rich ambience of the perfect September morning.

Glen and *Little Emily* came into the harbor before I'd finished eating, and obviously Glen hadn't been out to haul; he wasn't dressed for it. He waved to me from the mooring.

"Go meet Glen," I told Chad, who threw back his head to sing out his view-halloo and then went streaking down the wharf, scattering every unsuspecting gull and sea pigeon in the harbor. I went inside and began making more French toast.

I heard Glen and Chad greeting each other, and their boisterous progress up the wharf. So Glen was happy this morning; another bonus. He'd been out to see Fee, he told me over his meal.

"I should have said more to her yesterday," he said. "It was on my mind all night. But the news brought me up with a round turn. It's kind of a momentous occasion, my sister having a baby. Especially when we were shoved together more than most brothers and sisters. The poor kid, she deserved more from me yesterday than what she got."

"How'd you manage without Julian knowing?"

"Oh, I didn't say anything about the baby. But she could tell by the way I acted. Times were when we never needed words, and I guess we haven't lost the knack yet."

"I'm glad," I said, "and now I'll tell you my news." I began with Gideon's call; I saw no need to let him know about my earlier and probably criminal behavior.

37

When the grandparents returned from church, I told them about Janine but asked them not to mention it. "She's in somebody else's hands now," I said. "The police want to keep her a secret a while longer."

After that Glen and I took our rods and went trolling for mackerel well to the south'ard of the islands. The bluefish were still making things hard for the mackerel fishermen, but just to be out there was good enough, jogging back and forth across the lightly ruffled blue water. We saw occasional sails—Kenneth's Friendship sloop was out there; the speeders considerately kept their distances, and another lobster boat with a family fishing party trolled not far from us, but not near enough to bother.

When you're out there like that each hour seems to go on for three times its length. This occurs when you're scared out there, too. Time stops, and you think you'll die before it begins again and gets you safe to port. But on a day that's all sunshine and blue skies and blue seas, with just enough breeze to cool you off and make the water dance and sparkle, it was like living in the Land of the Lotus-Eaters, where it's always afternoon.

We didn't get any huge mess of mackerel, but we had enough to share with my parents and grandparents, and I designated one of mine for Gideon's cat. We went around to the camp to stoke up James and shut him in for the night; he was very gracious, especially to Glen.

We went from Gideon's place to Glen's and had our broiled mackerel there. He brought me back late, and I went to sleep quickly. But I dreamed about the murderer, as if he had been keeping just out of sight all day and was now reminding me that it wasn't over, he was still around. I wondered if he'd have dared to show up if I'd stayed the night with Glen.

Monday began as another exquisite day. Glen stopped in and had breakfast with me while the sky was still the color of ripe peaches. He was very sunny, which was natural after last night; he was feeling better about Fee, and he was glad that Janine had been found alive instead of murdered.

"Glen, did you mean it when you said you'd go to Scotland with me in the spring?" I asked him. "You weren't just indulging the kid?"

"I meant it," he said in surprise. "I'm counting on it."

So in spite of the murderer, I was rather cheerful when I walked down on the wharf in the sunrise with him and Chad, who did his bit by clearing the area of an insolent pair of mallards.

I was anxious to get to Maddox to leave mackerel with my parents and begin collecting my Scotland material, but it was far too early for anything to be open yet in Maddox; besides, with fishermen still arriving, and the school bus due soon to pick up the Temples, I'd be taking a chance on being seen when I turned off at Gideon's mailbox. So I had hot bran muffins with Gram, and she told me it had been on the six o'clock news last night that a local man had been taken in for questioning on the Fox Point case. Janine had not been mentioned.

"I should think they'd give out the news of her," said Gram, "to see if anybody makes a move. I know all about these police dodges from watching television."

"I wonder if Lieutenant Jensen watches those shows," I said.

"Of course nobody's writing the script for *him,*" she observed. "He has to do all the work himself."

I was just about to leave for Gideon's when Clem Jr. called me and told me Gideon was on the way home. Walking.

"I wanted to take him all the way, but he said he'd been confined for nearly twenty-four hours, and he needed to walk or he'd be flying. I took him as far as the Whittier line. I'll be down to Fox Point this afternoon to get Janine's things."

"How is Janine?"

"Fine, considering. She's a good distance from Maddox and anxious to let her father and Tracy know she's alive, but Jensen wants to keep it quiet for a few days more. I don't know, Eden." He sounded weary. "They may decide to use her as a decoy, hinting that she really knows something which she doesn't—in order to move this affair toward a conclusion."

"We seem to be getting deeper and deeper," I said. "What will Mrs. Thatcher think about your collecting her clothes?"

"That it's just a part of tidying up for Kenneth, I hope. I'm Janine's guardian, so it should appear logical for me to take charge of her possessions. By the way, Mrs. Thatcher's roasting a chicken for Gideon, a kind of apology."

I went down and told Gram that Gideon was on his way home, and I was going to start now and wait at his camp for him. She filled a small carton with bran muffins, doughnuts from the crock, and raisin turnovers. "These ought to put some meat on his bones," she said.

I had just turned off the road into the hidden spot when I heard a car coming down Sunday Hill. It almost slowed to a stop by Gideon's mailbox. Feeling melodramatic I peered through spruce boughs and saw Kenneth and Gideon getting out.

When I emerged from behind the trees, both looked at me without surprise. "Hello, Eden," Kenneth said. "Look what I picked up. He gave me quite an argument, but I finally talked him into the car."

"You wouldn't think this boy could be so persuasive," Gideon said. "Now I know how he manages to keep his business in the black. No offense, son."

"None taken," said Kenneth. He looked different this morning from the way he'd been the last time I saw him. Worn, somehow, and his smile was too quick and didn't reach his eyes. Well, why shouldn't he be grieving like the rest of us?

"I hear Mrs. Thatcher's upset," I said to Gideon. "She wants to apologize to you, on account of her relations being so impetuous."

"Well, I'm going back to finish tuning the piano by and by," said Gideon. "But no apology is necessary. I consider myself lucky, because Billy the Kid didn't shoot first and cry afterwards. . . . Hey! what's all this?"

I was holding out the carton. "Gram sent it along with me. It's all carefully arranged not to arrive in fragments unless you stub your toe and land on top of everything." James is so courtly, I was looking forward to seeing him this morning."

"He'll always be at home to you, Eden," Gideon said.

"Here." On impulse I added the foil-wrapped package of cleaned mackerel. I'd give my parents some out of the next batch. "Share with James."

"We thank you kindly, and thank Mrs. Winter for all the benisons." He was so dignified in his old fatigues, with his Allagash hat held respectfully under his arm and his untidy hair standing every which way. "By the way, I was able to clear Robbie and myself at one fell swoop," he said offhandedly. "I'm pretty sure. Of course they fingerprinted me first."

"He must have been saving the news for you, Eden," Kenneth said.

"Oh, I'd have told you, son," Gideon said, "even if she hadn't been here." He leaned against the mailbox with a spacious air of leisure. "At nine-thirty that night I was sitting under the window of a house overlooking Bugle Bay, listening to Robbie playing Mendelssohn's "Songs without Words" for a lady who shall be nameless"—he inclined his head in a courteous bow to her—"but who is doubtless one of Jake Rigby's oil and gas customers, and that is how she probably met Robbie. He was playing by the light of a branched candlestick, like Liberace," he said dryly. "I don't own a watch, but there was a striking clock on the mantel. Sounded off every fifteen minutes. A nuisance, but useful for an alibi."

"*Robbie?*" I was incredulous and delighted. "Robbie and an older woman? Who is she? I must know her!"

"Far be it from me to bandy a lady's name about. But she's the best kind for a boy like Robbie," he said seriously. "In her late thirties, perhaps. Not my idea of a charmer, but then I'm considering what Robbie needs, someone to fuss over him and believe he's a genius. The desert was blooming like a rose that night, believe me! Something for a lonely woman, something for a lonely boy. He won't have to be unchivalrous and name her if he'll agree that he was playing Mendelssohn at that time, and he'll be doing us both a favor."

"Just what I need," Kenneth said. The laugh was humorless.

He shook hands with Gideon. "Keep the faith, Gideon."

"Thank you, son," Gideon said. "Well, I guess I'll go home and have a word with James. He'll be wanting an explanation."

We watched him start down the track over the ledges and moss, with crows ahead of him warning of his return. As he disappeared, Kenneth murmured, "There goes a happy man."

"Do you think he'll go to jail for resisting arrest?"

"I think all charges will be dropped. He shouldn't have been arrested in the first place." He turned back to the road. Out in the sunlight his skin looked greyish-sallow, and he seemed newly thin, with a hollowed look about the temples.

"You look terrible!" I exclaimed. "What did you mean about needing a favor? Did you mean an alibi?"

"You've got it. Bright little Eden, right on the mark. Come on to Fox Point with me. I haven't been there since it happened, but I know I have to do it sometime."

I got into his car with him, and neither of us spoke on the drive back to Fox Point. I had never once seriously considered Kenneth as the murderer, but now the trite warnings danced in my head. *He's a loner. One of the quiet ones. The neighbors always say, "But he was such a nice guy!"* His grimly preoccupied expression didn't help. I tried to sit as if I were comfortable with him, not poised to jump, and I was ashamed but I couldn't help it. Nothing was safe anymore, and I didn't really *know* Kenneth at all.

When we stopped outside the front door of the Fox Point house, I barely restrained myself from leaping out of the car.

Mrs. Thatcher let us in, sputtering, "That fool of a boy! I've given him and his mother a piece of my mind, believe me! When I think—Oh, Lord! It's a mercy he didn't panic and pull the trigger!"

"Gideon doesn't blame anybody," Kenneth said, "and he'll be back this afternoon to work on the piano."

"I'll have some good food for him to take home," she said. "Now, is there anything I can get for you folks? I can stir up a coffee cake in about two shakes."

"No, thanks, Nell," Kenneth said. "We're taking a walk down to the shore."

"Real handsome down there this morning." She nodded at us. "Good to see you, Eden. You're looking better."

As we went around the end of the house I said, "I see you're still avoiding going in."

"To tell the truth; I don't think I could talk in there. I hope you didn't mind my refusing coffee cake for you."

"I didn't want any. I couldn't eat any more than you can talk." Outside I had a good chance to run for it. For God's sake, Eden, this is *Kenneth,* I excoriated myself. But how well do you really know what he could do?

We crossed the lawn, waving at Roy on the riding mower some distance from us. The last time I'd walked here had been with Fee. I could see us now, like two tiny brilliantly sharp figures seen through the wrong end of the binoculars; leisurely and innocent, with our first experience of hell day ahead of us.

We had reached the bank above the shore. I said hurriedly, "I'll go mad now trying to guess who Robbie's girlfriend is, and I'll have to figure it out all by myself." Stop jabbering, Eden.

"I had an early morning session with Jensen," Kenneth said. "Fingerprints and all. If I didn't mind, Mr. Rigby. Just a process of elimination." He looked ruefully at his hands. "He didn't tell me if I was eliminated—after that I didn't want to go to the shop, and I certainly didn't want to run home to Mummie and tuck myself in with my teddy bear. It's quite a shock to find you're on the short list. This isn't self-pity talking, Eden," he said dryly. "It's unadulterated terror." You and me both, I thought. Instinctively, I took his hand, and it was very cold in mine.

"You shouldn't have stayed a solitary so long," I said inanely. "You haven't got a girlfriend to get you off the hook."

"Or a boyfriend, either." He smiled at my expression. "I'm used to that story, Eden. What poets used to call the love that dares not speak its name is plastered all over the place these days like campaign posters. Nobody ever used to question an old bachelor. He could be shy with women without everyone automatically assuming that he had another sexual preference, as they put it."

"Not everyone," I corrected him. Odd! Holding his hand, I felt a little better. But I could still be fooled; the Esmond girls had been fooled. How did it happen that I was always alone with these people? "Come on down to the beach," he said.

We went by way of the wharf, down onto the white sand littered with faded blue mussel shells and black wisps of dried seaweed. It shifted softly under our feet as we walked, and the sun was hot on our heads and shoulders. Kenneth drew my arm companionably through his; to hang onto me, my ugly suspicion suggested. A few hundred feet offshore someone was hauling his traps; the boat was from St. David's, across the river, and she needed a muffler. The radio was turned up above it, to hard rock.

"If he drove along Main Street making that much noise," Kenneth said, "he'd be up in court the next day." The lobsterman waved sociably at us, and we waved back. He looked about sixteen.

"Deaf as a post by the time he's twenty," I said. "And he's just as happy as if he had sense. Kenneth, what's your motive?" I was actually asking it, somewhat hoarsely. "You knew for weeks that you were Mrs. Rigby's heir. Why would you want to hurt her?"

"Don't you know that loners are supposed to explode all at once and commit massacres?" Reading my mind. The water ran down my back. "According to Morris Hearne, she found out that I was going to tear the house down and sell the land for a few million. So she told me she intended to change her will, and I took an ax, like Lizzie Borden."

The room burst open before me in an explosion of blood. How could it be even more terrible to remember than it had been to discover? I was nauseated again and thought I was going to desecrate the white sand. But I didn't, and his tight hold on my arm kept me from staggering.

"Nell Thatcher called me; she was so upset," Kenneth's even voice went on. "Morrie and Esmond had been here to see Mrs. Rigby. They were paranoid because Morrie'd found me here one day. So he told her that I was queerer than a three-dollar bill—Morrie's phrase—and I'd never raise children in that house. In fact, it was all over town what would happen to it before she was cold in the ground if she left it to me. At this point Nell was ready to charge in with news of a fake catastrophe with the hot water heater or the stove, but Mrs. Rigby didn't need her. She was like a rock. She said the property was hers to do whatever she liked with, and then she ordered them out. She never mentioned it to me, and neither did Miss Emma."

The monotone didn't change, as if he didn't trust himself to let his voice go free. The St. David boat was heading out toward the islands, leaving a diminishing wake of noise behind her, and the returning quiet was like balm on a burn or a black fly bite.

"Here, let's sit down," Kenneth said.

38

With a reviving sense of letting go, I thought, *I believe him.* The relief was sweet.

The granite whaleback at the far end of the cove was pleasantly warm, and now we could hear the birds again and the nearly silent creep of the water on the sand.

"So I came to see them," Kenneth said in that flat tone, "without letting them know Mrs. Thatcher had called me. I told them I intended to live in the house some day, but I didn't want that day to come for a long time yet. Then I introduced the proof that I didn't prefer little boys, or big boys, either."

"What kind of proof?"

"Jean Whittier," he said.

"The *Cruikshanks'* Jean Whittier?" I asked stupidly.

"Is there any other? I wish you could see your face."

"I'm flabbergasted," I said. "Too much keeps happening, and I'm running out of emotional reactions. Pretty soon I'll be just letting my mouth hang open and saying, 'So what else is new?' Oh, hell!" I grabbed his hands and kissed his cheek. "Now I'm excited, and I want to know more."

"Well," he said moderately, "Jean and I are the best-kept secret in Maddox since my grandfather's great affair. Clem Jr. knows, and a close friend of Jean's; that's all. They've covered for us from time to time. Jean's family's savings went with my grandfather, by the way. That's one of the reasons we've had to keep quiet. The Maddox Whittiers haven't officially spoken to the Rigbys since the day they found out who robbed the bank.

And Mrs. Whittier rules by threat of a fatal heart attack if she's disturbed about anything. If she hadn't had one of her spells that night, Jean and I would have been together.... I swear the woman's psychic. Her timing is always perfect."

"My parents could tell you a few yarns about Mrs. Whittier," I said. "I should think by now you'd have worked up some ways to disturb her right out of the way."

"Don't think I haven't," he said ruefully. "But I'm a murderer in fantasy only. And fantasies makes me feel guilty enough."

"How would your mother feel about Jean?"

"In her own way she's as bad as Mrs. Whittier. She likes having a safe old bachelor for a son. A non-deserting Rigby male. My father deserted her for his quarries, and then the granite industry failed. So he died. Now *he* should have remained a bachelor and hired a housekeeper instead of marrying one. But he wanted a son to carry on the name. Not that he ever took much notice of his son," he said without bitterness. "My mother must have been damned thankful to have a boy the first hop out of the box, so she didn't have to try again. She still tells me what a hard time I gave her when I was born. Well, I got over feeling guilty about that, and then I was sorry for her because he gave her so little attention."

"I'd have been sorry for her, too, then," I said. "But your father's been dead a long time. He was dead long before we came back to Maddox."

"Yep, and I stopped being sorry for her when I realized she was as weird as he was." It was an astonishing statement from the master of understatement.

I'd never thought of Kenneth as handsome, though I liked his looks; but now, quietly infused with justified and passionate resentment, he was handsome. I was preoccupied with that until the quizzical cant of his head recalled me.

"You still with me, Eden?"

"Yup. Have you been able to talk freely with Jean about this?"

"God, yes! We've talked in circles for about twelve years too long!" he said savagely. "When I left Jensen this morning I was sick, and not only from fear that I couldn't prove I was sailing alone that night. I was suddenly forced to see myself as I am, and Jean too; a couple of dimwits waiting for their mothers to die. That's the blunt truth of it. And now that I know what real terror is, I wonder what in hell we were afraid of, all those years?"

His sudden grin took me by surprise. "I hate to tell you this, Eden, since you were my only fan besides Jean for so long, but the quiet and mysterious *me* was all a fake."

"Well, dammit!" I said. "You go get Jean this minute and walk down Main Street holding her hand, in the face and eyes of the whole town. And if Jensen doesn't have anything on you, how can he get you into court? He can't torture you into a false confession."

He reached out and took my chin between thumb and forefinger; I'd have died for this about nine years ago, and even now I had a pang, knowing that it had been Jean way back then. He didn't say anything, just held me like that, not quite smiling, while my thoughts rushed the heat into my cheeks. I was nearly overcome with guilt because I'd even suspected him.

"I was always your adoring public, Kenneth," I said. "I might just drop Jean's mother an anonymous postcard. If it killed the old bat, you'd have only one mother to contend with."

He released my chin. "Who'd ever have believed that little Eden would be telling me what's what?"

"Tell *me* something. Why did Mrs. Rigby make you her heir? If I shouldn't ask, don't answer."

He reached down and picked up a big mussel shell from between his feet and began slowly scooping sand and methodically pouring it into a little pile. "I used to write to my grandfather," he said, keeping his eyes on what he was doing. "When I was eight years old I found his picture up in the attic in a trunkful of his clothes, uniforms, books, and so forth. His name wasn't ever mentioned, but we kids talked about him on the sly. Pretty potent stuff, having a great criminal for a grandfather. We didn't know he'd been a hero first. When I found this picture—wow!" He whistled. "Here's this handsome guy in the riding pants and boots, the Sam Browne belt, the wings. He seemed too young to be a grandfather, but the way he looked into my eyes, he could be both father and friend. Well, I wasn't about to share him, so I never told the others. He and I did a lot of things together and had long, long talks about everything. This was all in my imagination until the time came when my mother wouldn't let me try out for Little League."

"For heaven's sake, why not? Was she afraid you'd get hurt?"

"Oh, no. But the coach's father used to collect our trash once a week, and some of the boys were not, quote, Our Kind, unquote. I was feeling so grim I wrote a letter to my grandfather and told him all about it. I needed more than an imaginary conversation. Then I took the letter up to Mr. Cruikshank's office on the way home from school. I asked him to send it; I knew he could, because I was always listening at doors trying to find out more about my grandfather, and Mr. Cruikshank was sometimes mentioned."

"Did he send it?"

"About a month later he gave me the answer," Kenneth said, "and he didn't have to tell me not to show it. I wrote to my grandfather for the rest of his life, and when he died, Marianne wrote and told me how it had happened, and what I'd meant to him. She and I wrote after that, still through the Cruikshanks. When we were kids, Clem Jr. kept all my letters for me in his room. They still exist in the safe at my office."

"I feel like crying," I said, "but the way things have been lately, if I get started I won't be able to stop. So tell me what your grandfather said about Little League."

"He sympathized, but he told me to try to find something that wouldn't cause conflict until I was old enough to make my own decisions. He'd always liked tennis, and maybe I'd turn out to be as good as he was. So that's when I asked for a tennis racket and lessons for my birthday, and my mother was *so* happy. Little she guessed how much she owed to the family desperado."

"It's a fantastic story, Kenneth," I said. "It kills me that my ethics forbid me to use it."

"Hold onto those ethics, kid—I'm trusting you with my soul." We both laughed. It was a relief we needed.

"Did you ever tell him about Jean?" I asked after a pause.

"Yes, but not as if she and I were dirty secrets kept from our mothers. I lied by omission, and he died while we were kidding ourselves that *this* year, *next* year, we were going to face them."

"Don't be too hard on yourself. You couldn't help it if you'd been raised to be your mother's devoted protector."

"*Protector!* Do you know how many clubs and committees she's run with an iron hand, until people got fed up with her? How in hell could I believe she'd fall apart if I crossed her? The Harpies and the rest would have gathered around to hold her hands, and she'd have had the time of her life."

"Do you call them the Harpies, too?"

"Doesn't everybody? Except my mother. She doesn't know where I am this morning, but she'll have to know eventually that I'm a suspect." His mouth twitched. "Boadicea will then fasten the scythe blades to the wheels of her Buick and go out to mow down the enemy."

"And where will you be? Cheering her on?"

"I think I'll tell her a few other things. She might as well get everything at once; the first shock ought to numb her for the rest."

"I hope you prepare Jean for this, so she'll back you up."

"I'm telling her first. She's been quietly reaching her desperation point. We both want children, and they won't wait forever. Of course her mother may have a genuine heart attack just to spite her, but—" He kicked over the sandpile. "It roils my gut to think what it took to make me act."

He straightened up and said brusquely, "There's another well-kept secret in Maddox. I'll share it with you if you'll keep on remembering your ethics."

"I don't know if I can keep my head," I said. "All this attention from you is rekindling my early fires."

"Thanks, Eden, I thrive on adoration. You know the Deering Fund?"

"Sure. Scholarships, no-interest student loans, outright grants, helping small businesses get started, all kinds of other good works."

"And it's stopped a sheriff's sale more than once and kept a few roofs over quite a few heads. Well, in 1927 the Deering Fund was nearly defunct, through the bank's bad management. That wasn't Guy's fault; the fund was his father-in-law's baby. The Jarretts had handled it ever since Paul Deering established the fund, back in the 1890s."

I was watching him like Chad waiting for that plastic lid to be thrown; any time now I'd begin panting. Kenneth went on, maddeningly at leisure.

"Paul Deering left Maddox because he expected to be made captain of a new vessel his father had built, and he was passed over for a more experienced cousin. Eventually he worked his way to the Great Lakes and was hanging around the ships there looking hungry when a small owner who liked the cut of his jib took him on as a hand. He rose to become the owner's heir, and he turned the line into one of the biggest grain carriers on the Lakes."

"And because somebody took a chance on him, he wanted to pass it on?"

"Yes. Originally the fund was to assist the young of Maddox, and the Jarrett Bank was to manage it. Old Ezra Jarrett did all right, but his son was a damned poor excuse for an investor, and he was too stubborn to hand the management over to Guy. So it was practically dead when Guy left." He turned my hand over and appeared to be reading my palm. "The fact that the Deering fund has been alive and healthy all these years is due to my grandfather.—That brought you up with a round turn, didn't it?"

"I can't believe it," I protested. "I don't mean I don't believe *you*—" I was almost stuttering—"but how can it be? And never mentioned?"

"Because nobody knows. I didn't until recently, but I believe Miss Emma." A small halt in his voice, and he looked away for a moment.

"She swore to me that Marianne didn't know about the embezzlement. She was wrong-headed and immoral to elope with a married man, but she thought love was an excuse for everything. She'd even convinced herself that Guy's children would be better off without their parents' quarrels. But she believed the money was his own, made on the stock market, and that they kept moving from place to place so his wife couldn't chase him down. Marianne wanted desperately to make some contact with her own family, even if she didn't intend to ask for forgiveness. But Guy kept telling her to wait, it wasn't safe.

"Marianne's desperation grew as they hurried from place to place in Europe; this wasn't how it was supposed to be. She *had* to let them know she still loved them; she *had* to explain to Emma why she hadn't confided in her. So within six weeks of the elopement, when they'd taken a flat in Paris, secretly she wrote separate letters to Emma and her parents through Duncan Heriot, the twins' grandfather. Everybody knew he had friends who'd stayed in France after the Armistice, so a French postmark wouldn't cause comment in the post office. Her parents never did write, but Emma did, in a roaring blaze of accusations and recriminations. And this was how Marianne found out about the embezzlement; she and Guy were living on half the town's savings, including her parents', and Emma's conservatory account, built up bit by bit over the years.

"So she gave Guy an ultimatum. All the money had to be returned, or she would leave him. She loved him, and she was just beginning her studies with a teacher she worshipped, but she was ready to give it all up. Guy was frantic; he didn't want to lose her, but he didn't want to give up his dream of the good life abroad.

"And then he remembered the Deering Fund. He was a wizard at making money, and the stock market was still climbing. He even found a donor, a man from down east Maine with whom he sometimes had drinks in a sidewalk café while Marianne was having her lessons. This man was another reprobate who found it expedient to live abroad; he was a bootlegger who'd absconded with money due his bosses. He and Guy worked out a deal.

"There's such a thing as honor among thieves, sometimes," Kenneth said ironically. "Or maybe Maine crooks are different.

"Guy used his stolen money to make money, as he'd intended to, in those insane days before the Crash. He began laundering large amounts of it through the down east bootlegger, who transferred it to the Maddox Board of Selectmen with a covering letter composed by Marianne. In it he explained that he was always interested in the small coastal towns of his native state, and it was his hobby to contribute to the further education of bright young graduates who might otherwise miss out, especially gifted girls. Their financial needs should be given first place, but after that worthy citizens could be helped at the discretion of the trustees; he was an admirer of Paul Deering and hoped his gifts could be administered through the Deering Fund.

"It worked; Emma's education was assured, along with that of some others. With impeccable timing Guy got out before the Crash. He and Marianne lived adequately, not lavishly, through the worst times, and she was able to keep up her studies. The fund stayed alive, and when the economy began to recover, so did the fund. By the time the 'donor' died, the fund was making money through the hands of a responsible broker and was administered by a board of honorable citizens, none of whom knew that Guy Rigby had given back to the town much more than he'd taken; even though he could never make up for his original act."

The story wasn't incredible, because I could believe in the young Marianne's determination and Guy's frenzy of compromise. But that the revived Deering Fund was the product of two exiled lawbreakers, conceived over drinks in a Parisian sidewalk café—that was the mind-boggling bit.

"If I put all this in a novel," I said, "it would be called too pat, too contrived, too soap-opraish. And that it *was*, and still *is*, a secret makes it only more so."

He seemed both amused and pleased by my bedazzlement. "Sometimes I've wondered if the Cruikshanks ever suspected. But Miss Emma found out when she went to France after Guy died. There were no more secrets between them then."

"How soon did you see them after they came home? Were you excited?" Marianne was alive for me again, and I wasn't going to let her go. "Tell me, what was it like?" I begged.

"I saw Marianne within two days. She was magnificent, but she didn't knock me speechless; it was as if we'd been talking together just the week before." He looked away from me, out over the cove. "Eyes bluer than that water," he said absently. "She needed no defense, you know. She didn't explain, she didn't apologize. It was Miss Emma who told me about the fund, when I found her alone one day."

We sat in silence for a little while, each drifting in private reverie. Then reality was back, chilling the sunshine and greying the sea. Someone had taken an ax to the little girl who'd worn her best dress to whitewash the henhouse; someone had butchered the tall young girl who owned a stage when she set foot upon it. I said in a small stiff voice, "What are you going to do about Fox Point?"

"Can you believe this? Esmond asked me to sell them part of the land!

I think they're actually convinced that I'll sell the whole place to them once I'm convicted."

I couldn't help wincing. "Don't, Kenneth."

"Oh, I'm not pitying myself now. I keep remembering how Esmond looked. He was all but drooling."

"What did you tell him?"

"That I was considering giving it all to the Audubon Society. He turned a dirty green. Bile, I think they call that shade."

He pulled me up from the rock. "You really want to know what I'm going to do about Fox Point? Just what I told Marianne. We're going to move into the house. She wanted children in it, and so there will be."

We embraced spontaneously. "I had to wait a long time for this, dammit," I grumbled into his shoulder, "and now I'm hugging you because of another woman. Kenneth, I do love you, and I hope you and Jean will be trimming a tree here this Christmas."

39

We walked hand in hand down the hill to where I'd left my car. "When I drove along here with Gideon this morning," he said, "I felt a lot different from the way I feel right now. Now if by some miracle Janine would turn up alive," he said, "both for her sake and mine—"

"Nick Raintree's got no alibi, either," I interrupted rapidly, to stifle my eager desire to tell him Janine was safe. "He's very nervous, too, if that's any comfort to you."

"All I know about him is that one of my mechanics says he has a record in another state."

"He borrowed a pinky to go sailing, and she didn't want to turn around and come back," I said. "Neither did he. They picked him up off the Florida Keys."

"Good for him!" said Kenneth. "I wish he'd made it to South America. I wish I'd taken Jean and made a run for it. Just sailed and sailed over the horizon."

"The world forgotten, by the world forgot," I said. "Or something like that." Somebody driving by blew his horn at us, and Kenneth swung up our laced hands over our heads. The horn tooted again, exuberantly.

"Gosh, now we're an item," I said. "That man's like *Time* for getting the news around. Well, all things come to her who waits.... Think of Gideon having a happy reunion with James. At least all's right with their world, for the time being." I knocked on a tree trunk.

He stood by while I backed out, and when I drove away he was still standing by Gideon's mailbox. I waved again, but his head was bent, and he was looking at the ground. I may have been convinced, but that didn't put him in the clear.

Amidst the litter of appeals and unwanted catalogues in our mailbox, there was a thick envelope from my agent's office; that would mean three copies of the new contract. When two of them went back, half my advance would be sent to me.

I did mental arithmetic as I drove in, subtracting the agent's commission, adding the remainder to my bank account. Compound interest is a mystery to me, but still I had a comforting idea of the result. My journey to Scotland was paid for; first there'd be all the delicious getting there, of course; going up through England by train, stops at York and in Brontë and Wordsworth country; then Edinburgh and the Highlands, and out to the Hebrides.

I had enough plans now to bury the murderer, and this was all owed to Nick, for giving me that jolt; but Glen didn't need to know that. Bless you, Nick. Please don't be the murderer.

The color of the blood hadn't faded yet, that would take a long time, but eventually I would stand on another shore with it all left behind me. *To the Hebrides.* What a lovely phrase, what a potent incantation. When we came back, perhaps the scarlet would have dulled a little. When there were children at Fox Point, it would almost go away, and then we could remember Them as they would wish to be remembered.

In my own life the Hebrides would be only the beginning; maybe not every year, but every other year, we'd spend a month or two on distant coasts, under alien skies. Who'd ever have thought old Glen would be so willing? See, Eden, he still has surprises for you, after all these years.

Chad missed me when I came into the yard, being busy in the store with Gramp, but Toby made up for the absence; he came at a lope across the parking lot, the turned-down tops of his boots flapping. He was carrying a small brown paper bag.

"Judas, you're harder to catch than a flea. That ain't very complimentary, but it's the best I can do right off the bat." He gave me that winsome grin. "I've got something for you. Had it quite a while, but it's not the kind of thing you carry around casual."

"A diamond bracelet!" I said. "Just what I've always wanted." I carried my armful of mail up the steps, and he followed me.

"Gorry, I'm sorry it's not diamonds," he said. "But it's a kind of cunnin' little thing. It will go good on your windowsill, or you could use it for a paperweight." He followed me into the kitchen, where I dropped the mail onto the table.

"How are Shasta and the baby?" I asked.

"Great! Oh, hey, she got your check, and she was some tickled. She's going to write to you." He watched me sort the mail. "The baby weighs eight pounds now, and she's real good. Fern was out, and Shas called me." He was feeling pretty smug. "I trotted Derek around on my shoulders, so he'd know he was still an important little guy to me, and I took him a new truck. Shas got her divorce started. I don't figger Richie'll give her much trouble; he's in such a pucker to be free he almost can't stand it."

I finished picking over the mail and forebore kissing the envelope of contracts, though I felt like it. "Well, where's the present?" I demanded. "Come on, I can't stand the suspense."

Fairly sparkling in anticipation of my surprise and pleasure, he opened the paper bag and took out something wrapped in paper towels. Then he carefully folded back the towels, as if the three-colored money kitten were alive, and he didn't want to wake it.

I couldn't believe it at first. I was stunned into muteness, my face cold and stiff. I knew Toby was hurt and bewildered, but I couldn't do anything about that; I was back in the book alcove at Fox Point a few mornings ago, looking around for something familiar and comforting to touch, something that should have been there but was missing. And now I knew what it was.

Praying for it to be pure coincidence (surely there could be other money cats), I picked it up and turned it over. Underneath, there was the name *Phronsie* which had been incised in the soft clay before the firing.

"Oh, Toby." I nearly whispered it. "How did you come by this? How did you get into that house? How *could* you?" I meant it in two ways. "Everything's kept locked up, and there's someone there night and day."

"I know I stole her," said Toby candidly, "but the place wasn't locked, and there was nobody there. I figgered they didn't think much of the kitty. She was stuffed away in a drawer. I left everything neat," he added with pride.

"When was this?" I was still struggling to stop the pinwheel spinning in my brain.

"The day of Sonny's funeral. Hell, I was out there by myself, digging on Tamarack, and I saw them leave for here, so—" He shrugged, but without his usual savoir-faire; it must have been the way I was looking at him. "Hell, I didn't mean any harm and didn't do any. Just looked the place over. I've got this curiosity, you see, it's like a disease. I didn't take anything but that." He nodded at the kitten. "Hell, there wasn't anything to take anyway. Some good antique stuff, but it was too big. I was awful tempted by this little yawe model; she'd look real pretty on my mantel when I get a place for Shas and me and the kids, but—" He shrugged again. "Now this, I just wanted her because I thought you'd like her."

"What island was this, Toby?" I asked, but I knew.

"Heriot," he said uneasily.

"It's true, they didn't think much of it," I said. "Hiding it away in a drawer. And they may never miss it. But even if I wanted to keep it—you know they come here." Good God, the way I was babbling I sounded as if I were condoning, even conspiring.

"Christ, I forgot that!" He whacked the side of his head. "Look, I can sneak it back when they go out to haul together.... Eden, are you mad as hell with me?"

"I don't know if I'm so much mad as disappointed. Toby, if you're going to be a father to Derek and my namesake, you've *got* to stop thinking that going through other people's houses and helping yourself is a perfectly normal occupation, or hobby, or however you see it. Would you want Derek and Eden Michelle growing up as little thieves?"

"No!"

"Then you'd better watch your own light fingers, and that curiosity of yours. It's a terrible thing to rummage through people's personal things, even if you don't take anything. You know you're probably going to jail for a while, but when you come out you'll be making a brand-new start as a husband and father, and that doesn't mean burgling your way through a brand-new list of houses."

He looked at his feet, he looked at the ceiling, he looked out the window. He blinked like Chad when you shake your finger at him.

"Listen," he said desperately, "I can return that cat, and they'll never know she was gone, but not today, they'll be getting home any time now. You hold onto her for safekeeping. I'm living at home, and the little kids are like a batch of raccoons for going through everything. She could disappear when my back's turned." He gave the kitten a tender look.

"All right," I said. The Barry household must have been a den of miniature looters all practicing to be *big* looters like their older brothers. "But if you don't come for her soon, I'll come after *you*."

"I promise," he said forlornly. "Look, I'm sorry, and I'm still going to give you something. Something *honest*."

"A nice mess of clams would do fine."

His reaction was incandescence. "That's a deal!" He left happily; as he crossed the yard to his truck he began whistling "Morning Has Broken." The long sweet notes went joyously up like singing birds, and each one was a darning-needle stab in my temples. I had always loved that song, until this day.

I felt behind me for a chair and dropped into it before my legs gave way and sat hunched there contemplating the cat. The first thing was to avoid people while I reassembled my scrambled brain; Glen most of all, because I couldn't drop this on him before I knew myself what to think. I got up and put it away in the top drawer of the chest in my room.

I'd been hungry when I came down the road; now I was suddenly doubled up with peristaltic cramps. After they'd sent me to the bathroom enough times to make me feel ten pounds thinner, I set out for a walk to Winter Head, where now there were quite a few empty houses. Chad caught up with me, and this time I didn't send him back.

Having no other human listener for a sounding board, I talked out loud to myself as I wandered over uncut lawns starry with fall dandelions and alive with young goldfinches and across the rich-colored autumn tapestry of a meadow to the sou'westerly shore of the head, where I could see the horizon without having to look at the islands. Chad scattered a few sandpipers, who simply settled down again behind us. He nosed breathily through the tidal rubble while I talked.

"The last time I saw the kitten was on the Sunday before." I meant before the murders, but I still couldn't say it easily. "Fee was playing with it, showing it to Robbie, making a fuss over it. Was there some way she could have slipped it into a pocket and taken it away with her?"

Chad may not be bright, but he knows a question when he hears it. He cocked his head at me and looked extremely intelligent.

"It's not like her," I told him. "She was never the least bit dishonest. But how else could it have gotten out to Heriot Island? Unless they gave it to her. But they certainly didn't on that day; I walked to the wharf with her and she didn't have it then, not with that fancy dress."

Chad was putting his all into his response. I took his big head in my hands and kissed the top of it. "Don't be so worried. Leave all that to me, and you just be a happy dog." He rushed off down the beach and pounced on a thick rope of kelp, backing away to pull it free of a tangle, and growling all the time.

"What about the next day, then?" I asked. "Monday? Maybe she dropped in with a gift of lobster or crabmeat. But if they gave it to her then, why should she hide it?"

But she couldn't have gone there on Monday. Early that morning they'd grounded the boat out beside Julian's brother's wharf on the mainland. She'd been out for the entire week after that.

I found a patch of sand and lay down on it with my arms under my head and watched the slow sailing of the clouds. The kaleidoscope resumed its spin. There *had* to be a simple reasonable explanation, and it *had* to be right there in plain sight; I experienced the panic of someone suddenly losing half her vision.

Chad came up dragging his prize and stood over me, blotting out most of the clouds. He managed to flap the broad, wet, sandy apron of kelp onto me and then began barking at me. In self-defense I sat up and threw off the kelp; he grabbed it and ran away again.

"The day Fee went to the doctor," I called after him, "she could have stopped at Fox Point, and Mrs. Thatcher would have let her in. I didn't see the cat when I was there earlier, but that doesn't mean it *wasn't* there then. Maybe Nell washed it after the police had dusted it for prints, and she hadn't put it back in the same place. Fee wouldn't have taken it while they were alive, but when she went there afterwards, imagining she felt all these influences and so forth, she could have taken the kitten on impulse, thinking it would never mean anything to anyone else, not what it represented to *her*."

It was all so logical, I could even see myself doing it. Or could I? I wasn't Fee. I'd have probably asked to buy it from the estate, and Kenneth would have said, "Take it."

Fee *could* have taken it, but Julian would have disapproved; that was why it was hidden. In her own mind she was convinced that it wasn't theft, that she was doing something right and justified. I could see her plainly, sitting in her kitchen or on the doorstep when Julian was asleep, holding the kitten in her cupped hands, her eyes shut or fixed on a certain star as she tried to hypnotize herself into being a receiver of those messages she wanted so passionately to hear.

The picture made gooseflesh on me, but it was a sensible explanation and that was all I wanted. I got up and played with Chad for a while, throwing a plastic toggle and trying to trick him into splashing overboard. But he'd never go in over his ankles.

We used up a couple of hours roaming around Winter Head. I dreaded returning to the Hayloft, even though I had now rationalized Toby's discovery. It was a kind of solace to put all the blame on him; if he hadn't been where he had no right to be, I wouldn't have suffered this traumatic jolt. I might never have thought of the kitten again, never have realized what I had been looking for on that day. Now I had to work my way around this unpleasantness as if it had never happened, and the presence of the kitten in my bureau drawer was going to make it difficult to forget that first numbing instant. Besides, when Toby returned it, he was likely to give in to temptation and lift *Sea Swallow.*

And while I was waiting for him to return the cat, what if Fee discovered it was missing? She could go as hysterical as she'd been when we found Sonny's body, which would be hard enough on her even if she weren't pregnant. Alternatively she could take its absence as a sign and be over the moon about it. She wasn't my down-to-earth, pragmatic, skeptical Fee these days.

I tramped wearily home, sighing at intervals until I caught myself at it and found the view distasteful. At the mailbox I remembered my contracts, and this seemed to exorcise the kitten, reminding me that life went on.

40

My notebook didn't work any more, and I was tempted to burn it without reading, except that as a writer I'm a compulsory keeper of any story I've written which might be even remotely useful some day. So I buried it in Job Winter's sea chest. I slept that night simply because I was too tired to stay awake, and if Phronsie had been a live cat, purring by my feet every time I shifted them or prowling around the Hayloft poking at anything movable, she couldn't have disturbed me more than did her presence in a nest of scarves and handkerchiefs in a closed drawer.

I slept, but I was conscious of twisting from side to side, belly to back, all night. Then came the busy early-morning dreams as I paddled just below the surface of consciousness; the weird montages, the optical illusions; unknown faces suddenly blazing at me out of darkness, with the fierce bulging stares of people in daguerreotypes. Isolated statements, ordinary and colorless in themselves, were now invested with a sinister emphasis.

"She has gone to get it." Who is *she,* and what has she gone to get? "Have you seen Roger yet?" Roger *who?* And why do I hear it as a life-or-death question?

A small house silhouetted black against a green-gold sky tumbled unhurriedly off a cliff. "I heard from Ariadne yesterday," a sexless voice announced as the house fell apart in slow motion. "And who the hell is Ariadne?" I snapped, and lunged out of bed.

It was just before sunrise, and the boats were going out, the gulls coming in. On land the chickadees were busily breakfasting in the alders. The day would brighten to beauty, and here I was with my innards crawling;

Janine was safe, but I had exchanged one set of apprehensions for another. In Maddox Kenneth Rigby was waking, if he had slept at all, to his own apprehensions. Out on Heriot Island Fee might have discovered that the cat was missing, and she was either panicked by the loss or jubilantly positive she'd received a message.

I signed my contracts and walked up to the mailbox in a dewy hush. Back in the harbor someone's radio went on, and there was no avoiding the morning news as the sound carried relentlessly across the water and up the driveway to me. I heard that Janine Wolcott, who had been missing since the murders of two elderly sisters and sixteen-year-old Ira Neville, Jr., had contacted the State Police. She had been in hiding ever since that night, afraid for her life. She was now in seclusion in a place known only to the investigating officers, and it was hoped she would be able to provide important evidence to lead to the murderer.

So that was that, and I was still tired. I thought I'd never get over being tired, and I would have liked to be a snail, snug in my shell in the deep grass at the far end of the orchard. *How we should slumber, how we should sleep, far in the dark with the dreams and the dews.* Just thinking those lines made me yawn.

A pickup came down the road behind me, and I recognized the engine. Talk about your *deus ex machina;* it was Glen in his truck. I stood in his way, wigwagging, making a joke of it while I felt like bursting into sentimental tears and blubbering, "God bless you."

"Give me a half-hour to throw some food together, and I'll go with you," I said. "That is, unless you've got a date with another gorgeous mathematician."

"There's a sexy seal out on the Seal Rocks," he said. "She's got a big crush on me, but we can avoid her. It'll be a long day, I'm going to shift traps. You sure you want to come?"

"A long day away from here is what I want," I said.

We left the harbor in the full splendor of the sunrise. He had food in his lunch box, but I had packed plenty more of it, filled two thermos bottles, and added an extra jug of water. I was dressed for work and wishing that when the day was done we could anchor in some hidden cove for the night, where we'd have been as snug as those snails at the foot of the orchard. But hidden coves exist now only in romantic fantasies.

We broke off work in a few hours to have a mug-up, anchored by one of Glen's buoys well to the south of the islands. The sea was calm, and the sun was hot. There were nine lobster boats in sight, working among the buoys that spangled the sea with dots of every color in the spectrum.

A few boats moved in clouds of fluttering, swooping gulls as the men emptied old bait over the side. We saw *Island Magic* in such a cloud, out off the St. David light.

"Do me a favor, Glen?" I asked. "Can we just keep to ourselves? It's nothing to do with *them,*" I lied fervently. "It's just that I've reached a point where I don't want to talk to anyone but you, not even Fee."

"Sure," he said. Lovely word. "But if they spot us, nothing I can do about it."

"I know that. But given my druthers, I just want to be alone with you. You're so restful."

"Thanks."

"But not when I don't want you to be," I said.

He gave me a pawky sidewise look. "Care to step into my cabin, lady?"

"I'd love to!" I said effusively. "And we can make bets on who'll be the first man to come alongside and see if you got caught in a riding turn and went down with one of your traps."

"It'll be Sprig," he said, "knowing damn well that you're with me, and we're not overboard and drowned. Come on, let's get back to work."

We went down by the Seal Rocks to pick up some traps where the sexy seal liked to lie around in the sun, alternately in disguise as a mammoth sack of dirty laundry and an immense grey pottery gravy boat tipped up at bow and stern. Of course, in the water she was all satiny grace and big brown eyes.

"She may be a woman under an enchantment," I said. "Don't ever risk a fishy kiss to break the spell, she's probably better-looking as a seal than she ever was as a woman."

Sprig Newsome came alongside as we were heading away from the Rocks. He made the obligatory remarks about female sternpersons and then said he was going in. "She's taking on water. Damn' stuffing box again, I guess."

"Want a tow?" Glen asked.

"Nope. It's flat-arse calm, not as if she'd have to pound all the way in. No sense telling you two to behave yourselves. That's what you do best." He sighed. "Hell, what a waste."

All that day *Island Magic* never approached us. They fished in St. David territory, which meant all their gear was to the east, and they'd have had to run a long way to talk to us. We didn't go in until after five o'clock. I'd done my share of taking out lobsters and measuring them, slipping elastic bands over the keepers' claws; putting fresh bait in the traps, getting each one ready for Glen to shove overboard at the exact moment to reset it in the right place. Glen did the lifting of the traps to be shifted, stacking them on the stern.

When we were heading home, the sun was low in the west, and the blue ripples were constantly changing patterns of gilt filigree. The gulls were going home, too, flying out as we came in. Sitting on the washboard, I was blissful with my aches. Nothing, not even the kitten or the murderer, could reach the depths in which I would sleep tonight.

The tide was almost as low as it had been when we left this morning, and everyone had gone home but Sprig. His boat was beached beside the big wharf, well braced so she couldn't fall over on her side.

"I was right," he called to us from under her stern. "I'll have her back on the mooring at high water tonight."

Glen was going to a meeting of the volunteer fire department that night, so he didn't stay for supper. I accepted an invitation to eat in the main house, if I could have a bath first, and I was about to take the telephone off the hook before I got into the tub, but it rang. I swore, and then answered.

Nick. So much had happened since the last time we'd talked, it felt as if a year had passed. "When can I see you?" he asked curtly. "It's been too long."

A rock dropped into my stomach with a nauseating *splat,* and I sat down. All I could think was that somehow he'd made the connection between Janine and me; someone had recognized me in front of the police barracks Sunday morning, and now the word was out. Punch-drunk as I was from all the shocks I'd been trying to absorb, I could now see with a preternaturally clear vision that his whole long story about being involved with a drunk was false. I'd whiffled about it before, but now I was certain at last.

"Are you there, Eden?" he asked, more gently. "Are you all right?"

He had wept for Marianne and Emma. Crocodile tears? "I'm all right," I said. "Just reaching the fracture point."

"I won't keep you long. But I've been thinking about some things we planned that we never got to do. It's not because I forgot about them."

"Me, neither," I fibbed.

"You're one of my first friends in this place."

"And you told me about eloping with *Halcyon,*" I said. "Look, Nick, I can't make any dates right now, but if you want to take a chance on catching me, come any time. If I'm here, I'm here." Not alone. "And if I'm not—"

"You're not," he said and laughed. It was such a pleasant, natural sound, very disarming. A man may smile and be a villain still, I reminded myself and then forgot it and went to my bath.

After supper with Gram and Grampa, I did the dishes, and then, because it was such a lovely evening, and I didn't want to shut it out just yet, sleepy as I was, I took Chad for a walk. Dusk would come quickly on, so Chad and I didn't lollygag out on the end of Winter Point but made a quick circuit across the lawns and yards of departed summer residents. There were a few interesting scampers and rustles in the shrubbery, but Chad obediently stayed with me; my fingers hooked into his collar helped. I felt comparatively peaceful when I turned down our driveway in a twilight as still and clear as blue-tinted water in a jar. The readiness for sleep was taking over, as sweetly as the night was approaching.

Chad ran ahead of me toward the back door, heading for his water dish; but suddenly he veered to the right and was off down the yard to the orchard barking, with me behind him ineffectively yelling his name.

That night Chad fulfilled for the third time one of his major ambitions. He made a grab at a porcupine's tail as it went up an apple tree and received the prize, a bloody mouthful of quills. He was leaping up the trunk, still trying as the porcupine went out of reach. He could bring forth only a choking wheeze. I held him by the collar with both hands, yelling for somebody to come with a leash; it was the Temple boys who reached me first, but they'd pounded on the back door as they passed by, and Gramp followed them down to the orchard.

It's a good thing both grandparents have strong hearts. Chad's open mouth—he couldn't possibly close it—was indescribable. It certainly took my mind off everything else for a while. Uncle Early was called, and he and Gramp took Chad to Maddox to Dr. Mayne for what would be a long session; Aunt Eleanor took Gram home with her for the evening. We've all been through this before, but Chad is the only one who doesn't seem to learn from it.

Will and Ben stayed with me for a while. They'd been so horrified by Chad's mouth and his suffering eyes that Ben hadn't been able to keep from crying, and Will was close to it. Their father had gone to the firemen's meeting, and their mother to a Tupperware party; with Will in the seventh grade now they considered themselves too old for a sitter, and they had been left alone, after they promised to obey all the restrictions and to go to bed at their usual time.

I cheered them up with soft drinks and cookies and told them that by now Chad would be painlessly asleep, and the vet would be already beginning the long job of pulling out the quills. Then I tried to get them to talking about themselves, but they wanted to discuss Janine. I let them wonder out loud and exchange their theories with each other until night was well and truly upon us, and then I said I was sleepy and sent them home.

"Yeah, we're supposed to hit the hay, too," Will said.

"And no TV first, either." Ben sounded injured. They left, racing each other. In about three minutes I heard a door slam over at the Temple house, and a light went on in the kitchen.

My own kitchen was somewhat illuminated by the security light that had gone on at dusk, and I undressed by it. When I was in my pajamas and robe, I went out on the deck to listen to the night. Close to me there were crickets, and from afar the distinctive drone of Jon's seiner as the eternal quest for herring went on. Then, much closer, the pulsing murmur of a boat slowly entering the harbor. The red and green running lights became visible, though the boat was not, and they moved eerily above their constantly fracturing reflections to the almost melodious engine sound, as if some craft from outer space were taxiing along the water trying to find the place to stop. One gets to know all the engines, and this one belonged to *Island Magic.*

"Oh, *damn!*" I whispered. I was aching for my bed, and Fee was coming to talk about Janine and bring me the latest news from Out There; my unlighted windows wouldn't deter her if she thought I was home. She'd just as soon wake me up. As *Island Magic's* voice ceased in the harbor, I thought of hiding in the open chamber and letting her think I'd gone with someone for the evening, but my tiresome conscience wouldn't let me. Best friends don't run and hide.

And then I remembered the kitten; Chad's adventures had made me forget it for a time. Now I felt as if the words *that cat* were printed across my forehead in Day-Glo orange, and Fee would see them even before I put the lights on. Then I almost did run, but it was too late.

41

They borrowed Sprig's empty mooring, and with Julian rowing Sprig's skiff, they came into the spectral outermost reach of the light on the wharf; at first specters themselves in a ghostly craft sliding on corpse-white phosphorescence, stirring it with each gentle dip of the oars. Then they became substantial, though the intensifying illumination leached their skin and clothes of color. Fee saw me up on the deck and called, "Hey, where is everybody? Not a light in the place but a couple out on the points." Her voice was almost shockingly loud in the night, and it made me wince, I was so tense.

"Everybody's up the road, for one reason or another," I called back, wishing I had sat on my conscience and locked myself into the open chamber. As soon as the skiff touched the float, Fee was out and up the ramp, running along the wharf like a ten year old and across the lawn toward the house.

"Isn't it sensational?" she cried. "Janine's alive! I've been rejoicing all day, but we couldn't get here till now." She bounded up the steps and squeezed me in a hug that hurt my ribs. "I knew I couldn't sleep tonight till you and I talked about it. I wonder where she's been. Do you think we'll ever know?"

"In time, I suppose." I faked a big yawn. "Let me go—I'm feeling fragile. I was out with your brother all day, shifting gear, and I'm too drunk with air and exercise to wonder about Janine or anything else. I'm just glad she's safe," I added through another yawn. "How come you picked up Sprig's mooring instead of tying up at the car?"

She sat on the railing. "We heard him on the radio this morning telling somebody he was going to put his boat on the beach, so I thought we could use his mooring and not be cluttering up the car in the morning, in case we were still here. If you and I go on yakking half the night, Julian will fall asleep so I can't budge him."

"Sprig's coming back," I started to say, but she went on talking. "He could sleep on the floor, and I could bunk with you. Couldn't I?" she asked, tentative all at once. "Or is Glen coming back tonight?"

"Nope," I said, exasperating myself. Why couldn't I be coy about it, if I didn't want to lie outright?

"*Good,*" she said, clearly all set to make a night of it. She swung a leg over the railing and sat astride it, looking down at the wharf where Sprig's boat lay quiet on the high tide, made fast bow and stern, her bow on a level with the wharf planks. Julian stood under the light, gazing down into the cockpit; then his head came up, and he seemed to be staring out through the glow to the dark beyond.

"Must be fish jumping out there," Fee said. "He hears everything, like Chad. Where *is* Chad, by the way?"

I told her about the porcupine, and she moaned in sympathy. "Oh, my God, the poor dog! I hope they get all the quills out. What if one works into the brain or something?"

"Hasn't happened yet." I knocked on the railing. Sitting with my back to the light, I could pick out the stars in the northern sky. The Big Dipper glittered over us.

"Haven't you heard a thing about Janine?" Fee asked. "Don't you have any idea where she is?"

"I was out with Glen from about six this morning until after five this afternoon. All I heard was the early morning news. Why didn't you ask Milton?"

"I did, but he wouldn't answer," she said seriously. "All he or any of them ever said was that Sonny and Janine were nearby." She crossed her arms over her chest and hunched her shoulders. "Freezes me just to think of it. Sonny practically on our doorstep, as if somehow he'd made it on his own. After that, what else could we think but that Janine was dead, too?"

She paused, and I could hear her quick light breathing, as if she'd been running.

"But you knew she was alive before anybody else did, didn't you?" she asked.

I was glad I was turned away from the light. "Where'd you ever get that idea?" I tried to sound entertained.

"I saw Janine at the funeral. I know you talked with her, and she told you where she was hiding, right?"

I was temporarily beyond speech and afraid to move an arm or a leg for fear I'd start shaking. How much of the truth could I tell; should I tell any of it? She didn't seem to pick up my agitation.

"Hey, mind if I put the teakettle on?" she asked. "I could stand a cup of coffee." She went in and put on the light.

"You should drink milk, for the baby's sake," I called after her.

"Oh, shut up," she said good-humoredly. It sounded so perfectly natural that I relaxed all at once and followed her into the kitchen.

"Yep, I saw her. I looked around at a squirrel and saw her and thought it was a hallucination."

Fee, taking mugs from the cupboard, said, "Mm-hm."

"Well, after all your talk about the Ouija board, I had to check up on myself, to know if I was seeing things or not. So I discreetly excused myself and left."

"And I followed," she said. "Not right away. But I began having this feeling when you didn't come right back. My scalp prickled," she explained earnestly, waving a mug at me. "That's always a good sign. I thought you needed me. That you were sick or had twisted your ankle or something. So I snuck away, too, and then I heard the voices. I crept up, remembering the broken twig that always gives somebody away in the old Indian stories, and you and Janine were just parting. So then I had to creep right back, so you wouldn't know I'd followed."

"Why, for heaven's sake?"

She measured coffee into the two mugs. "It was your secret," she said soberly, keeping her eyes on the spoon. "We never did spy on each other, and Janine didn't know I was there. It wouldn't have been fair to her, either. You gave her your word you wouldn't tell—I heard that, at least. But now—" She looked across at me with bright merry eyes. "Come on, Edie, tell me! Where was she, and where is she now?"

"I really don't know, Fee! Cross my heart—Scout's honor—" I made all the appropriate gestures, with mental reservations; I was being honest about one part of her question, anyway. "Clem Jr. took her somewhere."

"But did she tell you *anything* that day before I came along? If I had a hint to work on, something tangible that she remembered—"

"I couldn't make any sense of it. Maybe the police can, but then maybe she's really got nothing to be afraid of."

"But can they hypnotize her?" The kettle began to boil, and she poured water into the cups; the steam came up around her face. "So she'll remember something she blocked out?"

"I don't know if they do that or if it's just on TV shows," I said. Fee began looking in the cookie tins.

"You should eat this shortbread before it gets rancid," she said.

"Eat it then. And pour some milk for Julian." I went back out onto the deck. Behind me Fee sneezed twice and asked rhetorically what brought that on. Talk about unseen influences, spooks or not, they were so thick about me I could hardly breathe. Julian had left the wharf and was standing on the lawn with his hands in his pockets. "Come on up, Julian," I said.

"I've been listening to the crickets," he said in his slow deep voice. "There's one in our house."

"A cricket on the hearth is good luck," I said. Surely Julian didn't know she'd stolen the kitten and would never understand her doing it. So that solved tonight's problem; I couldn't possibly bring it up, but one day I would, and Fee would either be mortified, furious with Toby, or blithely unrepentant, saying nobody else could appreciate the kitten as she did, but to satisfy my and Julian's puritanical standards, she would confess all to Kenneth and ask to buy it.

The three or four fists that had been wringing out my stomach like a soaked Turkish towel let go so suddenly I almost staggered. I *was* a mess.

"Edie!" Fee called. The nickname always put us back to being thirteen.

Julian said, "It's going to breeze up. I smell herring." So did I, a clean, sharp, deep-sea tang from the southeast. The crickets went on industriously all around us, and then Fee called again, so we went inside. The steaming mugs, the glass of milk, the tin of shortbread, were all on the table. Fee stood in the doorway of my bedroom, holding out her hand. The kitten lay on her palm.

"Have you been in my house while my back was turned?" she asked unbelievingly. "Rummaging through my things?"

"What are you talking about?" I said foolishly. I was burning but still felt like turning up the collar of my robe.

She was so pale that her grey eyes looked dark, and there was a tremor in her voice. I took that and the pallor for weakness, as if she might faint. I was feeling rather fragile myself.

"I would never go through *your* bureau drawers without permission," she said.

"You just did."

"That's different!" Energy flamed up in her. "You were here, too, and all I wanted was—" She could have said *a handkerchief,* but I saw the actual instant when her romantic inspiration quickened. "I was *led* to that drawer."

"By Milton?" I asked sardonically. "Come off it, Fee, you were poking around, hoping to find something from Janine. A note Clem Jr. mailed for her, maybe. You've been obsessed with curiosity about her, and you won't believe I don't know anything. Why don't you admit it? There's nothing disgraceful about plain nosiness." I even tried for a laugh, but it was impossible because she simply stood there staring at me, with the kitten in her open hand. Julian had been mildly amazed until now, when suddenly he saw the kitten. His expression changed to pleasure.

"Where did you get that?" He went around me toward her, reaching for it, but she put it behind her. "I was saving it for your birthday, love," she said tenderly.

"I guess I can wait, then, and make out like I'm surprised." He smiled at me. "You sent so many good names I'm having a hard time choosing."

"Just shut your eyes and point," I said, keeping my eyes on Fee. My long-suffering stomach was beginning to roil. "How did you get it, Fee?" I asked. "You tell me, and I'll tell you. Julian, why don't you go outside so Fee and I can tell each other secrets?"

Always accommodating, he moved toward the door. "*Julian!*" she snapped. "You stay *here.*"

I shrugged. "Either one of them gave it to you, or you just took it. But I'm not telling you how *I* got it, unless we're alone."

I was attempting, probably foolishly, to keep Toby out of more trouble. I knew Fee wouldn't make too much fuss, especially if she'd lifted the kitten and didn't want Julian to know. But he was so rigidly upright, I was afraid he'd go hunting Toby up and have him arrested, if he didn't shake the living daylights out of him first.

"They gave it to me that last day," Fee said tiredly, putting her hands in her pockets and leaning against the wall. She smiled sadly. "I haven't been able to look at it since."

"That Sunday?" I asked. "I don't remember your carrying anything down to the boat."

"I saw them one more time," she said. "I went back Monday morning with some lobsters. See, we hauled before we grounded the boat out for work, and I took them four lobsters, and they gave it to me then.—Well, actually I was pretty shameless about admiring it, so what else could they do?" She started to laugh, and it turned into a sob. She wiped her nose on her sleeve like a child.

"Here, Julian, you might as well have it now," she said thickly, and gave him the kitten.

Delightedly he set the kitten on his big palm, lifting it up to look into the half-shut eyes.

"So you see," Fee said, "*whatever* Janine told you about that night, it had to be a lie, because we had no boat. *Island Magic* was high and dry. Now tell me how you got our Phronsie. Yes, that's the name, lover," she said, smiling at Julian; she was almost beautiful.

"Phronsie," he repeated slowly, tasting the strange syllables.

This was no nightmare. I was awake, and it was all really happening. I felt as I did when I walked into the bloody room at Fox Point. *This is real. I cannot wake up from it, no matter how I try.*

It was the instant when the man takes the step off the window ledge into space; or presses the trigger; or kicks away the stool under his feet.

"But you had your dory," I said.

"Hold her, Julian," Fee said in an ordinary voice. I heard the kitten clatter on the table, and I snapped out of my paralysis. I was no bird hypnotized by a snake, but before I could dive toward the door, I was caught and hugged against his chest too tightly even to kick his shins; in any case, I was barefoot. My breasts were hurting terribly, and I felt as if my ribs were slowly caving in, forcing the air out of my lungs. He is the one, I thought with perfect clarity. He is the murderer.

Fee turned off the lamps and moved around the room to sit on the edge of the table, half of her visible in the light from the wharf, the other half lost in shadow. And you are the murderer too, I thought, wonderstruck.

"Now tell me what Janine told you," Fee said, still sounding like my own Fee. "You've been like a hen on a hot griddle ever since that day. I know you too well—I could feel it, I could all but see it. And you can laugh at ESP, but you've seen the aura around Julian and me. That's why you went through my house while my back was turned, looking for clues. You and Glen were plotting against me."

"You're crazy!" I gasped. "Let up, Julian. I can't talk."

Fee nodded at him, and there was a slight loosening of his arms across my chest.

"Janine didn't see anything but a big black figure. And Toby Barry swiped the kitten the day of Sonny's funeral and gave it to me for a present. I made him promise to put it back where he found it, first chance." I squirmed angrily in Julian's embrace. "Come on, you two! What *is* this? Fee, I thought you'd stopped at Fox Point on the way home from the doctor's and lifted the kitten then. That's *all* I thought."

She sat there immobile in the grotesque lighting; I could see the shine of one eye. The breeze had arrived and was making that familiar little sound around my window and through the screen door. It occurred to me that I would never hear it again after tonight. They wouldn't let me go now. She was no longer my Fee, and this was no longer my life, but something to dispose of. If I'd had an instant or the breath to scream, who'd have heard me?

They tell about going beyond fear; maybe that was how people managed those speeches from the block. "When *did* you steal it?" I asked. "The night you killed them? And why did you kill them?"

"That's none of your business," said Fee. "Clem Jr. will tell me where she is. He'll do anything for me."

"Not that," I said. "The minute you ask, he'll know why."

"Then I won't ask him, I'll find out another way," she said with a nonchalant air of power. "And you'll never be able to tell on me, will you?"

She got up and went over to the screen door and looked out. Now there was a faint sloshing around the wharf spilings and a gentle thumping and, through these small noises, the sound of a truck driving in. She shut the door before I could attempt a yelp.

"Sprig," she said casually. "Coming down to see how his boat's lying. We'll let him get out of here first. Then there'll be nobody around to save poor Eden when the Mad Killer catches up with her. We'll be safe back on the island when the news gets out, and I'll cry for you, Eden darling. I really will."

I wondered how my chances were now to give Julian a good, hard, twisting pinch in a place that he couldn't ignore; but Fee was between me and the door, and she was strong.

"Were they dead by the time you took the ax to them?" I asked. The smile went.

"Don't you dare mention them to me!" she snapped. "You've got no right. They were *my* grandmother and *my* great-aunt! Do it, Julian, and we'll be out of here as soon as Sprig goes up the road again." Wouldn't you love her for *your* very own great-aunt? she'd once asked me.

"He came down to put the boat on the mooring—" I grunted as Julian's arm drove the wind out of my lungs, but I went wheezing on. "When he finds his skiff at the wharf and your boat out there, he'll be back in—"

"Then he'll meet me tumbling out of here in hysterics," she said calmly. "We just found you dead. He'll stop wondering about anything else, he's been so crazy about you for so long.... Poor Sprig," she said. "Poor *me,* finding my best friend dead and still warm."

The door behind her was driven open so suddenly that she was propelled forward, almost fell flat, was caught by a chair, and doubled over the back of it. Glen stood in the doorway, hands thrust out before him in the classic police pose, yelling, "*Freeze!* We're taking you all in for unlawful assembly!" Behind him Sprig was laughing. Fee was slowly straightening up; I don't know what her face was like.

"Glen, they're trying to kill me!" I could hardly speak, but was twisting with a strength I didn't know I had. The imaginary revolver disappeared, and he switched on the lights.

"If this is a joke, it's a damn' poor one," he said frigidly. "Let her go, Julian."

"Don't do it, lover," Fee said. She must have still felt invincible at this point, until Glen wrestled her back against him as Julian had held me, except that *his* right arm went hard across her throat. Her eyes widened and bulged, but she choked out, "Get rid of her, Julian."

"And I'll kill Fee before your eyes, Julian," Glen said. I could hardly recognize his voice.

"You heard me, lover." Immobilized, she was still fighting. Insane, insane! I thought. *My Fee.*

"And you heard me, Julian," Glen said inexorably. "I will drop her dead at your feet, the way your cat gives you a dead mouse. That's what *dead* means, Julian. Like the boy on the beach you never thought would show up again. Well, Fee'll be just another dead body a couple of minutes from now if you don't let Eden go."

"He'll never hurt me, lover," Fee said. Glen forced her head back with his arm under her chin, but she was still trying to hold Julian with her eyes. "I'm his twinnie, we were always two against the—" The last word was cut off.

"I'm doing it, Julian," Glen said. "I'm killing her right now."

I was suddenly free, holding myself up by hanging onto the counter. Glen still held Fee in that crippling grip; Julian stood staring with his mouth open. There seemed to be a lot of shifting shadows and small noises outside the screen door, and they weren't from the wind.

"You sit down, Julian," Glen ordered. "Never mind what she says. I'm boss here now. Tell him I'm boss, Fee." He jerked his forearm against her throat, and she said painfully, "Yes, you're boss."

Julian still didn't move; he was too quiet. Nick came in behind Glen and Fee and walked around the table. I wasn't surprised. His purposeful appearance was all of a piece with the whole affair. But Julian's wide amber eyes didn't flicker away from Fee and Glen. Nick took him by the back of the neck as he had taken Lucas that day and said, "Sit down, chum."

Julian sat. There was nothing else he could do. He rested his big hands on his knees and kept on gazing at Fee, waiting for her to take charge as she always had. Glen released her and instantly she turned and wrapped her arms around him, crying in wild, loud, ugly sounds.

"I had to do it, Glen!" she wailed. "But it wasn't only for me—it was for you, too, it was for *you!*" Julian stirred nervously, but Nick still held him by the neck.

Glen's face looked grey and aged. "Just what was for me, for God's sake?" he asked. She made an immense physical effort to quiet herself.

"She wouldn't acknowledge us! She wouldn't listen, and after we rowed all that distance that night because I couldn't wait any longer to tell her I knew Dad was hers and Guy's!" Gulping, snuffling, she groped for something to wipe her face. Her hand fell on a dish towel, and she wiped her face and blew her nose and went on through sobs, "But she lied to me! She pretended to be so damn' kind and understanding, and Miss Emma was fluttering around trying to pat me and saying, 'But listen to the music, dear,' but I knew the truth, and I couldn't make *her* admit it, that Dad was hers and Guy's." She gripped Glen's shoulders and backed off to look imploringly into his face. "I *knew* she was lying. I *knew* from the first that Guy was our grandfather just as much as he was Kenneth's and Edith's! We had the *most* right to Fox Point, because she was *our* grandmother, not theirs! She had him while she was away at school, and Grandfather Heriot worshipped her so much he'd do anything for her, so he adopted the baby."

"Goddamn it, Fee. You *know* who Dad was!" Glen was in torment, and there was nothing I could do. Sprig spoke from outside, his drawl more pronounced than usual. "I told the kids to call the police and to wait out by the mailbox for 'em." He reached inside the door to snap on the deck light, and disappeared.

"I worshipped her," Fee said piteously, "but I couldn't let her go on lying and pitying me, making me feel like a kid having a tantrum. So I hit her and knocked her down, and when Miss Emma came to help her—silly old fool—I hit her, too, and then we had to make it look as if somebody broke in." She drew a long whistling breath and rushed on. "I sent Julian for the ax, and he did a pretty good job of it if I do say so. Didn't you, lover?" She turned her wet, blotched, swollen face toward him, and he nodded confusedly.

"Well, they found out old Fee was nobody to trifle with," she said proudly. "They knew then I was as tough as Mary Ann Esmond. They both knew all right. They were still alive when Julian came back with the ax."

Nick's free arm held me rigidly upright. His fingers hurt, digging into my ribs, but I rejoiced in the pain; I was alive.

"You should've seen us when we got through!" Fee's laughter combined with those deep belly-wrenching sobs was indescribable. "What a mess!" She might have been talking about clam-flat mud. "Julian went upstairs looking for Janine; that was why he was on the stairs when those two idiotic kids came barging in. That girl ran like a deer and where the hell she went I still don't know. Miss Priss here wouldn't tell her best friend."

We were as mute as Julian; she was the only one, seemingly, with the faculty of speech. With her eyes sparkling she said in a ghastly parody of her old mischief, "And afterwards I scooted back to swipe the kitten, to give to Julian on his birthday."

That meant she'd gone twice past three butchered bodies; and she could stand there smiling at us as the troopers came up the steps.

And then she winked at me.

42

Fee began to cry again when she was handcuffed and taken down the steps. She kept straining toward Glen and begging him to help her. It was hideous. He never moved from where he stood or spoke. I went to him, but I don't think he knew I was there and touching him.

It was a time of orderly chaos, when those in charge knew exactly what they were doing, and the rest of us were flung away from the center of the vortex as if by centrifugal force and remained where we were tossed. I saw and heard it all as if I were a recording machine, knowing that eventually I would have to think on my own, and there was no way I could help Glen. The yellow deck light poured down on us, the blue lights on the cruisers kept revolving, radios boomed and crackled as if with arcane intergalactic messages. Sprig's voice was uncharacteristically authoritative as he ordered away a few ghouls who'd heard the call on their scanners and arrived by cars and one motorcycle, which made more noise than anything else, and left with a deliberate uproar when Sprig made his point.

A thin man in slacks and a sports jacket seemed to keep appearing here and there, and I wondered hazily what he was doing. I saw the Temple boys' faces whitely hovering about the perimeters and felt I should do something about them until their parents got home, but I didn't know what. I hoped my grandparents wouldn't arrive in the midst of this scene in their driveway; I didn't know if I could get my wits and words together to explain. This is how we worry and niggle at superficial details to keep the Unthinkable at bay.

Docile and speechless, Julian went where he was guided. It took Glen and the woman trooper to finally get Fee into the other cruiser, and I could scarcely imagine what he was going through. Fee must have known, when she and Julian were put into separate cars, that the island had ceased to exist for them and that they would never be together again, but she hadn't a look or a word for him. When they drove away she was screaming inside the car, "Glen, I did it for *you!* For *you!*"

When the second set of tail lights disappeared around the corner by the mailbox, the rest of us stood there in silence, the boys at a respectful distance. Then Glen cleared his throat and said with a careful ordinariness, "Well, I'd better get moving."

"I'll go with you," I said at once.

"No, you won't," he said without raising his voice. "I don't want you near the place." I knew better than to insist. He was having all he could do to hold himself together.

"I'll drive you up," Sprig said, "and don't argue."

"Thanks. Nick, stay with her till her folks come home, will you? And thanks for helping out. If he'd exploded, he could have smashed up the place and us with it."

"I've seen those quiet ones in action before," Nick said. Glen walked quickly away out of the light toward the parking lot, and I wanted to run after him; we had not held each other since he'd burst into the Hayloft. But he had forbidden me.

I caught Sprig by the arm. "Bring him back here, no matter what he says," I said. "He's not going home alone tonight."

"I'll bring him back if I have to knock him out. You hang in there, kiddo." He squeezed my shoulder and went after Glen.

When his truck had gone up the road, the night returned the crickets to us and the audible swash around the wharf; the breeze was cold on my sweat-dampened skin, but I couldn't make myself go into that kitchen. I tied my robe tighter.

"Eden," Nick began, and then the man in the slacks and sports jacket came to us from an unmarked car we hadn't noticed in the parking lot. It was as if I couldn't see his face, even dimly; he was just a courteous voice and glasses that reflected the deck light. He showed me his badge and said he would like to have my statement.

"Where's Jensen?" I asked childishly. "I *know* him."

"I work with him," said the man. "He'll see this, I promise you."

I said to the Temple boys, "Your folks will be home soon, expecting to find you in bed."

They seemed spellbound, unable to move or speak.

"Come on, guys," Nick said. He started them off with a hand on each back between the shoulder blades and went with them across the dark parking lot. The officer and I sat on the top step under the light, and I told him how it was. A separate Eden stood off and contemplated in wonder the way this one could pick and choose her words. The fact that I could do it at all was due to my still being somewhat numb. I left out the kitten, with some fuzzy idea of not adding to Toby's list of crimes; I said Fee had been very excited when she came in and kept talking about Janine's being alive and what she must know; and then she'd announced that whatever Janine said about her and Julian, it had to be a lie because their boat had been on the beach that night. Then I had foolishly said, "But you have a dory," and Fee had seemed to go mad before my eyes.

Here my impetus died, but he appeared to be satisfied. "Thank you, Miss Winter," he said. "Will you be alone here? Is there someone you can call?"

"I'm here," said Nick, coming forward out of the dark. I don't know how long he'd been there.

The officer said good night and went to his car; the sounds of water and the rising breeze masked his footsteps. When the car backed around and drove out, I turned off the deck light and went down a few steps to get away from the wharf light. The dark seemed friendlier. Nick sat beside me and put his arm around me. I leaned against him, but I didn't cry. Save your tears until you've really got something to cry about, my mother used to advise me when I was small. Maybe this was it, but I had no more tears.

"The kids are drinking cocoa loaded with marshmallows and watching an old western on TV," he said. "There was no sense in telling them to go to bed, but I told them to stay put until their parents come.... They saved your life tonight, you know, but I don't think they realize it."

"You'd better tell me." I sagged more heavily against him, unable to help myself.

"Well, after our little talk earlier, I didn't want to wait, I wanted to see you tonight. So I drove down and parked off the road and walked in, taking a chance on finding you home. But then I saw the place was dark. I was about to leave when I saw some action on the wharf, so I went down there. Sprig was just about to put his boat off, and Glen was standing on the wharf, and here were these two kids. One of them says, 'Hey, Sprig, don't forget your skiff. She's tied up on the other side of the wharf.'"

"How the hell did that happen?" Sprig asked. "Who used it?"

"Fee and Julian," the boys told him. "They're on your mooring, and they're up at Eden's now."

They all looked up at the Hayloft windows, which showed no inside light, but simply reflected the light from the wharf. "If they're up there," Sprig said, "they must be having a séance."

"He was kidding," Nick said. "But Glen wasn't. 'Like hell they are!' he said. 'I'm going to break up that foolishness once and for all.' Then he tried to lighten up. 'Come on, you two, join the SWAT team,' he said. 'See how it's done.'"

They had gone up into the parking lot, walked along behind the rose hedge, and approached the house from the back. The two boys came tiptoeing behind, hoping nobody would notice them and send them home.

"Glen was the first up the steps," Nick said. "We heard voices through the door, but not what they were saying. Well, you know the rest, you were there." His voice dropped off into an abashed silence, and he tightened his arm around my shoulders.

"They knew Sprig was here," I said, "but the wind was rising so we didn't hear Glen drive in. And if those kids hadn't been flitting around like bats—" I left it at that. But I could see Fee rushing down these steps, throwing herself at Glen and screaming, "Somebody's killed Eden!"

"I can say this all to you," I said to Nick, "because I have to say it aloud to someone, but I can't ever say it to Glen. I don't know what he and I can talk about now, for the rest of our lives. That's what she's killed, besides *them.* Honestly, I don't know if I can ever make myself go up these steps and into my kitchen again."

"Run away with me then," said Nick. "We haven't got *Halcyon,* but my car's all gassed up. We'll just go, right now, and never look back."

"Don't tempt me," I said. "If you *did* have *Halcyon*—" I stood and started up the steps as if to the gallows.

He came with me. "For you I'd steal another one," he said. "We'd go *now,* as soon as you could get dressed."

The kitten lay sleeping in the middle of the table where Julian had dropped her. I could not have smashed her any more than I could have killed a live kitten, but I didn't want ever to see her again. I put her in a bottom drawer I hardly ever opened. In the bathroom I doused my face with icy water and combed my hair. When I came out, Nick said, "If you could get drunk, you wouldn't have to think for a while."

"Until I woke up," I said. "Besides, Glen's coming back."

"Maybe," he said. Exhausted, half-drowned by alternate waves of acceptance and rejection of events, I longed giddily for any escape, to be hurled like a science-fiction heroine out of one world into another or to be a time traveler into another century; across the room from me, Nick's jeans and knit shirt became the anachronism instead of the gold earring and the Elizabethan beard, as if he were a messenger sent to fetch me back.

"You look bushed," he said roughly. "Sit down."

I did, more or less collapsing on the couch. "Thanks for being such a good friend, Nick," I said.

"Don't ever forget I wanted to be more," he said. "That's why I came down tonight, to talk to you about it. I'll always feel they killed something for me, too." His tone was neither accusatory nor self-pitying. "I've never forgotten the night we watched the moon rise. I never will, and I hope you never do, either. But there's another *never,* bigger than all the others. You'll never turn away from Glen now. No matter how he is after this, you'll always be there just in case he needs you. Like tonight, the way he was for you." Then he turned his back on me, and began clattering around the sink. "Isn't it a cup of tea they always offer, with plenty of sugar in it for shock?"

"If a person could turn a key on her thoughts, Nick," I said, "and never take them out again, who knows what would be possible?" It was a strange thing to say, and I couldn't tell him about the picture that went with it, of us driving away through the night into a future uncluttered by any past whatever, not even a wispy memory of what we'd been.

"Get some rest, if you can," he said. "You need the strength." He sat down in my rocking chair with a book and tilted back with his heels on the window sill.

43

There was nothing I could do for Glen that night but hold him as he had held me on the night of the murder. When he had been quiet for so long that I thought he had actually fallen asleep, he said clearly into the dark, "I'd have killed her, and she knew it. I wanted to do it, and she knew that, too."

What answer could I make? Then he continued. "It was a pretty queer thing, this strong feeling that I wanted to see you again tonight." A curious echo of Fee's words, and Nick's. "*Had* to, it was so damned strong, as if there was something I was supposed to do or say." His voice dragged with weariness. "Made me walk out on the poker game after the meeting. I thought you'd be asleep after the day we'd had and wouldn't take kindly to being waked up and asked if you were all right. So I'd sneak in and take a look at you and then bunk on the couch, and we'd have breakfast together."

How sweetly sane it sounded, yet how remote, as if we'd lost sweet sanity forever.

"Sprig was fooling around with his boat," he went on, "so I didn't want to be too damn' obvious about going up your steps and having to listen to a lot of bad jokes tomorrow. I went down to see if he'd caught the leak, and here were these two kids who were supposed to be in bed. Then Nick Raintree showed up. He didn't say what *he* was down here for."

"Just out wandering around, he told me," I said untruthfully.

"When the kids said they were in from the island and up here with you—" He couldn't say their names. I tightened my arms, which were already aching. "I was mad," he said after a pause. "Sprig made a joke about a séance, but by God it was no joke to me. I thought, when she starts coming in here at night to drag you into her foolishness, it's too much." He stopped again, as if he had to collect more breath, and either he was shaking, or I was. "I tried to make it sound like a goddam foolish joke, coming up here to wreck the fun." The vibration ceased suddenly; long shuddering breaths began and then died away as if life itself were leaving the body in my arms, he was so cold and quiet. Then he roused himself again.

"I had to call Julian's folks for him, and I'd rather have been shot. The whole tribe came, but he wouldn't look at any of them. Only wanted to talk to me. The place was a madhouse. They had to have a doctor in to give *her* a shot to quiet her down, and Julian didn't know which end was up, just wanted me to tend to the cat and kittens." There was a catch in his throat. "Begging me to take care of the kittens, worried sick about them, and all I could see was him holding you, ready to strangle you when *she* gave the word. And your eyes when you saw me—oh, *Jesus.*" He put his face between my breasts, and, stroking his head, I wondered when he would be able to say her name again, if ever.

After that I told him my story, beginning with Toby's gift of the kitten; we weren't going to sleep anyway. Too much had to be said, and we might as well say it now. When I finished I tried to give him some comfort, though it was of the cold variety. "She's gone over the edge, Glen. It was happening right before our eyes, and we were too close to her to see it. But you *were* having a lot of uneasy feelings about her. They'll see how far gone she is. How could they miss it? They can't possibly call it cold-blooded, or premeditated, or—"

"She made it all up out of whole cloth," he said. "About their being our grandparents. She knew better."

"She wanted so hard for Marianne to belong to her," I said. "So after a while, after she'd dreamed the fantasy long enough, it had to be. That shows how far round the bend she's gone, Glen, and—"

He interrupted me again. "She knows who our father was. He was a Heriot all right, woods colt or not. On both sides. They were cousins and scared to let their folks know. Otherwise, where the hell did we get these eyes and noses?"

"She was so romantic," I said. "She never wanted him to be just ordinary. She thought the Guy-and-Marianne story was the romance of the century, and she wanted to be part of it."

"Don't talk any more," he said, laying his arm across me and settling deeper against my side.

He had either passed out or was giving a perfect imitation of a deep sleep when Uncle Early brought my grandparents and Chad home, well after midnight. I listened to the small hushed sounds and Uncle Early driving quietly out and was glad they could all go innocently to bed and sleep for the few hours left of the night.

"I'm sorry as hell for Clem Jr.," Glen said unexpectedly against my throat. "She wants me to call him first thing. I wouldn't do it last night. Let him sleep while he can. This is going to half-kill the poor bastard."

I slept a bit toward morning, until crows in the orchard woke me at dawn. Still narcotized, I wondered if they were hollering about the porcupine; if he was eating apples for breakfast.

And then I remembered.

Glen was making coffee in the kitchen, and we drank it in silence. I had avoided my reflection in the bathroom mirror, but I couldn't *not* see Glen, and the sight knotted my insides. I looked out at the fluffs and streamers of lavender-grey cloud faced with pink that deepened through red coral to cherry as I watched, and then began to fade in the light cast upwards when the sun rose behind the woods on the end of Fort Point.

"Clem gets up early," Glen said suddenly. "Might as well get it over with." I left him dialing and went downstairs to tell my grandparents.

They loved Fee, and they were shocked beyond speech. Gram dropped a plate and sat down suddenly; Grampa's blue winter eyes narrowed as against a blinding glare, and there was a perceptible stiffening around his mouth. But their toughness was no delusion. This was not a time for wailings and lamentations; we'd all be a long time getting over it, perhaps we never would, but at the moment there was too much to be done for us to go to pieces.

"I'll do that," said Gram, angrily pushing away any offers to pick up the broken dish. "And we'll let the rest of the family know that you're all right. You take care of Glen. I always thought that girl was too high-strung for her own good. Keep that fool dog out of my way." Rapidly she swept broken china onto the dustpan. I took Chad's head in my hands; he was only slightly chastened by his experience and his still-tender mouth. He wagged with great fervor. Some dogs are supposed to sense grief in people, but Chad is blessedly free of that gift.

Grampa reached down a hand and helped Gram to her feet and took the dustpan and brush from her. "Poor Emma," she said suddenly. "She never deserved a death like that. Nor Mary Ann either, though if she'd never run off with Guy—go back to Glen," she ordered me. Grampa gave me an encouraging smile, as if I were five and just learning to row.

"Yes, go on," he said. At the foot of the stairs I looked back, and he had put his arm around her and was murmuring something.

Glen had finished talking to Clem but didn't tell me how Clem had reacted, which was something else I didn't want to think about. "Come on out to the island," he said. "I'm supposed to pick up some things for her, and there's those cats to feed."

We left the harbor after everyone else had gone out, and Gramp and Uncle Early had come up to the house for a mug-up. It was a fine morning with an uneven southeast breeze patterning the water with rumpled patches of dark blue and broad satiny streaks of blue-white calm. I ached through my ribs, feeling as if a slight push would knock me down and I wouldn't bother to get up again. But then I'd see how Glen's flesh seemed to have been pared off his bones in one night; I knew how his eyes burned and stared behind the dark glasses, and then I'd glean from somewhere the strength to cope.

At the island the dory lay innocent on her mooring, a gull riding the bow. It was strange to be walking up from the wharf to the house in this fresh morning, with the same birds and the same sweet or pungent scents rising from the fields; the same slant of light across the chimneys and gables. Clouds of purple and lavender asters had appeared in the last week, and the ferns were turning bronze.

Did *she,* this morning, think of how it looked and felt? But such an agony of longing would be a normal reaction, and she must have traveled far beyond that. I reached for Glen's hand and walked awkwardly behind him up the narrow path, hanging on; he was hanging onto my hand just as hard.

Polly met us at the door, talking, winding rapturously around our legs. She had to be picked up, she insisted, and I did it; then she squirmed to be free and hurried off outside. The kittens had been out of their basket but tottered back to it at the arrival of strange giants. Without speaking, we agreed that I'd pick up Fee's toilet articles and a change of clothes; he filled Polly's dishes and then took the litter pan out, and stayed. As I walked around the bedroom collecting things I wished, quite lucidly, that I were taking clothes for her to be laid out in. If she and Julian had been killed outright in an accident last night, the grief we'd be feeling would be the purest felicity compared to the present reality. And this was just the beginning. If Fee had died yesterday, tomorrow we would have begun, however wretchedly, to mend.

The room was so suffocatingly filled with her presence that I had to go outside for a few gulps of air. Julian's brother's boat was coming into the cove, and Glen sat on a crate on the wharf watching the approach. Larry is a hulk like Julian, though not so handsome, and today he looked belligerent—a natural way to hide his anguish. I ran down the path to be with Glen in case Larry took a swing at him.

We stayed by the crate while Larry made the boat fast bow and stern, then climbed the ladder. He strode up the wharf toward us with his arms swinging as if he were heading into a brawl, both hands in fists. He stood over us; he would have been menacing had his eyes not been so red and his voice thick and hoarse from weeping.

"In the old days someone like her would have been burned for a witch," he said. "My brother never hurt anything or anybody in his life. God knows what she did to him."

Neither of us answered. He glared around at the gear on the wharf, at the tools visible inside the open fish house door. "I know what's his around here, you know."

"Take it," Glen said, sounding indifferent.

"He's got some stuff at the house, too."

"I'll go up with you," I said.

"You don't have to worry!" he lashed out at me. "I won't steal nothing!"

"I don't think that," I answered, following him up the path. He said things under his breath as we went along, not directed at me, I was sure, but as a way of relieving the dreadful pressure. When we came into the kitchen Polly lay in the middle of the floor, feeding her young. "Might as well drown that lot," he said morosely.

"We're keeping them," I said at once, wanting to sweep them all up in my arms and lock them away from him. But he simply shook his head as if to shake pain loose and tramped into the pantry. He collected Julian's razor and toothbrush from the shelf beside the sink, then walked heavily across the kitchen to the hall and into the bedroom. I followed him.

"Julian's chest is over there," I said, pointing. He grunted and jerked out the top drawer. I found a suitcase in a closet and put it near him, then I sat on the bed: I didn't care what he took of Julian's, but I didn't want those hands going through Fee's things. At the same time I marveled that protective instincts took so long to die.

I was doubtless misjudging him; he hated Fee so much that he probably couldn't have borne to touch anything of hers. "Larry, Glen's in the same boat as you," I said, to my own surprise. "Don't be too hard on him."

He never looked around. In a few moments Glen came quietly across the hall and stood in the doorway without speaking. Larry finished stuffing clothes into the suitcase and slammed the drawers shut; again he made a confrontation out of facing Glen.

"What about the boat and gear? It's half his."

"The boat'll stay tied up in Job's Harbor till we know what's what," Glen said. "You'd better talk to the warden about tending the gear. I won't interfere. No sense losing money."

Larry became as red as his eyelids already were. "By Jesus," he said in a congested voice, "I'll haul just half of it, for *him.* I'll fry in hell before I make a buck for *her.*"

"Oh for God's sake, man," Glen said wearily, "haul them all and keep it all. I told you I wouldn't interfere. Just take your stuff and get off the island."

"We've got Harrison Black already." He hurled it at us like a hand grenade. That well-known criminal lawyer is a summer resident of St. David. "He'll get Jule off!"

Glen shrugged. "I'll be back to get the rest of his stuff," Larry grumbled. When he went out, he stumbled into the side of the doorway. We watched him go down the path like a blind man helplessly driven by his own momentum, and I wished again that those two were dead, no matter how.

Crossing the cove, he swerved the boat as if to pick up the dory, but thought better of it. When I returned to the kitchen, Glen was sitting on the edge of the table, looking a dirty white. "We've been going for hours on black coffee," I said roughly. "There's food here. We'd better eat something, or we'll be keeling over. Light up the kerosene stove."

Obediently he did so. There was water in the pail beside the sink and I filled the teakettle, then went down into the cold cellar for eggs and bacon. I fried the bacon and scrambled eight eggs in the same frying pan and made toast over another burner. Glen fixed two mugs of tea, and we carried everything down to the wharf, accompanied by Polly. We didn't need plates. We ate the scrambled eggs out of the frying pan between us on the crate and held the bacon in our fingers. Polly tried to reach it, and we both fed her, appreciating her guileless presence. Glen began to look better, physically. "I can't leave this place alone!" he broke out suddenly. "It'll be picked clean in twenty-four hours. I ought to stay here myself, but goddammit, I can't! And I don't want anybody else in here. I don't know who I can trust."

"Me," I said bravely, wondering how I could sleep in Fee's bed. Well, what were sleeping bags for? "Look, we could bear it together, I think."

He didn't answer that but took my hand and got me onto my feet. We left Polly to clean out the frying pan and went out to the end of the wharf and sat there with our legs dangling over the water. I know I was trying not to see the dory; they might have been still rowing her home when I walked into the house at Fox Point that night.

It was near noon, the sun strong on our heads, ospreys whistling over the passage between Heriot and Tamarack. Monarch butterflies flickered above the goldenrod on the slope above the wharf. We heard the oncoming boat before she came into sight around Tamarack; it was the Marine Resources patrol boat with two wardens and two men in civilian clothes whom they delivered at the wharf. One was Jensen, who introduced the younger man as Sergeant Harriman. By his voice I knew at once that Harriman was the man who had taken my statement last night; he was a neatly built, tanned man with pleasant hazel eyes behind nontinted glasses.

"They told us at Job's Harbor we'd find you here," Jensen said. They had brought me my statement, typed; I read it, had no corrections to make, and signed it. Harriman went up to the house, and Jensen stayed on the wharf with us.

"We haven't touched anything up there," I said. "We picked up some things for them, that's all."

"We don't expect to find anything," Jensen said candidly. "From what we've been hearing, it seems nothing was left to chance."

Glen flinched as violently as if he'd received a rope-end across his open eyes. I ignored his pride and put my arm around him. Jensen had a few questions for us, and his impersonal manner made it as easy as possible. When he and the sergeant were through with their inspection, we took them back to Job's Harbor. Clem Jr. had called and left a message; he wanted to see Glen that afternoon at half past two, at his home, and this time Glen asked me to go with him.

He drove back to his place to clean up, and I picked him up in time for him to go to Tenby first, with Fee's bag. We parked around the corner from the red brick jail behind the courthouse so I didn't have to gaze directly at it. I would have left the car and walked away from the area while I waited, but I was afraid of meeting someone I knew; Gram told me that the news of the attack and the capture had been on both radio and television news. Tenby streets are rich with shade trees like those in Maddox, and the jail is incongruously surrounded by handsome old houses. They offered something restful for my aching eyes; if I shut them, I had no escape.

Glen was back in about half an hour. He said nothing until we were halfway to Maddox. Then, staring straight ahead with his eyes half-shut against the glare of the sun on the road, he said tonelessly, "She says if that damned little crook hadn't gone through her house and found the kitten, she'd have gotten away with it. She says nobody could have proved anything. They scrubbed and painted the dory, and they bagged the clothes and sneakers they wore that night with rocks and sank them out by Davie's Rock." Looking sidewise I saw him wetting his lips before he could go on. "They threw the ax overboard between Fox Point and the island."

"She has to be insane," I said helplessly. He didn't speak again until we met Clem Jr. on his front porch. His children had obviously been told to stay away. He looked gaunt and ill, but he spoke as he always did, with an added undercurrent of compassion. He invited me to make a pot of coffee, so I knew he wanted a few minutes alone with Glen. I didn't want to know anything about that, so I took my time. Glen told me later it was almost the hardest thing each man had ever had to do; Clem to talk about the murders, and Glen to listen.

Jensen hadn't needed a Ouija board; he'd had something to go on from the first. Not so much the two sets of bloody footprints, one large and the other smaller and narrower, and the traces upstairs, but the almost complete bloody print of a big hand on the banister. This was the clincher, and the reason for fingerprinting all the males who'd known the sisters and who had no alibis for that night. He'd also been checking out any of the county's known bad actors who were not in jail at the moment. Julian had seemed to be out of it from the first, with the boat grounded in St. David on the night of the crime and ten miles of water between Heriot Island and Fox Point. But at a family cookout on the evening when Fee was preparing to corner me about Janine, Jensen watched some teenagers racing dories, and he remembered the Isles of Shoals murders, committed by a man who'd rowed ten miles out from Portsmouth and back again.

So even if they'd been able to leave me dead and get away without being incriminated, Jensen or Harriman would have been out on the island the next morning to take Julian ashore for the routine examination. When Fee bragged about having left nothing to chance, she hadn't known about the print on the stair railing. So their destiny was awaiting them; but I would have still been just as dead.

Fee was blaming everyone, from Marianne to the Temple boys. She was furious with Julian for leaving that print. Clem Jr., who had been all morning at the jail as she gave her statement, looked as if he'd spent a season in Dante's Inferno. He had called the man he considered the best criminal lawyer in Maine, but Fee must be persuaded to cooperate with him. She wouldn't listen to *him;* would Glen try? Glen nodded bleakly.

"Will there have to be a trial?" I asked.

"I don't know. There'll be the probable-cause hearing, and there'll be no doubt about the decision to hand it over to the Grand Jury. I'm afraid there'll be no doubt about the indictment either. After that, I don't know, Eden. Sainsbury will have to get together with Harrison Black and the prosecutor. If they'd all agree to leave Fee and Julian to the mercy of the court, they can simply be sentenced without a trial. But we have to take it one day at a time."

"If they call it insanity—" I couldn't give up. I wanted some crumb of comfort for Glen, if he was hearing us; the way he looked, he could have turned us off like a radio.

"Black will probably use that for Julian. He's very confused right now, which may be in his favor. But—" Clem doodled on the yellow legal pad. He didn't need to finish. "See if you can get through to her, Glen."

"Yes," Glen said as if from the depths of sleep. He stood up, looking only at me. "Let's go home, Eden." When we were in the car, he said in that dead voice, "She never asked for you. She never said she was out of her mind to want to hurt you. I kept waiting for it."

44

We moved onto the island that night, to stay until we had everything ready to be moved. The good side of it was that we were away from telephones and a road running right to the door. We camped in the fish house, with our sleeping bags and a camp stove for cooking; there was a curious comfort in falling asleep to water sounds under the floor, the little gurgles and bold rhythmic swashings and smackings around the spilings. It was a better sedative than a drug after the visits ashore.

These were harder on Glen than on me, because I could stay put at the harbor or go no farther than Whittier's Store for groceries. Glen had to see Fee several times a week, and there were meetings with Clem and Thomas Sainsbury, the criminal lawyer.

We would hurry back to the island after these times, loaded with gifts of food from the family freezers as well as what I'd bought. We walked the shores in all weathers, avoiding High Ledge Cove where Sonny had come ashore. If it was wet and cold, we had a fire of old laths in the potbellied stove in the fish house. Some days I didn't go to haul with him, but stayed in to pack clothing, books, pictures, the lovely old quilts, and other keepsakes. I hadn't known how I could manage it, but I did it because I had to. The presence of Polly and her tribe was as much company as Chad would have been.

Bail was denied, which was a relief. Fee refused to consider a plea of temporary insanity, the only one possible; she insisted that she had simply been provoked into a reasonable rage by her grandmother's stubborn denial of her, and she always referred to Marianne as her grandmother and a wicked old woman. After striking the two women she wanted to make it look as if someone had broken in and attacked them; this was simply a matter of self-preservation. "Wasn't this *sane?*" she demanded.

Nothing, nobody, could move her from this stand. She seemed to be arrogantly confident that everyone would understand that she had to act as she did. Sometimes she bragged that she would walk out of the courthouse a free woman; Glen didn't tell her that we were staying on the island and packing up her possessions as if she would never be back. When he went to see her, he never knew which Fee he would find. She still didn't ask for me, and I was glad of that; I was in mourning for *my* Fee, not the one in the county jail. If she'd asked me to come, I don't know how I would have faced her.

She didn't mention Julian, either. He was lost without her. He kept asking for her, and when neither she nor her messages came to him, he became so quiet that he soon ceased to speak altogether. He was finally judged unfit to stand trial, and it didn't need a Harrison Black to bring about that decision. Some day he may be released from the institution where he is now confined, but at the moment it's doubtful.

Sainsbury and the district attorney did what Clem Jr. had hoped for; they agreed to have Fee throw herself on the mercy of the court. Not that *she* wanted to do it that way. No, she wanted a full-scale jury trial, the possibilities of which had been giving both Glen and me some ghastly nights, and the days weren't much better. She was given a life sentence, and when she heard this, she laughed and said to the judge, "A life sentence doesn't mean anything these days. I'll be out. You can't keep me in, because it was justifiable homicide."

At some time in our lives, without our knowing it, she had passed an invisible frontier and become the dangerous citizen of another country. We wondered about the Ouija board, Milton, her talk of unseen presences: had it all been an act, or had she really been trying to find out if the sisters would some day speak through a genuine medium and name her? No wonder she went into hysterics when Sonny's body turned up, as if he'd made it on his own (her words) to confront her and Julian.

Julian's family blamed, and still blame, Fee; well, they have a right. For a while there was talk of a suit on the grounds of her being an evil influence on him; the family frankly wanted the island, which would go for a million dollars or so the way island real estate is priced now. But Harrison Black convinced them that even he couldn't accomplish that miracle; Fee had been the instigator, but Julian had swung the ax, and he had been prepared to break my neck. Fee gave Clem Jr. power of attorney, and he signed her share of the boat and the traps over to Julian, so his family has the use of them now.

Jon's seining crew loaded *Juno* with the trunks and the fine old pieces of furniture Fee had brought from the old Heriot house. *Little Emily* transported the cartons of dishes and other treasures that would make an antique dealer salivate, and everything was put away in Grampa's open chamber for storage. Sprig moved into the house on the island when we left it, on a long lease. For a bachelor whose life as a free spirit was somewhat trammeled by the conservative parents with whom he lived, the lease was very nearly a passport to Paradise. Not that Sprig went into such an ecstatic description, but he looked volumes, as they say. He hadn't been there two weeks before he had a housekeeper (a local euphemism). She was originally an island woman from Penobscot Bay, and she considered a town even as small as Whittier to be grossly overcrowded. They have kept Polly; Ben and Will Temple took two of the kittens, Uncle Early another, and Detective-Sergeant Harriman asked for the little female, who had insisted on sitting on his foot that day he examined the house.

I will love and mourn my Fee for the rest of my life. She went away somehow without my knowing, and left a changeling, but that does not erase or even diminish the Fee of my childhood and youth. She *is* those years. The changeling is locked up under her name.

Epilogue

It is an April day twenty months after that September. I write at the kitchen table in Aunt Noella's house, and our boy watches me from Jon's old playpen, meditatively gnawing at the rim. If he catches my eye, he gives me his gorgeous, sunny smile; I arrange for him to catch my eye quite often. He is a year old, a bright, blond little boy with amber eyes. It is only the eyes that remind us of Julian, and then not always. We never think of Julian as his father. He is ours, older brother of the children to come.

My premonition in the hospital, when I saw Eden Michelle for the first time, was half-right. I received Fee's child in my arms when he was a week old; but she was not dead, except perhaps to me. Glen drives south once a month to see her. The tension grows brutally for a week ahead, and he comes back looking too old. Why does he do it? Because she pleads with him not to forget her, and then half the time she devotes the visit to making him more miserable than he already is. She has yet to show remorse and harangues him for not continuing her fight for their rights. The last few times he has come back angry; a good sign.

We were married at Thanksgiving in Grampa's living room. Sprig stood up with Glen, and I asked Janine to be with me. All our lives Fee and I had planned to be each other's maid of honor, and so I wanted no one, but I woke up one morning thinking of Janine, who was now living in Clem Jr.'s family. She was so far over the moon about my very simple ceremony that I wondered how she'd have reacted to a big production in a church. She and Sprig were the only people from outside my family; Glen had wanted no one else, either. Afterwards we had a wedding supper, and because everybody insisted it would be good for us, we went to Boston for a week and then came back to the cabin on Bugle Bay.

But we both wanted to be on the harbor side, though *not* in the Hayloft; just to go up the steps nauseated me. So a modest bank loan and our fund for the Hebrides trip went into enlarging and remodeling Aunt Noella's house into a place with big windows to bring in the harbor and the sky, and a wide old-fashioned porch, glassed in the winter and screened in the summer. At the center of the house we have a fieldstone fireplace.

I completed the notebook novel that winter in the cabin on Bugle Bay, while we were waiting to move. It has paid off the bank loan; how's that for black humor? Escapism with pay.

We moved into the house in April, and *Sea Swallow* was set on the mantel before one other thing was brought across the threshold. In a week we drove to Portland to get the baby at the hospital where Fee had been taken to give birth. She had eagerly signed the papers before he was two days old, but she still didn't want to see me. It came to me then that if she hated me it was because she couldn't face me. I have to think she too has her moments of mourning, as I have.

Ronnie is a good and happy baby. He is a rich baby because he owns the island, rich too because he has a large family of many generations who love him (my parents *dote*) and a number of honorary aunts and uncles. These include the Temple boys. Some day we will have to decide what to tell him about his birth parents, but that's a long time away. We have much to do first, beginning this summer when we go to the Hebrides at last, with Ronnie on his father's back.

Toby Barry is out of jail. He came in the other day with Derek and Eden Michelle; she is a dark little pixie with the Barrys' fine features, and she is as quick moving as a grasshopper. They brought a teddy bear Shasta made for Ronnie.

"We'd ought to make a match of Ronnie and Michelle," Toby said, watching the three children playing on the floor. "Don't matter if she's a dite older than him. A feller needs an older woman. Shas is a year and a half older than me, and she's got a hell of a lot more sense."

"Well, you can't ever tell what will happen, Toby," I said. He doesn't know that his gift of the kitten nearly got me killed, and he has never asked me what I did with it.

"Jesus, no!" he exclaimed, then rolled his eyes toward Derek, who was gazing reproachfully up at him. "*He* came out with that the other day, and Shas like to hit the ceiling. You can talk about Jesus in Sunday school and your prayers, but not like swearing. Ain't that right, Derek?"

"Ayuh," said Derek stolidly.

"'Course I wasn't really swearing. More like awe-struck, when I think of everything that's happened around here."

"We don't talk about it, Toby," I said. "We can't. How about a mug-up all around?"

Kenneth and Jean live at Fox Point. She lost their first baby in the early months of pregnancy, and now they are adopting. Both their mothers are alive and healthy, joined in an uneasy alliance as expectant grandmothers to the same children. Gideon keeps the piano tuned, and the Thatchers are still there.

Janine and Tracy are going to Bates next fall and will room together. Tracy is almost slim now, and she *does* have bones like Marianne's. Janine cleans house for her father on a regular basis and prepares a meal and eats it with him; he is sober most of the time. She tells me that she still dreams sometimes that Sonny is alive and has just come home to her, and she wakes up crying, but she is able to cope.

The Hearnes have found some suitable property upon which Esmond can exercise his architectural genius. The Harpies still convene on Main Street but are sadly lacking in their old verve. Jake Morley is the same hail-fellow-well-met type he's always been, but his wife has ascended to a Higher Plane, so to speak, since Jane has begun appearing on the covers of the biggest high-fashion magazines, looking absolutely smashing.

Clem Jr. is seeing one of his clients outside the office. She is a very nice woman, a widow. For him, as for all of us, Fee is a wound which will never heal completely but may close enough for us to live our lives in spite of it.

As for the Winters, we go on in force. "Tough," Gram says with a new emphasis, as if to convince herself. We gave Ronnie the middle name of Winter, for luck. Jon has moved into the Hayloft; like Sprig, he feels it's time for a bachelor establishment, but unlike Sprig he doesn't require a housekeeper. He knows too many girls and is quite a busy bee among the flowers whenever he is ashore.

Chad has not yet learned about life and porcupines, but he has a new craze besides barking at sea pigeons, chasing a plastic lid, and lugging dirty socks around. He adores lying beside the playpen while Ronnie drops toys on him.

Nick was gone before the wedding. We get occasional postcards from distant places. I remember all our conversations; we didn't have so many that it's easy to forget one. I remember how disturbing he could be, without even knowing it, I'm sure. Or perhaps he did know; perhaps he wanted to see it in my eyes when I was compelled to admit, even in silence, that the way I was living wasn't the way I'd intended and expected and desired.

I'd never intended my life to be quite the way it is now, either. But Glen was willing to kill his sister, his twin, for me; and you don't take that for granted. You don't simply set it aside somewhere like a spare pair of socks in case your feet get cold. You fit the rest of your life around it.

At Easter this year Jean and Kenneth held an Open House at Fox Point. Among the guests were some of those from that first Afternoon: the Cruikshanks, the Carvers, the Highams. Sydney Carver played Mendelssohn on Miss Emma's Amati, and if there was any reason to believe she was with us then, that was it. Robbie Mackenzie was home from Boston, where he is studying, and played Marianne's piano for the first time. I don't believe anyone so much as shifted a foot during the whole performance of Liszt's B Minor Concerto.

"I didn't know he was capable of such fire," Tillie Higham whispered to me at the end. Her eyes were wet, but jubilant with discovery. "It's as if Marianne bequeathed him that as well as money."

God shall wipe away all tears, it says somewhere in Revelations; perhaps he wipes away all blood as well. I remember them alive now more than I remember them dead. I play their music, and I see them making it. I hear their voices, Marianne's irony, Emma's young laughter. I have their memories, from that afternoon when they played the old songs for me and showed me themselves as children. Julian and Fee, alive and locked away, are not as real to me sometimes as little Emma wanting to play her violin by the Maddox flagpole, with her dog beside her holding a hat; and a leggy Marianne poises her hands over the keys, looks properly exalted, and sees herself as St. Cecilia, waiting for the roses.

The kitten is buried very deep at the foot of the orchard, where the woods begin.